Professor Bernard Knight, CBE, became a Home Office pathologist in 1965 and was appointed Professor of Forensic Pathology, University of Wales College of Medicine, in 1980. During his forty-year career with the Home Office, he performed over 25,000 autopsies and was involved in many high profile cases.

Bernard Knight is the author of twenty novels, a biography and numerous popular and academic non-fiction books. *The Elixir of Death* is the tenth novel in the Crowner John Series.

THE ELIXIR
OF DEATH

Bernard Knight

POCKET
BOOKS

LONDON • SYDNEY • NEW YORK • TORONTO

First published in Great Britain by Simon & Schuster UK Ltd, 2006
This edition published by Pocket Books, 2006
An imprint of Simon & Schuster UK Ltd
A CBS COMPANY

3 5 7 9 10 8 6 4 2

Simon & Schuster UK Ltd
1st Floor
222 Gray's Inn Road
London WC1X 8HB

www.simonandschuster.co.uk

Simon & Schuster Australia
Sydney

A CIP catalogue record for this book
is available from the British Library

ISBN 978-1-84739-991-5

Typeset in Baskerville by M Rules
Printed and bound by
CPI Group (UK) Ltd, Croydon, CR0 4YY

Author's Note

In the twelfth century, little distinction was made in the West between the various peoples in the Levant and Middle East, so names such as 'Saracens, Turks, Moors, Arabs, Mohammedans and Mussulmen (from Mosul)' were all randomly applied to them. Even the great Saladin, leader of the Saracens and major adversary of Richard the Lionheart, was actually a Kurd.

A further historical note about the fanatical Nizari branch of the Isma'ili sect is given at the end of the book, indicating that the present-day strife between Shi'a and Sunni Muslims has been going on for well over a thousand years.

Palestine, the Roman name for 'The Holy Land', was then part of a collection of Christian kingdoms, which extended up into Asia Minor, mostly ruled over by French noblemen. This Christian land was often known as Outremer, meaning 'beyond the sea'.

In spite of the long voyages involved, piracy and coastal raiding were common around the southern and western coasts of Britain long after the well-known Viking period, carried out by marauders from as far away as Spain, North Africa and even the eastern Mediterranean.

Alchemy was a mystical and secretive precursor of chemical science, but with a deep philosophical content. Its origins go back to ancient China, where a 'Pill of Immortality' was claimed to have been developed about 300 BC. After the collapse of Romano-Greek culture, alchemy was rescued, like other disciplines such as medicine and astronomy, by Arabic philosophers such as

Geber, until it came back into Western consciousness in the Middle Ages. Here its main objectives were the search for the 'Philosopher's Stone', which could transmute base metals into gold, and the related 'Elixir of Life', which, like the Chinese pill, could heal sickness and prolong life.

One of the problems of writing a long series such as 'Crowner John' is that regular readers will have become familiar with the background to the stories and may become impatient with repeated explanations in each book. Those coming new to the tales, however, still need to be 'brought up to speed' to fully appreciate some of the historical aspects, so in this tenth episode, to avoid slowing down the action in the text, the Glossary has been expanded and a note offered here on the functions of the coroner, one of the oldest legal officers in England.

Though there are a couple of mentions of a coroner in late Saxon times – and he may have existed in pre-Conquest Normandy – the office of coroner really began in September 1194, when the Royal Justices at their session in Rochester, Kent, proclaimed in a single sentence, the launch of a system which has lasted 812 years – so far! They said, 'In every county of the King's realm shall be elected three knights and one clerk, to keep the pleas of the Crown.'

The reasons for the establishment of coroners were mainly financial, aimed at sweeping as much money as possible into the royal treasury. King Richard the Lionheart was a spendthrift, using huge sums to finance his expedition to the Third Crusade and for his wars against the French. When he was kidnapped on his way home from the Holy Land, he spent well over a year imprisoned in Austria and Germany and a huge ransom was needed to free him. To raise this money, his Chief Justiciar, Hubert Walter, who was also Archbishop of Canterbury, introduced all sorts of measures to extort money from the population of England – indeed, the first taxation on property began then.

Hubert revived the office of coroner, which was intended to collect money by a variety of means relating to the administration of the law. One of these was by investigating all deaths which were not obviously natural, as well as serious assaults, rapes, house fires, discoveries of buried treasure, wrecks of the sea, and catches of the 'royal fish' (whale and sturgeon). Coroners also took confessions from criminals and fugitives seeking sanctuary in churches, recorded the statements of 'approvers' who wished to turn King's evidence, attended executions to seize the goods of felons and organised the ritual of Ordeals and trial by battle.

As the Normans had inherited a multiple system of county and manorial courts from the Saxons, the coroner also tried to sweep more lucrative business into the new royal courts, which gave him the title of 'Keeper of the Pleas of the Crown', from the original Latin of which (*custos placitorum coronas*) the word 'coroner' is derived. Although he was not allowed to try cases, he had to record all legal events to present to the Royal Justices when they came on their infrequent visits to the 'assize' towns. The actual recording was done by his clerk, as the vast majority of people were illiterate, including the coroners themselves. Reading and writing were almost wholly confined to those in holy orders, of which there were many grades, apart from actual priests.

It was hard to find knights to take on the job, as it was unpaid and the appointee had to have a large private income, at least twenty pounds a year. This was supposed to make him immune from corruption, which was common among the county sheriffs. Indeed, another reason for introducing coroners was to keep a check on the sheriffs, who were the King's representative in each county. They were notorious for their dishonesty and embezzlement – in 1170, the Lionheart's father, Henry II, had sacked all the sheriffs and heavily fined many for malpractice. The sheriff in the earlier books, Richard de

Revelle, was actually the sheriff of Devon in 1194–95. He was appointed early in 1194, then lost office for reasons unknown, and came back later in the year, but was fired again the following year. As is the case with his successor, Henry de Furnellis, many of the characters in the books actually existed, especially the churchmen of Exeter. The names of the Devon coroners are not recorded until early in the thirteenth century.

Attempting to use 'olde worlde' dialogue in historical novels of this era is quite futile and unrealistic, as in Devonshire at the time of this story most of the common people would have used Early Middle English, of Germanic origin, totally incomprehensible to us today. Some would still have spoken a Celtic language, similar to Cornish, Breton and Welsh – and the ruling classes would have spoken Norman French. The language of the clergy would have been Latin in which all documents would also have been written.

The only money in circulation, apart from a few Byzantine gold coins, would have been the silver penny. The 'shilling', the 'mark' and the 'pound' were nominal accounting values, not actual currency.

The daily wage of a manual worker would have been one or two pence, more for skilled craftsmen. Pennies were cut into halves and quarters for the purchase of small goods.

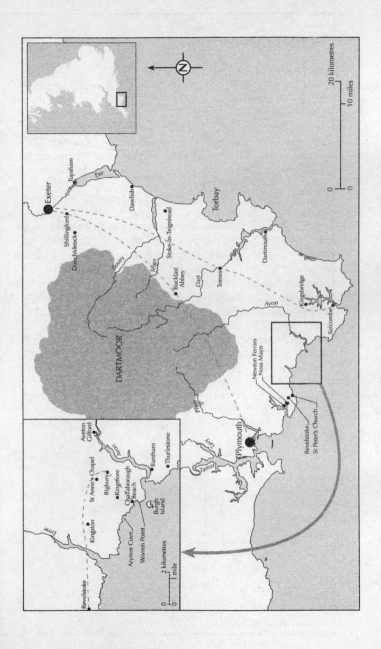

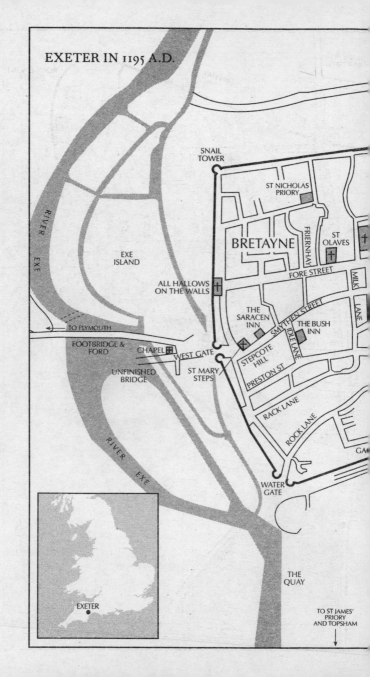

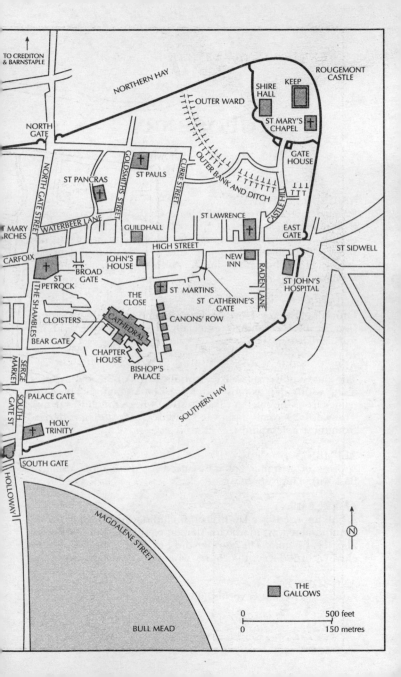

TO CREDITON & BARNSTAPLE

NORTHERN HAY

ROUGEMONT CASTLE

SHIRE HALL

KEEP

OUTER WARD

NORTH GATE

ST MARY'S CHAPEL

NORTH GATE STREET

ST PANCRAS

GOLDSMITH'S STREET

ST PAULS

CURRE STREET

OUTER BANK AND DITCH

GATE HOUSE

CASTLE HILL

MARY CHES

WATERBEER LANE

GUILDHALL

ST LAWRENCE

EAST GATE

ST SIDWELL

CARFOIX

HIGH STREET

JOHN'S HOUSE

BROAD GATE

NEW INN

RADEN LANE

ST PETROCK

THE SHAMBLES

ST MARTINS

ST CATHERINE'S GATE

ST JOHN'S HOSPITAL

THE CLOSE

CANONS' ROW

CLOISTERS

BEAR GATE

CATHEDRAL

CHAPTER HOUSE

BISHOP'S PALACE

SERGE MARKET

PALACE GATE

SOUTHERN HAY

SOUTH GATE ST

HOLY TRINITY

SOUTH GATE

HOLLOWAY

MAGDALENE STREET

N

THE GALLOWS

0   500 feet
0   150 metres

BULL MEAD

GLOSSARY

ABJURING THE REALM
Sanctuary seekers (q.v.) could leave England if they confessed their guilt to a coroner and then walked in sackcloth, carrying a wooden cross, to a port nominated by the coroner. If no ship was readily available, the abjurer had to wade up to his knees in every tide, to show his willingness to leave the realm, never to return.

AGISTERS
Officials of the royal forests who regulated 'agisting', the admission for a fee of animals, especially pigs, to feed on the fallen nuts and acorns.

ALE
The almost universal, weakly alcoholic drink of the lower classes, along with cider, as most water was contaminated. The name comes from the 'ale', a village festival where much was drunk. The words 'wassail' and even 'bridal' (bride-ale) are derived from these celebrations.

ALEMBIC
A piece of alchemic apparatus used for distillation, usually a flask with a long spout.

AMERCEMENT
A fine imposed by a law officer, including the coroner, for the innumerable ways in which a person could fall foul of the complex legal system. The coroner did not collect the fine, but his clerk recorded it for the courts, which decided upon payment.

ANCHORITE
A religious hermit or recluse, living alone in a remote place.

ASSARTING
The extension of the cultivated area of a village by cutting back the surrounding forest. The cleared area was termed 'the waste' until the tree stumps were removed.

BAILEY
An area, around either a castle mound ('motte and bailey') or the inner or outer ward of a larger castle or fortified manor-house.

BAILIFF
As used in this book, an official of a manor who supervised one or more villages in respect of the agricultural work. He had manor-reeves under him and was responsible to the steward of the manor-lord.

BARTON
A farm, usually for the sole benefit of the manor-lord.

BOTTLER
A servant responsible for providing the drink in a large household – the origin of 'butler'.

BRANDY-WINE
Strong distilled spirits were rare in medieval times, ale, cider, mead and wine being the main alcoholic drinks. However, some 'brandy-wine' (burnt-wine) was imported from France.

BRETAYNE
The north-west medieval slum district within the walls of Exeter, so named because when the Saxons invaded they pushed the Celtic 'Britons' into the least desirable corner of the city.

COB
A building material made from clay, straw and often dung, which was plastered on to wattle panels fixed between the timber frames of a cottage.

COG
A medieval trading ship, similar to a Viking longboat, but higher and wider, with more vertical stem- and stern-posts. Part decked,

with a single mast and sail, it had a steering oar, as rudders were not yet used.

COTTAR
A low-grade villein, an unfree man in the feudal system. He had no field-strips to cultivate, but had a toft and croft (q.v.). He worked at various tasks, such as hedging, thatching and labouring.

CROFT
A plot of ground on which a 'toft' or cottage was built, to house either a freeman or a villein.

CRUCIBLE
A container, usually of stone or pottery, for melting substances at high temperature in a furnace.

CULF
A Celtic word for a thick chunk of bread.

CURFEW
The closing of the city gates from dusk to dawn. Derived from *couvre-feu*, the covering or extinction of domestic fires at night, owing to the ever-present risk of conflagration in buildings mostly made of wood.

CURRAGH
A boat like an elongated coracle, made of tarred fabric or skin stretched over a light wooden frame. Still used in the west of Ireland.

DEODAND
An object that has caused death, forfeit to the Crown after a coroner's inquest, where the jury decided its value. It could be a knife, a horse or even a mill-wheel. Sometimes, the proceeds of its value to the Treasury were given to the family of the deceased.

DESTRIER
A large warhorse, capable of carrying a man in armour. Oxen were used as draught animals, as horses were too valuable.

DISTAFF
A stick for holding raw wool or flax, from which a thread is drawn during hand spinning.

ELECTRUM
An alloy of gold and silver, known to the ancient Egyptians.

EYRE
The periodic visitation of each shire by the Royal Justices, to hear civil and criminal cases. This later became the Eyre of Assize, but there was also a much more infrequent General Eyre, which was a searching inquiry into the administration of the county. Because the eyres moved so slowly around England – often years elapsed between visits – judges of lesser rank, called the Commissoners of Gaol Delivery, came to clear the prisons.

FIRST FINDER
Whoever discovered a dead body in any but the most innocent circumstances, became the 'First Finder' and had specific legal obligations which, if not carried out to the letter, attracted a heavy fine. He had to knock up the four nearest households and initiate the 'Hue and Cry' (q.v.) and report the find at once to the village reeve or bailiff or equivalent officer in a town. These must then notify the coroner without delay and protect the body *in situ* until his arrival.

FLUMMERY
A bland food like blancmange, often made of oatmeal with fruit and honey.

FURLONG
From 'furrow', an eighth of a mile, originally the length of a furrow on a square field of ten acres.

HONOUR
The land held by barons and lords from the King, whether large estates or single manors.

HUE and CRY
When a crime was discovered, especially the finding of a dead

body, the four nearest households must immediately turn out and raise the alarm in village or town, running through the streets to seek the offender. Failure to do so would result in an amercement (fine) levied upon the community.

HUER
A lookout on the shore or cliff, who spots shoals of herring or pilchard for the fishermen to harvest.

JUSTICIAR
One of the King's Council, a baron or bishop, who acted as a deputy when the King was abroad. In the late twelfth century, Hubert Walter, the Chief Justiciar and Archbishop of Canterbury, was virtually the regent of England, as Richard Coeur-de-Lion never returned after 1194.

KIRTLE
A lady's dress, sleeved and of ankle length. A fashion-concious age produced innumerable variations in style.

LEMAN
A mistress or unmarried consort.

MATINS The first of the nine religious offices (services) of the day. Matins took place soon after midnight, later in the winter.

MARK
A nominal value, not actual currency, worth two-thirds of a pound or 160 pennies, which were the only coins.

MURDRUM FINE
(See 'Presentment').

MURRAIN
A disease of farm animals, especially sheep, though it covered a range of ill-defined ailments.

ORDEAL
Though sometimes used to extract confessions, the Ordeal was an ancient ritual in which suspects were subject to painful and often fatal procedures to determine guilt or innocence by semi-

magical means. These included licking a red-hot iron, picking a stone from the bottom of a vat of boiling water (or even molten lead) or walking barefoot over nine red-hot ploughshares. If they suffered no significant burns or their injuries healed quickly, they were judged innocent – otherwise they were hanged. Women were bound hand and foot and thrown into deep water; if they sank, they were innocent. The Ordeal was abolished by the Vatican in 1215.

OSTLER
A man or boy who tends horses.

OUTREMER
Literally 'over the sea'. The several Christian kingdoms established in the Holy Land and adjacent areas in Syria and Asia Minor, following the capture of Jerusalem during the First Crusade.

PALFREY
A small, docile horse, suitable for use by a lady.

PALIMPSEST
A reused parchment. Until paper was introduced into England in the fourteenth century, all writing was on sheep- or goatskin (parchment) or lamb or kid-skin (vellum). Owing to its cost, old writing was often scraped off and the surface used again.

POUND
A nominal sum of money, worth 12 shillings or 240 silver pennies, which were the only coins in circulation, apart from a few foreign gold bezants.

PRESENTMENT
When someone was found dead, other than from obvious disease, a relative had to make 'Presentment of Englishry' before the coroner, to prove that the deceased was a Saxon (or Welsh, Irish or Scots). The Norman administration, following revolts after the Conquest, assumed that all slain men were Normans until proved otherwise, and if proof were not forthcoming the village was amerced with a heavy murdrum fine. Within half a century of 1066, this became almost meaningless because of

intermarriage, but the fine was continued for several centuries as a cynical means of extorting money from the population.

QUARREL
A type of cross-bow arrow, a bolt with a pyramid-shaped head, which could not easily be removed from the flesh.

QUIRE
The part of a cathedral where the priests held their services, separated from the common public in the nave by the rood screen. Later it became known as the 'choir'.

REEVE
There were various grades, the lowest official in a village being the manor-reeve, who organised the daily routine of the workers on the land. He was elected by his fellow villeins, theoretically to protect their interests at the manor court. A sheriff (shire-reeve) was the King's representative in each county.

ROUNSEY
An ordinary saddle-horse, for general riding, smaller than a destrier or warhorse

ST RADEGUND
A sixth-century Frankish queen, who founded a monastery in Poitiers. In the twelfth century there was an altar to her in Exeter cathedral.

SANCTUARY
The right of a fugitive from the law to evade arrest by hiding in a church for up to forty days. At the end of that time, he either confessed his guilt to the coroner, 'abjuring the realm' (q.v.), or was locked in and starved to death. If he emerged, he could be beheaded by anyone.

SENNIGHT
A week or 'seven nights', similar to a fortnight (fourteen nights).

SHINGLES
Wooden tiles for a roof, an alternative to thatch or stone tiles.

SHRIEVALTY
The office of sheriff.

SUMPTER
A packhorse for carrying goods.

TRANSMUTATION
The goal of alchemists for many centuries, the conversion of base metals into gold. Claims were made for all kinds of processes, usually involving mercury, sulphur, lead, silver and copper.

TRENCHER
Plates were rarely used at mealtimes, a thick slice of stale bread being placed on the scrubbed boards of a table to accommodate the food. Afterwards, especially at feasts, the used trenchers were given to the poor and the beggars who gathered at the door.

UNDERCROFT
A semi-basement of a castle keep or manor-house, usually used for storage. For defence reasons, it was accessible only from outside. The main door to the building was on the floor above, and the wooden steps granting access could be thrown down in case of attack.

VULGATE
The Catholic Bible, translated into Latin by St Jerome in AD 405. The Church resisted an English translation until the Reformation, as losing their monopoly of interpretation by priests, would have weakened their authority over the lay public.

CHAPTER ONE

November 1195

In which Crowner John is called to the shore

'He should never have been at sea this late in the season!'

The coroner's deep voice competed with the wind whistling past the ears of the two horsemen. They waited on the seaward end of a long ridge, high above the beach, while a third man laboured up behind them, his pony trudging wearily after the tedious journey west from Exeter.

'Not this far down-channel, now that we're well into the autumn,' agreed his henchman, a huge dishevelled Cornishman astride a large brown mare. Gwyn of Polruan had ginger hair poking from under his shabby leather hood and a bushy moustache of the same colour hanging down on either side of his mouth. All were damp from the spray and fitful rain that half a gale was hurling at them from the west, under dark clouds that scudded across the afternoon sky.

'Are you sure that's Thorgils' vessel, Crowner?' asked the thin figure on the pony, as he pulled alongside them. Thomas de Peyne was the coroner's clerk, his sallow face looking as miserable as the Dartmoor pony on which he sat side-saddle like a woman.

'Of course I'm not sure!' snapped Sir John de Wolfe. His meagre patience was worn even thinner by almost two days' riding from Devon's county town. 'But the bailiff claimed that it was – and I see no reason to doubt him.'

Gwyn, having been a fisherman farther down the coast before he became Sir John's bodyguard, considered himself an expert on things maritime. At least he knew more than the other two, and now he pointed with an air of authority down to the mouth of the river, where the low tide had exposed a broad expanse of sand. It lay about a quarter of a mile below them, beyond the steep slope of coarse grass that ran down to the rocks at the water's edge.

'That cog is just like Thorgils', though it's too far away to see any details,' he declared. 'But it could well be the *Mary and Child Jesus.*'

At these holy words, Thomas de Peyne crossed himself reverently, as he did many times a day. 'That bailiff said that some of the crew have perished, but we must hope that God decreed that our friend was not one of them,' he piped, his squeaky voice contrasting with the gruff tones of his companions.

They looked down through the rain to the beach at the foot of the bluff where they now sat on their weary horses. The hull of the boat lay on its side, its broken mast digging into the sand. The heavy surf had pushed it up to the high-water mark, only a few yards from the foot of the low cliffs.

'Just as well there are no spring tides at this time of the month,' bellowed Gwyn above the wind. 'Otherwise she would have been battered to pieces on those rocks.'

The coroner grunted, his favourite form of reply, and continued to study the vista below. He always liked to get any new scene firmly fixed in his mind before speculating on what might have happened. In front of him, a stretch of sand a few hundred paces wide joined the mainland to an island, which was now accessible across the beach until the tide rose again. It was only a few acres in extent, the rocky base rising to a low hill covered with sparse turf. On

top of it was a stone hut, hunkered down against the gales
that so often threatened to tear it from the small islet.

To his right, the southern coastline of Devon stretched
far away in the direction of Plymouth, the cliffs visible for
miles between the squalls of driving rain. This whole
coast, from Dartmouth sixteen miles behind them, right
down to Cornwall, was indented by a series of fjord-like
river valleys that cut into the coastal plain that lay below
Dartmoor. Below him to his left was the mouth of one of
these, the River Avon, whose narrow vale penetrated
deeply into the lonely countryside. A few villages were
dotted among the heathland that was all that could survive the frequent Atlantic gales – only in the sheltered
dales were there woods and cultivation.

At high tide, the winding valley of the Avon was
flooded for several miles inland, but now the estuary was
almost all sand. The river made a final double bend
before it flowed across the wide beach into the sea,
between St Michael de la Burgh Island and a low headland on the southern side. They had approached on a
track from the north and the wreck now lay below them,
driven ashore by the westerly wind almost on to the rocks
of the promontory opposite the island. De Wolfe wondered whether the bodies had been found on the same
beach.

'Where do we find this bailiff fellow, Crowner?'

Gwyn's voice broke into John's reverie and made him
suddenly aware of being wet, cold and hungry. Though
he and Gwyn had suffered far worse conditions over the
years in campaigns stretching from Ireland to Palestine,
there was something uniquely depressing about the bone-
chilling damp of a Devonshire autumn.

'A fire, some food and a warm place to sleep would be
more than welcome,' Thomas piped longingly, as if reading his master's thoughts.

De Wolfe stared down once more at the derelict vessel,
abandoned on its desolate beach. 'No point in going

3

down there now – it'll be dark in an hour or so,' he grunted. 'We'll come back in the morning, after we've seen these corpses.'

Pulling his horse's head around, belatedly he answered Gwyn's question before moving off along the ridge. 'The bailiff said he lived in Ringmore. That's the manor about a mile west of here, inland from the sea.'

'We should have made the bastard come with us,' grumbled Gwyn. 'It was hard enough finding this damned place, not having someone local to guide us.'

'The poor fellow said he had to hurry back home, as his wife was in childbed!' objected Thomas. His compassion was mixed with his usual desire to contradict everything said by his burly colleague.

The bailiff of Ringmore, one William Vado, had arrived at the coroner's chamber in the gatehouse of Exeter's Rougemont Castle early the previous morning. He had ridden the thirty-five miles in a day and a half, forcing the pace to carry news that had the coroner and his two men saddled up within the hour. They stayed that night in Totnes Castle, the bailiff having parted from them earlier to hurry home to his wife. By late afternoon of the following short November day, they had reached the place overlooking the River Avon that Vado had described.

Now John de Wolfe led the way towards Ringmore across the undulating heathland behind the cliffs. It was deserted apart from some scraggy sheep and a few goats lurking among the bracken and stunted gorse bushes bent over by the prevailing winds. There were only sheep tracks to follow, and John saw that down to his left was another smaller beach at the end of a valley between the cliffs, with a few ramshackle fishermen's huts above the water's edge. The only guides they had to these parts were some instructions offered by the bailiff, together with a rough sketch map hastily drawn on a scrap of parchment by the steward at Totnes Castle.

4

They crossed this valley higher up and a few minutes later reached the head of yet another glen, where a small stream cut its way down to the sea. Here a lonely village nestled in the valley where, protected from the worst of the winds, trees softened the landscape and some strip-fields backed on to the dwellings. Ringmore was little more than a collection of tofts and crofts around a tiny Saxon church. Below it on the slope was a large tithe barn and a fortified house within a rectangular wooden stockade. The cottages were all built either of lime-washed cob on wooden frames or of weathered timber, with roofs of thatch or turf.

'Not much of a place, is it!' grumbled Gwyn, who, though born in Polruan, an equally undistinguished fishing village at the mouth of the Fowey river, had adopted the airs of a city dweller after twenty years as a largely absentee citizen of Exeter.

'As long as they've got somewhere with a sound roof and a fire to dry ourselves by, I don't care what it looks like!' whined little Thomas, his thin shoulders shivering under the threadbare black cloak that enveloped him. He wore a shabby pilgrim's hat and his pallid, thin face peered out miserably from under the wide, floppy brim.

John let his old warhorse Odin pick his way carefully down the slippery rutted track that served as the village street, heading for the larger house that lay inside the palisade of old stakes.

'Does a manor-lord actually live in this God-forsaken place?' grunted Gwyn, looking around at the humble dwellings, most of which were wattle-and-daub huts.

The coroner shook his head, drops of water flicking off his dark, beetling eyebrows. 'The land belongs to Totnes, that's why the steward there could draw us a map. But someone must have ruled here years ago for there to be a manor-house, poor though it looks.'

It turned out that the bailiff now occupied the old

place, using it as his base for looking after several villages hereabouts that belonged to the lord of Totnes. This was a legacy from the days of the Conqueror, who gave many parcels of land in this area to his supporter Judhael, who built the castle at Totnes to subdue the local Saxons and Celts.

They rode up to the gate in the stockade and found William Vado hurrying out to meet them in the gathering dusk. He was a stocky fellow of about thirty years, with a square face, a bulbous nose and lank yellow hair that was a legacy from his Saxon mother. He wore a thigh-length tunic of coarse brown serge, clinched with a wide leather belt. Cross-gartered breeches and wooden-soled boots clothed his lower half.

William waved to a couple of skinny lads who emerged from a barn inside the compound and they hurried forward to take the bridles of the visitors' horses.

'You found us, then, Crowner?' he asked in a thick local accent. 'Come inside and get some food and drink inside you.'

It was the more sympathetic Thomas who thought of asking after his wife, as they all dismounted and trudged through the mire of the bailey towards the old manor-house.

'She's well, thank you,' answered William Vado. 'A girl again, I'm afraid. Another useless mouth to feed.' He sounded bitter, and they soon learned that his wife had had seven previous children, five of which had died in infancy, leaving two other girls alive.

John looked about him with interest as they crossed the yard and climbed a few steps to the house, for this was one of the original manors that dated back to the early years of the Norman invasion, now well over a century earlier. It was a square, single-storeyed block, built of massive oak timbers on top of a masonry undercroft, with a stone-slabbed roof as a safeguard against fire-arrows. The interior was almost all taken up by the hall, but two rooms had been partitioned off for the family, secure behind a pair of stout iron-banded doors. These remote coastal villages were occasionally ravaged by pirates who came ashore to rape, pillage and replenish their food and fresh water – not only French privateers, but men from as far afield as the Mediterranean.

The hall was lit by unglazed slit windows, through which the fading daylight dimly penetrated. A large fire-pit occupied the centre of the hall, ringed with whitewashed stones outside a circle of baked clay. The smoke from the heap of burning logs wafted upwards before spreading out to escape through the slits beneath the roof timbers, though some of it circulated back down again to irritate the eyes and throats of the dozen or so people scattered about the hall.

'We can only offer you a place to sleep on the rushes,' said the bailiff apologetically. 'My wife and her womenfolk and the children are swarming about the other chambers like bees in a hive. But there's food and ale aplenty and some wine if you're so inclined.'

'Drying off is our first need,' rumbled Gwyn, shrugging off the frayed leather cape with the pointed hood. He draped it over a stool facing the fire and stamped his cold feet on the floor rushes, disturbing a rat that was foraging for fallen food scraps.

Within a few minutes, they were seated on benches at a nearby trestle table, enjoying the warmth of the flaming beech logs. A pair of serving girls, little more than children, brought platters of spit-baked fish, cold pork and boiled beans and cabbage, with thick trenchers of coarse bread to lay on the table as plates. As usual, the kitchen was in a hut behind the house and the bare-footed maids had to run back and forth through the mud to bring the food to the new arrivals.

'Have some mulled ale to warm you up, sirs,' invited Vado, taking a thick poker from the fire and plunging the red-hot iron into a gallon jug of ale. With a hiss and a sizzle, the turbid liquid almost boiled, and before it could cool he splashed it into a row of crude eathernware pots standing on the table.

Thomas, who disliked ale even more than rough cider, sipped his with ill-concealed distaste, but John and Gwyn gulped the warm fluid gratefully and pushed their pots forward for a refill, while they wolfed down the food. Around them, rough-looking men sitting at other trestles or standing around gazed curiously at these outsiders from the big city.

'Tell us the whole story again, bailiff,' commanded de Wolfe, through a mouthful of gravy-soaked bread. 'Has there been any more news since you returned?'

William Vado, sitting at the end of the table, beckoned to a large, brawny fellow standing nearby, who came and sat with them.

'This is Osbert, the manor-reeve. He can tell you at first hand, as it was he who brought me the news.' The reeve was a villein who was in theory elected by his fellows to represent their interests before the manor court, but in effect was usually the appointee of the lord, who needed someone in every village to organise the day-to-day running of their agricultural labours. Obviously ill at ease in the presence of a knight who was a senior law officer, the village foreman haltingly told his story.

'I was going down to Challaborough beach the evening before last, as someone said they saw a cask washed up. It may have been flotsam full of something, like raisins or wine, so I was prepared to report it.'

He said this virtuously, though everyone, including the coroner, knew very well that he would have been more interested in acquiring salvaged goods for the village – or even himself – rather than for either his lord or the King, to whom all such flotsam legally belonged.

'Anyway, I saw no cask, but when I was on the sands, a crabber came running round from Warren Point and said he had found a dead body!'

Vado explained that Warren Point was the end of the bluff where they had looked across at Burgh Island.

The onlookers in the hall drew perceptibly nearer to the table, eager to hear the story again, though Osbert had regaled them with it many times over the past day or so. Drama and excitement were in short supply in such a remote place as Ringmore.

'Who was this crabber?' demanded de Wolfe. 'He must be accounted as the First Finder.'

This announcement was met with blank stares from both bailiff and reeve. 'We don't really understand this new crowner business, begging your pardon, sir,' confessed the bailiff. 'All I was told last year by my lord's steward in Totnes was that, unless they died in the bosom of their family, all corpses must be reported to Exeter without delay.'

De Wolfe sighed and dropped his small eating dagger on to the table. It was over a year since the Chief Justiciar had revived the old Saxon office of coroner, but most of the minor officials in England still seemed ignorant of the procedures.

'Listen, for Christ's sake! It's simple enough!' he said with his tongue in his cheek, for it wasn't simple at all. 'When someone dies suddenly, whether of violence or poison or anything other than sickness or old age, then whoever comes across the corpse is the "First Finder". He has to raise the hue and cry by knocking up the four nearest households and starting a search for the killer, if one is suspected.'

'What if it's just a child who falls into the millpond, Crowner?' objected a toothless man standing amongst the listeners. 'Or a lad who gets gored by a bull? We've had both those this past autumn. Are we to go racing round the village, looking for a murderer who doesn't exist?'

'Then use your common sense, man!' snapped John irritably. 'But they still have to be reported to the coroner.

The reeve or bailiff must inform me without delay, either directly or through your lord's steward.'

There was a disbelieving rumble from the group of village worthies.

''Tis a mortal long ride to Exeter, just to say that some old fellow has broken his neck falling from a hay-wagon,' complained another man.

'It's also the will of King Richard's Council,' rasped the coroner. 'I didn't make the laws, but it's my job to see they are kept. Any breach of the rules means an amercement against the offender or his village, so it doesn't pay to flaunt them.'

At the mention of fines, the small crowd fell silent and watched sullenly as John de Wolfe picked up his knife and began hacking again at his trencher. Gwyn grinned to himself under the shelter of his ale-soaked moustache – he had heard all this before at a dozen places across the county, as the over-taxed population digested news of another means for the Lionheart's ministers to screw more money out of them to pay for his German ransom and his French wars.

'So tell me again about these corpses,' demanded John, belching and picking up his ale jar to wash down the salty fish and the fatty pork.

Osbert picked up his tale where he had left off. 'I don't know this crabber's name, but I can find out in the morning. He's from up Bigbury way, I know him by sight. Anyway, he takes me to the high-water mark and shows me this body – and damn me, if there wasn't another one, fifty paces away.'

The bailiff, sitting with a jar alongside the coroner, took up the tale.

'When Osbert came back with the news, I went down with two other cottars and searched all along the shore of the bay, this side of the river. We found another dead 'un, then came across the vessel itself, beached fairly high up between the Warren and Sharpland Point.'

'Why did you think the ship belonged to Thorgils of Dawlish?' bleated Thomas. 'Could you read the name on its bow?'

William Vado shook his head sadly. 'I've got no learning, sir. But when we found these poor dead shipmen, I sent back for our priest to shrive them. He's the only man hereabouts who knows his letters and he said the cog was called the *Mary and Child Jesus.*'

Osbert piped up again. 'The crabber, who sells his catch and some other fish in Salcombe, says he's seen the vessel berthed there in the past and knew it came from up Dawlish way.'

De Wolfe nodded, as he knew that Thorgils the Boatman, as he was universally known, called at all the South Devon ports to collect cargo for his endless runs back and forth to Normandy and Brittany.

'But this was no ordinary shipwreck, you claim?'

Vado shook his blond bullet-head. 'They were knifed, Crowner! No doubt of it, though I make no claim to being either a soldier or an apothecary. That's why I rode straightway to Totnes to ask my lord's steward what was to be done.'

'And the bodies and the wreck? You have made them secure?' demanded the coroner.

The bailiff nodded virtuously. 'The cadavers are in the church here. We couldn't leave them on the beach till you came. With tides rising with this moon and the wind freshening, they might have been washed back out to sea. Couldn't do anything with the ship until she's lightened of her cargo, but I've set a man and a boy on guard at the head of the beach to keep off any pillagers.' His face darkened as he contemplated the neighbouring villages. 'Those bloody people from Bigbury and Aveton would strip the wreck down to her last dowel-pins, given half a chance.'

De Wolfe turned to his officer. 'Gwyn, how many crew does Thorgils usually carry?'

'Three or four, besides himself, so there's at least one not accounted for. Was he carrying goods for you on his outbound voyage?'

The coroner nodded. 'He took a cargo of wool bales and some finished cloth from Topsham across to Harfleur. I don't know what he was due to bring back. We had no orders for him, but he's hardly likely to have come back empty.'

John de Wolfe was in partnership with Hugh de Relaga, one of Exeter's two portreeves, the leaders of the city burgesses. When John had given up campaigning a couple of years earlier, he had invested the loot he had accumulated in two decades of fighting abroad in a wool-exporting business with de Relaga. Though he was only a sleeping partner, he derived a steady profit from the enterprise, more than sufficient to fulfil the legal necessity of a coroner having an income of at least twenty pounds a year. This requirement was in theory a safeguard against corruption, as the King's Council naively thought that anyone with such riches would have no need to embezzle from public funds.

When the visitors had finished the food on the table, they pulled their stools around the edge of the fire-pit and sat with the bailiff and a few of the other villagers. Their pots were refilled by the young servants, and as darkness fell outside rush-lamps were lit and set on sconces around the walls, adding a dim light to the flames that flickered from the fire as more wood was stacked on to it. This was a time of day that John enjoyed, feeling a warm glow from the food and ale inside him and the radiance of the fire outside. Though he was as fond of a woman's company as any man, he felt most at home with plain and sturdy men such as these, telling tales of old battles and country yarns of ghostly hounds and evil spirits roaming the moors.

There were several former archers among the company tonight, and they could match the tales that Gwyn and John could spin about campaigns in Ireland and France, though unlike the coroner and his officer none had been out to the Holy Land on the last Crusade. The dozen men of Ringmore sat absorbed in the talk, this advent of strangers from Exeter being a welcome novelty in the humdrum life of the village. They sat listening to this pair of big men, for Thomas said almost nothing, the little clerk being half asleep on his stool as he nursed his unwanted ale.

After a couple of hours swapping yarns, the fatigue of the day and the quarts of ale began to take their toll. The bailiff drifted off to lie with his wife and new baby, while the other men stumbled out into the darkness to find their own tofts.

A couple of older servants carried out palliasses of hessian stuffed with dry ferns and laid them around the fire-pit for the visitors. Wrapped in their freshly dried riding cloaks, the coroner's team gratefully settled down for the night, and soon the hall echoed with Gwyn's snores, which drowned the rustle of rodents in the straw and the dreamy whimpers of the dogs that slept among the men around the fire.

By dawn, the wind had dropped and the rain had cleared away, so that a watery blue sky streaked with high streamers of cloud greeted the King's officers as they trudged up the muddy track between the manor-house and the little church. After quickly breaking their fast on oatmeal gruel and coarse rye bread, with the promise of a better meal later on, they had followed William Vado and his reeve Osbert out into the bailey, where two other men were waiting. One was the sexton, a cottar whose duties included looking after the church, the other the village priest himself, a burly man with cheeks and nose covered with a network of purple veins, which suggested to John that his contacts with the spiritual world came mainly via a wine flask.

Introduced by the bailiff as Father Walter, the custodian of souls in Ringmore mumbled some curt greeting and set off ahead of them to his church, built in Saxon times. This was a small structure of weathered stone, a bare box barely a dozen paces long. It was roofed with wooden shingles, most of which were thick with moss. There was no bell-arch nor porch – it was just a rectangular room with one door and half a dozen arrow-slits for lighting. It compared poorly in both size and construction with the tithe barn next door, indicating the relative importance which the Archdeacon of Totnes assigned to pastoral duties against the collection of taxes.

The parish priest crossed the churchyard inside its ring of old yew trees and hauled open the creaking door to admit them. In the pale morning light, de Wolfe saw a bare chamber with a simple table at the far end serving as the altar, bearing a tin cross and two wooden candlesticks.

'There they are, God rest them,' muttered Walter rather grudgingly, and joined Thomas in making the sign of the Cross. In front of the altar, on the floor of beaten earth, lay three still figures, the upper part of each covered by an empty sack to serve as a shroud.

John de Wolfe stalked towards them, his characteristic stoop making him appear to the bailiff like some large crow as he hovered over the bodies. Bending, he pulled the sack away from the nearest corpse and Gwyn did the same for the other two.

'God blast whoever did this!' snarled the coroner. 'It *is* Thorgils, just as I feared.'

'And I recognise these other two,' boomed Gwyn. 'They're his crew members, though I don't recall their names.'

The three cadavers lay pale and waxy on the floor, dressed in the simple attire of shipmen – a short, belted tunic of faded blue and stout breeches, their feet bare.

Gwyn bent and picked up one of the hands of the man in the middle.

'Still some death stiffness remaining, so they've not been dead more than a couple of days in this cold weather.' He squinted at the skin of the palms and finger-pads, which was wrinkled and sodden. 'Yet they were long enough in the water to get washerwoman's fingers.'

John stood silently, looking at the faces of the three victims. Thorgils was a grey-bearded man of about sixty years, the other two were stocky seamen probably in their twenties. As de Wolfe stood in pensive contemplation of a man he had known for much of his life, the bailiff stole a look at the coroner. He saw a tall, sinewy man who gave an overall impression of blackness. At forty-one, De Wolfe still had hair the colour of jet, which he wore longer than most Norman knights, swept back from his forehead and curling down to the nape of his neck. Luxuriant eyebrows of the same colour overhung deep-set dark eyes and his long, gaunt face carried a big hooked nose. Though he had no beard or moustache, his cheeks were usually dark with stubble between his weekly shaves with a sharp knife. The only relieving feature of this forbidding visage was the full lips, which the bailiff suspected were a sign of latent passion and a fondness for the ladies. De Wolfe's garb suited his face, as he wore a long sombre grey tunic under his mottled wolfskin mantle. One of the archers had told Vado that during the campaigns in Ireland the coroner had been known as 'Black John' from his predilection for dark clothing and often equally dark moods.

De Wolfe suddenly moved, jerking the bailiff from his contemplation of the coroner. 'Let's see these wounds, Gwyn,' he commanded, bending to the corpse of the ship-master. Between them, they unbuckled Thorgils' wide leather belt and raised his tunic.

'Look on his back, Crowner,' muttered the bailiff, starting forward to help. Turning the body over on to its bearded face, they soon saw that there were two stab wounds in the ship-master's back, between the shoulder blades. The tunic had corresponding cuts, though there was little more than pinkish discoloration on the surrounding cloth. When they looked at the two younger men, the findings were much the same, though one of them had three stab wounds.

Thomas de Peyne, still sensitive to these sights of fatal violence even after more than a year in the coroner's service, held his hand to his mouth and murmured between his fingers.

'Why so little blood, Crowner?'

'They've all been in the damned sea!' grated de Wolfe, his temper made even shorter by the sight of a friend so callously slain – even if he had been cuckolding him for years.

'Whatever blood escaped has been washed away,' added Gwyn, ever eager to show his expertise in matters of violence. 'That's why the tunic is hardly soiled. He must have been pitched into the water soon after the knifing, so that the blood had no time to congeal in the cloth.'

William Vado and the men from the village hovered behind the coroner and his men, staring with interest at their activities. Rough countrymen such as these were no strangers to death, whether of animals, their families or their fellows, for life was hard in these remote areas, where disease, accidents and sometimes winter starvation carried off many people before they reached middle age. Murder was quite uncommon, however, and this was a novelty that they had no intention of missing, their eyes following the coroner's hands as he traced the outline of the wounds.

'These are peculiarly wide stabbings, Gwyn,' growled de Wolfe, pulling the edges of one of the wounds apart with his fingers. 'Surely more than two inches across. What sort of knife made these?'

The Cornishman, crouching down alongside his master, scratched his russet hair, which was as dishevelled as a hayrick in a storm.

'Not the usual dagger, Crowner! Yet they seem too clean cut for a broadsword. And you don't dig someone two or three times in the back with a sword!'

John grunted and slid a forefinger into one of the holes. He frowned, then pulled it out again and stuck the bloody digit into several more wounds, moving to the other bodies to test them in a similar fashion. His finger penetrated up to the knuckle and when he pulled it out, there was an obscene sucking sound which made the sensitive Thomas shudder.

'Very odd! I get the feeling that the tracks curve inside the body, rather than go straight in,' de Wolfe muttered, almost to himself. Wiping his finger on the tunic of the youngest corpse, he stood up and stared down again at the bodies. 'No other injuries . . . not that the poor devils needed anything more.'

'And no sign of a fight, for their fists are free of any injury,' added Gwyn. 'Stabbed in the back unawares by some cowardly bastard.'

De Wolfe glared at his companion. 'I think you mean "bastards",' he corrected. 'One attacker couldn't do this alone without the two other sailors fighting back! The crew must have been jumped by several assailants at the same time.'

'Especially if there was another seaman whose body hasn't been found,' cut in Thomas, his sharp mind overcoming his repugnance at the morbid scene.

'Cover the poor devils up again!' commanded the coroner, stepping back to allow the village men to spread the sacks over the victims.

'There's nothing more we can do for them, but I'll have to hold an inquest later this morning.'

'What about the corpses?' asked Thomas. 'Will they be buried here or taken back to their homes in Dawlish?'

De Wolfe shrugged. 'It's a hell of long way to carry them, either on a cart or slung across the back of sumpter horses. I'll have to ask the families what they want done.'

'You knew these men before this?' asked the bailiff.

'I knew Thorgils, the ship-master. He was the main carrier for the goods our merchant enterprise send across to Brittany and Normandy – sometimes even to Flanders.'

He saw no point in mentioning that Thorgils' wife Hilda had been his mistress on and off since they were both young. The lissom blonde was the daughter of the reeve of Holcombe, one of the de Wolfe family's two manors on the coast near Teignmouth. Though five years older, John had grown up with Hilda, and by the time she was thirteen they were lovers, albeit clandestinely in the hay-loft or out in the woods. He had gone off to the wars before he was twenty, and though they had reconsummated their romance at intervals over the suceeding years, she had eventually married Thorgils, a much older man, while John had been pushed into his loveless marriage with Matilda de Revelle seventeen years earlier.

As John stood over the slain body of Hilda's husband, he felt a twinge of conscience that he had wronged this old man, even if Thorgils had never known about it. De Wolfe also had to suppress a voice in his head that told him that Hilda was now free, a delectable widow still only in her thirties. His conscience was not troubling him in respect of his own wife, but because of his regular mistress Nesta, the Welsh tavern-keeper with whom he was almost sure he was in love.

As he stood pensively staring at the hessian-covered corpses, he felt the eyes of the other men upon him, waiting expectantly for his next move.

'Are we going to look at this vessel now, Crowner?' prompted Gwyn.

With an almost dog-like shake of his shoulders, John jerked himself back into the present and uttered one of his characteristic throat-clearing noises, which could mean almost anything. Marching towards the door, he beckoned to the others with a sweep of his hand, and a few moments later they were back in the manor bailey, climbing on to their horses, which had been made ready by the youthful grooms.

William Vado rode ahead of them and Osbert the reeve and two other men loped easily behind them, as the horses went at a mere walking pace along the rough track out of the village. They retraced their route of the previous evening towards the bare downs behind the cliffs, but then descended the little wooded valley that led to the fishing huts that John had seen on the small beach. Although the rain and wind had died down, it was much colder, and the first chills of approaching winter were in the air. John wore leather riding gauntlets, but most of the other men had rags wrapped around their hands to keep some feeling in their fingers. The two village men, who seemed to be some sort of assistants to the reeve, were bare-footed, but their horny soles seemed impervious to both sharp stones and the cold. When they reached Challaborough beach, the bailiff turned left along a track that followed the edge of the low cliffs that formed Warren Point, the promontory opposite Burgh Island. Sheep scampered out of the way as they turned the corner above the estuary, where William Vado led them down a gully out on to the beach.

The firm sand stretched for many hundreds of yards, both over to the island and far across the river to sand dunes on the other side of the estuary, towards Thurlestone, named after the huge perforated rock pillar on the shore. The tide was coming in, but the surf was still far off, a long way short of the wreck, which lay away to their left. As they crossed the wide beach, de Wolfe noticed the imprints of bare feet running ahead of them, and soon they were met by a ragged old man, swathed in an uncured cow-hide, and a boy of about twelve, shivering in a threadbare tunic.

'This is the pair I left on guard,' explained the bailiff, though what such a frail-looking couple could do against

a determined band of pillagers was beyond John's understanding.

'Haven't seen a soul, William,' said the old man in a
quavering voice. 'Naught but a couple of tide fishermen
going across to Bantham strand.'

They walked up to the beached vessel and circled it as
it lay on its side on the sand. There was a line of seaweed
on the beach just above it, showing the limit of the high
tide. A typical trading cog, it was about forty feet long and
had the general shape of a Norse longboat, but broader,
with a high freeboard and almost vertical stem- and stern-
posts. It was half decked, there being no planking over
the central section of the hull, which was used for carrying cargo. Thomas, the only literate one among them,
read out the name chiselled into the upper strake next to
the stem-post.

'*Mary and Child Jesus*,' he intoned reverently, crossing
himself again. 'It's Thorgils' boat right enough.'

As they had just seen the ship-master's body lying in
Ringmore church, this confirmation seemed superfluous,
but John let it pass. He turned to Gwyn, as the authority
on seafaring matters.

'What's to be done about this? Is it a total wreck?'

The Cornishman pulled at the long, drooping ends of
his ginger moustache as an aid to thought. 'She's sound
enough at the moment, until the rising tides throw her
on to those rocks.' He indicated the jagged reefs at the
foot of the low cliff, fifty paces away. Advancing right up
to the deck of the ship, he inspected the damage before
continuing.

'The hull is not breached, so she should float if she was
upright.'

'So why is it lying on its side?' snapped Thomas, ever
ready to contradict the coroner's officer.

Gwyn pointed to the canvas cover that had been
stretched over the single opening that occupied half the
deck area abaft the broken mast. It was ripped across the

top and the lower part was bulging outward, as objects pressed against the inner side.

'The cargo has shifted, that's why. Whatever they have in the hold has tumbled to one side and capsized her.'

'At least it hasn't been stolen yet!' said de Wolfe, with a touch of sarcasm. He clambered on to the bulwark, which was half buried in wet sand. The deck rose vertically in front of him and, with Gwyn's help, he tore down the tattered canvas. There was a rumble and they both stepped aside hastily as several kegs and boxes rolled out of the hold, having lost the support of the hatch cover.

The bailiff joined the two larger men as they peered into the gloomy cave that formed the entire inside of the hull. Thomas, sniffing miserably at a dew-drop that dangled from the end of his long, pointed nose, cautiously held back with the other men from the village. A few dozen barrels and a collection of crates lay on the lower ribs of the hull. Several kegs had cracked and a smell of wine permeated the air inside.

Gwyn hauled at one of the casks to gauge its weight, then did the same to a crate. 'These are damned heavy. No wonder she keeled over when they shifted!'

'Why should that have happened?' demanded John. 'Thorgils was one of the best ship-masters along the coast.'

'Not if he was dead, he wasn't!' retorted his officer. 'With the crew stabbed or thrown over the side, the vessel would have broached to in the strong winds and waves we've had these past few days, especially this close to the shore.'

He pointed a hand the size of a small ham towards the stern.

'With no one at the steering oar nor men to attend to the sail, she would have been thrown on her beam ends and this cargo would have tumbled to one side, preventing her from righting herself.'

'So what happened to whoever murdered them? Did

21

they drown as well?' asked Thomas, but no one answered him. The coroner had stepped over the coaming of the hatchway, and as his eyes became more accustomed to the gloom he walked along the planking between the now horizontal ribs.

'This isn't only cargo – someone has been living down here,' he rasped.

Gwyn and William Vado followed his pointing finger and saw four sodden mattresses floating in the few inches of water between the ribs. They were no more than sacks filled with straw, some of which was spouting from the torn end of one bag.

'There's some pots and a broken jug there, too,' observed the bailiff. 'Maybe the crew lived down here?'

'No, they would take turns to be on watch and to eat and sleep in that shelter near the stern,' said Gwyn. He indicated the remains of a low structure abaft the hatch, which had been smashed but was still recognisable as a wood-and-canvas hut, little larger than a privy.

'So Thorgils must have been bringing some passengers back from wherever he had been,' mused de Wolfe. 'I know he took our goods to Harfleur at the mouth of the Seine, but God knows where he went after that.'

There seemed nothing else to be learned from the vessel. There were no bloodstains on the planking, but given the battering the cog had received from tide, wind and rain, this was to be expected, even if at least three men had been slain there.

'What's to be done about the ship, Gwyn?' demanded the coroner. 'Can she be saved?'

The ginger giant made a show of deep thought, pursing his lips under their hairy fringe and staring first at the vessel, then at the line of rocks at the top of the beach.

'Have to be quick – a few more rising tides and she'll be pounded to bits. But if this cargo can be taken out of her, then she'll float upright and could be towed upriver on a flood tide.'

'Why take her up the Avon?' asked the coroner.

'Because then she could be beached somewhere safe a mile or two inland, until she could be remasted and sailed back to Dawlish,' reasoned his officer. 'Or a rough mast could be jury-rigged, enough to get her to Salcombe or even Dartmouth for repairs.'

De Wolfe stood immobile for a long monent, as the glimmerings of a plan came into his mind. The bailiff thought that he now looked more like a black cormorant than a crow, as with his hands on his hips the drape of his dark cloak resembled the outstretched wings of one of those seabirds drying itself on a rock.

'I'm seizing this vessel and her cargo in the name of the King,' announced de Wolfe formally. 'It is part of my duties as coroner to confiscate wrecks of the sea, as well as royal fish – the whale and sturgeon – to the use of our sovereign.' He cleared his throat. 'At least until I hold an inquest . . . it may be that I will decide to restore the property to the rightful owners.'

'The owner's dead!' objected Thomas, with unusual boldness.

'Then to his heirs!' snapped John. 'And the cargo was not his property, he was just the carrier. I need to discover the truc owners.'

He glared at Thomas. 'No doubt you've got writing materials in that bag you always carry,' he grunted, indicating a shapeless pouch that hung from his clerk's shoulder. 'So make a tally of every one of these casks and boxes. I want them all accounted for when they're carted back.'

'Back to where, Crowner?' asked the bailiff.

'I don't know yet. Enquiries will have to be made among various importers.Thorgils usually dealt with merchants in Exeter or Topsham.'

He turned to Gwyn once again. 'You said this vessel will have to be towed. How can that be brought about?'

'Once she's afloat, given calmer weather like we have

today, then a couple of pulling boats can drag her out towards the middle of the estaury. The incoming tide will take her up without effort, as long as the towing boats keep her bow to the middle of the stream.'

De Wolfe spent the next ten minutes giving orders to William Vado and his reeve, using his authority as the King's law officer to impress on them that there would be trouble if his wishes were not carried out. The cargo, which thankfully was only about half a full load, was to be carted back to the tithe barn at Ringmore, and the coroner promised dire consequences if any of it went missing. He was only too well aware of how goods and even the fittings and timbers of a stranded ship could vanish overnight. In fact, one of the purposes of the coroner was to try to stop the depredations of the locals on what was royal booty.

'And what about moving the vessel?' he demanded. 'Can two boats be found, together with some men who have a knowledge of these matters?'

William consulted the old man with the smelly hide cloak, who apparently was a beach scavenger who lived in a hut near the mouth of the river. After a muttered discussion, in accents so thick that John missed half the words, the bailiff turned back, somewhat abashed.

'He says it could be done, but the men would wish for payment, as they would lose their fishing for that day.'

John nodded curtly. 'We'll no doubt be able to find them a few pence for their trouble. They only need to beach the craft in a safe place, then I will send a shipwright down to see what needs to be done.'

As they began walking back along the beach, Gwyn came close to his master and murmured in his ear.

'Why are you concerned with the vessel, Crowner? Thorgils is dead.'

John tapped the side of his curved nose. 'Firstly, I feel I should do what I can for the widow Hilda. That vessel is worth nothing to her smashed on the rocks.'

'I thought the coroner had to sell salvaged wrecks for

the benefit of the King's treasury?' grunted his officer. He was well aware of the long history of John and Hilda and wondered what the coroner was planning.

'It's up to the coroner and his jury. As with deodands, there is a discretion to give some or all of the value to the widow or surviving relatives.' He was referring to the object that caused a death, such as a sword, a cart or even a mill-wheel. Normally this 'deodand' was confiscated for the Crown, but its value could be given to the dependants, especially if the dead victim was the breadwinner and his demise had caused hardship to the family. But Gwyn was still curious about the coroner's motives.

'D'you think Hilda would want to keep on Thorgils' seafaring business? She will be a comfortable widow anyway, with that fine house in Dawlish and no doubt quite a few pounds sitting in his treasure chest.'

John was quite ready to talk about his plans with his trusted companion of more than twenty years.

'It occurs to me that as Thorgils carried abroad almost all the goods from my enterprise with Hugh de Relaga, it might be more sensible for us to run the vessel ourselves. When she has overcome her grief, I will put it to Hilda that she could enter our partnership, as a passive member. We could have the use of the *Mary and Child Jesus* and she could share in the profits.'

As they trudged across the sands, Gwyn gave a broad smile that was almost a leer. 'You must like living danger-ously, Crowner, to take as a partner such a lovely woman, when you have two other ladies in Exeter who are only too well aware of your partiality for her.'

'This would be purely a business arrangement, man!' he snapped. 'Where's the harm in that?'

'None, though I suppose you will need to go to Dawlish quite often to discuss that business,' replied Gwyn, with an innocent expression that did not fool his master.

Thomas, who had been limping behind listening to this exchange, piped up with a practical question. 'Beg pardon, Crowner, but you are no ship-master! How will you manage such a venture, which is so foreign to your nature as a soldier and a knight?'

'Pah! I'll leave that side of the matter to Hugh de Relaga. He can appoint one of his clerks to run the business or find some former shipman to advise him. If the portreeve thinks that he can make more profit, he'll find a way, never fear!'

As they were nearing the bottom of the gully, their conversation lapsed, but privately Gwyn was still worried. He feared that John's proposed intimacy with Hilda, even if allegedly only commercial, would be ill received by certain ladies in Exeter. He knew that de Wolfe's youthful romance with the blonde Saxon and his irregular adultery with her over the succeeding years, was more than just casual lust. The Cornishman cared nothing for any problems with the coroner's wife Matilda, with whom Gwyn shared a virulent mutual dislike – but he was concerned about anything that might cause another rift between the coroner and Nesta, the landlady of the Bush Inn.

His anxious ruminations were suddenly interrupted by shouting from behind them, coming from the direction of the river, where it fanned out across the sand in its last rush towards the sea. The old flotsam-raker stopped and stared in that direction. 'It's one of the beach fishers,' he said in a quavering voice. 'But there's a packhorse and some other men coming up behind him.'

The bailiff and his manor-reeve began walking towards the man who was hollering and waving his arms to attract their attention. A beach fisher was one of those shore-dwelling folk who scratched a living by catching crabs in the rocks and by pegging out baited lines at low tide, following the next ebb back to retrieve any fish that might have been hooked. The coroner's trio waited for the men to approach and saw that the last pair were leading a thin packhorse across the shallow delta of the river.

'There's something strapped across its back,' observed Gwyn, shading his eyes from the glare of the weak sun on the sea. 'It looks like another body.'

Minutes later, this was confirmed, as when the group arrived they saw a limp shape draped over the sumpter horse's bare back, held on by a rope tied around the beast's belly. William Vado came up and repeated what he had just heard from the other men.

'Crowner, these are fishermen from Bantham, just across the river. On Monday, they found this young man washed up on the beach, still alive, but near to death.'

Gwyn gently lifted up the head of the corpse, which had been drooping face down against the rough hide of the pony.

'Little more than a lad, by the looks of him. Dressed like a seaman, the same as the others.'

'Must be the missing one from the crew,' suggested Osbert the reeve. The compassionate Thomas began shriving the dead boy in murmured Latin, repeatedly making the sign of the Cross on himself as if he were in a cathedral quire, not shivering on a wintry beach.

'He was still alive when you found him?' demanded de Wolfe. 'Did he say what had happened?'

One of the fishermen, the one leading the pony, shook his head.

'The poor lad died on us within a couple of hours. He was half drowned when we found him on the beach, then he began retching and gasping.'

'We took him to our hut on the Ham, where we had a fire and warmed him up, intending to take him back to the village,' said the other man, a gaunt figure with a hacking cough that suggested advanced phthisis. 'But he never made it. We were going to bury him above the high-water mark, as is done with the corpses of most washed-up shipmen, but then yesterday we heard that there had been others found over here, so we thought we'd better bring him across.'

'Did he get his wits back at all before he died?' asked Gwyn.

The haggard fisherman looked at his mate first, then shrugged.

'Nothing that made sense. He came round a bit and mumbled, but old Joel said the only word he could make out sounded like "Saracens".'

John sighed at the obtuse way of speaking of these rural folk.

'Who's Joel, for God's sake?' he demanded.

The man pointed up to the top of Burgh Island. 'He's a hermit who lives up there in the stone cell of St Michael. A bit crazy, but useful, as he acts as our huer, spotting shoals of pilchard and herring for us.'

'If the boy said it was Saracens, perhaps the vessel was attacked by Barbary pirates?' suggested Thomas. 'Remember what happened at Lynmouth last year, when that galley appeared? They were Turks or some brigands from beyond Gibraltar.'

It was true, conceded de Wolfe, that both the Channel coast and the Severn Sea were visited by these swift rowing vessels filled with bloodthirsty villians, not only from Moorish Spain but from as far away as North Africa or the Levant. Though the distances were great, they seemed to have no difficulty in reaching these islands, where abundant trading ships and coastal villages offered rich pickings. Some even set up camps on islands such as Lundy or along the coast of southern Wales.

'Has this young fellow been injured in any way, like the others?' he demanded, waving a hand at the lifeless form slumped across the packhorse.

'Not that we could see, sir,' said the first fisherman. 'He died of having his tubes and lights filled with sea water and sand.'

His emaciated companion gave him an uneasy glance once again.

'There was one other thing, my lord,' he muttered,

playing safe with John's rank. 'The same day, when we went to attend to our fishing lines at Aymer Cove, a mile or so up the coast, we found a curragh.'

A curragh was a kind of elongated coracle, a light boat large enough to hold six men. It was made of canvas daubed with pitch, stretched over a frame of hazel withies.

'Every cog carries a curragh, lashed upside down on its deck,' said Gwyn. 'It's used for getting ashore when the vessel can't come against a wharf – or even as a life-saver if she sinks.'

'No doubt it was washed off the *Mary* when she lost her crew and was capsized,' said John.

Both fishermen shook their heads emphatically. 'Not so, sir! The boat was undamaged and had been dragged up above the tide-line,' said the thin man.

'There was a keel mark in the sand where it had been pulled up,' confirmed the other fellow. 'And there were two paddles left inside. Someone had landed there, no doubt of that.'

'It may be nothing to do with the *Mary*,' objected Thomas stubbornly. 'If this poor lad mentioned "Saracens", surely that means it was attacked by pirates.'

'Was the curragh one you recognised?' asked Gwyn.

The sick-looking local shook his head. 'We know every boat for ten miles along this coast. This was a different style from the few we fishermen build, it was the sort that trading vessels carry.'

De Wolfe rubbed his bristly face, now black with four days' stubble since his last shave. 'So it seems that someone came ashore – and there's nowhere they could have come from other than a ship, unless it was St Brendan himself!'

His allusion to the Irish monk who centuries before had allegedly explored the deep ocean in a curragh was lost on these untutored folk.

'And the only ship around here is stranded on this very beach – and its boat is missing!' said Gwyn with morbid satisfaction. 'Too much of a coincidence not to think that the killers used the curragh to get ashore.'

'But why, for God's sake?' demanded de Wolfe. 'Why slay a few poor shipmen and let the vessel become wrecked. It wasn't even for the cargo, for that didn't amount to much – and anyway, it's still in the vessel.'

No one had an answer for him, and after he had made a quick check of the young sailor's body, the fishermen set off with the packhorse to deliver the corpse to the church, where it could lay with the other victims. John then discussed with the bailiff and reeve how best to manage the removal of the cargo and get the stranded cog towed to shelter. After the promise of a small reward, the fishermen and the crabber agreed to help and Osbert the reeve was dispatched upriver to negotiate for a couple of pulling-boats and the men to handle them, so that the *Mary* could be hauled off on the following day's tide, while the weather still held calm.

Then they set off after the pony with its unhappy burden, and before mid-morning were back in Ringmore, where they thankfully warmed themselves again in the hall of the manor-house and ate a more substantial breakfast of bread, sea-fish, eggs and fat bacon, before the next stage in their legal proceedings.

CHAPTER TWO

In which Crowner John calls upon a new widow

It was past noon before the coroner could begin his inquest, for they had to wait for Osbert the reeve to return from Bigbury, a village farther inland, where he was seeking men to salvage the cog. He was needed for the proceedings, as he had been declared First Finder. This time, John de Wolfe had a double jurisdiction, not only in respect of the dead men, but also concerning the wrecked vessel.

None of this had much impact upon proceedings in the tiny manor of Ringmore that day. De Wolfe was the second-most senior law officer in the county, and his superior, the sheriff Henry de Furnellis, was an elderly, easygoing man who was only too content to let John get on with his job in whatever fashion he chose. In this, he was quite different to his predecessor, Sir Richard de Revelle, who was also John's brother-in-law. He had recently been expelled for malpractice, mainly at John's instigation, a fact that made the coroner's married life even more fraught with problems. As he went down to the churchyard for the inquest, de Wolfe remembered with a twinge of unease that his brother-in-law's main manor, Revelstoke, was only a dozen miles farther down the coast, and in fact could just be seen from where they had stopped to survey the wreck. He shrugged off the thought, as he could conceive of no possible way in which Richard could become involved in this present matter, even though John was always suspicious of any of his activities.

At the gap in the moss-covered stone wall that surrounded the neglected churchyard, John found that the surly village priest was directing everyone across the overgrown area to another opening on the far side, which led to the large tithe barn, standing lower on the sloping terrain.

'I thought it more seemly for your deliberations to take place there, rather than in my consecrated church,' growled Father Walter, who seemed ill disposed to offer any help to the representatives of the Crown. 'I had the bodies laid out there, together with the new one that you sent.' With that, he loped off to indicate that he wanted no more to do with them.

'Useless old bugger!' growled Gwyn, who had little time for clergymen, other than his friend Thomas. 'I'll wager he's off to find a skin of wine, even at this time of day.'

'That's why he's stuck in a God-forsaken place like Ringmore,' replied John. 'The bishop and his archdeacons send the drunks and deadbeats to places like this, where they get even worse.'

After the manor-house, the tithe barn was the best structure in the village. It was a substantial building of massive oak frames, boarded with panels of woven hazel withies plastered with cob, a mixture of clay, dung and bracken. The steep roof was thatched with oat straw, mottled with moss and growing grass. There was a pair of doors tall enough to admit an ox-cart piled with hay, and now, at the start of winter, the barn was half full of this sweet-smelling fodder. Heaps of turnips and carrots lay on the floor and piles of threshed oats occupied a boxed platform raised up on large stones in an attempt to keep the rats away. Though a tenth of all this was destined for the church, the contents of the barn represented most of the winter stores that the village hoped would keep them alive until late spring.

Floor space was limited, and the four corpses were laid in a row just inside the wide-open doors. The coroner stood in the entrance to conduct the proceedings, which were opened by Gwyn in his role as coroner's officer.

'All ye who have anything to do before the King's Coroner for the County of Devon, draw near and give your attendance!' he roared in his bull-like voice. With his wild red hair and whiskers, he cut a fearsome figure in his coarse woollen tunic, over which his worn leather jerkin fell open to reveal the huge sword hanging from a wide belt, supported by the leather baldric over his shoulder.

His audience consisted of a score of men from the village, rounded up earlier by the bailiff to act as a jury. In theory, all the males over fourteen from the four nearest villages should have attended, in case any of them knew anything about the deaths under investigation. In a hard-working farming and fishing community this was patently impossible. Though the object of a jury was to provide witnesses, as well as adjudicators, finding so many men and boys from such a wide area was quite impracticable in the time available. John knew this very well and was content to carry on with the handful of men who might know something about the matter, which included Osbert, the fishermen and the crabber. Even old Joel, the recluse from the island, was there, a tall, thin man who looked like an animated skeleton dressed in a ragged robe of hessian, with a poorly cured sealskin cape stinking around his bony shoulders. In spite of his scarecrow appearance, he held himself erect and had the remnants of authority about him, which made the ever curious Thomas wonder as to his past history.

De Wolfe knew full well that his inquiry would be futile at this early stage, but being a man who stuck rigidly to his royal mandate, he pressed ahead with the formality of the inquest. The first matter was that of 'Presentment of Englishry', which again was a foregone

impossibility, given that a hundred-and-thirty years after
the Norman invasion, intermarriage had blurred the distinction between Norman and Saxon. And if proof could
not be produced, a murdrum fine was levied, so 'presentment' had become merely a cynical device for
extorting money from the population, especially as all
deaths other than those from obvious disease were eligi-
ble, even if they were due to accidents or the occasional
suicide.

John de Wolfe still had to apply the outdated procedure, however, and he began his inquest by glaring
around the bemused villeins and freemen of Ringmore,
demanding to know whether anyone could prove the
identity of the corpses. As the dead men were strangers
washed up on a nearby beach – and presumably came
from Dawlish, over thirty miles away – there was little
chance of anyone present knowing anything about
them, but one fellow spoke up in a rather truculent
voice.

'I hear that one of them is called Thorgils, so with a
name like that, how can he be anything other than of
Saxon blood?'

From the size of his bulging arm muscles and his
leather apron scarred with burns, John assumed that he
was the village blacksmith. The coroner knew that the
smith was doing what he could to avoid the murdrum
fine – usually of several marks – being imposed on the village, as they would all suffer from having to scrape
together the hundreds of pennies needed. He replied,
but tempered his words with a reassurance.

'A good point, but I need much better proof. In the
absence of any family, then presentment cannot be made
and my clerk will so record the fact.' He jerked his head
towards Thomas, who was sitting on a small stool just outside the doors, with his writing materials before him on
an empty keg. 'But no murdrum fine will be imposed
until the Justices in Eyre consider the matter, which might

be a year or two in the future. And if the true culprits of this heinous crime are found before then, you will not be amerced.'

A murmur of relief rippled round the half-circle of jurors, echoed in the background by the group of anxious wives who were clustered around the gateway into the churchyard. Women had no voice in these matters, but they suffered just as much when penalties were imposed on their village.

The few witnesses were called one after the other, to haltingly say their piece. Osbert described how he had been called to view one body and then found another two. The fishermen repeated their story about discovering the dying boy and the mysteriously intact curragh. The hermit Joel, who had a surprisingly deep and cultured voice for such a wreck of a man, related how he had heard the word 'Saracens' pass the lips of the dying lad, but he could add nothing more of any use. Then John instructed Gwyn to march the jury past the four pathetic corpses, so that they could see the wounds on three of them.

'It was a large knife, with a wider blade than the usual dagger,' he pointed out in his sonorous voice. 'The younger lad has no wounds, but you have heard how he soon expired from the effects of the sea, being half drowned when they found him on the shore.'

Gwyn marshalled the men back into line outside the barn, so that the coroner could address them again.

'There is much more to be learned about this affair, but I must reach a verdict now, so that the dead men may be given a Christian burial. There is no doubt that three of the seamen have been stabbed to death. It is impossible to be sure what happened to the boy, but common sense would suggest that he managed to jump over the side of the vessel when they were attacked. Thus he escaped injury, but perished in the waves.' He glowered along the line of men, his dark head thrust out like a vulture. 'So make up your own minds and get one of you to tell me what you decide.'

There was a muttered discussion lasting less than a minute, then the blacksmith stepped forward. 'Crowner, we go along with what you said. The three men were slain, but we can't be sure about the lad.'

De Wolfe nodded his agreement. 'It shall be so recorded. Now I have to consider an easier matter, that of the vessel. The *Mary and Child Jesus*, a trading cog out of Dawlish, was owned by Thorgils, one of the murdered men. It was washed up on the shore at the mouth of the Avon and as no living thing survived aboard, I now declare it a wreck of the sea.'

Ancient law stated that a stranded vessel that was totally abandoned became the property of the Crown. If anyone survived on board, the boat and its cargo remained the property of the owners. There had even been cases where it had been successfully pleaded that even a dog or cat left on the ship had prevented the declaration of a wreck.

'I also take the cargo into the King's custody and I command that it be kept safely.' De Wolfe scowled around the small crowd to impress the point upon them. 'My clerk has a complete inventory of what was in the vessel and I expect every single item to be there when arrangements are made for its collection.'

He knew only too well that the contents of a ship – and even the structure of the vessel itself – were an irresistible attraction to poor coastal communities. In fact, the Curia Regis had placed wrecks within the coroner's jurisdiction in an attempt to reduce the pillaging that went on, often with the local lord's consent or even active participation.

The inquest was soon over, and all that remained for John to decide was the fate of the corpses.

'If we wait until we get back to Exeter before sending a cart down here to fetch them, they'll be stinking by the time they reach Dawlish,' said Gwyn, in his typically blunt fashion. It was true that a clumsy ox-cart trundling along the atrocious tracks of South Devon would take many days to make the round trip. William Vado confirmed that there was no carter in Ringmore or any of the nearby villages who would be willing to make the long journey to Dawlish. Eventually, de Wolfe compromised by paying for a local carter to convey the dead men as far as Totnes, where the coroner promised to make arrangements for them to be taken on to Dawlish.

Their work in the village done, the trio saddled up and by noon were on their way eastwards, the coroner grimly promising the bailiff that he would be back as soon as there was any news of what had occurred on that lonely coast.

It was the afternoon of the next day when they reached Dawlish, as John had stopped to visit his mother and the rest of the family at Stoke-in-Teignhead, a village just south of the River Teign, not far from where it emptied into the sea at Teignmouth. He had been born and brought up there and had a great affection for the place, where his sprightly mother Enyd, spinster sister Evelyn and elder brother William still held the manor. Their usual effusive hospitality extended not only to John, but to Gwyn and Thomas as well, who were always welcome there. They were plied with food and drink, which the ever hungry Cornishman attacked with gusto, while John brought the family up to date on recent events. In fact it was difficult to get away, and only John's pleading that he must call at Dawlish on the way home allowed them to get back on the road. His family had been saddened to hear that Hilda was now widowed, for she was the daughter of the reeve at their other manor at Holcombe, farther up the coast. They had all known her since she was a child, but the unbreachable gap between a Saxon villein and the son of a Norman manor-lord made it impossible for John's youthful romance with Hilda to flourish. Privately,

Enyd would have preferred her as a daughter-in-law to Matilda de Revelle, but it was not to be.

As the three men rode out of the wooded valley of Stoke, John's mother gazed after them with a twinge of anxiety, as she was well aware of her son's partiality for women and the affection he felt for Hilda. Enyd was also very fond of his Welsh mistress Nesta, especially as she herself had a Welsh father and a Cornish mother. As John vanished beyond the trees, she hoped that Hilda's new availability would not put her son's life in greater emotional turmoil than usual.

The riders reached the ford at the mouth of the Teign, where thankfully the tide was low enough for them to cross, then went northwards up the coast for a few miles. Dawlish was a village that straggled above the beach, where a small river gave shelter for the vessels that were pulled up on to its sandy banks. Most were fishing boats, but there were two trading cogs lying there, smaller than the wrecked *Mary*.

'I'll leave you to it, Crowner,' said Gwyn tactfully, as they reined in in the centre of the hamlet. 'I'll be in the alehouse when you've finished.'

'And I'll be in the church, praying for the souls of those poor shipmen,' added Thomas rather haughtily, preferring God's house to a tavern.

John led Odin down to the river to drink, then tied the reins of the big grey stallion to the rail outside the inn, giving orders to a runny-nosed lad who acted as ostler to find hay for their three steeds. Then he loped up a short side lane from the village street, making for the largest house in Dawlish, which lay behind the usual collection of ramshackle dwellings.

Thorgils had done well from his cross-Channel business, after many years of sailing back and forth with goods in either direction. Some five years before, he had used some of his accumulated wealth to build this fine house, modelled on some he had seen in Brittany. It was all in stone, the only one in this village of wooden dwellings, and had an upper storey, supported in front by two pillars, like a house he had admired in Dol.

John de Wolfe threw his mantle back over his shoulders as he approached the front door, made of heavy oak with metal banding. Suddenly, he felt apprehensive at being the bearer of such bad news. Though he knew that Hilda had never been in love with her husband, who was more than twenty years older, he was well aware that she had felt affection and respect for him and that Thorgils had always treated her courteously and generously. She had married him twelve years earlier, when John was away fighting in the Irish wars. Though a little piqued and slightly jealous, de Wolfe had been glad that she had found security and comfort, as although his brother William was a most benign lord in Holcombe, the life of an unfree peasant in a small village did not equal that of the wife of a wealthy ship-master.

He straightened his habitually stooped shoulders and rapped on the door with the hilt of his dagger. A moment later it opened and Hilda's maid, a pleasant, round-faced girl called Alice, gazed out at him in surprise.

'Is your mistress at home?' he asked gently, for he knew the girl from previous clandestine visits when Thorgils had been on the high seas. The maid stood aside for him to enter, then led him down a short corridor between two rooms. The house did not have the usual cavernous hall with an upper solar attached – instead, an open wooden stairway rose at the end of the passageway. The girl clattered up the steps before him and went into a chamber at the back of the house, one of the pair that occupied the upper floor. He heard her excitedly announce that Sir John had arrived, then he followed her into the room. Hilda was seated on a padded bench next to an open window that looked over roofs towards the shore. The Saxon woman, now in her mid-thirties, was slim and supple and had long blonde hair falling to her waist, unconfined in braids or a cover-chief when she was at home. She rose quickly as he came in and gazed with pleased surprise at her former lover.

'John, what are you doing here? I had no idea that you would call on me today.' Then Hilda noticed his expression and her gaze faltered.

The next few minutes were very uncomfortable for John as he broke the news as gently as he could. Alice stood uncertainly near the door, as her mistress was held close against the breast of this fierce-looking knight. Hilda's eyes filled with tears, but much to John's relief she held back from sobbing, as he would rather face a thousand of Saladin's warriors than one weeping woman.

'He was a good man, always kind to me, like another father,' she murmured into his tunic. 'I'll miss him, though he was away at sea for much of the year.' Hilda turned her beautiful face up to John, causing him to think inconsequentially how different it was from Nesta's. Where the Welsh woman had rounder features with a snub nose, Hilda's face was longer, with higher cheek-bones and a slim, straight nose below her blue eyes.

He led her back to her chair and drew up a stool to be close to her side.

'There are many practical matters to be dealt with, Hilda. But I will do all I can to help you with them.'

She nodded, drying her moist cheeks with the hem of her sleeve, then ordered the maid to fetch some wine and pastries. When the girl had rather reluctantly left the room, Hilda laid her hand on his.

'There has been a very special bond between us for many years, John. I wish with all my heart that I could have become your wife, instead of Thorgils', but it was not possible.' She leant across and kissed his stubbly cheek. 'But we must not turn this tragedy to our own advantage – I am a new widow and you have your Nesta.'

De Wolfe knew that he was being gently warned off, and it reinforced his determination to be faithful to his

Welsh mistress, if not his wife. Yet a trace of disappointment niggled in his mind, though even that was soothed by her next words. 'Time may alter matters, John, so let us have patience.'

The wine and a platter of meat pasties appeared and as Alice seemed determined to play the chaperone by crouching in a corner, John led the discussion on to the practical matters he had raised. He told Hilda of the arrangements to bring back the bodies of Thorgils and the other Dawlish men and promised to send Thomas de Peyne to see the parish priest this very afternoon, to organise the funeral.

When he enquired about money, she assured him that her husband, conscious of his years and his dangerous occupation on the high seas, had made ample provision for an unexpected death. A document had been drawn up by an Exeter lawyer leaving everything to her, as there were no children alive by his previous marriage and they had had none themselves.

'I have the key to his treasure chest, which he always told me to use as my own,' she said sadly. 'The house is valuable and he owned two other smaller ships and a warehouse in Topsham which brings in a rent, so I have no concerns about my survival.'

She asked about the *Mary and Child Jesus*, expecting to hear that it was a total loss, but John explained that it might well be saved and brought back into service.

'But I have no experience as a shipowner, John. What am I to do with these three vessels? Shall I sell them?'

He had no wish to burden her with business matters so soon after learning that she was a widow, but he briefly explained that he would talk to Hugh de Relaga and see whether they could work out some new venture.

'But forget that for now, dear woman,' he said gruffly, as he rose and patted her shoulder awkwardly. 'I will attend to all these matters. Have you someone who can come and keep you company at this unhappy time?'

She smiled sadly. 'With Thorgils absent so much, I am so often alone, apart from Alice here. With the winter coming and the ships laid up, I was looking forward to his company. Now I will go home to Holcombe for a while to be with my family.'

John assured her that his brother William, manor-lord of Holcombe, already knew of the tragedy and would do anything necessary to help her.

As he was leaving, with a promise to return for the funeral, Hilda clutched his arm.

'Who can have done such a terrible thing, John?' she asked, in a voice that quavered with emotion. 'The wife of a shipman always accepts the perils of the sea. Every time he left, I wondered if it would be the last I would ever see of him, because of some tempest or shipwreck. But that he should be stabbed to death, along with his crew, is beyond my comprehension!'

John put a long arm around her shoulders and hugged her to him, ignoring the curious stares of the maid.

'I'll not rest until I find the answer to that question, Hilda. This is a very strange crime, but I'll get to the bottom of it, even if takes me years and a journey to Cathay and back!'

The coroner's next journey was not as far as Cathay, but was the ten miles into Exeter, which they reached just before dusk, when the walled city was closed at curfew. Gwyn did not enter through the West Gate with his master, but went around the south side to reach the village of St Sidwell, where he lived in a hut with his wife and two small sons. With his clerk lagging wearily behind, John de Wolfe walked his horse up Fore Street to the central crossing of Carfoix and straight on into High Street, the town plan having been set down a thousand years earlier by the Romans. A thriving, bustling city, Exeter was developing quickly, many of the old wooden houses being rebuilt in stone, so that a confused mixture of styles lined the crowded streets. Not yet paved, these lanes were of beaten earth, dusty in the dry and a morass in the rain. A central gutter sluggishly conveyed all the effluent down to the river, including most of the rubbish and filth that householders and shopkeepers flung out of their doors.

Just past the new Guildhall, a narrow alley opened on the right-hand side. This was Martin's Lane, one of the entrances into the cathedral Close, the large open area around the massive church of St Mary and St Peter, whose twin towers soared above the city. The coroner had his house in the lane, but this evening both he and his clerk carried on up High Street towards the East Gate, then turned up Castle Hill to Rougemont, the fortress perched on the northern tip of the sloping city. John wished to discover whether any more cases had been reported during his absence down in the country. Thankfully, the guardroom had no messages for him and with Thomas close behind, he climbed to his cheerless chamber high in the gatehouse, which stood astride the entrance to the inner ward. He had hardly sat down behind his table when a voice came from the doorway.

'The sheriff sends his compliments, Sir John, and asks if you could attend upon him.'

The voice was that of Sergeant Gabriel, the grizzled old soldier who headed the garrison's men-at-arms at Rougemont, so called on account of the colour of its local sandstone. He had stuck his head around the tattered hessian curtain that hung over the doorway to de Wolfe's chamber. It was a bleak, draughty garret, spitefully provided by the former sheriff, Richard de Revelle, when he was reluctantly obliged to find some accommodation for his brother-in-law, the new coroner. De Revelle had seen the introduction of these upstart coroners as a threat to his own interests, especially his opportunities to extort and embezzle from the inhabitants and taxes of the shire of Devon. The knowledge that one of the King's motives in setting up the coroner system was to keep a check on rapacious sheriffs made it an even more bitter pill to swallow.

De Wolfe received the sergeant's message with a lift of his black eyebrows, as he sat in the lengthening gloom at the rough trestle table that acted as his desk. This, together with a bench and a couple of milking stools, was the only furniture in the room. Thomas de Peyne was on one of the stools on the other side of the table, his tongue projecting from the corner of his thin lips as he began lighting a rush lamp with a flint and tinder to check the parchment roll carrying his account of the Ringmore inquest.

'Did he say what he wanted, Gabriel?' demanded de Wolfe.

The old soldier shook his head. 'Not a word, Crowner! But a herald came with messages from Winchester when you were away. The day 'afore yesterday, it was – so maybe it's to do with that.'

His head vanished, and with a groan at the stiffness in his back and legs after so much riding, John rose and went after him, with an unnecessary admonition to his clerk to get the inquisition finished before the day was out.

The steep spiral staircase in the thickness of the wall led back down to the guardroom.This was just inside the archway that led from a drawbridge spanning a deep ditch separating it from the outer ward. The tall, narrow gatehouse had been built by William the Bastard, one of the first stone structures he put up after the Conquest, mainly to guard against a repetition of the revolt that the citizens of Exeter raised against him. Below it, the large outer ward was defended by a bank topped by a stout wooden palisade and contained most of the garrison and their families, living in a motley collection of huts and sheds.

The inner ward was protected by a castellated wall cutting off the uppermost corner of the old Roman fortifications. John walked across this towards the keep, a two-storeyed building in the far corner, beyond the Shire Hall, which was the courthouse for the city. The only other stone building there was the tiny garrison chapel of St Mary.

De Wolfe tramped through the mud churned by horses, oxen and soldiers' boots into a slippery brown paste, until he reached the wooden steps going up to the entrance to the keep. As a defence measure, this was set high above the undercroft, a gloomy basement partly below ground level which housed the cells of the castle gaol. The upper doorway gave directly on to the hall, a large chamber occupying most of the main floor, the remainder holding a few rooms for the sheriff and castle constable. The floor above was a warren of stores, offices and living accommodation for clerks and more senior servants.

John looked around the crowded hall and its scattering of tables where men were talking, eating and drinking. Although it was late in the day, more were standing in groups or tramping impatiently about waiting for an audience with clerks and officials. A big log fire smouldered in an open hearth against one wall, the smoke wreathing upwards to blacken the old ceiling beams even more. He acknowledged a few waves and greetings, then went to the first door on the left of the hall where a man-at-arms in a leather cuirass and round iron helmet with a nose-guard was leaning against the wall. As soon as he saw the coroner, he sprang to attention, banged the butt of his spear on the ground in salute and opened the door for John to enter.

Inside, he found the sheriff, Henry de Furnellis, beleagured behind a table covered with rolls and parchments. Candles and rush-lights were lit on the table and in sconces around the walls. A clerk hovered beside him, waving more documents for the sheriff's attention.

'Thank God for an interruption!' boomed de

Furnellis. 'Sit down and give me an excuse for a drink and a respite from these bloody rolls.' As Henry was no more literate than John, his clerks had to read him every word and transcribe any responses from his dictation, as Thomas de Peyne did for the coroner.

John was quite familiar with Henry's chamber and went to a shelf to fetch a large jug of cider and two pewter mugs. He filled these and placed one before the sheriff, before dragging up a stool and sitting down on the opposite side of the table. They both took deep draughts of the cloudy fluid, then Henry gave a sigh of satisfaction and wiped his lips with the back of his hand. 'I needed that, John! The county farm has to go to Winchester next week and these accursed clerks are driving me mad with their accounts.'

The 'farm' was the twice-yearly payment of the taxes collected from Devonshire and had to be taken in coin personally by the sheriff, to be accounted for by the clerks of the royal exchequer. The two men talked for a few moments about the state of the local economy and the fears they had that the next farm might be much reduced, if the coming harvest was as bad as could be expected after this foul summer. Though Exeter itself was booming from its trade in tin, wool and cloth exports, most of the population elsewhere in the county lived off the land and were ever vulnerable to the effects of the weather.

De Furnellis reached across to refill their tankards. At sixty, he was almost two decades older than John, another old soldier who had been rewarded for his years of faithful service by being appointed as sheriff. In fact, this was the second time he had been sheriff of Devon, as early the previous year John's brother-in-law had been appointed, but owing to suspicions of his favouring Prince John's rebellion, Richard had been suspended and Henry had filled the gap for a few months, until de Revelle was reinstated. Now that the latter had finally been disgraced and ejected, de Furnellis had once more rather reluctantly accepted another term as sheriff. He fervently hoped that it would only be temporary and that he could go back into retirement once again.

After another swallow, the coroner banged his mug on to the table and got down to business.

'I've got some news for you, Henry, from the south-west of your domain. But first, what's this about a royal messenger coming while I was away?'

'That's why I wanted to see you, John. As well as a lot of official nonsense for me from the Chancery and from the justices about their next visitation, there was a message from Hubert Walter which concerns us both – especially as you are so thick with him.'

He said this without sarcasm, as de Wolfe's friendship with the Justiciar was well known. Hubert had been King Richard's second-in-command on the Third Crusade and had been rewarded by being appointed both Archbishop of Canterbury and Chief Justiciar, the highest office in the King's Council. Now that Richard Coeur-de-Lion had gone back to France, apparently never to return, Hubert Walter was virtually regent in his place, the most powerful man in England. John de Wolfe had fought alongside him in the Holy Land and had been part of Richard's body-guard on the ill-fated journey home, when the King had been kidnapped in Austria and imprisoned there and in Germany for well over a year, until the Justiciar had nego-tiated his release on payment of a huge ransom.

'What's this message about? Is Hubert calling us to clean the rust from our swords and go to help the King in France?'

John said this jokingly, but there a wistful undercurrent in his voice, as he still missed the excitement and com-radeship of the battlefield, after twenty years of campaigning.

Henry de Furnellis grinned and shook his head. He was a heavily built man, slow of movement and deliberate in speech. His ruddy face carried a large nose, though this bucolic appearance was enlivened by a pair of bright blue eyes. He had cropped grey hair and a drooping moustache of the same colour. A mournful mouth above loose skin on his neck gave him the appearance of an elderly deer-hound. Picking up a curled page of parchment from his cluttered table, he waved it at the coroner, who could see a heavy wax seal dangling from it which he recognised as that of the Justiciar.

'Like you, I can't read a bloody word of it, but Elphin said it was important.'

He beckoned to his chief clerk, who was hovering near the door to the inner chamber. This led to the sheriff's sleeping quarters, but though his predecessor had spent much of his time there – sometimes with a lady of ill repute – Henry had his own town house near the East Gate and rarely used the bedchamber. The tonsured clerk, a spare elderly man, came forward and took the document to read to John.

'It's from Hubert Walter, Crowner, and after the usual greetings, he is, quite emphatic that the contents should also be communicated to you.'

He cleared his throat and went on. 'The Justiciar says that he has had information from his spies in France that King Philip Augustus is once again encouraging Prince John, Count of Mortain, to foment rebellion against his brother, our sovereign lord, Richard. The intelligence is very vague, but there are rumours that agents have been sent to England, mainly to raise funds to recruit and equip another army for the purpose.'

De Wolfe looked across at the sheriff and shrugged. 'Nothing new in sending spies across the Channel – it happens all the time, in both directions.'

'I have not quite finished, sir!' rebuked Elphin, and dropped his eyes back to the parchment. 'Though they gleaned little more than hints and rumours, his spies heard whispers that the far west of England was involved and also that Moors might be implicated in raising money.' Elphin bent to put the message back on the table as he said his final words. 'The Justiciar says he has sent this warning to the sheriffs of all the western shires, from Cornwall to Dorset, with an admonition for every law officer to be vigilant.'

'What do you think of that, John?' asked de Furnellis. 'You have been involved in several brushes with those who adhere to the Prince's cause – mainly involving your dear brother-in-law.'

The coroner was silent for a moment as he chewed over the scanty information, then he cleared his throat with one of his non-committal rasps.

'The Count of Mortain has been quiet lately, as far as I've heard. I had hoped that he had learnt his lesson last year, when the Lionheart came back from captivity and trounced his forces at Tickhill and Nottingham.'

'King Richard was too damn lenient with his young brother!' growled Henry. 'He should have locked him up for a few years, as their father did with their mother, Queen Eleanor. Instead, the soft-hearted fellow has now given back most of John's land that was confiscated.'

'If he's thinking of new treachery against the King, he'll certainly need money to rebuild support,' mused de Wolfe. 'I wonder what sending agents to the west hopes to achieve in that direction?'

'And what's this business about Mohammedans?' demanded de Furnellis.

A few more minutes' discussion brought them no enlightenment, and with a shrug of dismissal de Wolfe went on to tell the sheriff about the wreck of Thorgils' ship and the murder of its crew. The sheriff listened with interest, but had no suggestions as to who might have perpetrated this strange slaying – nor what could be done about it, without further information.

Henry, though nominally responsible for keeping law and order in Devon, was a somewhat reluctant enforcer and was more than content to leave the more energetic de Wolfe to deal with suspicious deaths and other crimes of violence. The coroner's remit, vague though it was, covered a whole host of matters, from sudden deaths to rape, from severe assault to fires and from wrecks to catches of the royal fish. In addition he had a wide-ranging obligation to attend to many legal matters, such as preparing evidence for the King's Justices, who came at long and irregular intervals to the city. He also had to attend executions and Ordeals, take confessions from sanctuary seekers and those who turned King's evidence by wishing to 'approve', as well as holding inquests on deaths and finds of treasure trove. It seemed that Henry de Furnellis also wished him to gallop around the county to seek out and arrest wrongdoers, though at least he had assured John that at any time he could call upon Ralph Morin, the castle constable, to turn out with men-at-arms from the garrison for any policing that was necessary.

When the cider was finished, the overworked de Wolfe left the harassed sheriff to the mercy of his clerks and went back to his chamber, to tell Thomas that he was at last going home to face his wife.

John rode sedately down to Martin's Lane and delivered Odin to Andrew the farrier, who had stables on the left side of the alley, right opposite the de Wolfe residence, one of several tall, narrow wooden houses. The front was relieved only by a heavy door and a shuttered window at ground level, plain timbers reaching up to the steep roof of wooden shingles.

Pushing the door open, he entered a small vestibule where, with a sigh of relief, he hung up his cloak and slumped on to a bench to exchange his mud-spattered riding boots for a pair of house shoes. To the right was an inner door into his hall, the main room of the house, but he turned left and went around the side of the building. The vestibule was continuous with a narrow covered passageway which led to the back yard. Here the kitchen shed, the wash hut, the well, the privy and a pigsty competed for space in an area of beaten mud, in which a few chickens pecked around. Plaintive bleating came from a small goat, destined for the next day's dinner, which was tethered to a ramshackle fence.

From force of habit, de Wolfe glanced up a flight of steep wooden steps that rose from the yard to the door of a room built out high on the back wall of the house. This was the solar, the only other room in the dwelling, which acted as his wife's retiring room as well as their bed-chamber. Beneath the timber supports of the solar was a box-like structure where his wife's body-maid, Lucille, lived. There was no sign of either of them, so John turned into the kitchen hut, where their cook-maid lived and worked.

'Mary, I'm famished!' he growled. 'I can't wait until supper-time. What have you got to eat?'

A dark-haired woman in her mid-twenties was stooping over an iron pot that was simmering on a small fire in a pit in the centre of the shed. She turned and stood up, a smile spreading over her handsome face.

'Welcome home, Sir Crowner!' she said in slightly mocking tone. 'I wondered if you still lived here, we see so little of you.'

John grinned at her familiar manner and leaned forward to kiss her cheek. They had had many a furtive tumble in days gone by, but now Mary thought more of keeping her position in the household than rolling in the hay with the master. Since John's relations with his wife had deteriorated, and especially since the nosy Lucille had arrived, she was afraid of her former indiscretions being discovered.

The cook-maid ladled some hare stew into a bowl for him and set it on a rickety table that was the only furniture, apart from a stool and a straw-filled mattress in the corner, which was her bed. As he sat to eat it, Mary placed a hunk of barley bread in front of him and poured a quart of ale into an earthenware pot.

'That will keep you from starving for another hour, perhaps?' Her manner was one of affectionate bantering, as she was his ally against the two other women in the household. Without her ministrations, he knew that he would go unfed and unclothed as far as Matilda was concerned. She cared nothing for domestic matters, being obsessed only with religion and maintaining her social status as wife of the county coroner and sister to the former sheriff.

'How has she been?' he asked, as he sucked the meaty stew from a spoon carved from a cow's horn.

'Fretting as usual, as she has been ever since she got back from France a few weeks back. And she's wrathful over the fact that you've been away for two nights, God knows where!'

He grunted sardonically, as it was the same old story with Matilda. She had pushed him into this job as coroner the previous year, seeing an opportunity to flaunt herself as the consort of the King's Crowner. Yet when he had to be absent on his duties, she complained endlessly that she was left alone and neglected, heedless of the fact that when he was there, she spent most of the time either scolding or ignoring him.

'Where is my dear wife now?' he asked.

'She'll be on her knees at St Olave's until supper-time, listening to Julian Fulk gabbling his Latin.'

John dipped the last of his bread in the dregs of the stew. 'She doesn't understand a bloody word of it, but she keeps going there. God's offal, if I didn't know her better, I'd think she was enamoured of that fat clerk.'

The cook had squatted on her bed while de Wolfe finished his food and drank the rest of his ale, an easy companionship settling over them. He began telling her of his trip to the south-west of the county, and she was saddened to hear that Hilda was now a widow. Mary was well aware of her master's various infidelities and had met Hilda several times in the past.

'Who could have done such a thing?' she asked, echoing the widow's words. 'And why, if none of the cargo was taken?'

As they discussed the mystery, his old hound Brutus ambled in from where he had been sleeping in the wash house and John fondled his smooth brown head as he spoke.

'This affair will take me down to that area more than once, I'm afraid,' he said. 'So my wife will have no lack of opportunity to nag me about being away from home again.'

Mary chuckled. 'That's nothing to what you'll suffer when she finds out that this affair will often require you to visit the Widow Hilda!'

Her husband's amorous wanderings were no secret from Matilda – in fact most of Exeter was well aware of his fondness for the ladies and for the landlady of the Bush Inn in particular. It was true that almost every prominent knight, burgess, merchant and even many men of the cloth had a mistress or two tucked away somewhere – and the booming trade in the city's brothels suggested that men of all stations in life were little bothered by the Seventh Commandment.

Mary's remark cast a gloom over John's mood, for until then he had forgotten that resurrecting his contact with Hilda, however innocent it might be, was bound to cause more trouble with Matilda. And a little niggle in his mind also suggested that the news might not be too well received at the Bush tavern in Idle Lane.

Though most people ate their main meal of the day around noon, a modern fashion was creeping upon the upper classes to have a substantial supper in the evening. Matilda de Wolfe, never wishing to be outdone by her cronies, had embraced the trend, and when the light had faded on that autumn evening, she and her husband sat down to eat grilled salt fish, then boiled bacon with cabbage and beans, followed by the last of the season's apples, stewed in honey. Mary was an excellent cook, which was why Matilda tolerated her, though relations between them were frigid and distant, as the lady of the house suspected that something had been going on between the maid and her husband. True, she thought the same of almost every woman with whom John came into contact, but she gave the benefit of the doubt to Mary, as eating good food was close to Matilda's heart. In fact, her brief sojourn in Polsloe Priory, where some months earlier she had decided to become a nun, had ended not so much from a failure of religious faith, but from distaste for the dull food and drab raiment, as she was also addicted to fine clothes.

Now they sat in their gloomy hall at either end of a long table, hardly speaking a word, as John's attempts at relating the saga of the wrecked ship and murdered crew had been received in stony silence, once he had revealed that the vessel belonged to Hilda's husband and that, by inference, the attractive blonde was now a widow.

De Wolfe felt his short temper rising, as she so blatantly snubbed his genuine efforts to be civil to her. He sat chewing on the fatty bacon, ripping the tough rind from his teeth with fingers that he felt would be better employed in squeezing the life out of her thick neck. He glared at her from under his black brows, seeing her as if sizing up an adversary on the battlefield. Thickset and heavy, she was not ugly, but was still totally unattractive to him. A square face carried a downturned mouth that gave the impression that there was a permanent bad smell in the vicinity. Her small eyes were heavy lidded and pouches of loose skin beneath them matched those that drooped beneath her chin. Her mouse-brown hair was rarely visible, as she always wore close-fitting wimples and cover-chiefs that made her look like the nun she had fleetingly been after a particularly severe rift between them had sent her in a fit of outrage to the nearby priory of Polsloe.

When they had finished the food, they retired to the hearth, where they sat before a glowing fire, while Mary brought in a jug of wine decanted from a keg and two pottery cups. As they slumped morosely watching the flames and sipping the red liquor from the Loire, de Wolfe again tried to break the oppressive silence by telling her of his plans to get his partner Hugh de Relaga to take over the three ships that had formerly belonged to Thorgils and use them to transport their goods.

'He could get Eustace, that smart young nephew of his, to look after that side of the business – he wanted to get experience of the coroner's work, but I fear he's not really suited. Or nearer the truth, my clerk is jealous of his position and sees him as a threat.'

John was certainly lacking in foresight and tact, as this speech put him in double trouble with his surly wife. First, she hated any mention of Thomas de Peyne, that 'fallen and perverted priest', as she called him, despite the fact that he had recently been fully exonerated from his alleged crime in Winchester. So devoted was she to 'men of the cloth' that the notion of a priestly sexual offender was poison to her ears. John's second faux pas was to mention again anything to do with Dawlish, as even an oblique reference to Thorgils' ships reinforced her awareness of Hilda's new availability.

'If all you can think about is that brazen woman down at the coast,' she snapped, 'then you can sit alone to slaver over your fornication!'

Hauling herself to her feet, she stomped her way to the door, yelling at the top of her voice for her maid Lucille to attend upon her, leaving John with mixed feelings of annoyance at her rudeness, but relief at being left in peace. He sat by the fire finishing his drink and scratching Brutus under the ear until he was sure that Lucille had finished fussing over Matilda's preparations for bed, setting out her night-shift and primping her hair. There was a small slit in the wall high to one side of the hearth which communicated with the solar, and long experience had trained him to recognise the various sounds that came through it when his wife was up there. She usually berated Lucille for being too rough with her hair or failing to fold her clothes properly. Sometimes the maid would get a slap from her short-tempered mistress and burst into tears. Finally the sounds would subside and John knew that Matilda would be on her knees saying her prolonged prayers before collapsing on to the thick feather mattress on the floor which was their loveless matrimonial bed.

When he was satisfied that all was quiet up above, he threw a couple more oak logs on to the fire and went out to the vestibule for his cloak. Brutus, who knew the routine perfectly, loped after him and when the front door was opened unerringly turned right and set off ahead of his master in the direction of the Bush Inn.

Below Southgate Street, the city of Exeter sloped sharply down towards the river, so much so that one of the lanes was actually terraced, giving it the name of Stepcote Hill. John's destination was Idle Lane, a short track that led from Priest Street, so called from its abundance of clerics' lodgings, across to the top of Stepcote Hill, where the infamous Saracen Inn was situated, a haunt of harlots and thieves. The Bush was the only building in Idle Lane, so named from the waste ground that lay around it after a fire some years earlier. The tavern had recently been rebuilt after its own disastrous fire, which had destroyed everything except the actual masonry walls. It was a square, solid structure, with a high thatched roof that came down almost to head height and gave ample space in the loft for many straw mattresses, rented at a penny a night. There was also a small partitioned bedroom where the attractive landlady slept and often entertained the King's Coroner for the shire of Devon.

This gentleman now ducked his head under the low lintel of the doorway and followed his hound into the large tap room that occupied the whole of the ground floor – a floor of beaten earth covered in fresh rushes, as Nesta was unusually particular about cleanliness, a rarity in the inns of Exeter.

After the chilly evening outside, the fug in the room was both welcome and familiar. A glowing fire in the hearth pit near one wall kept the place warm, and as the logs tonight were dry there was relatively little smoke circulating to smart the eyes and irritate the throat, before it seeped out under the eaves, as there was no chimney. However, the smells of sweat, spilt ale, unwashed bodies and cooking, made up for the lack of fumes, though none of the patrons ever noticed this miasma.

De Wolfe sat at one of the rough tables near the hearth, a wattle screen shielding his back from the draughts from the open door. This was his acknowledged seat, and if someone was already sitting there when he arrived, they hastily found another perch. He looked around and nodded to acquaintances in the crowded taproom, which was filled with men standing with quart pots or sitting at the few other tables scattered around the room. At the back, there was another door leading out into the yard, where the cook shed, the brew-house and the privy were situated, though most patrons lined up against the back fence when ridding themselves of the residue of their ale. Alongside this door was a row of casks and tall crocks, containing the ale and cider brewed by the landlady, which was indisputably the best in the city, as was the food that came from the hut outside.

Brutus slid under the table, peering out hopefully to see whether any of the patrons who were eating had some scraps to throw down to him. As John lowered himself on to his bench, an old man with a lame leg hobbled across with a pottery tankard of best ale.

'Evening, cap'n!' he said, as he had done hundreds of times before. Old Edwin was a former soldier, wounded in the foot and blinded in one eye at the battle of Wexford – the same Irish campaign in which de Wolfe had fought. Edwin had a touching regard for the coroner as a fellow soldier and always used his military title of captain – though privately he always thought of him as 'Black John'.

'Is your mistress about, Edwin?' asked John.

'Out in the cook shed, scolding one of the new girls, sir. Since we opened again after the fire, we've had a couple of useless doxies who couldn't boil water, let alone fry an egg!'

De Wolfe supped his ale and had a few words with several men standing near by, one of whom was the master carpenter who had organised most of the rebuilding of the inn, at John's expense. This was the second time he had ploughed money into the tavern, as several years ago he had come to the rescue of Nesta when her husband had died of a sudden fever and left her to run the debt-ridden inn. John had known Meredydd when they campaigned together, as he was an archer from Gwent in South Wales, the home of experts with the longbow. When he gave up fighting, he followed John back to Exeter and took over the ailing Bush, but died before it became profitable. John had come to the aid of his widow and their friendship developed into intimacy and – even though the taciturn John was loath to admit it – into genuine love. More recently, Nesta had narrowly escaped death when the inn was deliberately set on fire and, once again, John came to her rescue by financing the rebuilding.

'Here she is now, cap'n,' croaked Edwin, his dead white eye rolling horribly as he passed by again with a handful of empty ale-pots. The coroner looked up expectantly, his usually dour expression softened and a rare smile lit up his face at the sight of his mistress threading her way through her patrons. She gave many of them a cheerful greeting or a playful tap on the arm, as her pleasant manner was almost as much an attraction at the Bush as her good food and ale.

'Sir Crowner, I thought you might have left the country, it's so long since I saw you!'

She stood over him, grinning mischeviously as she used the half-mocking title that told him she was teasing – though there was a hint of reproach at his recent absence that reminded him of his maid's similar complaints.

'God's teeth, woman, it's good to see you! My arse is near worn away from sitting on a horse these past few days.' He reached up to pull her on to the bench alongside him and hugged her close. 'I've been halfway to the bloody Scilly Isles to see a shipwreck.'

He gave her cheek a smacking kiss, to the benign amusement of the regular patrons around them. They all knew and approved of the affair between their coroner and the comely ale-wife, not a few of them envying his luck at being able to bed such a pretty dame. Although twenty-nine, some dozen years younger than de Wolfe, she still had a shapely figure, with a small waist and a full bosom under the kirtle of fine green wool that covered her from neck to ankles. The Welsh woman was not small, but she came only to the shoulder of the lanky knight. Her face was round, though she preferred to think of it as 'heart-shaped', with a tip-tilted nose and lips like Cupid's bow. Her grey-green eyes complemented her glossy auburn hair, which now peeped out rebelliously from under a white linen coif, a close-fitting helmet that was tied under the chin.

As she snuggled up to his side, he brought her up to date on his doings since they had last met at the weekend, telling her of the journey to the south-west coast and the wreck of the *Mary and Child Jesus*. He tried to tread delicately around the fact that Thorgils was dead, as Nesta was well aware of Hilda's existence and of his dalliances with the blonde from Dawlish. In fact, Nesta had met Hilda several times and had got on well with the other woman, even though she knew that John still had feelings for her. Now she expressed her genuine distress that Hilda had been made a widow in such tragic circumstances and pressed him for more details of the death, which he was unable to provide.

'It's a complete mystery, *cariad*,' he said in the Welsh tongue that they used together, as, thanks to his mother's ancestry, he was fluent in that Celtic language. 'The whole crew knifed, apart from the lad who must have jumped or been thrown overboard. The vessel was left to drift until it beached, but the cargo was untouched. I don't understand it at all!'

Nesta always liked to hear about his cases and he enjoyed telling her about them, as she had a quick and lively mind that often produced useful ideas. In addition, she heard most of the gossip of the county, as the Bush was the most popular inn for travellers passing through the city, and on more than one occasion she had been able to offer him titbits of information that helped him in his investigations.

'Who could have done this, John?' she asked. 'Where did they come from and where did they go?'

He shrugged as he finished his quart and Nesta immediately signalled to Edwin to bring a refill. 'There were signs that someone other than the crew had been living below decks, so presumably Thorgils had brought some passengers across the Channel. It could only have been them that committed the crime.'

Nesta looked dubious. 'Why couldn't it have been an attack from a raiding ship? There have been many reports of Barbary pirates along the coast.'

De Wolfe shook his head. 'Unlikely, because the curragh that the vessel carried was missing and one was found intact and dragged up on the beach not far away.

Almost certainly, they abandoned the ship and made their way ashore.'

When John went on to tell her of the message that Hubert Walter had sent down to the sheriff, the landlady's fair eyebrows lifted. 'Maybe the two things are connected! Couldn't these men who went ashore be French spies? They killed the crew to prevent them telling of their illegal landing!'

De Wolfe had half-heartedly toyed with this idea himself, but had dismissed it as being too much of a coincidence, even though there was no better explanation on offer. 'Thorgils would never have agreed to anything underhand, like bringing infiltrators to these shores.'

Nesta shook her head impatiently. She was a woman of quick decisions and firm ideas. 'There need be no question of that, John. They could have bought their passage as genuine travellers, like hundreds of others. If Thorgils was bound for Salcombe or Dartmouth, they could have requested passage to one of those . . . then when it suited them, they rose up, slew the crew and rowed themselves ashore.'

John grudgingly admitted that she could be right. 'But why? And why go ashore on such a remote and God-forsaken bit of the coast? There's nothing there.'

'Exactly! And so few people to see them arrive!' she said triumphantly. 'Once ashore, they could go anywhere, as long as they were careful. And your intelligence from the Justiciar specifically mentioned the West Country.'

John suddenly realised that he was pressed against a warm and shapely woman and abruptly lost interest in hypotheses about French spies.

'I have other intelligence that tells me that the ladder I see at the back of the room leads up to the loft!'

He squeezed her thigh under the table and she rolled her eyes at him wickedly. 'I thought you might have forgotten that you most urgently instructed the master carpenter over there to rebuild my little chamber in the loft. I was beginning to think that it was a waste of good timber!'

He stood up and stooped over her. 'I very much regret the loss of our fine French bed in that fire, sweet woman! I have ordered a new one from St-Malo, but until it arrives I think we can make do with a palliasse on the floor!'

chapter three

In which the coroner attends another corpse

Over the weekend, Matilda was in a glowering sulk, but her husband was so used to this that he took little notice. They rarely met, except at mealtimes and on opposite sides of their wide mattress on the solar floor. On Saturday, John spent the afternoon at Bull Mead, the large field outside the south wall of the city, which was used for tournaments and other public spectacles. Today, there was a local jousting and archery contest, where young bloods and older men came to show off their amateur talents. The jousting was not in the knightly class, with destriers and lances, but a succession of youths and aspiring squires knocked each other about either on foot or from the backs of borrowed ponies and palfreys.

John, as a well-known and respected soldier, was sometimes persuaded to act as judge on these occasions. With Gwyn at his side clutching his inevitable meat pasty and jug of cider, he sat at a trestle table at the side of the field and adjudicated on the enthusiastic if often inept efforts of the lads from around Exeter to emulate the stars of the tourney fields elsewhere. Old King Henry had forbidden the major tournaments, fearing the death of too many expert knights – and the risk of training forces for barons who could rise up against him in rebellion. But his son Richard Coeur-de-Lion, ever with an eye to making money, had licensed four tournament grounds in various parts of England, charging a fee to all participants. None of these was in Exeter but the authorities – including de Wolfe – turned a blind eye to smaller events, which were useful in keeping potential foot soldiers trained to fight the French, as invasion had several times been threatened.

The two old campaigners sat on their stools and watched critically as the young men thrashed about on the field, belabouring each other with staves or laying about them with swords made of whalebone, which, though they could deliver a nasty whack, were never lethal.

'God's truth, Crowner, were we ever as clumsy as some of these when we were young?' demanded Gwyn, as one lad managed to trip over his own staff.

'Probably, when we first began,' grunted John. 'But we had to learn fast, in real battle. Those down there are doing better with their bows.'

He pointed farther down the field, where butts had been set up with straw targets for the budding archers. This activity was being overseen by Sergeant Gabriel from the castle, a crack shot with the cross-bow in his younger days. There was a royal ordinance which said that every man over fourteen had to practise with the bow each week, to keep in training for possible conscription. This rule was widely ignored, especially in the towns, though in the villages outside, regular practice with both longbow and cross-bow was looked on as a useful recreation and was often enforced by manor-lords and barons, who might need proficient troops for purposes of their own.

John thoroughly enjoyed his afternoon and afterwards, as the shadows lengthened, he made his way back to the South Gate, Gwyn going off eastwards towards his home in St Sidwells. As he strode through the cathedral Close, he saw a familiar figure coming towards him, one that stood out from the crowd by virtue of the colourful raiment that he wore. John's friend and partner, the portreeve Hugh de Relaga, was addicted to garish clothing and today was arrayed in a vermilion tunic down to his knees under an open surcoat of lime-green cloth. On his head was wound a capuchin of blue velvet, the free end hanging over one shoulder.

Hugh greeted him cheerfully, the round face above his short, corpulent body beaming with genuine pleasure. 'Where have you been these past few days, John?' he enthused. 'I have been wanting to pour money into your purse, as we have done so well with that last shipment of cloth to Flanders.'

John took him by the arm and steered him around towards Martin's Lane. 'Come in and have a cup of wine, friend. There is something I must discuss with you.'

A few moments later they were sitting at John's hearth, drinking his best Anjou red from heavy glass goblets that he brought out only on special occasions. Matilda was again on her knees in St Olave's church, but even if she returned unexpectedly, John knew that she would be quite civil to de Relaga, as he was always amiable and attentive to her and was one of the few of John's acquaintances whom she tolerated.

'I regret to tell you that we have lost our good friend Thorgils the Boatman. We urgently need to discuss how our merchandise is to be shipped abroad in future.'

He explained the whole story of the wreck and the death of the ship-master and his crew. Hugh was shocked at the news, as he had known Thorgils for many years. Then he listened to John's proposition about taking over the ships themselves.

'It would not only solve the problem of transporting our own goods,' declared de Wolfe, 'but it would be a profitable business in its own right. With the increase in commerce between Devon and the ports across the Channel, we could increase our income by shipping wool, cloth and tin for other merchants.'

Hugh rapidly became enthusiastic about the idea. 'There are three vessels, as I recall. Could we manage them all?'

'Two are smaller than the *Mary*, but are quite seaworthy and already have masters and crew, now idle and unemployed. We would need to repair the *Mary*, which seems not to be a great undertaking, then find a shipman and crew for her. Thankfully, it's now November, so we have ample time until sailing begins again in the spring.'

They went on to discuss how Hilda, who had inherited the ships, could be brought in as a sleeping partner and share in the profits. They decided to delicately broach the matter with her on Monday, when they would both attend Thorgils' burial in Dawlish.

Two days later they rode down to the coastal village for the sad ceremony. Gwyn came with them, as there were always outlaws lurking in the woods along the high roads and whenever he was out of Exeter the brawny Cornishman rarely allowed his master out of his sight. Hugh also brought one of his retainers and the four of them trotted down to the port of Topsham to take the little ferry across a hundred yards of tidal water. Then they carried on across the marshy land that occupied the lower end of the valley of the Exe to reach the hills that ran down to meet the sea at Dawlish.

The corpses of the seamen had arrived on a cart the previous night and after a sad ceremony were laid to rest in the churchyard. Hilda was her usual dignified self, doing all she could to console the wives and children of the other dead sailors, assuring them that they would not go hungry now that their menfolk had gone. John looked at her with a mixture of pride, compassion and longing. Only the sensation of Nesta looking over his shoulder prevented him from rekindling his passion for the willowy blonde.

When the burial service had ended and after the plain coffins were lowered into the sandy soil, Gwyn and Hugh's servant sought the nearest alehouse, while Hilda led John and Hugh de Relaga back to Thorgils' house, which was now hers. Hugh had not seen it before, and his eyebrows rose as he saw the elegant stone pillars holding up three arches which formed the front of the lower storey. Compared to the usual wooden dwellings and the cottages of plastered cob that surrounded it, it was almost a palace, and he was keener than ever to get this lady into partnership.

In the large room upstairs, the maid served ale and wine, and platters of fine wheaten bread, cheese and savoury pastries were handed around. Though sad, Hilda seemed to be bearing her new widowhood with equanimity and was quite willing to talk business with the two men from Exeter. The portreeve did most of the talking, and they soon agreed on a mutually advantageous scheme, which could later be put in writing and sealed by one of the few lawyers in the city.

'Will I need to take any active part in this?' she asked. 'I have no knowledge of business and cannot even write my own name!'

Hugh's cherubic face creased in a smile. 'All you need do, dear lady, is buy a larger treasure chest, as I have no doubt that John will be coming down quite often to add more silver to it!'

Even this jocular reference to frequent future visits to Dawlish caused a worm of unease to wriggle in the back of de Wolfe's brain. The other night, when he had gone up to Nesta's bed, their lazy conversation after making love had drifted to his proposition to include Hilda in the partnership. He immediately sensed a stiffening in her voice, and she enquired several times how often this would require him to travel to Dawlish. The mild tenseness passed off quickly, but left him with a wariness and a resolve to tread very softly with Nesta where any mention of Hilda was concerned.

Here in the blonde woman's solar, he sighed at the thought that now two women were looking on Hilda as a threat – his wife and his mistress.

*

That week, there were fewer cases to deal with than usual and at home Matilda was no better and no worse, spending most of her time either praying or staying with her cousin in Fore Street. She ignored him at mealtimes and at night he contrived to stay out of her bed until she was asleep.

With Nesta, he was careful to avoid any mention of Hilda and the concern he harboured over her nascent jealousy thankfully subsided. When she asked him whether there had been any news of who might have killed the ship's crew, he kept the discussion strictly to the Ringmore end of the story – not that anything had been reported from there to give him the slightest clue as to what might have happened.

'I must go down there again soon and see if any local news has surfaced,' he said. 'To be honest, I have no idea where to start looking, unless someone in that locality comes up with some information.'

Towards the end of the week, another matter began to absorb their attention, though it was mainly Thomas de Peyne who was involved.

At last the time had come for him to go to Winchester to be received back into the bosom of his beloved Church, following his absolution from the alleged crime that had led to his ignominious ejection from the priesthood. When he was teaching in the cathedral school there, a malicious accusation of indecency had been made by one of the girl pupils and Thomas was lucky to escape with his neck intact. As an unfrocked priest, he almost starved for a year, until he walked to Exeter to throw himself on the mercy of his archdeacon uncle, who found him a clerk's job with the new coroner.

Now he was to attend the cathedral there on Thursday of the following week for the brief ceremony that would restore him to grace. Originally, John was going to send Gwyn with him as a companion and bodyguard on the long journey, but fortuitously the sheriff's trip to the exchequer to deliver the county taxes coincided with Thomas's appointment. Henry de Furnellis readily agreed to having the clerk tag along with his party, which would be escorted by Sergeant Gabriel and six men-at-arms, to make sure that the large sum of silver coinage would be safe from prowling outlaws.

In addition, after this had been arranged, Archdeacon John de Alencon, Thomas's uncle, decided to include himself in the party. He claimed to have ecclesiastical business in Winchester, but the coroner suspected that he was keen not only to see his much-maligned nephew vindicated, but to savour the chagrin of his fellow canons in Winchester, who had so readily accepted the downfall of his young relative.

They were to leave at dawn on Monday, spending two nights on the journey, which was almost a hundred miles. By Friday, Thomas was already in a fever of excitement, hardly able to credit that the nightmare of his long period in the wildnerness was now almost over. He persuaded Gwyn to shave his tonsure down to his scalp, scraping off every vestige of thin mousy hair from the top of his head. His uncle bought him a new black robe to replace the patched, threadbare garment that he had worn for more than two years. Nesta gave him a pair of strong leather boots and Gwyn's present was a new shoulder bag of doe-hide to carry his writing materials. John, bereft of any original ideas to celebrate this happy event, handed him a purse containing a hundred silver pennies, the equivalent of more than four weeks' wages. The little clerk was overcome by the kindness of his friends and babbled his thanks to each of them, tears of gratitude mingling with his joy.

Monday morning could not come soon enough for Thomas, but then on Sunday, at about the ninth hour of the Sabbath, just as the nearby cathedral bell was tolling for Terce, de Wolfe was in the stable across the lane from his house. He was waiting for Andrew the farrier to finish saddling Odin, as John felt that the big stallion needed some exercise down on Bull Mead and perhaps a canter down the Wonford road and back. Just as Andrew was tightening the saddle girth, a figure appeared in the doorway from the lane. So often in the past, it had been Gwyn arriving with some news of a fresh body, but this time it was Sergeant Gabriel. John's first thought was that he had come with some news of a change of plan for the sheriff's departure for Winchester the next day, but the grizzled old soldier had news of a different kind.

'A fellow from Shillingford has just turned up at the gatehouse with some nasty news, Crowner!' he exclaimed, with an excited gleam in his eye. 'Their manor-lord has been found dead, on account of his head being lopped off and gone missing!'

John stared suspiciously at Gabriel, but he knew that the sergeant was not much given to humour or practical jokes.

'Shillingford? That's the honour of Sir Peter le Calve! Dead, you say?'

His tone carried incredulity, as in peacetime manor-lords were not expected to be murdered.

'Dead as mutton, Sir John! Beheaded, he was – and no sign of his nut anywhere!'

'Is Gwyn up at Rougemont?'

'I'm sure he is, Crowner. Playing dice in the hall, last I saw of him.'

De Wolfe turned to the farrier, whose jaw had dropped at this bizarre news. 'Get Odin ready for the road, Andrew, while I go for my cloak and sword. Gabriel, get back to the castle and tell Gwyn to saddle up and meet me back here, as quick as he can.'

As the sergeant turned to hurry away, the coroner called after him.

'And send whoever brought the message down with him.'

As the farrier fussed with Odin, John went across to his

house and sought out Mary to tell her that he would be missing his dinner once again. When he told her where he was going, she asked whether she should fetch Thomas.

'No, leave the poor little fellow in peace today. No doubt he's praying in the cathedral, practising for next week. He'd be in no fit state to do any work, anyway.'

He stalked to the vestibule and pulled on a pair of riding boots, buckled on his sword and slung his mottled wolfskin cloak over his shoulders, securing it over his left collar-bone with a large buckle and pin. Then he went back to the stable to wait impatiently for his officer to arrive.

It was a short ride to Shillingford, as the village lay little more than two miles to the west of the Exe, on the high road that led to Ashburton, Buckfast Abbey and distant Plymouth. Going at a brisk trot, the three horsemen covered the distance in half an hour, long enough for de Wolfe to get the story from Alfred Clegland, the manorial servant who had brought the news. A short, red-faced man with bristly fair hair, he was the falconer, an unusual person to act as messenger, as he explained as he rode alongside the coroner.

'The bailiff has got a terrible flux of his bowels, or he would be the one to come, sir. Our steward is in such a fevered state over his master's death that he could hardly sit a horse, so I was sent to fetch you.'

His story was that Peter le Calve, the lord of Shillingford, had gone hunting in his park the day before, accompanied only by his houndmaster and one of his adult sons.

'They had little sport, so the houndmaster said, until near to dusk, when the dogs raised a fallow deer in the woods. My lord and his son William split up, going off in different directions. And that's the last they saw of Sir Peter.'

The falconer related this with morbid fervour, and

John had the impression that their lord was not all that popular with his subjects.

'So who found the corpse?' demanded Gwyn, riding on the other side of Alfred.

'Nobody, not last night! When he didn't come back nor answer to the horn, William broke off the chase and with the houndmaster began searching the woods. But it soon got dark and they had to give up and go back to the village for more men.'

'Couldn't the hounds have found him by scent?' asked John, who unusually among men of his class had little interest in hunting.

Alfred was scornful. 'Them bloody dogs is useless! Comes of having a drunk for houndmaster. They couldn't find a turd in a privy. The only smell they know is that of a deer or a fox.'

'So who discovered him – and when?' demanded de Wolfe, his patience wearing thin.

'When the master failed to come back after a couple of hours, we tried going into the woods with pitch brands, but it was useless, especially as it started to piss with rain, which put out our torches. By dawn, when he was still missing, the whole village was turned out to search.'

By now, the road was entering the dense woods that surrounded the village of Shillingford, and they had time only to learn from the falconer that it was the manor wheelwright who had made the ghastly discovery. On the bed of a stream that ran through the forest, Sir Peter le Calve was found lying on his back, in a state that was more graphically described by the wheelwright when they arrived at the village.

Shillingford was a relatively small manor, a series of strip fields, pasture and waste surrounding a cluster of houses, the church and an alehouse. It was encircled by dense woods, which were slowly being cut back by assarting to provide more land for cultivation and beasts. The hall was in the centre of the hamlet, an old wooden structure like that at Ringmore, set inside a wide circular bailey fenced off with a ditch and stockade. John de Wolfe knew the lord slightly, though le Calve was an older man. They had been campaigning in the Holy Land at the same period, but the coroner had not fought alongside him, and since John had returned home from Palestine their paths had not crossed. Indeed, John had heard that Peter was now something of a recluse and rarely left his manor, except to travel to his other possessions in Dorset. He knew that le Calve was a widower for the second time and had two grown-up sons, but that was the extent of his knowledge of the man, apart from the fact that Peter's father had also taken the Cross, back at the time of the so-called Second Crusade, well over forty years earlier.

As they rode into the village, dust and fallen leaves were blown up from the track by a cold easterly wind, as November had turned dry since they returned from Ringmore. The place looked miserable under a leaden sky and John shivered in spite of the weight of his riding cloak. The depressing atmosphere was not helped by the sight of sullen bondsmen standing by the gates of their crofts as the coroner rode past. The village seemed to have come to a standstill with the loss of its lord, and there was an air of apprehension hanging over the place, as if the inhabitants were waiting to be blamed for this latest tragedy. The harvest had been bad and it needed a strong hand at the top if hunger was to be avoided during the winter that lay ahead, so the sudden death of their lord was an added uncertainty.

The falconer led them through the open gate of the manor-house bailey, where they found a score of people milling about uncertainly. Most were the servants belonging to the house and to the barton down the road, the farm that belonged directly to the lord to supply his needs. On the steps of the manor-house, a two-storeyed building with a shingled roof, a stooped old man waited for them, wringing his hands in nervous concern.

'I am Adam le Bel, Lord Peter's steward,' he quavered in a high-pitched voice. 'His sons are in the hall and wish to speak with you, sir.'

He led the way into a gloomy hall, made of ancient timbers that must have been felled when the first King Henry was on the throne. A large fire-pit lay in the centre, with a ring of logs like the spokes of a wheel smouldering on a heap of white ash. There were tables and benches set around it and at one of them a group of men sat with pots of ale. Two of them immediately got to their feet and advanced on the coroner. They were well dressed compared to the others in the hall, and John rightly took them to be the sons of the dead man.

'I am Godfrey le Calve and this is William,' said one, a tall, spare man of about thirty-five, touching his brother on the shoulder. William was a slightly younger version of Godfrey, otherwise they could have been taken for twins. Both had long chins and Roman noses, with brown hair shaved up the back and sides to leave a thick mop on top.

'This is a dreadful day, Sir John,' muttered William. 'Who could have done such a terrible thing?'

To John, his words echoed those uttered about the murdered ship's crew.

'My condolences, sirs. I knew your father only slightly, but there is always a bond between us old Crusaders. Where is his body now?'

'Left where it was found, Coroner,' said Godfrey, somewhat to de Wolfe's surprise. Though the victims of all sudden deaths were supposed to be undisturbed until the law officers examined them, in practice many were hurriedly moved, especially those in the upper ranks of society.

'In view of the grim circumstances, we thought it best to wait for your presence, Crowner,' added William. 'Being so close to Exeter avoids much delay.'

They marched out of the hall ahead of John and his officer. A ragged procession of steward, reeve, falconer and a man who turned out to be the wheelwright trailed after them. In the bailey, Godfrey turned and explained to de Wolfe that it was not worth mounting horses, as the distance was short and the terrain easier to navigate on foot.

More servants joined them as they took a path that passed the fields and then crossed the pasture and waste land to the edge of the trees. The ground was undulating, and a quarter of a mile into the wood there was a small valley with a sizeable stream running at the bottom. They scrambled down through a heavy fall of autumn leaves to a place where the brook ran over flat stones, some of the rocks projecting above the water.

'This is how I found the master, sir,' exclaimed the wheelwright, who had run ahead of them and was pointing upstream, where the rivulet made a sharp bend through the cut-away banks of red soil on either side. When John and his officer got down to the water's edge, they could see around the corner, and even their eyes, hardened by years of fatal injury and maiming in battle, were shocked by the sight.

Across some flat rocks, his feet in the running water, was the body of a man, lying on his back. His arms were outstretched, as they were lashed at the wrists to a fallen branch laid crossways underneath him. His neck ended at a bloody stump and through a tear down the front of his long tunic his entrails protruded on to his ripped belly.

'He's been castrated as well, sir!' volunteered the wheelwright, with a melancholy relish. Either the two sons had very strong characters or they had no great affection for their father, for they splashed up the stream ahead of John and stood over the mutilated corpse while John and Gwyn caught them up.

'Our sire was not the most popular of manor-lords,' admitted Godfrey with surprising frankness. 'But surely no one would wish a death like this upon him!'

The coroner clambered out of the water and stood on

the table-like rock, his officer standing ankle deep in the stream on the other side of the body. They looked down at the bloody remains, taking in all that was to be seen. Peter le Calve – for they assumed it was he, in spite of the lack of his head – wore a long woollen tunic of a green colour, though much of the front and sides were now almost black with blood, except where splashes of water had diluted the gore to a pink hue. The garment was ripped from the neck-line down to well below his waist. A coil of his bowels lay amid clotted blood on his belly, and below this a ragged wound indicated where his genitals had been crudely removed.

Gwyn reached down and took hold of his leg below the knee, attempting to lift it. 'Stiff as a board and as cold as ice,' he muttered. 'He's been dead a goodly time.'

John slipped a hand into the dead man's armpit, but could feel no vestige of remaining warmth. He looked up at the elder son. 'Your father went missing at dusk last night and was found soon after dawn?'

Godfrey nodded, his rather equine face now pale as he stood over the ravaged corpse. 'We were all out at first light and he was found within the hour.'

'Then no doubt he was killed last night, so the miscreants could be well away by now,' growled de Wolfe. Even though hardened by past experience, the manner of this death was one of the worst he had seen, especially as it savoured of a crucifixion.

'Can we not move him now, Sir John?' asked William, who was as pale as death himself. 'This is not a fitting way for any man to be left, especially a lord in his own manor.'

John rose to his feet and nodded. 'I agree with you! A Crusader deserves better than this. We must get him back to the village.'

Godfrey shouted over his shoulder at some of his servants who were clustered anxiously a few yards away. He ordered them to find a litter to carry the body, and some of them jogged away back towards the manor.

'We'd best get him off these stones and on to the grass, Crowner,' suggested Gwyn. He drew out his dagger and bent to the nearer wrist of the corpse, intending to slash through the bindings that held the victim to the willow bough, but De Wolfe stopped him.

'Wait a moment! Let's look at the way he's tied, in case there's something useful to learn.' With Gwyn's hairy head close to his, he peered at the lashings and felt them with his fingers.

'Tied with two simple half-hitches,' declared his officer, a former fisherman. 'Nothing special about the knots.'

'No, but what about the cords themselves, Gwyn? How many local outlaws or robbers carry silken cords with them, eh?'

Gwyn grunted his surprise and touched the bindings, rubbing his thick finger along them. 'God's knuckles, so they are! Soaking wet, they looked black, but I think they are red.'

The coroner now told him to release the lashings and as the wet cords had pulled so tight that the knots were almost impossible to untie, the Cornishman cut them through and held them up for inspection. The two sons came nearer and agreed that their father had been tied down with cords of dark crimson plaited silk, somewhat thicker than a goose quill. They were wet and rather dirty, but were certainly not common hemp.

'The ends are frayed – looks as if they've been cut from a longer length,' said the ever practical Gwyn, stowing them carefully in the pouch on his belt. When the corpse was lifted off, the thin branch revealed nothing of interest, being a fallen bough with a broken end.

'Not specially cut down for this purpose,' said Godfrey, who seemed less affected by his father's bizarre death than his younger brother.

'No, there's plenty of such wood within fifty paces,' agreed the coroner.

The falconer and the wheelwright carried their lord's

body reverently to the bank and laid it gently on the grass.
John checked that there was nothing left on the rock
where the corpse had lain, then came across and had
another look at it.

'There can be no doubt that this is your father?' he
demanded, looking up at Godfrey and William. Both men
shook their heads.

'Those are his garments, certainly,' replied William.
'But you're not suggesting that someone placed his clothing on someone else?'

'Stranger things have happened,' grunted de Wolfe.
'Though I admit it's highly unlikely. But is there any other
way you can identify him, without his head?'

'He had a scar on the side of his chest,' offered
Godfrey. 'It came from a spear wound at the battle of
Arsuf, so he told us.'

John well remembered Arsuf in the Holy Land, for he
was there himself. In September three years previously,
Richard the Lionheart had marched down from Acre
towards Jerusalem and at Arsuf, Saladin tried to stop him
with a massive army. Richard, the superb tactician, won
the day, though the battlefield was strewn with the corpses
of both sides and many more were wounded. John himself had a small scar on his arm from a Moorish arrow,
and now he bent to look at a beheaded corpse to seek
more severe evidence of that fateful conflict. When he
pulled the torn tunic aside, sure enough there was a white
puckered scar running for a hand's breadth horizontally
across the left lower ribs, which both sons confirmed was
identical to the one they had seen on their father. But
John's attention was now elsewhere, for pulling the clothing aside had revealed something else. Just above the scar,
smeared with blood, was a wide slit, the pouting edges
exposing the muscle beneath the skin.

'Mary, Mother of God, he's been stabbed as well, poor
bastard!' Gwyn's irreverent voice boomed out as he bent
for such a close inspection that his bulbous nose was

almost touching the corpse. 'And haven't we seen wounds like that only a few days ago?'

The stricken onlookers watched as the two law officers poked and prodded at the gash in the dead man's side.

'Very wide indeed, Gwyn, as well as deep,' said de Wolfe grimly. 'But surely this must be a coincidence?'

Godfrey and William le Calve stared at each other, bemused at what was going on. 'What importance can this have, Sir John?' asked William. 'Surely in the presence of the other mutilations, this can have little significance?'

De Wolfe explained that recently they had seen similar unusual knife marks on the crew of a wrecked ship.

'But that was thirty miles from here and in very different circumstances, so I fail to see how it can have any connection,' objected Godfrey.

'I would like to agree with you, sir,' said John thoughtfully. 'But I must keep an open mind on the matter for now.'

Together with Gwyn, he explored the rest of le Calve's body, but found no other injuries, and by then several villeins had hurried up with a crude stretcher made of a pair of poles with ropes strung between them.

A short time later, the corpse was laid on a table in one of the side rooms of the manor-house and decently covered with a blanket. The parish priest was called and stayed to mumble Latin prayers over it, though there was no suggestion yet that the body be moved to the church, as was the usual practice.

'Thank God our mother is no longer with us, to have to witness such a devilish act,' muttered Godfrey. 'She died seven years ago, Christ rest her soul.'

John had noticed a handsome, well-dressed woman hovering in the background as they brought the lord back to his hall for the last time, but he was tactful enough not to enquire who she was.

'What happens now, Crowner?' asked the bemused

elder son, still grappling with the fact that he was suddenly the new lord of Shillingford.

'I must start my enquiries,' replied de Wolfe. 'Though
as it is a Sunday, I cannot open an inquest today, but I
must question those people who may have any knowledge, while their memories are still fresh.'

The two sons remembered their obligations to visitors
and invited the coroner and his officer to have some meat
and drink before they began their investigations. More
logs were placed on the fire and when they were all seated
at one of the tables, servants brought wine, ale and cold
meats with fresh bread and slabs of hard yellow cheese.
Godfrey and his brother took some wine, but ate nothing,
which was hardly surprising, considering the ghastly sights
they had seen that morning. Adam the steward and some
of the senior servants, such as the bottler, the falconer
and the hunt-master, hovered in the background, with
lesser mortals behind them, all wanting to share in any
dramatic revelations that might come along.

'I'll need to speak to all those who had any part in both
the hunt yesterday and the finding of the body this morning,' announced John, as he finished his impromptu meal
and drained the last of his wine. Godfrey, gradually assum-
ing his new role as the head of the household, gave orders
to his old steward to round up everyone who was needed
and soon a motley, shuffling group of men assembled in
the hall.

John sat at the table as soon as the remains of the food
had been cleared, with a brother on either side of him, as
this was not a formal inquisition. However, to save taxing
his memory until he returned to Exeter, de Wolfe asked
Godfrey whether Adam le Bel, the only literate man
among them, could write a summary of the facts, and the
wrinkled old steward sat at the end of the table with quill
and parchment. Gwyn stood near by and acted as a master
of ceremonies, motioning the wheelwright forward as the
First Finder. He had little to say except that he happened

to be the first man to come across his lord's body in the stream and had hollered out in panic to bring the rest of the searchers to him.

Then the huntmaster reluctantly stepped forward, turning his pointed woollen cap restlessly in his hands as he stood before this grim-faced officer from Exeter. He was a lean, stringy fellow with a yellowish tinge to his face and a nose blushed with fine veins, suggesting too strong a liking for the ale-cask.

'Tell me what happened last night,' demanded John abruptly.

'Not a lot to tell, sir,' said the fellow hesitantly. 'We had little sport all afternoon, until the light was fading, when one of my beaters raised a deer. I think Sir Peter had been irked by the lack of excitement until then, for he dashed off to the left, waving to Sir William to circle round to the right. I went with the younger master and that was the last we saw of our lord.'

In spite of further probing by the coroner, it seemed he had nothing else to tell, and several other retainers who had been following the chase gave the same story. Peter le Calve had rushed off on his horse through the woods and had not been seen alive again.

'How far was the spot where you separated from that place on the stream?' John asked William, as Godfrey had not been at the hunt.

'Not more than half a mile, Crowner. If darkness had not overtaken us, I suspect we would have found him within the hour.'

As an aid to thought, de Wolfe rubbed his chin, which was relatively free of dark stubble, as it was only the previous day that he had had his weekly wash and shave. Even this mannerism failed to stimulate any profound ideas about advancing his investigation, but to fill the time he asked the steward a question.

'Your bailiff, I was told he was absent due to an illness. Where was he last night?'

Adam le Bel looked up from the parchment that he was laboriously completing. 'On his cot, no doubt, Crowner! He has been laid low these past three days with a bloody flux. I visited him yesterday morning in his toft along the road there and he seemed a little better. His wife said he had taken a little gruel, without it immediately passing through him.'

John grunted and accepted that, even if improving, the sick man was hardly likely to have been in a fit state to be involved in his lord's murder. There seemed no one else to interrogate, and John was driven to ask general questions of the throng that now half filled the hall of the manor.

'Has anyone any further light to shed on this tragic happening?' he shouted at them. 'Have there been any strangers here in the past few days?'

There was a general murmuring and shaking of heads, but no one volunteered any information. The new manor-lord came to their rescue.

'Unfortunately in that respect, Sir John, we are on the high road to Plymouth, so strangers are passing through all the time. Few stop here, as we are so near Exeter, but some call at the alehouse for food and drink.'

This seemed to trigger someone's memory, as an elderly man stepped forward, leaning heavily on a staff and deferentially tugging at a sparse lock of dirty grey hair that hung over his forehead. He was dressed in little better than rags and had a strip of filthy cloth wound around his right leg, from which yellow matter leaked down on to his bare foot.

'Begging pardon, sirs, but I saw some strangers on the lane to Dunchideok yesterday afternoon, a couple of hours after dinner-time.' His quavering voice was weak, and Godfrey beckoned impatiently to him to come nearer.

'What's all this, Simon? Who did you see?' He turned aside to the coroner to explain. 'He's an old cottar, a bit mad. He cleans out the privy pits in the village, which is why he's always getting these purulent sores.'

'I was sitting on the bank, master, my leg being so foul. Three men passed me, jogging on palfreys towards Dunchideok. I couldn't see any faces, they had deep hoods over their features.'

'Can you describe anything else about them?' barked de Wolfe. Hooded men in a village could be significant, he thought.

'Yes, sir. They had black habits down to their feet, bound with cords around their waists.'

Godfrey gave an impatient snort. 'For God's sake, Simon, they were just monks! Benedictines, no doubt. There are hundreds of them about the countryside. Buckfast is one of their great houses.'

'What about this lane?' asked John, reluctant to give up even the most unpromising clue. 'Does it go anywhere near those woods?'

This time William answered. 'Not really, it's just a track to the next village. There's a hermit's cell there. I suppose monks could be visiting that for some reason.'

The crestfallen Simon stepped back among his sniggering fellows, and there now seemed little left to keep the coroner in Shillingford. With a promise to return the next day to formally hold an inquest, so that burial could be arranged, he and Gwyn went out to reclaim their horses and leave an uneasy and chastened manor behind them.

On the short ride back to the city, de Wolfe chewed over the strange affair with his officer, partly to sort out the details in his own mind.

'Who would want to kill Peter le Calve, anyway?' he mused. 'He's getting on in years, certainly older than me. And he takes no part in politics or county affairs – in fact, I'd almost forgotten he existed, as he never attends any tournaments or feasts in Exeter.'

John pondered for another score of Odin's hairy hoof-beats on the track.

'And look at the manner of his death! Lashed to a pole, beheaded, gutted and his twig and berries cut off!' he muttered.

'That was no casual robbery,' said his companion. 'And anyway, his purse was still on his belt with some coins still inside.'

'And where the hell is his head and his manhood?' persisted John. 'Have they been taken away as trophies?'

'Could this be to do with witchcraft or the black arts?' queried Gwyn, almost nervously. As a Cornishman and a Celt, he had a healthy respect for pagan supersitions, as a recent outbreak of witch-hunting in Exeter had revealed. De Wolfe, though having similar Celtic blood in his own veins courtesy of his mother, had no time for magic. 'Those wounds were made with good sharp steel. And what are we to make of that stab wound, eh?'

Gwyn took a hand from his reins to scratch his unruly red thatch.

'It was a strange one, Crowner, just like those on poor Thorgils and his crew. But one swallow doesn't make a summer.'

'True enough, but how many three-inch knife wounds have we seen since we came back from Palestine?'

There was no answer to this, and in silence they walked their steeds down into the ford alongside the unfinished Exe Bridge, to reach the city's West Gate on the other side of the river.

ChAPTER fOUR

In which Thomas rides off to Winchester

Early the next morning, a cavalcade assembled in the inner ward of Rougemont, watched by a small group of onlookers which included John de Wolfe, the constable, Ralph Morin, Gwyn and even Nesta. The occasion was no great novelty, as it was a regular event that took place twice a year – the transporting of the county 'farm' to the royal exchequer at Winchester, one of the twin capitals of England.

But on this raw day in early November, the spectators had come to see off Thomas de Peyne on the journey for which he had been yearning for almost three years. He was near the tail-end of the little procession that was forming, waiting impatiently alongside Elphin, the sheriff's chief clerk. Behind them were two mounted men-at-arms and immediately in front were four sumpter horses. Each of these had a pair of large leather panniers slung across their backs, containing the coin extracted as taxes from the shire of Devon. Two more soldiers rode ahead of these, the head ropes of the packhorses attached to their saddles. Beyond these, Thomas could see the erect figure of his uncle, Archdeacon John de Alençon, sitting astride a grey mare alongside Henry de Furnellis's bay gelding, the whole retinue being led by Sergeant Gabriel and another two men-at-arms.

The horses bobbed their heads and some neighed restlessly or scratched at the ground, making their harness clink and rattle. Gwyn looked with a critical soldier's eye at the convoy, but could find only one real fault.

'That little sod puts us to shame, Crowner!' he grumbled, poking a finger in the direction of their clerk. 'Hanging over the side of his saddle like a bloody nun, even when he's got a decent horse!'

John had decided that Thomas's broken-winded pony was not reliable enough for such a long journey and had hired a palfrey for him from Andrew's stable, but the clerk still insisted on having a side-saddle.

'At least he'll be able to keep up with them, thanks to the heavy load on those sumpters,' replied the coroner. 'Though I don't know how he'll manage on the way back.'

'Perhaps he won't come back,' said Gwyn. 'Maybe they'll make him bishop in Winchester to make up for the injustice he's suffered.'

Nesta kicked him on the ankle in mock anger.

'He'll be back, I know it! The faithful little fellow swore to me last week that he'd never leave you in the lurch, John, not after what you've done for him.'

De Wolfe gave one of his grunts, as this was too emotive to suit him. He turned to watch as the powerful figure of Ralph Morin had a final word with the sheriff, then walked up to his sergeant to give him the order to start. With a thudding of hoofs and a jingle of harness, the cavalcade slowly moved off towards the arch of the gatehouse, accompanied by waves and shouts from the onlookers. Nesta flourished a white kerchief at Thomas and called out 'God speed you!' as two tears of happiness for the excited clerk ran down her cheeks. John raised a hand in courteous salute to the sheriff and his friend the archdeacon and turned it into a wave for Thomas.

'Try not to fall off that bloody nag!' yelled Gwyn, covering his affection for the little priest with mock ferocity, and as the clerk waved back in farewell, they saw that he too was weeping tears of joy.

As the last soldier vanished over the drawbridge, John

felt curiously lonely, as if someone close to him had died. Nesta seemed to sense this and slipped her arm through his. 'He'll be back in a week or so, John. Be glad for him – he's waited so long for this redemption.'

As usual, the pretty woman always overflowed with kindness and compassion, and de Wolfe squeezed her arm with his in a mute token of affection. But the feeling of loneliness persisted when de Wolfe and Gwyn went up to their dismal chamber in the gatehouse for a jar of ale and some bread and cheese. Though nothing was said, they both missed the little man sitting at the end of the table, his tongue protruding as he hunched over pen and ink, concentrating on forming the fine Latin script on his parchments.

Their workload had declined again, with no outstanding cases other than the mystery of Thorgils' ship and the bizarre happenings of the previous day. It was just as well, as with Thomas absent for up to a fortnight, every time there was an incident John would have to borrow one of the sheriff's clerks to record his business.

'We could have asked that Eustace if he'd stand in as clerk for a time,' muttered Gwyn, through a mouthful of bread.

De Wolfe shook his head. 'Thomas will only sulk when he finds out, so better leave him to running these ships when the season comes.'

He swallowed the last of his ale. 'Now what in hell's name are we to do about these deaths? We must go back to Shillingford after dinner today and at least hold the inquest – not that that will get us any nearer solving the problem.'

The big Cornishman brushed breadcrumbs from his worn leather jerkin, then hoisted his backside on to the sill of one of the window slits before replying.

'There's a feeling in my guts that we haven't heard the last of whoever killed Peter le Calve. And what about those stab wounds?'

The coroner picked up a small knife that Thomas used to sharpen his quill pens and absently jabbed the point into the bare boards of the trestle table.

'Once again, I got the impression when I put my finger in the wound that it curved back on itself slightly. It's strange, but not enough to get excited about. Both were two-edged blades and very wide indeed, compared with our usual daggers . . . but you know as well as I do, any knife can be rocked back and forth to widen the slit it makes in the skin.'

Gwyn nodded reluctantly. 'Or the victim can move on the knife, which does the same thing,' he conceded. 'A pity we can't see inside the body – maybe the track deep in the vitals would tell us more.'

'The Church would have a fit if we suggested doing that,' grunted John. 'Yet I once heard from a Greek physician with us in the Holy Land that Egyptian physicians in Alexandria were dissecting both corpses and live criminals, centuries before Christ.'

The practical Gwyn was not very impressed. 'Much use that is to us today! It's a wonder that the damned bishops and priests let us look at the outside of cadavers, let alone probe the insides!'

For some reason that even John had never been able to discover, his henchman had a rooted antipathy to the organised Church and all its minions – their clerk being the only exception. Now, with Thomas gone on his way to be reinstated in his beloved Church after a belated acceptance in Winchester that the accusations were maliciously false, the coroner and his officer felt deflated, and they itched for something to divert them. Eventually, Gwyn went to find a game of dice in the guardroom and John took himself off to see Hugh de Relaga, to discuss their profits from the wool business and to talk some more about using Thorgils' ships when the spring sailing season came along.

*

As the sheriff's cavalcade wound its way eastward, a much more modest group was wending its way in the opposite direction, about thirty miles south-west of Exeter. As well as the difference in numbers, it was a much more bizarre sight than the orderly column led by Sergeant Gabriel. On the narrow track that wound through lonely heathland and woods near the upper reaches of the Avon estuary, three horses trudged along, one behind the other. The last was a packhorse, burdened by wicker panniers on each side and bedding rolls across its back. It was led by a huge man on a pony much too small for his bulk. He was dressed in a shapeless tunic of brown canvas over blue breeches, his calves bound by cross-gartering. The giant, even larger than Gwyn, was completely bald and had a red face with a large hooked nose, but what made his features most grotesque was the total collapse of his mouth, the lips being indented so much that his chin seemed to come up to almost meet his nostrils. When he opened his mouth, the cause was obvious, as he had not a tooth in his head – nor a tongue. Fifteen years previously, Jan the Fleming had had all these removed by the public executioner of Antwerp, after the irate burgomaster of that city took exception not only to his seducing one of his daughters but having had the gall to claim that she had invited him into her bed. Almost before the bleeding had stopped, he was bundled on to the first ship to leave the Rhine and ended up in Scotland, a country he had never even heard of before. This was how he came to be servant and bodyguard to the man on the leading horse, the contrast between them being as great as could be found anywhere in Christendom.

Alexander of Leith was a tiny man, yet he rode a large palfrey which would have better suited his acolyte. He sported what seemed to be a long kilt, the fabric of green-and-red tartan falling down to his calves, pleated sufficiently to enable him to sit astride his horse. Alexander's upper half was enveloped in a loose tunic of dirty white linen, on which were embroidered many cabbalistic signs associated with alchemy. His puny shoulders were shrouded in a scalloped leather cape which sported a hood that came to a sharp point above his head. Like Jan the Fleming, he had a peculiar face, but in a quite different way. An abnormally high forehead, fringed by white hair, rose into his hood, but his dense, bushy eyebrows were jet black. Wizened features, which suggested that his age was well past three score years, were relieved by a pair of little gimlet-sharp black eyes. This visage was rounded off by a soft-lipped, purse-like mouth under which was a white beard confined to the tip of his chin but which nonetheless fell down his chest like a dog's tail.

As they jogged along, he mumbled continuously to himself, perhaps to compensate for the permanent silence of his tongueless servant. They were strangers to this area, having jogged slowly for the past week from Bristol, which, in spite of his Scottish origins, had been the home of Alexander of Leith for the past ten years.

Now, hopefully, they were on the last lap of their journey, if only they could find their destination. The retainers of Prince John, Count of Mortain, who now spent much of his time at his restored possessions in Gloucester, had given Alexander a crude map drawn on parchment, which he studied every few miles and which provoked new bursts of muttering. Earlier that morning, they had awoken in a barn where they had spent the night, rode to a village where they bought bread and ale and received some more directions to Bigbury, alleged to be about ten miles distant. Now the little man turned in his saddle and yelled back at the Fleming in strangely accented English.

'Another couple of hours should see us there, you great useless oaf!'

Abuse was his normal form of address to his bodyguard, given and received without any apparent rancour. When he twisted to face Jan, however, the Scot fancied he

could hear a clinking from the load carried by the
sumpter horse, and he came to a stop.

'Did you pack those flasks well enough this morning,
you dumb animal?' he snapped. 'If any of that glassware
gets broken, I'll whip you within an inch of your life!'

The Fleming grinned amiably and made some finger
signs that only Alexander could interpret. Then he got off
his horse, an easy task as his stirrups were already almost
touching the ground. Walking to the patient packhorse,
he rummaged around in the panniers and rearranged
something, which gave rise to a muted rattling of porce-
lain and glass. With more signs that must have meant
satisfaction, he climbed aboard his nag again and they set
off, hoping to come across some local who could confirm
that they were on the right track for this Bigbury.

After another half-hour, the monstrous Fleming spied
a boy herding goats near a thicket away to their right, and
he attracted his master's attention by clashing a small pair
of brass cymbals that hung on a leather thong around his
neck. When Alexander turned, Jan pointed, and the little
alchemist turned his horse off the track and walked it the
few hundred paces to within speaking distance of the lad.
The Fleming watched the youngster staring slack-jawed at
this apparition, but the Scotsman seemed to get a satisfactory response, for he came back to the track and waved
at his servant to continue.

A mile farther on through the undulating countryside,
the alchemist saw the smoke from a village some distance
ahead, which he assumed was Bigbury, but following the
goatherd's directions, he turned left on to a path that
meandered through trees. These became more dense as
they went much deeper into the forest, but hoof marks in
the damp ground showed that the track was still in use,
though it was in a very remote area. After another half-
dozen furlongs, they came into a large clearing that was
dotted with scrubby bushes and some saplings. In the
centre was a small hillock, standing about twenty feet

high. It had a flat top and was obviously artificial, some blackened and rotted wooden foundations indicating that this must be the remains of an old 'motte and bailey' castle, now abandoned and derelict. Around the base of the mound was what was left of the bailey, an overgrown bank and ditch with the ivy-covered remnants of a stockade extending out to surround an egg-shaped enclosure. A few derelict huts still remained within this compound, and from one of them some thin smoke escaped from under the edges of the dilapidated thatch. Alexander of Leith came to a halt to survey this dismal place, then took from his belt a small pewter horn shaped like a trumpet. Putting it to his flabby lips, he blew a series of discordant blasts which sent birds flying in alarm from the nearby trees. A moment later, a rickety door scraped open and a figure appeared from the hut – a tall man, well dressed and with every appearance of a gentleman. He stared across the clearing, recognised the pair and beckoned energetically as he shouted, 'You have arrived on the very day we calculated, Alexander! Come on in, this place is not as bad as it looks!'

Just before noon that morning, the coroner went back to Martin's Lane for dinner, resolving once again to try to be more pleasant to Matilda. Their relationship seemed to get more strained by the week, and he was aware that he himself was far from blameless in this respect. Regularly, he would try hard to appease her, only to be rebuffed by either indifference or outright abuse. Then his short temper would flare up and make the situation worse than it was before.

Since her brother had been dismissed as sheriff, largely because of John's accusations of corruption, Matilda had been more difficult, and nothing he could do or say was acceptable in her eyes. She blamed him not only for Richard's downfall, but also, as the sister of a disgraced sheriff, for her own loss of face and prestige among her peers, mostly the snobbish wives of rich merchants who were her cronies at St Olave's church. John had bouts of conscience and compassion over her grieving for this brother who turned out to have feet of clay, but his repeated efforts at reconciliation were constantly rejected.

Today, his attempts at conversation at dinner-time were met only with grunts or stony silence, especially when he told her of the new sheriff's departure for Winchester and unwisely mentioned that the despised Thomas had travelled with him.

'We should never have married,' he groaned to Nesta, later that afternoon. 'Neither she nor I wanted it – we were pushed into it by our parents. Old Gervaise de Revelle wanted his daughter married off to the son of a manor-lord – and my father saw a chance to get his younger son into a rich family, for the de Revelles have lands at Revelstoke, Tiverton and in Somerset and Dorset – not that I have a cat's chance in hell of seeing a penny from them!'

'I wonder who you would have wedded instead of Matilda,' mused Nesta, wistfully. They were sitting by the hearth in the taproom of the Bush, with a quart of cider, a cold lamb shank and a bowl of flummery on the table, and a salivating Brutus beneath it.

'God knows! Perhaps some simpering third daughter of another baron or manor-lord,' he muttered. 'Certainly no chance of her being a beautiful Welsh girl with red hair and a bosom straight from heaven.'

Even the flattery failed to deflect a sudden barb from the landlady.

'Maybe it would have been a willowy Saxon blonde from the seashore?'

Once again a warning bell sounded in the back of John's mind. He had not expected Nesta to become so jealous of Hilda, especially as she had seemed so much at ease with her when they had met some months earlier.

John had not bedded the attractive blonde for a long time, though in spite of his genuinely deep affection for Nesta, he could not deny to himself that he might succumb again if the opportunity arose. He managed to turn Nesta's attention to other matters. He told her of his return visit to Shillingford that afternoon, where he had held a frustratingly short inquest over the body of Sir Peter le Calve, which, as he had expected, turned up no new evidence at all and was merely a legal formality to get the meagre facts into the record. The sons were concerned about burying their father without his head, but John assured them that if and when it turned up, there could be an exhumation and the missing part reunited with the rest.

After this rather grisly account, John lightened the conversation by wondering how Thomas was faring on such a long journey, as he was probably England's most reluctant horseman. The sheriff's party would take three full days to cover the hundred miles to Winchester, stopping overnight somewhere around Dorchester and then Ringwood. Nesta asked whether the clerk would have to be reordained into the Church, but John had questioned his friend the archdeacon about this and was quite knowledgeable on the matter.

'It seems that whatever crimes a priest has committed, he can never lose that status which was bestowed by God,' he explained. 'Once a priest, always a priest, it seems. But the Church can take away all the attributes of priesthood, ejecting him from any office he held and forbidding him to administer the Sacrament, take confessions or exercise his ministry.'

'So how does he get reinstated?' asked Nesta, with terrier-like persistence.

'John de Alençon says that during a celebration of the Mass in the cathedral, the bishop will publicly read out the judgement of the Chancellor of the Consistory Court, which decided that there is no longer any barrier to Thomas resuming his ministry, then bestow a personal blessing on him. And that's all that's necessary, except to find him a position afterwards to give him a livelihood.'

'But he's already your clerk – and wishes to remain so,' objected Nesta.

John smiled wryly. 'That's what he says now – and I'm sure he means it. But that's just his loyalty and gratitude. Before long, his deep desire to take an active part in his beloved Church will overcome him. His uncle says that he hopes to find him some sinecure in Exeter, so that he can combine the two jobs, though I'm sure he'll drift away little by little – and I'll not stand in his way when the time comes.'

'You are a kind man, Sir Crowner,' said the Welsh woman, squeezing his arm affectionately. They spent the next hour in amicable companionship before the fire, until it was time for him to go back to Martin's Lane for his supper.

The food he had eaten at the Bush in no way spoiled his appetite and Mary's poached salmon and eggs went down well with fresh bread and butter. Matilda's chronically depressed mood similarly failed to affect her partiality for well-cooked victuals and she ate everything the maid put before her, albeit in silence. Her husband sat hunched over his own trencher, wondering what was the point of a marriage in which the participants detested, disliked or at best were indifferent to each other. He felt trapped, as marriages could not be dissolved and an annulment was equally impossible after almost seventeen years.

After the meal, the same ritual was performed as on most other evenings – Matilda sullenly announced that she was retiring and went off yelling for Lucille, while he sat by his fireside, with his dog and his wine-cup, half-asleep and dreaming of old battles in which he and Gwyn had fought side by side. Eventually, when he judged that his wife was sound asleep, he climbed wearily up the steps to the solar and slipped under the sheepskin coverlet to sleep away his cares until the dawn of another day.

John's expectations of a good night's slumber were ill founded. Soon after midnight, he was awakened by an urgent tapping on the door of the solar. Though thankfully it failed to rouse the snoring Matilda, the old soldier was instantly alert and he jumped up from his mattress to lift the wooden latch on the door. Shivering in the thin undershirt that did service as a nightgown, he stared out and saw in the dim light of the half-moon a tonsured young man in a black cassock. He recognised him as one of John of Exeter's 'secondaries', a lad of about eighteen who was training to become a priest. This other John was one of the senior canons, who was the treasurer to the Chapter, responsible for all the finances and accounting for the cathedral. He was a good friend of de Wolfe, mainly because he was a staunch King's man, like John de Alençon.

'Sir John, will you please come at once,' the visitor hissed conspiratorially. 'The treasurer urgently requests your presence in the cathedral!'

John was not all that fond of attending church at the best of times and even less so in his shirt in the middle of the night. He stepped outside on to the platform at the top of the solar steps and pulled the door closed behind him, to avoid disturbing his wife.

'What the devil for?' he asked testily. 'What time is it, anyway?'

'Just after midnight, Crowner,' answered the youth anxiously. 'That's the problem. We should be starting Matins now.'

'What's happened, boy? Why does he want me at this unholy hour?' He used the phrase unconsciously, even though Matins was anything but unholy.

'Please, sir, I think you'd better see for yourself! I have to get back. The canon was most insistent that I brought you without delay.'

Grumbling, de Wolfe went back into the solar to feel for his tunic, hose and shoes, then followed the secondary down the stairs, where Mary was standing looking sleepy and dishevelled, after having to get up to let the young man in through the front door. She looked questioningly at her master, but he just shrugged and hurried after the other fellow.

The cathedral was a mere few hundred paces away, the surrounding Close opening out from Martin's Lane. As they approached the massive West Front, he saw a small crowd of people clustered around the small wicket set in the huge doors that were opened only on ceremonial occasions. The weak moonlight was aided by flickering flames from a few pitch brands set in iron rings on nearby walls, and John could see that the group consisted of black-cloaked clerics, a flash of white visible here and there where linen surplices were exposed. As he came near, he recognised several canons, among them Jordan de Brent, the cathedral archivist, the precentor and John of Exeter. The others were a motley collection of vicars-choral, secondaries and a few wide-eyed choristers peeping between the skirts of their elders.

'What's going on, John?' he demanded, as he strode up to his friend, the treasurer. He was a large man, normally ruddy faced and amiable, but tonight the coroner could see, even in the dim light, that he was pale and shaken. 'Come and see! I wish to God that de Alençon was here and not on his way to Winchester.'

The canon motioned him towards the small door, and the others stood aside to let them pass. Inside, the huge nave was almost in complete darkness, with only pale glimmers of moonlight penetrating from the clerestory window-openings high above.

John of Exeter walked rapidly down the centre of the

nave, his footsteps echoing on the flagstones of the great empty space. Ahead there was yellow light from the candles and rush-lights within the quire that separated the nave from the high altar. It was in this middle area that services were held. On either side, wooden stalls accommodated the participants in strict pecking order. To separate this august zone from the common herd in the nave, a high and very ornate rood-screen filled the lower part of the huge chancel arch. It was an intricate lattice-work of carved wood rearing up some fifteen feet, surmounted by a large gilded crucifix in the centre. Between this and the stone columns that supported the arch, each side of the top of the rood-screen was ornamented by a row of wooden spikes carved like spear-heads.

And on the third spike on the left side was impaled a human head, its genitals stuffed into its mouth!

An hour later, a shaken John of Exeter sat in his house in Canon's Row, on the north side of the Close, drinking wine with his namesake, John de Wolfe. He was usually an abstemious man, unlike some of his fellow canons, but tonight he was taking it to steady his shattered nerves, as the coroner attempted to reassure him.

'I've already had the head taken up to Rougemont,' he said. 'Later today, I'll restore it to his sons in Shillingford.'

The treasurer shook his head slowly. 'I can't believe that anyone would commit such sacrilege, John. What is the world coming to?'

De Wolfe scowled ferociously. 'I don't know either, friend, but I'm damned well going to find out! All these events are connected somehow, I feel it in my bones.'

The canon took another sip of wine, his hand shaking as he held the pewter goblet. 'It was good of you to climb up yourself and get that . . . that *thing* down from there. Everyone else was too squeamish to go anywhere near it, including myself.'

'I didn't mind getting the head, John, but I'm getting bit old to go shinning up rood-screens! It was fortunate that there was plenty of tracery in that carving to give me good footholds.'

In truth, even the hardened de Wolfe had felt some repugnance as he climbed up and came almost nose to nose with the bloody relic. As he hung on with one hand, he pulled the victim's private parts from its mouth with the other. The wide-open eyes stared straight into his and the dried lips, twisted into a rictus of final agony, almost kissed his own. Lifting the head by its hair, John wrenched the ragged neck-stump from the wooden spike and awkwardly clambered down, clutching the gruesome relics under his arm.

The senior canon shuddered again. 'I told the proctors to call some servants and get a ladder and buckets of water, to cleanse the blood from the woodwork. There was not much of it, thanks be to God, but we will have to carry out some sort of exorcism and rededication in the morning, to rid the place of this evil before we hold services there again. I have abandoned Matins, and we will have to hold our devotions in one of the side chapels until the quire is properly cleansed.'

The coroner made some non-committal noises in his throat, but his mind had moved to the crime, rather than its effect on cathedral protocol.

'Has this Peter le Calve or any of his family ever had any dispute with the cathedral or the diocese?' he asked. 'Perhaps over land or tithes?'

John of Exeter shook his head emphatically. 'Not at all, John. Before all this I knew virtually nothing of him, apart from his name. He supports his own church well enough in Shillingford, to the best of my knowledge. At least, the village priest has never brought any problems to our notice.'

He refilled their cups and took a gulp, rather than a sip. 'But if he had fallen out with the Church, surely it would be a priest who would suffer, not him. I can't imagine any Christian man committing such sacrilege.'

The coroner looked thoughtful at this remark by the treasurer.

'No Christian man indeed! What if it was a non-Christian?'

The canon stared at his friend. 'But we have no non-Christians, apart from a few Jews, who are respectable, harmless traders.'

'What about Saracens or Turks?' suggested John. Then he told the mystified cleric about the killing of Thorgils and his crew and the vague mention by the dying seaman of 'Saracens'.

'In addition, there are these stab wounds,' he added thoughtfully. 'In both Peter le Calve and the three shipmen, the wounds are much wider than the usual dagger-blade. And I get the impression that beneath the skin, they curve back on themselves.'

The priest, thankfully ignorant of such gruesome technicalities, was uncomprehending.

'What are you talking about, John?'

'These injuries could be explained by the use of oriental daggers, whose blades are very wide at the hilt and usually curve to their points.'

The archdeacon looked dubious. 'This is very flimsy evidence on which to start blaming Devonshire murders on Mohammedans, John.'

The coroner shrugged. 'I have to agree with you, but it still bears thinking about. As you say, what Christian would imperil his mortal soul by impaling the head of a murdered man on the rood-screen of your cathedral?'

The treasurer could only suggest some Barbary pirates attacking a ship off the coast, but this failed to explain their penetration inland to Shillingford and then into Exeter itself.

'How could such villains move around without being noticed?' objected de Wolfe. 'In every village, a stranger is noticed within a dozen heartbeats of his arrival! Unless they went slinking through the forest at night, there's no way that a gang of Turks in flowing robes and turbans could go parading through Devonshire to commit mayhem!'

They discussed the matter until the wine jug was empty, but made no progress with such poor evidence. The priest announced that he would not be able to sleep that night, as he had much to see to in view of the awful events of the past hour, but the coroner made his way back to his bed. In spite of seeing that grisly face dance before his closed eyes as soon as he lay down, within minutes John managed to slide back into a deep sleep.

CHAPTER FIVE

*In which Crowner John travels again
to Ringmore*

The missing head of Sir Peter le Calve was taken back to
his manor the next morning, slung unceremoniously in a
corn sack from Gwyn's saddle. The coroner and his officer had examined it closely in Rougemont before leaving,
the grisly object having spent most of the night in a
corner of the garrison chapel of St Mary in the inner
ward. The chaplain of the castle, a jovial Benedictine
called Brother Rufus, had studied it with them, having an
insatiable curiosity, especially about violent crime.

'Does the way it was cut off tell you anything?' he
asked, as the three men crouched over the decapitated
head, which lay on its left ear on the earthern floor.
Unlike the cathedral priests, the padre seemed to have no
qualms about desecrating his place of worship with such
an object.

'It's just a ragged cut, which could have been done
with anything sharp,' opined Gwyn.

De Wolfe agreed with him. 'The jagged edges are due
to the skin wrinkling up as the blade is dragged across it.
It was a keen knife, no doubt about it, for between the zig-
zags the cuts are very clean.'

'What about the bony part?' persisted Rufus. 'Could a
knife cut through that as well?'

John, still crouched on his haunches, picked up the
head, turning it up so that the stump of the neck was

uppermost. They peered at the pinkish-white bone, surrounded by beefy muscle.

'Again, a clean cut, no shattered bone. It's gone
through the gristle between the joints of the spine.'

'So not hacked off with an axe?' grunted the monk,
sounding rather disappointed.

'No, it could have been the same knife as cut through
the soft flesh,' growled Gwyn. 'Looks as if the killer knew
what he was doing – perhaps he had been a butcher!'

'You say "killer", but was this poor fellow dead or alive
when his head was cut off?' demanded the bloodthirsty
chaplain.

John shrugged. 'No way of telling, Brother. If he had
been still alive, there would have been a fountain of blood
from the pipes in his neck – but he was found in a stream,
which would have washed most of it away.'

'And remember, he also had a stab wound to his vitals,
which may well have been the cause of his death,' Gwyn
reminded them. 'I'd wager his head came off afterwards.'

John rose to his feet and motioned to his officer to put
the remains back into the sack. 'Whichever way it was,
he's dead – and he was murdered, so we have to discover
who did it. At the moment, only God knows, begging your
pardon, Chaplain.'

They left Brother Rufus to his contemplation of the
wicked ways of man and set off on the short journey to
Shillingford. An early morning carter had already taken
the news from Exeter to the village, and they found the
sons and their steward and bailiff waiting anxiously for
their arrival. Godfrey and William le Calve had the dis-
tressing task of formally confirming that the contents of
the sack were indeed the head of their late father and,
this done, the coroner suggested that, together with the
genitalia, it be reunited with the rest of the body without
delay. The surly parish priest was summoned and told to
get the sexton and dig up the coffin. An hour later, John
accompanied the brothers to the grave-side, where the

manor servants joined them in silence as the sexton replaced the head in an approximately correct position, packing it with cloths to hold it in place.

The priest muttered some dirge in Latin as the coffin-lid was nailed back and the mortal remains of the manor-lord were once again lowered into the red soil of Devon. As they turned away from the grave, John again noticed the pale woman standing inconspicuously in the background and guessed that this had been Sir Peter's leman.

A subdued pair of brothers offered them meat and ale in the hall and de Wolfe sat with them as he tried to squeeze out more information.

'He had no connection with the cathedral or any of its canons that you know of?'

Godfrey shook his head sorrowfully. 'None at all. He attended Masses here in our own church, as we all do. But he had no further interest in religion, beyond what is expected of everyone.'

The old steward, perhaps wiser in the ways of the world than the others, broke his silence with a more profound thought.

'Perhaps this sacrilege was aimed not at Sir Peter him-self, but at the Holy Church in general – some gesture of hatred or contempt?'

The others mulled this over for a moment.

'Both he and his father Arnulf had been Crusaders,' said William. 'But that should raise his esteem in the eyes of the Church.'

'But not in the eyes of Saracens,' observed the steward.

John's face swivelled to look at the old greybeard. 'Strange that you should say that, for it hovers temptingly close to certain ideas that I have had myself.'

Godfrey was scornful of this train of thought. 'Saracens! Crowner, this is Shillingford, about as unlikely a place to expect Turks and Mussulmen as anywhere in England.'

John was not prepared to share his scraps of information gleaned from the Justiciar, or his theory about the shape of the knife blade, so he let it pass, but he felt that the venerable steward might not be too short of the mark.

The denizens of the manor had no further information of any help, as no one had come forward to report any unusual happenings or the appearance of strangers in the village. Frustrated once again, the coroner set off for Exeter, arriving there in time to attend two Tuesday hangings, then go home for his dinner.

On Wednesday, John was determined to make some progress in investigating all these deaths. He resolved to revisit Ringmore and the banks of the Avon.

'We'll leave first thing in the morning,' he told Gwyn. 'Matilda will carp and gripe again at my absence for a few days, but to hell with her!'

Even at the Bush that evening, his announcement that he was riding off to the southern coast was received with raised eyebrows on the part of his mistress. He guessed straight away that she suspected that the part of that coastline might embrace Dawlish, so he made a point of emphasising that their path would lie through Buckfast and end at Ringmore, which seemed to dampen Nesta's hovering jealousy.

By midnight, he was sound asleep in his own bed, dreaming of shapely women, prancing horses and the sound of battles long past.

The hut that Alexander of Leith entered at the old castle at Bigbury was even worse inside than it appeared from the exterior. There was a fire-pit in the centre which was producing the smoke that he had seen lazily wreathing from under the thatch, but very little else. A rough table and a shelf on the wall held cooking pots and some dishes, as well as a few jars of ale and cider. Some piles of dried bracken in the corners appeared to be all there was in the way of sleeping accommodation. A bench and two milking stools completed the furnishings. The little Scot glared around in indignation.

'You don't expect us to live in this hovel?' he demanded, in his Gaelic-accented English. The target of his outrage was the man who had waved them into the bailey on their arrival. Raymond de Blois was a tough-looking Frenchman, with the appearance of a soldier but the manners of a gentleman. Of average height, he was lean and wiry, with a long clean-shaven face and short-cropped dark hair. He wore a calf-length tunic of good brown broadcloth, girdled with a heavy belt and diagonal baldric, from which hung a substantial sword and dagger. Alexander had met him before in France and at Prince John's court at Gloucester, and had been impressed by his courage and intelligence.

Now Raymond grinned at the diminutive alchemist and shook his head.

'Never fear, my friend, we've got better accommodation for you than this! A couple of loutish servants live in here – they are little better than outlaws. In fact, we encourage that notion, to keep off any curious peasants that may wander this way.'

He led Alexander outside again. 'I was just sheltering in there, to await your coming,' he explained. 'In fact, I have been waiting for three days, to be sure that I would intercept you, though in the event you were punctual to the dates we discussed in Paris.'

'What is this place?' asked Alexander, looking around at the overgrown courtyard and the moss-covered stones half hidden in long grass.

'I am told that it was one of the many castles that were hastily built some fifty years ago, during what the Normans called the "Anarchy", and later destroyed by their second Henry when he came to the throne.'

The Scotsman nodded knowingly. Though also a foreigner in England, he had lived here for many years and his wide knowledge of many subjects included some history.

'I was born during those times, after the first Henry expired and left no male heir after his son died in the White Ship tragedy,' he expounded. 'They say that for almost twenty years the country was racked by civil war between his daughter Matilda and his nephew Stephen.'

De Blois shrugged – as a Frenchman, both Normans and the English were his enemies, which was why he was here now, to aid his own King Philip in unseating the present ruler of these islands.

'The lands hereabouts, including this ruin, belong to Prince John, Count of Mortain, which is why he is able to arrange for our activities to take place here.'

Alexander looked about him, mystified. 'Am I to set up my crucibles among the weeds and distil my extracts beneath the trees?'

Raymond grinned and pointed past where Jan the Fleming was patiently holding the bridles of their horses.

'See beyond the farther palisade – or what remains of it? There is another ruin, but of a much older building.'

They walked across the bailey and out to the edge of the clearing, past the base of the castle mound. The smaller man now saw an area of tumbled masonry among the trees, nowhere standing higher than himself and swathed in moss and creepers.

'This is what is left of a Saxon abbey, ruined even before this castle was built. It is said that there was once a village here, abandoned after some pestilence ravaged its inhabitants.' De Blois strode towards the mouldering walls, beckoning Alexander to follow him. Almost entirely hidden beneath a straggling elder bush, a low doorway survived in a fragment of standing masonry that was covered behind by a pile of fallen stones and earth.

'Come inside, but watch your step. There is a stairway down to the right.'

Warily, holding the skirt of his long kilt clear of the rubble beneath his feet, the alchemist went through the opening and followed the French knight down a short flight of stone steps built into the thickness of the foundations. It was dark, but at the bottom, yellow light flickered through an arch. Alexander stopped in the doorway and looked with surprise at the sight before him. A wide undercroft, with a barrel-vaulted ceiling supported by thick pillars, stretched away for at least forty paces. He calculated that it must occupy the whole of the original building that once stood above them. The floor was flagged, unevenly in places, but it was better than the usual beaten earth, and though there was a dank smell, the dungeon seemed fairly dry. A fire burned in an open hearth to one side, but the smoke was conducted away up a chimney, which from the colour of its stones and mortar seemed to be a much later addition.

'This was the crypt of the old abbey,' explained de Blois. 'I am told that there were no coffins found here – it was quite empty when Prince John's men cleaned it up a few months ago and built that fireplace.'

The little Scotsman turned around slowly, surveying the long chamber, which, in addition to the fire, was lit by a dozen rush-lamps set on brackets around the walls. The wicks floating in their bowls of oil combined to give an acceptable light, once the eyes became accustomed to it. He saw half a dozen straw-filled palliasses along one wall and several tables and benches appeared to offer working surfaces for the paraphernalia of his profession. Alongside the hearth were two small furnaces, now cold, and some alchemical apparatus was set up on another table, with parchments and books on a nearby shelf. All that was missing were occupants.

'Where are these men I am supposed to work with?' he demanded.

Raymond shrugged in his Gallic fashion. 'I wish I knew! They are supposed to be labouring away here, in preparation for your coming, but they slipped away three days ago and haven't returned yet.'

His tone suggested that, whoever he was talking about, they were far from being his favourite people.

'We obviously sleep down here, by the look of those mattresses,' grumbled Alexander. 'But where do we get our food? There's no sign of any down here, nor in that miserable hut above.'

'Never fear, those two villeins cook for us in one of the other sheds. We keep a good stock there and they are out hunting and foraging every day,' explained the Frenchman. 'As the Count of Mortain owns the land, there's no fear of them being taken as poachers, so we get plenty of coney, hare and venison. They buy bread in Aveton and we get ale and wine sent in regularly.'

This allusion to external support sparked another question from the inquisitive Scot. 'This manor-lord I met in Gloucester a month ago – I understood that I was to meet him down here when I arrived?'

Raymond nodded as they walked towards the fire and sat on one of the benches.

'So you shall – as soon as you've had a night's rest after your long journey. As these other damned people have vanished, we may as well go tomorrow. It's but a few hours' ride from here to Revelstoke, where Sir Richard has his manor.'

The coroner and his officer rode off on Thursday morning, feeling strange without their clerk tagging along behind them. They certainly made better time without him, and were at their night's lodging well before the early November dusk fell. This time, they avoided Totnes and went twenty miles down the main high road towards Plymouth, where the Benedictines of Buckfast Abbey offered bed and board to travellers. For a modest donation, they secured a mattress in the large guest hall on the north side of the abbey yard and ate a plain but substantial meal in the lay refectory. Afterwards, they sat in front of the fire with jugs of ale and talked to other travellers for a while, but, weary from the saddle, they soon climbed into the dormer to seek their bags of hay. As they settled down under their cloaks, Gwyn was still thinking of his little friend.

'If that holy runt Thomas was here, he'd be on his knees in the bloody church half the night, praying that his backside would be less sore on tomorrow's journey!' he muttered to the shape next to him, dimly visible in the gloom.

'Perhaps I should be doing the same,' grunted the coroner. 'There was a time when I could ride all day and every day for a week and think nothing of it. But we're getting soft in our old age, Gwyn. My arse is aching just coming from Exeter today. Now shut up and get some sleep!'

The next morning they broke their fast with bread and hot oatmeal gruel, sweetened with the honey for which the monks of Buckfast were famous, then saddled up and rode off. The distance to be covered today was to be rather less, and they reached Ringmore by early afternoon. The bailiff, William Vado, was not overjoyed to see them, as law officers were never very welcome in any manor or hamlet – they usually meant trouble and often more fines. He was civil enough, however, and offered them food and a place near the manor-house fire for the coming night. He shook his head when John asked him whether there was any more news relating to the deaths after the wreck of Thorgils' ship.

'Nothing at all, Crowner. We've had no more corpses washed up, thanks be to Jesus Christ.' He crossed himself, reminding them again of the absent Thomas. 'The vessel is safe and sound, though,' he added on a more cheerful note. 'She was hauled up the river and beached at the highest tide of the month in a small inlet up near Bigbury. Roped to a couple of trees, she'll be safe there until your shipwright comes to repair her.'

John offered his gruff thanks to the bailiff for his diligence. 'We'll go and have a look at her tomorrow – I need to give my partner in Exeter some idea of what the repairs might cost.' The talk of ships sparked another thought in his mind.

'That curragh that was found on the beach – I need to see that, too. Where is it now?'

William Vado had a hurried conversation with Osbert the reeve, who was hovering behind them as they sat around the fire-pit.

'It's on our main beach at Challaborough, where we went last time you were here. Some of the fishermen have been using it, for it would be a pity to let it go to waste,' he added defensively.

'Then I must look at that too, to see if we can tell if it really came from the *Mary and Child Jesus*. If it did, then it should go back to her as part of her fittings.'

They decided to go to Challaborough beach before the light faded and made the short journey down the wooded valley to the sea. Once again to their left they saw the rocky shape of Burgh Island, with the tide fully in now, cutting it off from the land. The curragh was pulled up on the beach, upside down alongside the rude huts of the fisherfolk, and Gwyn, the self-styled marine expert, ambled over to inspect it. The black tarred fabric of the hull seemed sound enough, and when Gwyn and the bailiff turned the light craft over, the ribs and interlacing hazel withies that supported it were undamaged.

'Anything to show where it came from?' asked John, though well aware that no one there could read, even if there had been a name carved into the flimsy woodwork. Gwyn peered around the inside of the elongated cockleshell and shrugged. 'Only a sort of picture cut into the for'rad thwart,' he announced.

The coroner pushed forward and looked down at the first of the light planks that braced the curragh from side to side and provided seats for the rowers. In the centre was a crude carving, made with a knife. It was hard to make out at first, but when his eye became more attuned he saw a simple female figure with a wide ring around its head. Underneath was an angular squiggle that, thanks to the patient efforts of both Thomas and a vicar at the cathedral, John was able to recognise as a letter of the alphabet.

'It's a picture of the Virgin!' he declared with a hint of pride at his literacy. 'With the letter "M" for Mary under it. So it's definitely from Thorgils' vessel.'

The bailiff and the reeve looked glum at this, for it meant that their village would lose the use of the curragh before long, but they said nothing and waited for the coroner's next demand.

'The cargo from the boat – I trust it has been kept safe?'

Vado nodded, but looked a little uneasy. 'All in the tithe barn, Crowner.'

'And all intact, I trust?'

'Two of the kegs were damaged, sir. Brandy-wine began to leak from one, so we did what we could to save some of it in jugs and pitchers. The top of another containing some sort of dried fruit was stove in and spoilt by sea water.'

John covered up a grin with some face-rubbing and throat-clearing, as he guessed that all the French fruit and some of the wine had vanished into various tofts in the village. He did not begrudge this small loss, as it must have been a bitter disappointment to Ringmore when a law officer turned up to deprive them of the windfall that a wreck usually provided.

'I'll inspect what's left in the morning. Make sure no more goes astray, bailiff,' he warned.

Vado, happy that the matter was not being pursued further, led them back up the valley in the fading light. The steep track was deserted, and John asked whether there had been any sightings of strangers since the shipwreck.

'You said that the curragh was pulled up on Aymer Cove, your other beach to the west,' he growled. 'Whoever came ashore in it must have passed damned near your village.'

The bailiff shook his head, worried that he was being of little help to this powerful official. 'No one we don't know, sir. In these out-of-the-way parts, we get to know every move our neighbours make. Isn't that so, Osbert?'

The reeve, who was walking alongside their horses, bobbed his head energetically. 'Haven't seen a stranger these past three-month – and that was only a chapman selling his buttons and needles to the womenfolk.'

He paused to hawk and spit into the bushes. 'Richard the Saddler said he saw four monks on the road to Bigbury some time ago, but there's naught sinister about that. They were going to St Anne's Chapel, no doubt.'

De Wolfe looked across at Gwyn, who was riding alongside him.

'Haven't we heard that before somewhere?'

His officer nodded his hairy head. 'That old man in Chillingford had the same story, only there were three, not four. But the damned county is awash with priests and monks.'

The coroner turned back to the reeve. 'Did this sad-dler say what colour these brothers wore?'

'They were black monks, he said. He didn't get a close look at them.'

'Where is this St Anne's Chapel?'

The bailiff answered. 'About a mile inland, Crowner. It guards a holy well. No proper village, just a few crofts. The road turns back to Bigbury from there.'

De Wolfe pondered for a moment. 'So why would monks be going to this chapel from the direction of the sea? Surely they'd be coming from inland, if they jour-neyed from Buckfast or some other Benedictine house?'

William looked blankly at him and shrugged. 'That I can't tell you, sir. It does seem odd, looking back on it.

Maybe the parson has an answer – he's the only one who knows about priests and suchlike.'

John doubted he would get much help from the surly parish priest, but he stored the information away in his head for further deliberation. They reached the manor-house, and in spite of his earlier reticence the bailiff organised a good meal of fresh sea-fish fried in butter, with cabbage and turnips. A large jug of strong fortified wine was produced, presumably rescued from the allegedly fractured cask, and by a couple of hours after dark the coroner and his henchman were comfortably drunk and ready to lie down on their hay-bags around the smouldering fire in the hall.

The rest of the *Mary*'s cargo seemed intact when John surveyed it in the barn the next morning, so his next task was to speak to Richard Saddler, who they found sitting on a stool outside his dwelling next to the alehouse, boring holes in a sheet of thick leather with an awl. The coroner questioned him about the four monks he had seen, but learned little more except that it was about the time that the Dawlish vessel would have been lost. Time and date meant little to the inhabitants of rural villages; they were marked only by dawn and dusk, the Sabbath and saints' days. However, the finding of the curragh and the bodies on the beach provided a memorable marker in the humdrum life of Ringmore and the saddler was definite that he had seen the robed and cowled figures two days before that.

'We must enquire at this chapel place, in case other people have had sight of them,' he told Gwyn as they trotted out of the village an hour later. As expected, the surly Father Walter had been as unhelpful as usual when they called at the church, gruffly saying that he knew nothing of any monks passing through the neighbourhood. Now the reeve was guiding them up to St Anne's chapel and then across to the estuary of the Avon to look at the *Mary and Child Jesus*.

They climbed gradually up on to an undulating plateau, the strip-fields around Ringmore giving way to heathland and scattered woods until the track joined another which came north from Bigbury, a village a mile to their right, on the edge of dense forest. At the junction was a small chapel, a square room ten paces long, made of wattle plastered with cob, under a thatched roof. Across the track and down a short lane between scrubby oaks was an enclosed well, which, according to Osbert, was reputed to have curative powers, especially for the eyes.

'Is there anyone we can ask about these alleged travelling monks?' demanded John. The reeve slid from the horse he had borrowed from the bailiff and went into the chapel, returning with a bow-legged old man in a ragged tunic, his hair as wild as Gwyn's.

'This is the fellow who looks after the well and the chapel,' said Osbert. 'He lives off the ha'pennies that pilgrims throw into the well as thank-offerings.'

When the coroner asked whether he had seen four monks in the past couple of weeks, the man surprised John by nodding his head vigorously.

'Can't recall when, but it was less than a couple of Sundays past,' he wheezed.

'They came to pray in your chapel or visit the well?' asked John.

'No, walked right past, sir, turned down Bigbury way.'

When the coroner tried to get some better description, the old fellow pointed to his red-rimmed eyes, which John now saw were milky with cataracts. 'I can only just make out shapes with these poor things, sir. Dark robes and cowls, that's all I could see.'

There was no more to be gleaned from the guardian of the well, and they rode off again, de Wolfe thoughtful as he weighed up what little information they had.

'Is there anything to attract monks to this Bigbury place?' he asked.

Osbert was scornful. 'If you think Ringmore is of little

account, sir, wait until you see Bigbury! Nothing there
except a church, an alehouse and a handful of crofts.
They say it was once bigger, but was hit by a pestilence
long ago. It doesn't belong to the same manor as
Ringmore, it's on Prince John's land, though it's leased to
Giffard at Aveton.'

Here was another snippet of information that de Wolfe
stored away in his head, but now Gwyn was interrogating
the reeve. 'Where does this track go beyond Bigbury?'

'Nowhere, really. It ends up back at the headland
opposite Burgh Island, unless you want to turn off and go
down to the river's edge. From there you can go right up
to Aveton, when the tide is out.'

The Cornishman looked across at his master. 'So why
did four monks come down here, into the back of beyond?'

John shared his puzzlement, but had no suggestions as
to an answer. By now they were riding through more heavily wooded country and eventually came downhill into the
hamlet of Bigbury, which as Osbert had said, was little
more than a small cluster of dwellings around a small
church and an alehouse. They stopped to slake their
thirst with some surprisingly good cider and seek out
more information. There was plenty of the former, but
none of the latter. Though they questioned the garrulous
ale-wife and half a dozen villagers, no one owned to
having seen any monks at all, at any time.

'Damned strange, that!' grunted Gwyn. 'The old fellow
sees them coming down the road from that chapel, but
they never arrive here. There's no way that four black
monks could walk through here unseen!'

De Wolfe asked whether there was anywhere they
could have gone in between, given the heavily-wooded
country thereabouts.

'Nothing there, Crowner,' said the landlady emphatically. 'Only a ruin in the forest that used to be a priory in
my great-grandfather's time. Just ghosts and outlaws there
these days – not a place to go unless you have to!'

'If it was a priory, maybe these men were on some kind of pilgrimage?' suggested Osbert.

It was as good an answer as any other, and with a grunt the coroner upended his pot of cider and motioned to the other two for them to prepare to carry on with the journey. Half an hour later they were standing on the firm sand of the Avon estuary, well over a mile up from the sea, looking at the hull of Thorgils' boat. It was sitting upright in a shallow pool of water in a little bay at the side of the sinuous upper reaches of the river, lashed firmly by ropes to the trunks of two trees growing right on the edge of the bank.

John left Gwyn to to study the vessel, and he soon reported that there was no damage to the stout wooden hull and all that seemed necessary was a new mast, rigging and sail, as well as a steering oar.

'The men bailed her out with leather buckets and now when the tide's in, she floats as tidy as she ever did,' reported Osbert proudly. 'Come the spring, you'll be able to sail her out of here to wherever you wish.'

With nothing more he could think of investigating, the coroner and his officer said farewell to the reeve, who turned for home, while they headed up the track that followed the river bank up to Aveton at the head of the estuary. From here they made for Totnes and a night's rest, before the last lap the next day home to Exeter, where John glumly expected the usual black looks from his wife for yet again being absent for several days.

CHAPTER SIX

In which Crowner John visits his brother-in-law

Having arrived home on Sunday, the following week began quietly once again – especially in Martin's Lane, where there was almost dead silence in the de Wolfe household, as Matilda did her best to ignore her husband. Even Tuesday's hangings were a poorly attended occasion, and it was late that afternoon, an hour before curfew closed the city gates at dusk, that the returning sheriff's party trotted up to Rougemont Castle.

Amid shouts of welcome, cries of relief from the soldiers' families and a general tumult in the inner bailey, the dusty cavalcade dismounted and went their various ways. John and his officer clattered down their stairway and emerged just in time to meet the archdeacon and his nephew as they came across to the gatehouse. Thomas looked much the same, though there was a smug expression on his pinched face as he punched Gwyn on his brawny arm and pointed back at his borrowed horse.

'The fellow is almost as proud of that as he is of regaining his priesthood!' said John de Alençon, with a smile. Gwyn almost gaped as he looked across the courtyard and saw that Thomas now had a regular saddle instead of the female abomination that had so irked the Cornishman.

'You're a man at last!' he boomed, picking the clerk up from the ground and whirling him around in affectionate clowning.

De Wolfe saw the sheriff beckoning to him and suggested that they all adjourn to the keep for refreshment and to hear the news. In the crowded hall, Henry de Furnellis was welcomed back by his clerks, who began waving parchments at him. Ignoring them, the sheriff ambled to a table near the hearth and yelled for food and drink. As the travellers stretched and shrugged off their riding cloaks, the story of their week-long trip to Winchester unfolded. The archdeacon began by describing Thomas's restoration to his beloved Church, the little man almost wriggling with mixed delight and embarrassment.

'I have to admit that the bishop was magnanimous in his sermon,' said John de Alençon. 'He virtually apologised on behalf of the cathedral, its Chapter and the Consistory Court and welcomed Thomas back into the fold without reservation.'

Gwyn, standing behind the clerk as befitted his lower station in the presence of the sheriff and coroner, slapped his friend on the back, spilling the glass of wine he was clutching. 'It made a man of him, sirs! He even rides a horse like one now!'

The merriment and gossip went on for an hour, as the travellers unwound after almost three days on the road. Then one by one, they drifted away, the archdeacon going back to Canon's Row with Thomas, after the radiant clerk promised to meet them at the Bush later to give them a more detailed account of his visit to Winchester. The sheriff motioned to de Wolfe to come with him to his chamber and, over a flask of good wine, they sat at his table and discussed more official matters.

'I saw Hubert Walter at the castle after I delivered the farm to those exchequer vultures,' said Henry. 'He offered his felicitations to you and a little more information for both of us.'

'About this Prince John business?' queried the coroner.

De Furnellis nodded his grey head. 'It seems that some

more intelligence has come from the King's spies in France. Not much, but enough to confirm that dirty work is afoot to bolster the Count of Mortain's ambitions once again.'

He stopped for a long draught of red wine. 'There's no doubt that some scheme is being hatched in England and the whisper is that it is both related to money and that it is at least in part centred in a western county.'

'That could mean Gloucestershire,' said John. 'Since our king was unwise enough to restore some of the Prince's possessions, Gloucester has been his favoured abode when he is in England.'

Henry shrugged his tired shoulders. 'It could be, but it could also be down this way. Gloucestershire is not what most men think of when "the west" is mentioned.'

' Did the Justiciar have anything else to tell us?'

'An odd thing, John – very odd. He said that these agents on the Seine also had wind of some Levantine involvement in this plot.'

'Levantine? Did he mean Turkish or Saracen or what?' demanded de Wolfe.

'The word Saracen was not used, it seems. He said that Mussulmen were involved – but that could mean anyone east of Constantinople.'

The two men debated these obscure warnings for a while, but no enlightenment came. John told the sheriff of the sacrilegious exhibition of Peter le Calve's head in the cathedral and his lack of any leads about the perpetrators. Henry shook his head sadly at this further news about le Calve's hideous death.

'He deserved a more fitting end than that. He was a Crusader himself, and his father Arnulf fought with that bastard de Revelle's father in Outremer – a far better man than his son has turned out to be.'

John sighed at the thought that now occurred to him. 'With this talk of the possible involvement of Moors – and the fact that Arnulf le Calve was out there with old de

Revelle – it may be that I need to talk to Richard to see if he recollects any reason why the son of his father's friend might have been a target.'

De Furnellis stared doubtfully at John over the rim of his cup.

'That's a bit far fetched, John! It happened in Shillingford, for God's sake! A long way from Acre or Ascalon, both in distance and time.'

'I have to chase every hare that I can think of, Henry, as I've nothing else to go on.'

The sheriff acknowledged John's frustration. 'Rather you than me, for the less I see of Richard de Revelle, the better I'll be pleased. But if you think something may come of it, by all means pursue whatever lead you may have.'

When de Wolfe went home for his supper, he followed his usual practice of trying to make conversation with his wife, if only to salve his own conscience. When he told her that he was thinking of travelling to Revelstoke to see her brother, and explained the reason, he expected her usual carping complaints about his being away from home yet again. To his considerable surprise, she responded by saying that she would accompany him to her brother's manor, as she had not seen him for a considerable time.

'The western end of the county is a long ride for a lady,' he responded, with genuine concern for her comfort. It was the wrong thing to say, for she bridled and turned the comment against him.

'I suppose I'm not wanted once again,' she snapped. 'Perhaps you intend travelling via Dawlish!'

Holding his temper in check with an effort, John grunted that she was very welcome to go with him and suggested that they set out in two days' time, on Thursday. 'I hope the weather will be kind to us. It is now November, but we should miss the first snows, if we keep clear of Dartmoor.'

Once the notion had seized her interest, Matilda became almost civil, deciding what kirtles and mantles she should command Lucille to get ready. 'The girl must accompany us, of course,' she said firmly. 'No lady can travel without her maid beside her.'

John's heart sank. He could see this trip turning into a caravan of packhorses piled with feminine accoutrements.

'My officer and clerk will have to ride with us, of course,' he countered, hoping that Matilda's aversion to both Gwyn and Thomas might dissuade her from coming. He was out of luck, as the idea had now become so fixed in her mind that it seemed she would welcome even Satan himself on the journey.

'I suppose we could do with that Cornish lout as a guard,' she said loftily. 'He might be of some use in keeping off outlaws and footpads.'

Matilda retired early, announcing that she needed to sort out her gowns with Lucille and get extra rest in preparation for the rigours of the journey, so John was able to give Brutus his evening walk without waiting too long. As always, the dog took him to the Bush Inn, and John glumly related this latest complication to his friends in the tavern.

'I'll be stuck with my dear wife for at least five days, unless I can persuade her to stay with her brother for a while and return without her,' he muttered.

'Why does she want to go to see her brother?' asked Gwyn, who viewed with horror the prospect of being near Matilda for such a long time. 'I thought she had fallen out with him after his downfall.'

'It'll be nice for you, John!' said Nesta, sarcastically. 'A second honeymoon, you might say.' Since John had reported the widowhood of Hilda and announced his intention of taking her into partnership with Hugh de Relaga, Nesta was finding it hard to hide her jealousy. He felt wounded by this, as only once or twice had his thoughts strayed to the possibility of reviving his liaison with the blonde Saxon, and he had done nothing to nudge such thoughts towards reality.

Thomas, too, was unhappy about the thought of riding for days in close proximity to the master's wife, who made no effort to hide her contempt for him.

'Do you really need me, Crowner?' he pleaded. 'It's not as if this was an inquest or an investigation of a death, where I would be required to take down a record.'

John, mindful of his clerk's recent long ordeal on a horse, relented and said that he could stay in Exeter, at which Thomas's euphoria returned in full measure. He regaled his friends with a full account of his adventures in Hampshire and the glorious moments when the Bishop of Winchester brought him back into the bosom of his beloved Church. Nesta listened avidly, her eyes glistening with tears as Thomas told how even his parents, whom he had not seen for four years, came to the cathedral to witness his restoration. His father was a minor knight with a lease on a small manor five miles from the city and had severed all connection with his son when his alleged misdemeanour became known. Now they were reconciled and Thomas's contentment was complete.

The clerk, for whom one pint of cider was more than enough, left early to meet some friends among the secondaries and vicars in the Close, leaving Gwyn and Nesta to debate other matters with de Wolfe.

'Do you think confronting de Revelle will achieve anything, John?' she asked. 'You know how much he hates you these days.' Her previous spat of jealousy seemed to have been submerged by concern for his welfare.

'I can think of no other way for me to advance this obscure situation,' he replied. 'I just want some information about his father and his knowledge of Peter le Calve. I doubt I will get anything but a hostile reception from Richard, but at least the topic is not one that concerns himself or his misdeeds.'

Gwyn pulled at the bushy ends of his moustache, which hung down below his jaw. 'As long as the reception isn't a shower of arrows from the gatehouse of his manor! He'll be on his own ground there and not disposed to accept any liberties from you, Crowner.'

'I'll be the soul of discretion!' snapped John, which made Nesta smile, as, though her lover had many worthy qualities, tact was not one of them. Gwyn was still tugging away at his whiskers, usually a sign that he was worrying about something.

'This talk of Levantines or Turks or whatever you want to call them,' he growled. 'Why the hell should they be in the west of England to aid this bloody prince? There can't be an army of them, so what use can a few be, if the rumour is true?'

'And where are they, anyway?' added Nesta, typically getting to the heart of the matter. 'No one has seen so much as a turban or whatever they wear. How can it possibly be true?'

De Wolfe held up his hands in mock protection against their objections.

'It sounds unlikely, I know, but the King's spies are usually accurate. What Mussulmen have got to do with this money that's to be found, I don't know – perhaps they are going to make the stuff for Prince John!'

Alexander of Leith's foray to Revelstoke had been made a number of days before de Wolfe's journey there, and the alchemist was now back in the lonely ruin in the forest, still thinking about the visit they had made to the former sheriff.

When they had left Bigbury to meet Sir Richard de Revelle, Raymond de Blois had escorted the little Scot rapidly across ten miles of the western end of the Devon coast, with the grotesque Fleming hard put to keep up behind them. They had to go inland for half the distance to find a ford over the River Erme, another of the estuaries that cleaved the landscape, then aimed for the Yealm, the next fjord that cut deeply into the coast. De Blois had been here as an envoy – and a spy – several times before, covertly entering England by the western sea route on missions from Paris to the Count of Mortain. He spoke English, knew the terrain and had a mental map of the main tracks through the county, so was able to aim unerringly for Newton Ferrars, a fishing village on the Yealm. This vill was not his destination that day, but rather the manor of Revelstoke, a large honour occupying most of the peninsula south of the Yealm, which stretched down to the cliffs at the western end of the huge bay that arced from Bolt Head to Gara Point. He had visited Richard de Revelle before and knew his way to the manor-house, which stood on the high ground of the peninsula halfway between Newton Ferrars and Stoke Point. This was a headland behind which sheltered the little church of St Peter the Poor Fisherman, built by Richard de Revelle a few years earlier, in a moment of generosity augmented by the belief that it would aid his entry into heaven.

The trio reached Revelstoke early in the afternoon, as they had been delayed in fording the Erme because of the high tide. The manor-house was set behind a stone wall and a deep ditch as, being so near a lonely part of the coast, there was always the danger of sea raiders. Though a few crofts and tofts lay around it, the manor was more diffuse than the usual village, with some large bartons farming the extensive field systems that occupied much of the peninsula. There were more dwellings down at Noss, where crofts and fishing huts faced Newton across an arm of the branching Yealm river.

The bailey around the manor-house was guarded by a sturdy gatehouse, where a surly porter let them in as soon as he recognised Raymond de Blois. Inside, Alexander saw that the large bailey surrounded an imposing stone-built house of two storeys, with a number of timber outbuildings and barns at the rear. Jan the Fleming knew his place as a servant and took the horses off to the stables, leaving the Frenchman and the alchemist to be received by the steward. As they climbed the wooden stairs to the elevated door, this rather pompous head of the household staff bowed his head to the French knight, but gave only a cursory nod to the Scotsman, accompanied by a look of disapproval that suggested that such curiously garbed eccentrics were not welcome at Revelstoke. He led them inside the large hall, however, and indicated a table near the fire-pit where they could enjoy refreshments while they waited for the manor-lord, whom he said was presently with his wife in the solar. Servants rapidly appeared, bearing hot mutton pies, slices of ham and pork, together with fresh bread, butter and cheese. Washing these down with wine and ale, the ill-assorted pair ate in silence, their travel-chilled bodies warming up by the heat of the glowing logs. When they had finished, Raymond began to get impatient at being kept waiting for so long by a knight of equal rank to himself. Though he had met Richard de Revelle several times, both here and in Bristol, he did not like the man, thinking him a sly and supercilious fellow who could not be trusted.

Just as de Blois was working himself up to protest to the hovering steward that he did not like to be kept waiting, the former sheriff of Devonshire appeared in a doorway at the side of the hall. Richard was a slim man of average height, with a narrow face that appeared almost triangular, as he had a pointed beard of the same light brown as his hair, which was worn slightly longer than the severe crop favoured by most Norman gentlemen. He was an elegant dresser, favouring green in most of his tunics, such as the one he wore now, which had a crenellated pattern of gold embroidery around the neck and hem. A jewelled belt of soft leather ran around his waist, from which a purse dangled from plaited cords. His shoulders were covered with a surcoat of a darker green velvet and his shoes had long curled toe-points in the latest fashion.

The visitors rose to their feet as De Revelle walked across the hall, ignoring the bows of his steward and two other servants, to extend his hand to Sir Raymond, grasping his forearm in geeting.

'I regret my delay in attending upon you, de Blois, but my wife was indisposed,' he brayed, in his rather high-pitched voice. 'I am afraid that Lady Eleanor is of a somewhat delicate disposition.'

The Frenchman murmured some sympathetic platitudes, then turned to introduce Alexander of Leith. De Revelle regarded the apparition with obvious distaste, echoing the response of his steward.

'Does he speak our language?' he loftily asked Raymond in the Norman French that was his first tongue.

'Ay, and Latin and Gaelic as well – but I am more comfortable in English!' tartly retorted the little man, using the speech of the more lowly inhabitants of the islands.

Richard reddened, then regarded the strange tunic and long tartan kilt. He came to the conclusion that such eccenticity must betoken considerable academic and technical skill, and adjusted his manner accordingly.

'You are welcome, magister. I trust that you can help to achieve what is required?'

Alexander scowled, as he had also taken an instant dislike to this arrogant lord. But as they had a mutual purpose, for which he was to be well paid, he felt obliged to swallow his resentment.

'Much depends on these other people, sir. I have great experience of my art, yet have so far fallen slightly short of the desired goal. With the help that is promised by them, we shall suceed.'

The three men sat again at the table and Richard snapped his fingers at his steward for more wine.

'I have not yet set eyes upon these others who have

come to assist you,' he said to Alexander. 'Have you all that you require at this den which has been provided?'

'What I saw in the short time I was there seems adequate,' replied the Scotsman, cautiously. 'I too have failed to meet these alleged geniuses of my art.'

De Revelle's eyebrows rose as he turned to Raymond de Blois. 'Where are they, then? I thought it was agreed that it would be unwise for them to be seen abroad more than is absolutely necessary.'

The Parisian knight gave a very Gallic shrug. 'They seem to do as they please, Sir Richard. Communication is difficult, as only one speaks a bastard kind of French and none of them has a word of the English tongue. They seem to come and go as they wish, like ghosts in the night.'

De Revelle scowled. 'This is not satisfactory. The Prince would be concerned if he knew, as would your king. Have they achieved anything yet in their task?'

'I doubt they have tried – they seem to be waiting for Alexander here to join them.'

The talk continued for some time, consisting mainly of the former sheriff haranguing the others to ensure some action and to keep their associates in line. He ended with a stern recommendation to them to have a good night's sleep after the evening meal and to set off home early the next day to get on with the job that they had come so far to complete. Rising from the table, he bade them a curt farewell and, throwing his cloak dramatically back over his right shoulder, stalked away to his private chambers, leaving a Frenchman and a Scot united in their dislike of their host.

John's journey westwards was long and arduous, mainly because he was deprived of the usual gossip from Gwyn and the banter between his officer and Thomas de Peyne. With Matilda alongside him, stiffly upright on a decent-sized palfrey hired from Andrew's stable, conversation was as sterile as usual. The maid Lucille, muffled up to her thin nose in a dun-coloured cloak, trotted miserably on the other side of her mistress on another rounsey hired from Andrew's stable. Gwyn sullenly kept well out of the way, riding behind with the two men-at-arms that John had commandeered from the garrison to act as an additional escort. Normally, de Wolfe rode alone with Gwyn, but he felt that their efforts to repel any attack by highway thieves might be hampered by the presence of a lady, so he added this pair as a deterrent.

As with their last journey, they stopped at Buckfast for the night, rather than Totnes, for accommodation for female travellers was better in the large abbey hostel than in Totnes Castle. Though there were no nuns there, the hostel was run by lay servants, whose wives and daughters were employed in the segregated part reserved for women.

John was glad of the respite from the grim presence of his wife which he had endured during the many hours they had ridden from Exeter. He sat thankfully in the travellers' hall with Gwyn, their soldiers and a few other patrons, drinking ale and putting the world to rights with their gossip.

The next day, they were off again soon after dawn to cover the remaining twenty miles to Revelstoke, the last eight being through small lanes and tracks off the main Plymouth high road. As they went farther west, the already leaden sky darkened even more and a cold wind sprang up, with a few flakes of snow spinning in its icy breath. Around them, the countryside was hunkering down for the coming winter, the last of the leaves being whipped from the trees by the stiff breeze.

John had never been to his brother-in-law's manor before – he had never been invited. When they reached it, he was surprised by the extent of both the surrounding farmland and of the house itself. He wondered cynically how much of the money that Richard had embezzled in his various schemes had been invested in improving the property. As they reined up outside the gatehouse, he looked at the stone-tiled roof and castellated parapet that were visible above the boundary wall and wondered whether de Revelle was more concerned with defending himself against sea rovers or possible retribution from the king, if he was up to his old schemes again.

Once within sight of her old home, Matilda lost some of the icy impassiveness that she had shown throughout the journey. She became restless on her side-saddle, and John could see her biting her lip as they rode up to the gate. He wondered whether she was becoming anxious about their reception or whether a reunion with her disgraced brother was difficult for her to bear, since her former hero-worship had been so ignominiously undermined. As had often happened in the past, the sight of his wife in a state of obvious worry and unhappiness stirred both his conscience and his compassion. He leant across and touched her arm.

'He'll be glad to see you, never fear,' he growled, but Matilda made no response, other than to pull her arm away from his hand.

The porter, recognising the lord's sister, lugged open the gates and they walked their horses across the heavy timbers that spanned the deep ditch that ran around the walls. Inside the large compound, grooms came scurrying to take the horses and Gwyn and the two men-at-arms went with them to see that the beasts were fed and watered. John assisted Matilda to dismount and together they walked towards the steps to the hall, followed by Lucille, lugging a large parcel of her mistress's clothing. Warned by a blast from the porter's horn, the steward appeared, and his wrinkled face broke into an obsequious smile as he saw Matilda climbing up to the doorway into the hall.

'My wife is fatigued after the long journey,' rasped John, determined to take the initiative from the start and

not appear at any disadvantage in this house of a man he
despised. 'Please conduct her to Sir Richard and Lady
Eleanor at once.' Several servants appeared from side
doors and two women bobbed their knee to Matilda and
ushered her away, followed by another man carrying her
two large leather bags, which had been slung across the
backs of the soldiers' mounts.

As she vanished up a staircase in the wall, John turned
to the fire-pit and stood above the burning logs, rubbing
his hands to warm his fingers, his riding cloak still hanging from his shoulders. A fat priest sat on a stool opposite,
drinking ale and two other men occupied a bench to one
side, dressed in rustic clothing that suggested that they
were falconers or huntsmen. All acknowledged him with
nods, but made no attempt at conversation.

The steward hurried back and with much head-bowing
and gestures conducted the coroner to a side chamber,
where a fire burned in a small hearth with a chimney,
obviously a more modern addition to the structure of the
house. It was much warmer than the gloomy hall outside
and was well furnished, with several leather-backed fold-
ing chairs, a table, stools and a bench. John could see that
an inner door led to a bedchamber and he assumed that
this was to be the accommodation for Matilda and himself. The steward, who John later learned rejoiced in the
name of Geoffrey de Cottemore de Totensis, stood by as
an old woman and a young girl brought in food and wine
to set on the table. 'Lady Matilda is being entertained by
my lord and lady, sir,' Geoffrey announced loftily. 'She
says she will join you later. Supper will be served in the
hall soon after dusk.'

Having confirmed that Gwyn and the soldiers were
being cared for in the servants' huts at the back of the
manor, the steward strode out and John was left alone to
enjoy a hot pottage made of lumps of meat and bone
swimming in a mixture of herbs and vegetables. There
was a wooden bowl containing a large apple and an

orange, an ostentatious import from southern France. The bread and cheese were accompanied by a good Anjou wine, so John assumed that he was not going to be cast out of his brother-in-law's house that night. He ate heartily, keeping to the old soldier's dictum that one should eat, sleep and make love whenever the occasion presented, in case the opportunity never arose again.

When he had finished the food, he went to the window and pulled open the shutter that covered the narrow slit. The late afternoon was darkened by a heavily overcast sky, which had that pinkish-grey hue that suggested snow. A few flakes were still falling, but nothing was yet settling on the ground. John earnestly hoped that they would not get snowed in, as the shorter the time he had to spent under Richard's roof, the better he would be pleased. He wanted to be off again early in the morning.

He pulled one of the chairs nearer the fire and sat down with a pewter cup of wine. A few moments later he was snoring, dreaming that he was in an inn near Vienna, a sense of foreboding and recrimination clouding the scenes in his mind. It was a dream he had had many times during the past three years, but now it vanished as the creak of the door opening jerked him awake. In the failing light, he saw Richard de Revelle standing on the threshold, glaring at him. Rising to his feet, he faced his wife's brother and for a long moment the two men stared silently at each other.

'You are tolerated here for Matilda's sake, de Wolfe,' said Richard finally. 'I am told that, as far as you are concerned, your visit is upon official business. I doubt that you would have had the temerity to come for any other reason.'

His tone was flat, but there was an undercurrent of bitterness that was not lost on John.

'I need to ask you some questions, Richard. They concern your father.'

This was a surprise to de Revelle, who had expected

some stern interrogation connected to his own recent misdeeds. He had been ejected as sheriff by the Chief Justiciar several months earlier for illegally appropriating treasure trove destined for the royal treasury, but there were older, more serious allegations relating to his support for Prince John which might be revived at any time. But now to be asked about his long-dead father was as unexpected as it was welcome, if his own transgressions were not at issue.

'My father? You have come all this way to enquire about Gervaise de Revelle? You well know that he died many years ago.'

He stood aside as a servant came into the chamber with two three-branched candlesticks and placed the lights on the table. As he left, Richard waved a hand towards the chairs, inviting John to be seated. He himself went to stand in front of the hearth, hands behind his back, deliberately posing as the lord of Revelstoke to emphasise his ascendancy over his unwelcome visitor. Reluctantly, de Wolfe lowered himself into the chair, which creaked as he leaned back against the thick hide of the back-rest.

'This concerns a particularly brutal murder of one of our own kind, Richard,' he said sombrely. 'If you have been down at this end of the county for the past week or two, you will not have heard of the death of Sir Peter le Calve of Shillingford.'

His brother-in-law seemed to lose some of his naked antipathy at this news, as he stared at John in obvious surprise. 'Le Calve? Was he set upon in a robbery?'

The coroner described what had happened, holding back no detail of the macabre killing. All he held back was his vague suspicion that there might be a tenuous connection with other deaths, such as that of Thorgils and his men.

'But what has this to do with my father? He died sixteen years ago.'

De Wolfe had cause to remember that, as it had been a year after Sir Gervaise de Revelle had agreed with his own father to the disastrous marriage between his daughter Matilda and the dashing young warrior John de Wolfe.

'I have been told that Peter le Calve's father was previously a close friend of your own father. I am trying to find any clue in Peter's past which might explain why he was murdered in such a bizarre manner. I have asked Matilda, but she says she was too young to have any useful recollection of the elder le Calve.'

Richard was so relieved that the visit of the coroner was unconnected with his own past that he abandoned the hostile antagonism with which he had come prepared to meet de Wolfe. His brow wrinkled in thought as he pirouetted on a foot before the fire.

'I remember Arnulf, Peter's father. He was of Gervaise's generation and they campaigned together a number of times.'

'Including in Outremer, I understand,' prompted John.

'Yes, as a child and a younger man, I heard endless boring tales of those battles. But what in God's name can any of that have to do with Peter le Calve?'

De Wolfe sighed. 'I will be frank, Richard, I am grasping at straws. A Norman knight has been murdered in a terrible fashion and a cathedral desecrated in a most sacrilegious way. I have not the slightest notion of who did this, nor why it was carried out in such a wierd fashion, which seems to have some ritual significance.'

The appeal to his indignation at this assault upon Norman nobility struck a chord in Richard's aristocratic sensibilities, which were equally as snobbish as his sister's.

'It is certainly an outrage both to our class and to the Church!' he agreed. 'But I fail to see how his friendship with my father can enlighten you.'

John's fingers restlessly tapped the arm of his chair.

'Peter le Calve seems a highly unlikely candidate for some revenge killing. I fail to see how he could have engendered such hatred that he was sought out, crucified and beheaded. So I wonder whether he paid the price for some sin of his father?'

Richard looked uneasy at this. 'It is a theory with little substance, John. On that basis, given that my father and Arnulf le Calve shared so many campaigns together, then perhaps I am vulnerable as well!' He said this with an air of flippant bravado, but John detected an underlying concern in his voice. Richard de Revelle was not known for his personal bravery, and his ambitions had always been political, rather than military. He gave up his posing by the hearth and sat down opposite John, his elbow on the table and his fingers playing nervously with his small beard.

'The stories they told at the dining table and with wine cups around the fire were of many escapades in Ireland, France and especially the Holy Land,' he said.

'Any particular battles or sieges there?' demanded John.

'Damascus was the favourite, I seem to remember. They were both there in 'forty-eight.'

John grunted, contempt evident in his manner. 'The Second Crusade! The greatest fiasco this century. So they were at the siege, were they?'

Richard nodded, his anger at John's presence apparently submerged by this latest news, which, however faintly, might presage some danger for himself. 'And so were many others, both knights and men-at-arms. As far as I understand it, it was a military failure, but to hear those two older men talking, one would have thought it was a great victory.'

'But you heard nothing specific about the part your father or Gervaise played in it?' persisted John, worrying away at the problem like a terrier with a rat.

De Revelle shrugged his narrow shoulders under the

elegant tunic of fine green wool. 'I can't recall all those tales spun on winters' nights. I was either a boy or a young man, more concerned with my own affairs. But no, there was nothing special over and above two old men boasting over a flagon of wine.'

The coroner could get nothing further from his brother-in-law after several more minutes of probing, and he sighed in acknowledgement of a wasted journey across more than half a county. Richard sensed this and, perhaps anxious to draw the meeting to an end before John could move on to more sensitive matters, he stood up and moved to the door.

'We will go to table in an hour, John. No doubt Matilda will then tell you herself, but she has decided to stay here for a few days. I will see that she is escorted back to Exeter in due course. Meanwhile, I trust that your business will not detain you and that you will be ready to leave first thing in the morning.'

With that abrupt dismissal, he went out and, in spite of the previous marked softening of his attitude towards John, slammed the door behind him with unnecessary force.

When Alexander of Leith and his dumb henchman Jan returned to the derelict castle with their French guide, they found that the missing men had returned. After they had taken their horses to the stable at the foot of the castle mound, they went to the next hut, which served as their kitchen and refectory. Raymond de Blois marched in and stopped just inside the rickety door.

'You're back, are you?' he exclaimed. 'Where the devil have you been for the past few days?

The Scotsman peered around the tall Frenchman's elbow and saw three men squatting cross-legged on the dried bracken in front of the fire-pit. Two were tall, wiry-looking men of Moorish appearance with lean, dark faces and hooked noses over drooping black moustaches. They wore long shapeless habits of a thin white cloth unfamilar to Alexander, belted with cords from which dangled the sheaths of vicious broad daggers. Around their heads were wound lengths of striped cloth, the loose ends hanging down their backs.

The other man was older, probably well over fifty, but powerfully built, with a thick neck and large hands. His features were also those of a Saracen, with leathery tanned skin, deep-set eyes and a rim of black beard around his chin. He wore a more elaborate green turban, but his dress was similar to the others', except that around his neck hung a gold crescent moon on a heavy gold chain. The three men stared up at the newcomers impassively, but made no reply.

Raymond walked over to them and beckoned the alchemist to follow him.

'This is Alexander, with whom you will work,' he said to the seated men in carefully precise French. 'I trust now that you have returned to the duties for which you are being so handsomely paid, you will start your work without more delay!'

He turned to the Scotsman and laid a hand on his shoulder. 'This man with the green headdress is Nizam al-Din, a learned alchemist from the East, I'm not sure from where. He is the man that Prince John told you of when you were in Gloucester, being sent by the King of France. I hope you will work harmoniously together, for he speaks passable French.'

Nizam gave a perfunctory nod of greeting to his fellow wizard and curtly introduced the other two men.

'These are my servants, Abdul Latif and Malik Shah. They speak almost nothing of your language.' His own French was heavily accented and grammatically incorrect, but his meaning could be understood.

Alexander muttered some words of greeting, resolving never to trust these men and to be wary of ever turning his back on them. His main concern was to discover whether they had any new knowledge about the transmutation of metals, which had been his life's labour, along with the search for the related Elixir of Life.

Before he could take matters any further, the two peasants who acted as guards and labourers came in, followed by Jan the Fleming. Their names were Alfred and Ulf, two hulking Saxons of slow movement and even slower wits. Alfred had two large loaves of coarse bread under his arm and a pair of dead fowls swung from his other hand. His partner carried a small sack of grain and a gallon earthenware jar of cider.

'We stole these from a forester's dwelling,' muttered Ulf in English, his voice garbled to Alexander's ears by his thick local dialect.

'I hope that was far from here, as I ordered!' snapped de Blois. 'We don't want to be traced back to this place, especially if you robbed a forest officer.'

Alfred leered, showing two blackened teeth, the only ones in his mouth.

'Miles away, sir. We tramped near all the way to Modbury and back.'

'And right hungry we are from it,' whined Ulf, looking down at the fire-pit. Here a pair of hares had been roasted on spits, much of the meat having already gone down the Mussulmen's throats, accompanied by a mash of boiled wheat and vegetables which they ate with their fingers from small copper bowls set on the ground alongside each man.

Though he understood not a word of Ulf's speech, the meaning of the hungry glances was clear, and Nizam waved a hand at the remains. 'We shot these this morning on the way back. You are welcome to share it.' He did not elaborate on where they had been coming back from, and Raymond thought it pointless to pursue the matter. His main fear was that they would reveal themselves to the locals and ruin the efforts of Richard de Revelle and Prince John's officials in securing this remote place for their activities.

'These are awkward people to deal with,' he muttered to Alexander in his poor English. 'But we have no choice but to be civil to them if we want their assistance.'

A bench and stools were pulled up to the small trestle table and the knight and the alchemist sat to eat slabs of bread on which slices of hare were laid, cut by Jan, who took on the role of steward. Cheese was produced from an oaken chest, in which their victuals were stored away from rats, and ale was drawn from a small cask. Jan and the two Devon men sat on the other side of the hearth, and for a time everyone was occupied with their stomachs, the Mussulmen drinking only water from a nearby spring.

'Two chickens will not go very far between eight souls,' pointed out Alexander, between mouthfuls. 'How are we all going to eat while we stay here?'

Nizam's face cracked into a smile, which made him look more villainous than before. 'There is a dead sheep and a goat behind the hut,' he announced. 'Malik Shah is an expert with the bow.'

Again de Blois fervently hoped that this poaching had taken place at a considerable distance from Bigbury, as missing livestock would set any village buzzing like angry wasps. After they had eaten, Raymond beckoned Nizam and Alexander out into the approaching dusk and they walked over to the crypt of the old priory.

'It is time for you two to get together and discuss your work,' he said sternly, as they reached the bottom of the narrow stairway. 'The Count of Mortain and my king are very anxious for results. You came here because this county has abundant supplies of tin and some silver, so if you are successful in your endeavours, there will be no lack of the raw material.'

The few rush-lights that were lit hardly dispelled the gloom in the large underground chamber, and Nizam lit a taper from one and went around to generate a flame in each of the others.

139

'How long do you think this process will take?' de Blois asked the small Scot, who shrugged expressively.

'It has already been a thousand years since others began trying, so do not expect quick results. I feel that I am very near it myself, but I have to find out what this fellow knows – if anything!'

The Frenchman sighed, fearing himself marooned in this uncouth country for a long time. 'For God's sake do your best, man! These are difficult people to deal with and I would not trust any of them. If you have problems, let me know at once.'

He left the two wise men together, fervently hoping that their common interest in science would overcome the cultural gulf that existed between them. As soon as he had gone, Alexander bowed to Nizam and waved a hand at the apparatus already set up alongside the hearth.

'In the morning, I will unpack my equipment and arrange it alongside yours,' he said. 'Meanwhile, perhaps you will do me the honour of explaining your devices and how you intend to proceed.'

The impassive face of the Saracen again broke into a slight smile, and he led Alexander across to the bench and began explaining in a mixture of execrable French mixed with some Latin the function of his various flasks, retorts, crucibles and vessels set up there. Much of this was obvious and common knowledge to all alchemists, so that even with the language difficulty, Alexander could follow Nizam fairly easily. What was not obvious was the basic theory upon which the Mohammedan built his claim to successful transmutation of a baser metal into gold. But this was not surprising at a first meeting, as it was second nature for every practitioner of the art to jealously guard his secrets. However, the Scotsman was highly impressed when, after rather theatrical glances over both shoulders, Nizam fumbled into a hidden pocket inside his robe and pulled out a folded piece of soft leather. He unwrapped it carefully and held out something on the palm of his hand. It was an irregular lump of a blackish substance, about the size of a hazelnut. The Saracen prodded it with a forefinger and rolled it over. Embedded in the dark stone was a ragged area shining like silver – and at one edge of this was a tiny nodule that had the yellow gleam of gold.

CHAPTER SEVEN

In which Crowner John treads on dangerous ground

The coroner arrived back in Exeter with Gwyn and the two men-at-arms on Sunday afternoon. The long ride was without incident, though the weather had worsened and a light powdering of snow had settled on the tracks by the time they reached their night stop at Totnes Castle. On the second day, it had turned to rain and they were wet, cold and miserable by the time they entered the West Gate and walked their tired horses up the slope of Fore Street and into the centre of the city. At the castle, the soldiers vanished to their huts in the outer ward, seeking warmth, food and a welcome from their families, while John and his officer went into the keep to seek the first two commodities, though there was not much of a welcome. The sheriff was away visiting his manor outside the city, and there were only a few servants and clerks in the large, bare chamber.

They settled around a table near the fire-pit and were served with leftovers from dinner – boiled salt fish, a bowl of chicken legs, rye bread and some sliced boiled beef. There was plenty of the latter, as though most cattle were kept as draught oxen, some of the few dairy cows and young steers were butchered at this time of year, as there was insufficient fodder to feed them all through the winter. In fact, in the Welsh language that John learned from his mother, the word for November meant 'slaughter'. The two men ate in silence, but when they had had their fill, they pulled their stools nearer the burning logs to sit companionably with a quart of ale in their hands.

'So are we any the wiser after four days in the saddle?' grunted Gwyn. He looked across at de Wolfe, watching him in profile as he hunched over his pot, staring into the fire. The coroner's beak of a nose projected like a hook in front of cheeks darkened by almost a week's growth of stubble.

'None the wiser – but better informed!' growled John. 'There seems no reason at all to connect old de Revelle with the death of Peter le Calve.'

'What about this Second Crusade business?'

'What about it? God's teeth, how can that be connected with a death in Devonshire almost half a century later?' He spat into the fire and watched the spittle sizzle away on an ember.

The Cornishman drained his ale, leaving a wet rim on his luxuriant moustache. 'So what do we do now? There'll be rumblings in Winchester when they hear that one of our manor-lords has been crucified and beheaded. The next lot of Royal Justices to arrive in Exeter will give the sheriff a hard time if by then no one is chained in the gaol below.'

'As the King's Coroner, I'll not be too popular either,' agreed John morosely. 'But what can we do? Nothing, unless some new atrocity is committed.'

There seemed no answer to this, and their talk drifted on to other matters.

'What about the *Mary and Child Jesus*?' asked Gwyn. 'Are you sending a shipwright down there to size up the damage?'

'I'll talk to Hugh de Relaga tomorrow,' replied John. 'Though there's plenty of time now that winter's almost here, we still need to get an idea of the expense of refitting the vessel.'

143

He drained the last of his ale and stood up. 'And maybe they will want to get her around to a proper port. That creek on the Avon is not the best place to carry out repairs.'

Gwyn went off to settle his big mare in the castle stables, as there was nowhere near his modest home in St Sidwell to keep the beast. John slowly walked Odin in the gathering dusk down to High Street and a well-earned rest with Andrew the farrier. Then he gratefully entered his own house and sat with Mary for a while in her kitchen shed, telling her of the journey to Revelstoke, which was farther away than the cook-maid had ever been in her life. Though he had already eaten in Rougemont, Mary pressed him to one of her mutton pastries and a cup of cider while she listened to his tale.

'So when is the mistress likely to come back? And that nosy bitch Lucille?' she asked. Like John, she was savouring the house without the mistress. It was as if a dark cloud had been lifted from Martin's Lane while she was away.

'I don't know, but I doubt it will be more than a few days,' he said glumly. 'Since he lost the shrievalty, her hero-worship for her brother has vanished. Sooner rather than later, she will say something to offend him – and Matilda can't stand his wife, the icy Lady Eleanor, who thinks that she's only slightly less exalted than the Queen herself.'

The mention of King Richard's wife diverted their talk to Berengaria, a topic of endless speculation among both the aristocracy and peasantry of England. A Spanish princess, she had never set foot in the country of which she was queen and could not speak a word of its language. Mary was all the more intrigued by the matter, as John had actually been present at the marriage in Cyprus, on his way to the Crusade, and many a time she had made him describe the day, the story getting better with every telling.

As he was overdue for his weekly wash, shave and change of tunic, Mary heated water over her fire and he stripped to the waist in the doorway of her hut. With the water in a leather bucket, he laved himself with soap made from goose grease and wood ash, then scratched at his black stubble with a specially sharpened knife.

The handsome dark-haired Saxon woman looked longingly at his muscular body, but firmly decided against any weakening of her resolve not to share his bed again, even if her mistress and her prying maid were almost forty miles away. She had a comfortable job in the household and she was not going to jeopardise it again, even if the thought of John's enthusiastic embrace was very tempting. From the looks that he threw at her in return, she suspected that similar thoughts were going through his mind. His resistance came from a different source – a guilty conscience regarding Nesta in Idle Lane. An hour later, he was down at the Bush, resisting not more feminine advances but the offer of yet more food, as the landlady was trying to get him to eat another meal.

'Later on, *cariad*, later on!' he protested in Welsh. 'Every woman I meet wants to push food down my throat!'

'Did you eat in Dawlish, then?' she asked in mock innocence, forcing him to hotly deny having come back that way from Totnes. A mere novice when it came to understanding women's minds, he wondered why Nesta was taking so doggedly against Hilda these days, as a year earlier, when he had broken his leg on the jousting field, they had seemed the best of friends.

The little spat passed and, in between dealing with her maids and her drinking patrons, Nesta came to sit with him at the table behind the wattle screen next to the fire. After a couple of hours of pleasant dalliance, he was persuaded to eat again, and she went off to chivvy her two servant girls to get food for her lover. As she vanished through the back door to reach the kitchen shed in the yard, a small figure slipped in through the front door, his new cloak slick with raindrops. It was Thomas de Peyne, his lank hair plastered across his forehead by the downpour outside. His narrow face was radiant with excited pleasure as he slunk self-consciously through the drinkers to stand at John's table.

'Thomas, what brings you to venture into a den of sin – and on a Sunday, too!' jibed the coroner, knowing that taverns were not favourite haunts of his clerk.

'I've not seen you nor Gwyn for four days, master,' chattered the puny priest. 'So I've not been able to tell you my news! I thought I might find you here tonight.'

John motioned to him to sit down on the bench opposite. 'Calm yourself, Thomas. What great news is this?'

'The best, Crowner! I have been given a part-time post in the cathedral, so I will have both an ecclesiastical living and be able to continue as your clerk, as I vowed I would!'

De Wolfe's stern face broke into a smile of genuine pleasure at the young clerk's obvious delight. He leaned across and grasped a thin shoulder in a rare display of affection.

'I am greatly pleased for you, Thomas. I know it was your heart's desire. What is this new job – are you to be the next Bishop of Exeter?'

De Peyne smiled weakly at his master's attempt at wit.

'Not quite, sir! But I am to have a modest prebend as a chantry priest, with some duties teaching the choristers their letters – and I am to work in the archives above the Chapter House.'

'A prebend! Does that mean you will be a canon now?' demanded John, whose knowledge of the tortuous workings of cathedral administration was patchy.

Thomas giggled like a girl. 'Unfortunately not, I'm afraid. I will merely be a *preabenda doctoralis*, but that will give me a modest salary and the right to daily bread and candles.'

At this point, Nesta returned, and Thomas had to give

his news all over again. Nesta was suitably ecstatic and hugged the little man, giving him kisses on his cheeks, to his great embarrassment and secret delight. She made him explain his new status more fully, slipping on to his bench with her arm still around him.

'My blessed uncle, the archdeacon, arranged this for me, as it seems he has a chantry post in his gift.'

'What does that mean?' asked the landlady.

'When certain rich people die, they leave a bequest to the cathedral for Masses and prayers to be said for their soul in perpetuity. The money goes to pay for a priest, so I'll have to do this daily to earn my place.'

'What about these other tasks you spoke of?' demanded John.

'My uncle prevailed upon Canon Jordan de Brent to let me work in the scriptorium. It seems the cathedral archives have been neglected and need sorting and revising – a labour of love to me, but it is an added excuse to employ me, as is a small amount of tuition to the choristers, to improve their reading and writing.'

'It seems a lot of work for a stipend of a few pence and a daily loaf from the cathedral bakehouse!' said Nesta, though she did not want to dampen his excitement too much.

'And when are you going to have time to be clerk to the coroner?' added John, in mock anger.

Thomas hastened to reassure them. 'My Masses will be said at the crack of dawn, Crowner – and the teaching is but a few hours once a week. The work in the Chapter House archives can be done at any odd time.'

His master calmed him with a good-natured grin. 'I'm glad for you, Thomas, it's time things went well for you. But why did my good friend John de Alençon find such a hotch-potch of jobs for you?'

The clerk shook his head sadly. 'He said there is still antagonism towards me from certain of the canons, mainly because I am your clerk. It is the old business of

Prince John again, I fear. So the archdeacon had to circumvent their opposition by using means within his own personal power – and Canon Jordan is a genial man and a friend of my uncle.'

They chatted with Thomas for a while, then his reluctance to be seen for too long in a tavern on the Sabbath got the better of him and he vanished into the night, promising to be in the coroner's chamber in the castle early the next morning.

With no one at his house in Martin's Lane to censure him, John took the opportunity to stay the night at the Bush, so later he followed the delectable Nesta up the wide ladder to her little room in the loft.

A whole week went by and there was no sign of Matilda returning to Exeter. John began to think that maybe she would never come home again, and he settled into a pleasant routine. He went home at noon every day for his dinner, partly to please Mary, who was an excellent cook and fiercely determined to see that he was properly fed. In the evening, he went to the Bush for his supper and languorous entertainment up the ladder, where he stayed until he strode back to Martin's Lane for his breakfast.

The coroner's duties continued as usual, with executions twice a week, the county court and inquests scattered through the days as the cases required. There was nothing unusual among these – a fatal fire in a cordwainer's shop, a child crushed by a runaway cart, a rape in a back lane in Bretayne and a lethal stabbing outside the Saracen Inn. There was news that the Commissioners of Gaol Delivery might reach Exeter within three weeks, but such forecasts had so often proved wrong that Henry de Furnellis was making no special preparations for the King's Commissioners until he had confirmation of their arrival. They were not so grand as the Royal Justices, who came to hold the Eyre of Assize at much more infrequent intervals. The commissioners were supposed to present themselves every few months, to clear the gaols of prisoners awaiting trial – those who had not either escaped, killed each other or died of gaol fever.

If the commissioners did arrive soon, then both the sheriff and the coroner would have a considerable amount of work to do, both in preparing the rolls which documented the cases and in attending the court to present a wide variey of legal matters. This week seemed free of any serious problems, however, and John took advantage of it, especially as Thomas was settling down to his new duties in the cathedral. Now that he had a little money promised from his prebend, he was able to move out of the canon's house in the Close where he had previously begged shelter, sleeping on a mattress in a passageway of the servants' quarters. Now he bought a share in a small chamber in a house in Priest Street, near Idle Lane. There he bedded down with a vicar and two secondaries, on low trestle beds in each corner of the room. Lack of privacy, which was an uncommon commodity for all but the most wealthy, was more than compensated for by the fact that he was once again in the company of fellow clerics – a state halfway to heaven for Thomas de Peyne.

Only one event that week needed some delicate manoeuvring on John's part. As he had told Gwyn, he needed to speak to his partner, Hugh de Relaga, about the disabled ship down on the River Avon. On Tuesday, he called at the merchant's house in High Street shortly after dinner and caught the rotund portreeve dozing over a cup of Loire wine. Hugh jerked himself fully awake and pressed hospitality upon the coroner. When his even more rotund wife had poured wine for him, she tactfully retired to her solar and left the men to their business. John explained the situation and, after some discussion, they decided to employ a shipwright from Topsham to go down to survey the *Mary* and give them a report and estimate the costs.

'Why not ask the ship-masters from the other vessels that belonged to Thorgils to accompany him?' suggested de Relaga. 'They need to be brought into our scheme if they are to serve us faithfully – and their experience must surely be an advantage?'

De Wolfe readily agreed, but there was a complication in the proposal. Hugh wanted him to ride down to Dawlish to explain matters to Hilda and to arrange for the two shipmen to go down to Bigbury with the man from Topsham. Considering Nesta's jealousy, going to Dawlish was a dangerous venture. Either he went surreptitiously in the hope that she would not find out – or he would have to declare his intentions and their innocence before he went.

Later that day, as he loped down towards the Bush, he became angry with himself over the matter. He was a grown man, a Norman knight, a Crusader and a king's law officer – and here he was, worrying himself over possibly offending a mere alehouse keeper! He worked up a righteous indignation, which lasted all the way to Idle Lane, but as he approached the door of the tavern, his bravado evaporated.

'You could come with me, Nesta,' he heard himself saying a few minutes later. 'We could ride there and back between dinner and dusk.'

The Welsh woman pulled off her coif and shook her russet locks down over her shoulders. 'No, John, I can't leave this place unattended for half a day,' she said curtly. 'If you must go, you must go! But I don't see why the portreeve couldn't stir himself, instead of getting you to run his errands.'

John patiently explained that he knew both of the ship-masters and where they lived, so it was easier for him to speak to them.

'No doubt you do know them,' she said tartly. 'You must know Dawlish well and all those who live there, for you've visited often enough.'

De Wolfe kept his quick temper under control with an effort.

'Gwyn will be with me, Nesta. Shall I take Thomas as well to act as another chaperone?' he added sarcastically.

'Do what you like, John. Who am I to tell the county coroner how to conduct himself?' She got up from their table and began to flounce away towards the back of the taproom. With a groan of frustration, he went after her and grabbed her around her slim waist and propelled her towards the wide steps to the upper floor. She wriggled like an eel for a moment and began to squeal until she saw the amused faces of some of her patrons drinking near by. Her protestations diminished as he pushed her up the lower steps and as the pair vanished into the loft there was some good-natured cheering and banging of ale-pots by the approving customers. The only dissidents were two strumpets, who screamed abuse at their prospective clients sitting next to them, as token support for their sister who was suffering the usual domination by these pigs of men. However, upstairs in her little chamber, Nesta soon felt anything but dominated as she straddled her lover, her fit of pique forgotten as they both cheerfully kissed and wrestled on the feather palliasse.

By the end of that same week, Alexander of Leith was becoming a worried man. The apparatus that he and Jan had brought so carefully from Bristol on the back of a packhorse had been set up in the crypt and he had started work, continuing the experiments that had occupied him for the past thirty years. He had studied in various parts of Europe, including Paris, Montpellier, Granada and Padua, and had become expert in the arts of distillation, extraction and alloying. Though like most alchemists, his main interest was the creation of the Elixir of Life, the great prize was the transmutation of baser metals into gold. Though there were many who claimed to have suceeded, no claim had survived rigorous testing to exclude fraud. He himself had laboured at the quest in Scotland and more recently in Paris and Bristol and felt that he was nearer success than at any time in his long life. The offer by Prince John's chancellor to join this Moorish sage was readily accepted by Alexander, as he felt that maybe the legacy of Arabic learning might be the last link in the chain he had been trying to forge for decades. For was it not Geber, an Islamic, who had first proposed the Philosopher's Stone, seven centuries after Christ? Even the name 'al-chemy' came from the Arabic language, as indeed did 'el-ixir'.

So it was with disappointment that he viewed his first discussions with Nizam, in spite of the initial excitement of seeing a nodule of what seemed to be gold in the Muslim's palm. In a halting mixture of French and Latin, the Scot tried to elicit a coherent account of Nizam's theory and methods, but either because of the man's deliberate obfuscation or from genuine ignorance, he could make little sense of the Turk's vague ramblings.

When he asked to see the man manipulate his flasks, retorts and crucibles, he was given a fumbling display accompanied by an unintelligible monologue in the Turk's native tongue, and Alexander was little the wiser after five days than he was at the start.

Raymond de Blois had gone away again, ostensibly to secure more supplies of tin and silver and to meet an emissary from Gloucester at Revelstoke, but Alexander was determined to tackle him as soon as he returned, to get him to lay down the law to Nizam about his lack of useful cooperation. On Friday, with de Blois still absent, the little alchemist felt so frustrated that he decided to make a final effort and demand some decent information from the Mussulman – but after returning from a solitary noon dinner in the hut, he discovered that Nizam had disappeared, along with his two silent retainers and their horses.

'God's tits, where have they gone to this time?' he exploded to Jan, who was raking dung from the stable.

The hulking servant shrugged and made clear gestures, accompanied by guttural throat noises, that the three Asiatics had ridden off up the track to the road. A further pantomime told Alexander that they had been wearing dark cloaks with hoods, and his portrayal of a cross indicated that they had been dressed as monks. For a moment, the alchemist contemplated packing up and riding back to Bristol, but when his quick temper cooled, he decided to wait for Raymond's return.

He had a long wait, as the Frenchman remained away almost until dusk the next evening, eventually trotting in on a tired horse with a story that he had had to put the herald from Gloucester back on the right road to Totnes. He was in no mood to listen to Alexander's tale of woe, but after some food and wine served by the two Saxon guards, he unwound enough to sit by the fire in the crypt and consider what the Scotsman had to say.

'I'm beginning to think that this Nizam knows no more about transmutation than my dumb Fleming,' he began irascibly. 'I can get little sense out of him, and in spite of his having a speck of gold in his pouch, I doubt if he knows one end of a crucible from the other!'

De Blois tried to calm and reassure him. 'It must be the problem with language, magister. He was sent personally by my noble King Philip because of his prowess and reputation in your science. They met in Palestine and the King was so impressed by him that he brought him back to France. I was there myself, by the side of our sovereign, so can vouch for him.'

'But can you vouch for his expertise in alchemy, for there's precious little sign of it so far,' countered Alexander tartly. 'I feel I'm wasting my time here. I could be making more progress in my proper workshop in Bristol. And now the bastards have taken off again. They left yesterday. God knows where they've gone this time!'

Wearily, Raymond agreed to have a showdown with them when they returned. He angrily wondered where they had gone – this was the second time since they had arrived at Bigbury that the three Turks had vanished without explanation, even though he had lectured them on the need to lay low and keep out of sight of any of the local inhabitants. They had all brought monks' habits with them from France, as a necessary disguise to conceal their Moorish dress and features, but even these would not stand too close an inspection in daylight.

Raymond, guide and provider to this secret enterprise, did his best to pacify the indignant little Scotsman.

'We must persevere with this vital task, Alexander,' he cajoled. 'Sir Richard de Revelle has put himself at considerable risk and expense over this endeavour, and the messenger from Gloucester whom I have just left conveyed the concern of the Count of Mortain that success be speedily achieved.'

Reluctantly, the alchemist agreed to stay, but privately decided that he would carry on his researches alone, with little anticipation of help from the Mussulman, unless the latter demonstrated a radical change of attitude.

On Friday of that week, John de Wolfe took himself off to Dawlish with mixed feelings. On the one hand, he looked forward with disturbing enthusiasm to seeing Hilda, yet knowing of Nesta's disconcerting attitude he was almost afraid to mount his horse and commit himself to the visit. He took Gwyn with him, but left Thomas to his new-found delights around the cathedral. They trotted down to Topsham, led their steeds on to the flat-bottomed ferry for the short trip across the muddy estuary to the marshes beyond, then cantered across to the coast road at the foot of the low hills that led down to the sea and became cliffs farther south. Gwyn sensed his master's preoccupation and was well aware of the cause. Close companions though they were, it was not his place to offer advice, but he slipped in a few oblique hints when he had the opportunity.

'A fine woman, that Hilda! She'll have no trouble in getting herself a new husband in double-quick time!'

John scowled across at his lieutenant as they rode along side by side.

'Are you trying to tell me something, you old rogue?'

Gwyn innocently shook his head, his wild hair swaying like a corn stook in a gale.

'Just saying, Crowner, that's all! I'd make a play for her myself, if I wasn't a married man!'

'You mean just like me, don't you? Don't fret, Gwyn, I'm not going to throw a leg over her the minute I get inside her house. I've got Nesta breathing fire down my neck – and Matilda never misses a chance to remind me of my sins in that direction.'

His officer decided that he had better leave the subject alone and subsided into silence as they covered the last few miles to the little harbour. In the village, Gwyn diplomatically took himself to one of the two taverns, where John could pick him up when he had finished his business, innocent or otherwise. The coroner walked Odin down the lane that led from the creek where boats were beached and tied him to a hitching rail outside the solid stone dwelling that Thorgils had built.

Again the young maid was surprised to see him at the door, but with half-concealed giggles, simperingly she led him up the stairs to Hilda's solar. The widow had given up her mourning grey and looked elegant in a long kirtle of blue linen with a shift of white samite visible above the square-cut neckline. As usual indoors, her hair was uncovered and the honey-blonde tresses fell down her back, almost to her waist. John found it hard to remember her as the rosy-faced urchin with whom he had played in Holcombe many years before – and later as a lissom girl when they furtively kissed and coupled in the tithe barn. Looking at her now, serene, beautiful and self-confident, it was also difficult to accept that she was but the daughter of a manor-reeve, an unfree villein in his brother's employ – as she herself had been unfree until she had married Thorgils.

Hilda came towards him, her hands outstretched to take his, a smile of genuine pleasure on her face.

'John, it is so good to see you, no one is more welcome in this house!' She came close and, like iron chippings to a lodestone, his arms automatically came up to embrace her, though somewhere in his head warning chimes pealed as loudly as cathedral bells. Hilda's blue eyes and her full pink lips were inches away from his and he felt her breasts pressing against him as he held her. She stood immobile and he knew she was waiting for him to make the next move – or not make it. He realised that she was giving this old soldier the chance to attack or retreat, not forcing the issue but establishing where the watershed lay between prudence and abandonment. As he felt the heat growing in his loins, he groaned with longing and indecision, but then the vision of another pair of eyes, lips and breasts swam into his fevered mind. With a sudden movement, he pecked at her cheek with his lips and stood back, his hands sliding to hold her upper arms as they looked at each other gravely, the moment of decision reached – for now.

'I came to see if all was well with you, dear Hilda,' he croaked, then cleared his throat in one of the catch-all mannerisms he used to cover awkward pauses. Standing back, he saw that the maid was gaping at them, looking rather disappointed that they had not fallen to the floor in a frenzy of lust. Hilda led him to a chair and then sat opposite in another, after sending the maid scurrying to fetch wine and pastries.

'Tell me all your news, John. I have been quite out of touch since I came home from my stay in Holcombe.'

As he drank some of Thorgils' good Normandy wine and ate heartily of the pork and turnip pasties – for Hilda took little notice of the Church's edict regarding Friday fish – he brought her up to date on the plan to use the three ships to ferry goods from Exeter to other coastal ports, and especially those across the Channel. He wanted more details of the other two ship-masters, for in spite of his excuses to Nesta, he was not all that sure where they were to be found. The conversation flowed easily for an hour, though underneath was always their simmering awareness of their sexual attraction. The Saxon woman enquired after Matilda and patiently listened to John's bitter recitation of the hopelessness of their marriage, and his wish that the social gulf between them had been smaller before he had been forced into marrying de Revelle's daughter.

Then carefully, she asked about Nesta, whom she knew slightly and liked very much – though now she knew that the Welsh woman was an added barrier, in addition to Matilda. She suddenly came to appreciate that in fact if Matilda ceased to exist, she – Hilda – would be in a far better position to capture John de Wolfe than a lowly ale-wife, as there was no real reason why a Norman knight could not take her, a freewoman and the widow of a quite rich and respectable merchant, in marriage. Still, Matilda did exist and, being a sensible, realistic person, she felt no jealousy towards Nesta in a situation that was immutable.

John sat more easily as affection and admiration gradually replaced his lust and he settled down to enjoy the sight of her lovely face and body and the pleasant company that she afforded him. Eventually, the need to find the shipmen and to collect Gwyn from the alehouse before he became too drunk to sit on his horse drove him reluctantly to the door.

'Come to see me again very soon, John,' Hilda said without any trace of coquetry as he was about to leave. 'Let me know how our new venture is progressing and if you need a contribution to restoring poor Thorgils' vessel, you have only to ask.'

At the front door they kissed, and though this time it was fully on the lips, it was somehow chaste, as if a signal that for now they were as brother and sister. As John stalked away to untie Odin, he wondered whether Hell was a place where he was doomed to bounce for ever from one to another of an infinite number of women.

CHAPTER EIGHT

In which Crowner John examines some arrows

Though the cold persisted, the snow cleared away and bright crisp weather set in over the weekend. The sky remained blue, but dark clouds rolled in over John de Wolfe late on Monday afternoon, for not only did Matilda return, but she was accompanied by her brother Richard and his wife Eleanor, a haughty woman whose nature matched the frosty climate.

They were on their way to Richard's other manor near Tiverton at the eastern end of the county. He fervently thanked God that his house had no space for them to stay that night. Instead, they went to the New Inn in High Street, the best accommodation in the city, even if the cooking was inferior to that of the Bush. However, John did not get off scot-free, for Matilda invited her brother and sister-in-law to dinner on the following day.

'They provided me with bed and board for well over a week, John,' she snapped. 'The least I can do is to give them a good meal before they leave for Tiverton.'

Within minutes of his wife's return, his free-and-easy life had reverted to the familiar old pattern of silences at table, scowls at his every absence from meals and ill-tempered orders barked at Mary or Lucille. To avoid aggravating the situation on the very first evening, he desisted from his usual visit to Idle Lane and sat glumly at supper while Matilda, unusually loquacious, expounded on the luxuries of her brother's manor at Revelstoke, the excellence of his cooks and even the fertility of his fields. Her previous disillusionment with Richard seemed to have evaporated. He was now her idol once again, Matilda having conveniently forgotten his manifold sins and wickedness. By contrast, she was implying that her husband was all the poorer in substance and spirit for having treacherously stabbed her brother in the back when he finally denounced him to the Chief Justiciar. She now seemed to ignore the fact that Richard had committed the common crime of theft and the even worse one of treachery, both of which should have carried the death penalty, but which had been avoided by John's intercession.

Thankfully, Matilda was so full of her visit to the utopia of Revelstoke that she failed to make any enquiry about his own activities while she was away – but John knew that sooner or later she would get around to interrogating him about his journey to Dawlish and his scandalous attendances at the Bush Inn. After supper, she fired instructions at Mary concerning the lavish dinner that was to be prepared for the de Revelles the next day, then stalked off to bed, claiming fatigue after her journey that day from their night stop at Buckfast. Lucille pattered after her to get her undressed and settled for the night, leaving John to sit by his hearth, glowering into his ale-pot and bemoaning the end of his brief week of freedom. Even his hound Brutus looked miserable as he lay at his master's feet and rolled up his eyes so that the whites showed, in an expression of doleful sympathy.

The following day John de Wolfe spent the early part of the morning in glum anticipation of the approach of the noon dinner-time, but thankfully fate stepped in at literally the eleventh hour. It took a murder to avoid the ordeal of sitting down to a meal with three of the de Revelle family, but even Matilda must surely accept the urgency of attending another dastardly assault upon one of her beloved Norman county families. It began with the clatter of iron-shod hoofs on the cobbled floor of Rougemont's gatehouse arch, heralding the arrival of a messenger from Shillingford. This time it was one of the young stable grooms, perhaps chosen for his reckless speed on a horse. He gabbled his news to the soldiers in the guardroom and without delay he was hustled up the stairs to de Wolfe's chamber.

All three of the coroner's team were there. Thomas, having performed his paid Mass at an early hour, was now at his habitual task of making manuscript copies of cases for the next Shire Court. Gwyn was aimlessly whittling a piece of firewood with his dagger and whistling tunelessly through his drooping moustache. John was sitting moodily behind his table, but looked up as the groom came in, touching his shapeless woollen cap in hurried obeisance.

'It's the young master, Crowner,' he gabbled. 'Wounded real bad in the arm and the bloody steward killed stone dead!'

It took a few moments and a jar of Gwyn's rough cider to get a coherent story from the young fellow, but the upshot was that, early that morning, William le Calve had been walking with their steward, Adam le Bel, along the waste beyond the village fields.

'They were looking at the edge of the forest, deciding where the best place was to start felling trees, to assart more land for the livestock, as the strip-fields are now pushing well into the pasture,' explained the young man – in unnecessary detail, as far as the impatient coroner was concerned.

'So what happened, damn it?' he snapped, but the groom was hazy about the more vital parts of the story.

'Don't rightly know, sir, not having been there,' he muttered lamely. 'But they brought the old steward back dead as mutton and Sir William had a big wound in his arm, with a cross-bow bolt lying near by.'

An hour later, de Wolfe was listening to a more detailed account of this sketchy story.

The younger son of the lately deceased Peter le Calve was lying on a couch in one of the side rooms of the hall in Shillingford. It was a moderately comfortable chamber with a good fire in the hearth, clean rushes on the floor and some hanging tapestries to relieve the grimness of the grey stone walls. William was very pale and had obviously lost a lot of blood. His left arm above the elbow was expertly bound with a clean linen bandage and in the background the handsome lady whom John had glimpsed on his earlier visit was standing with an old serving woman, who clutched a pitcher of hot water and a towel. Godfrey le Calve was standing alongside his younger brother, solicitously resting a hand on his other shoulder, his face almost as pale as that of the wounded man.

'It was meant for me, you know!' he said shakily. 'The bolt that killed my steward.'

De Wolfe raised his eyebrows questioningly and William answered from his couch, in a voice tight with pain.

'I fear he's right, Sir John. No one would want to slay poor Adam, for the sake of Christ! Surely he was mistaken for Godfrey here.'

John mulled this over and felt inclined to agree. Two men shrouded in winter cloaks walking together, one recognisable as William le Calve – it might easily be assumed that the other was his brother, as Adam le Bel was about the same height as Godfrey.

'How severe is your wound, William?' he asked solicitously. The coroner noticed that the new linen around his arm was already becoming stained with blood. The lady in the dark brown kirtle stepped forward and laid gentle fingers on William's brow. Godfrey hurried to introduce her as Lady Isobel of Narbonne, a 'friend' of his late father.

'The bolt went right through the muscle, Sir John, and tore out sideways, so that there is a big open flap,' she said in a low, rather husky voice. In spite of the circumstances, de Wolfe's interest was aroused. He saw that she was about his own age, slim and good looking, with a dark beauty suggesting that she came from southern France or even Spain. However, with his amorous life already far too complicated, he pushed aside certain thoughts with a conscious effort and concentrated on the wound.

'He has lost much blood, I suspect,' he said. 'Was it much fouled?'

He well knew that the danger with any wound was that even if the victim survived the shock and blood loss, dirt carried in might lead to a fatal purulence. In fact, many archers deliberately stuck their arrows in ground contaminated by animal or human filth to increase the eventual killing power of their weapons.

Gravely, Lady Isobel shook her head. 'One can never tell, but it seemed quite clean and at least the bolt had fallen out. I washed the wound with hot water, then poured some brandy-wine into it, which I have heard can help to neutralise any poison.'

William looked up at her and winced, recalling his screaming agony of an hour ago, when the strong spirit cauterised the naked flesh inside his arm.

'You have been kindness itself, madam,' he whispered.

John turned to the anxious elder brother, eager to get on with the story.

'So what happened? Tell me from the beginning.'

Godfrey took the coroner's arm and led him across the room, to where Gwyn and Thomas were waiting just inside the door.

'My brother is shocked. I do not want to distress him more than we must. Come and see the other poor fellow first.'

He led the way into the main hall, past muted servants and a few manor officers, some of whom John remembered from his last visit to this tragic place, including the falconer and the houndmaster. They went outside and down into the undercroft, the semi-basement that was used as a storehouse. Here, on a couple of planks laid across some boxes, were the pathetic remains of Adam le

Bel, the steward of Shillingford. Covered with his own cloak, the old man still appeared dignified, even in death, when Godfrey uncovered his face.

'William and Adam here went out to decide where the men should start assarting later today. We need more arable land and pasture, so must push back the forest in places.'

'Were they alone?'

'The bailiff and the reeve went after them, but were some distance behind, as they stopped to chase some loose sheep back into a pen. They say they were a few hundred paces away by the time William and Adam reached the edge of the trees.' Godfrey stopped and gulped. He seemed a mild man and this revival of violence on his manor had unnerved him.

'So what did they see then?'

'The reeve says that suddenly our steward here seemed to stagger and fell against my brother. He thought he had had a seizure of some sort, as he was an old man, not in the best of health. Then a moment later, William yelled out and clasped his arm, before sinking to the ground himself.'

'What then? They ran to them, I suppose?' demanded de Wolfe.

'When they got to the pair, William was on his knees, grasping his arm with his other hand, trying to stanch the blood that was pouring out. Old Adam here was lying dead in the grass alongside him.'

'Did anyone see the attackers?'

Godfrey shook his head. 'I made particular enquiries of the bailiff and groom, but they saw nothing apart from the two victims falling. The bow-shots must have come from within the trees, as it was all open waste and pasture in the other direction.'

'Did anyone give chase in the forest?' demanded the coroner.

'Not until later – naturally, my two servants were more

concerned with stanching the flow of blood from my brother's arm and then getting help to bring him back here.'

'But later?' persisted de Wolfe.

'All this happened less than a few hours ago – you arrived so quickly, thank God. I sent the reeve, the hound-master and half a dozen grooms and labourers up there about an hour ago. They are still there, but I have had no report of them finding anything or anybody.'

John turned his attention to the still shape lying on the planks. He nodded to Gwyn and his officer took off the cloak and peered at the dead steward's left side.

'A quarrel sticking out just below his armpit, Crowner. Buried in about half its length, I'd say.'

As Gwyn lifted the corpse by its shoulder to offer a better view, John, Godfrey and Thomas bent to look at the side of Adam's chest. A thick rod of hard wood, about a hand's span in length, was projecting from the blood-stained yellow cloth of his tunic. The last few inches carried three flights of thin leather set symetrically around the shaft.

'The tip must be in his heart,' said Gwyn with grudging admiration.

'I wonder what the range was . . . it looks an expert shot.'

'We need to get it out. It may give us some clue as to its origin,' muttered de Wolfe to his officer. Gwyn nodded and moved around so that his great body was blocking the view of the less hardened Godfrey.

Thomas, who had been hovering behind, knew what was coming and retreated to the doorway of the under-croft as Gwyn reached behind for his dagger and pulled it from its sheath. With de Wolfe watching closely, he slit the tunic on either side of the arrow and ripped aside the torn undershirt beneath. An experimental pull on the shaft told him that there was considerable resistance inside, so with two bold slashes he enlarged the wound made by the crossbow quarrel and ran his blade down alongside it. With a few hard tugs and some more manipulation of his dagger, there was a squelching sound and the projectile suddenly slid out of the wound.

Thomas paled and turned to stare out of the doorway as Gwyn handed the bolt to his master, oblivious of the blood dripping on to the earthern floor.

'It's a hunting quarrel, Crowner. A nasty piece of work.'

John took the short arrow and examined the bloody front end. He stooped to pick up a piece of sacking that lay across a crate and wiped most of the blood away. The tip of the bolt was of iron, shaped like a four-sided pyramid, designed to cause more damage than a flat arrowhead. Now that it was less bloody, Godfrey stared at it with disgust.

'I've known Adam almost all my life. Now the poor man is dead from a mistake.' He took the short arrow from John's hand. 'This was meant for me, I'm sure.'

Thomas wandered back from the doorway, hoping that the more disgusting parts of the examination were over. 'Can you tell anything from it, Sir John?' he asked in his reedy voice.

'It's just an ordinary hunting quarrel,' replied the coroner. 'A deadly weapon at close range. I was hit by a Saracen bolt at Ascalon. Thank God it was a glancing shot which bounced off my chain mail, though I had a bruise there for weeks.'

'Speaking of Saracens, can I have another look?' asked Gwyn. He took the bolt from Godfrey and turned it over in his hands. Then to Thomas's disgust, he held it to his nose and sniffed at the flights, before passing it over to de Wolfe.

'Smell anything, Crowner? And look closely at the fletching.'

John had considerable faith in his officer's intuition and did as Gwyn suggested. His black eyebrows rose and he turned to the elder brother.

'Let's see the other quarrel, the one that injured William,' he commanded, and they made their way back upstairs. The bolt had been picked up by the bailiff when they rushed to William's aid and brought back to the hall, where it lay discarded on one of the tables.

The coroner picked it up, sniffed it and then compared it with the other one.

'Exactly the same – and the smell is identical,' he declared.

Godfrey and several servants gathered near by, staring at him blankly. They were all well used to cross-bow bolts, used in hunting everything from foxes to otters, but they had never seen anyone smell one before.

'What are you saying, Sir John?' asked Godfrey.

'Gwyn spotted it first. On the leather of the flights there are some faint hammerings. And they smell of spices or scent.'

He held out a bolt to le Calve and with a long forefinger pointed to some marks pressed into the leather of the triangular flights.

'That's Moorish writing, though God knows what it means. Together with that smell, it suggests that these bolts came from the Levant. And presumably so do the bastards who fired them!'

John de Wolfe was careful to delay his departure from Shillingford until well past the time when his brother-in-law and his wife would have left Exeter to ride on to Tiverton. He managed this by accepting the hospitality of Godfrey le Calve and having a good meal in the hall. Then he had another few words with William, to see whether there was anything at all he remembered which might help to identify the assailants. The younger brother was still very pale and thankfully showed no signs of fever from his wound mortifying, though it was early days yet. Lady Isobel sat with him and impressed John with her air of calm efficiency. He wondered what would become of her now that her protector Peter le Calve was dead. She was much younger than he had been and the coroner idly speculated that perhaps the affections of one of his sons might turn her way, though it was probable that they were already married themselves.

William had nothing to tell him, knowing only that his steward had suddenly stumbled against him, probably saving his life by knocking him out of the line of fire of the accurate killer in the trees. The second quarrel had sliced through the outer part of his arm and from then on he lost all interest in anything except his pain and bleeding.

The next activity that the coroner used to delay his departure was a visit to the scene of the crime. With Godfrey and several of the senior manor servants, he went with Gwyn and Thomas past the strip-fields behind the manor-house. These were still partly in stubble from the last harvest, though two ox-teams were slowly ploughing, ready for harrowing and winter planting. Beyond these were meadows where sheep and a few milk cows were competing with pigs and goats for the last of the autumn grass. A few lads were guarding them, with much yelling and waving of sticks.

This good pasture petered out into waste ground, which had been assarted earlier in the year and in which tree stumps and bushes still remained to be grubbed out and burned. The edge of the standing forest ran along like a dark wave at the top of a rising crest of land. Though many of the leaves had fallen, the trees were not yet bare and there was a mass of bracken, bramble and scrubby undergrowth along the edge to give cover to anyone lurking in the woods.

As they approached the spot where the hawk-master said the two men had fallen, they were met by the bailiff, the reeve and several villeins, who were emerging from the forest after searching for several hours.

'Nothing at all, my lord,' reported the bailiff, touching

his cap to Godfrey. 'We've been a mile in both directions. Nothing to see anywhere, not even a hoof print.'

A spattering of fresh blood blackened the grass where William had fallen. Standing near it, de Wolfe scanned the edge of the forest, which was about fifty paces distant. Then he loped to the nearest trees and pushed into the undergrowth, the brambles snagging his calf-length grey tunic. With Gwyn at his side and Thomas creeping uncertainly behind, he studied the ground, the trees and the bushes for a few yards each way and back into the darkness of the wood. As the bailiff had said, there was nothing to see – no strands of cloth caught on thorns or discarded arrows on the ground. On the walk back to the hall, he questioned the search party, which comprised most of the senior servants of the le Calve manor, asking whether any strangers had been seen since the previous day. The answer was in the negative once again.

'No mysterious monks this time?' he demanded, thinking of the old man's recollection when Peter le Calve had been done to death so horribly. Once again, there was much reluctant shaking of heads, and all that remained for John to do was to hold a quick inquest on Adam le Bel, to save him returning to Shillingford yet again. With the manor servants as jury and witnesses, he held his inquisition over the body of the old steward in the undercroft. As the circumstances were so straightforward, even if totally obscure, the formality took no more than a few minutes. In fact, the longest time was spent in waiting for Thomas de Peyne to inscribe the proceedings on a roll of parchment, a process that consisted mainly of recording the names of the jurors.

'Yet another bloody inquest with no result!' snarled John as the three rode back towards Exeter later that afternoon. 'The four shipmen, the lord of Shillingford and now its steward – all verdicts of "murder by persons unknown"! We're losing our touch!'

'What about this notion that we are dealing with

Saracens?' grunted Gwyn, pulling the collar of his jerkin closer against the biting east wind.

'It bears thinking about, as the signs are adding up,' replied the coroner. 'We have those curved wounds, which would fit a Moorish blade. Then those silken cords seem strangely oriental, as does the embossing on these leathern arrow flights and their spicy odour.'

Thomas, who, since he had taken to riding a horse like a man, was more able to keep up with them, spoke from John's other side. 'I also think, Crowner, that the mode of killing Sir Peter is significant.'

John turned his long face to his clerk and waited for him to elaborate. In spite of his often disparaging manner towards the little man, he was well aware of Thomas's intelligence and learning and had come to respect his opinions.

'I sense that his death was a deliberate insult to our Christian faith!' stated the clerk, emphatically.

Gwyn of Polruan groaned. 'To you, little turd, everything turns on your bloody religious fancies!'

'Let him speak, man!' snapped the coroner. 'What do you mean, Thomas?'

'The victim was subjected to a parody of the crucifixion, his outstretched arms lashed to that branch. Then his severed head was impaled not on some pole at a crossroads or on the Exe Bridge, but in the holiest of Christian sites in western England, our Lord's cathedral church of Exeter! Surely no Christian, however depraved, would go to such deliberate lengths to so contemptuously disparage our faith!'

De Wolfe nodded slowly, digesting the priest's earnest argument.

'And if not Christians, then they are likely to be Moors?'

Thomas eagerly agreed. 'Sir Peter had been a Crusader, like his father before him. Maybe this was a gesture of revenge for his taking the Cross against their own faith. There were many awful atrocities committed against them, which also affected innocent civilians.'

Gwyn was still dubious, though he never missed an opportunity to contradict the clerk. 'Both Sir John here and myself were at the Crusades, but no one has tried to cut off our heads! And what of the younger le Calve sons? They have never set foot in Palestine, but someone has loosed off cross-bow bolts at them.'

Thomas looked crestfallen at this logical demolition of his argument, but John came to his rescue.

'What you say has good sense behind it, Thomas. But we must wait and see what develops. God knows how we are to further this quest, as these attackers seem to melt away like the snow that is surely coming soon.'

He looked up at the grey sky and was glad to see the skyline of the city appear around the bend in the track-way. The return to Martin's Lane also meant, however, that he would soon have to meet the wrath of Matilda for absenting himself from lunch with his brother-in-law.

With a sigh, he touched Odin's flank with a spur, wishing he had to face Saladin and a thousand screaming Saracens rather than his wife.

CHAPTER NINE

In which Crowner John falls out with Matilda

The old hound Brutus slunk to the door of the hall, his tail between his legs. As he nuzzled it ajar and slipped out to seek solace in Mary's kitchen shed, he left a blazing row behind him.

'Does shaming me come naturally to you, John – or do you practise it daily until you reach this perfection?' snarled Matilda, standing by the long table, which was cluttered with the debris of the meal he had missed.

'I have the King's duties to attend to, woman,' he yelled back, his short temper now well alight. 'Duties which, as I recall, you were desperate for me to undertake last year when you insisted that I become coroner.'

Arms akimbo, fists placed on her thick waist, his wife abandoned all pretence of being a sophisticated county lady and descended to the body language and vocabulary of a fishwife from the quayside.

'Duties! Duties! By Christ and his Virgin Mother, have you no duties to your wife and family? My brother, who you ruined by your cheap jealousy and spite, gave you unstinting hospitality at Revelstoke barely more than a sennight ago, yet you insult him by deliberately shunning your duty as host for a mere single dinner.'

'Did I deliberately arrange for Willim le Calve to be sorely injured by a cross-bow bolt – and have his steward killed on the spot?' raved John. 'What would you have me do – tell the lord of Shillingford that I cannot attend his crisis, as my brother-in-law is coming to dinner?'

Matilda crashed her substantial fist on to the table, making the platters and pots rattle. 'You always have some glib excuse, damn you!' she shrieked. 'No doubt you waited until it was near dinner-time before you set off – and took good care not to return until Richard and Eleanor had left!'

There was half a truth in this, but John was in no mood to make any admissions.

'I went as soon as the messenger arrived, damn you! This attack is plainly related to the atrocity against Peter le Calve and, for all I knew, there was a chance of catching the murderers red handed! You are so proud of your Norman lineage, but would you now recommend that I allow fellow knights and manor-lords to be slain, with only casual regard for seeking justice? Eh? Answer me, woman!'

And answer him she did. The battle of words went on in the same vein for many more minutes, each combatant convinced of the righteousness of their own cause. From Matilda came a flood of accusations that she had pent up for months, blaming John entirely for her brother's downfall and dismissal from the post of sheriff. Since going to spend a week at Revelstoke, she seemed to have revived her adoration of her elder brother and, by inference, her husband's part in bringing him down became all the more dastardly.

This was a dispute that could have no solution, so entrenched was each one in their own attitude. Eventually, when both were red in the face and hoarse with shouting at each other, Matilda stalked towards the door, pushing him roughly aside as she went.

'I cannot bear to remain in the same chamber as you, husband!' she hissed. 'I am going to my solar and then to my cousin's dwelling in Fore Street. If I set eyes on you again today, it will be too soon.'

As she jerked open the door savagely enough to tear it from its leather hinges, he bawled at her retreating back.

'And if I set eyes upon you ever again, it will also be too soon!'

The slam of the door behind his wife actually shattered the wooden latch, but John was past caring whether the roof caved in on top of him.

'Bloody woman, this is too much to bear!' he muttered. Five minutes later, he was striding across the cathedral Close, his feet taking him blindly towards Idle Lane.

Alexander of Leith became a little more easy in his mind as the week went by, as he seemed to be making some progress with Nizam el-Din. Although their communication was still halting and imperfect, he began to follow the Turk's mixture of French and Latin more easily, especially when they discussed their mystic science, as much of the arcane vocabulary of alchemy was common to many languages.

After his initial exasperation at Nizam's proficiency in the procedures needed to pursue their research, Alexander rather grudgingly came to accept that the Moor knew something of what he was about, as he watched him juggling with flasks, retorts, pestle and mortar. As he worked, Nizam kept up a mumbled commentary to himself in a language the Scot could not place, though he assumed it was Arabic or whatever the fellow had learned at his mother's knee.

With the clumsy help of Jan the Fleming, Alexander had set up his own apparatus on the opposite side of the hearth, assembling a series of crucibles, retorts, distillation flasks and various other receptacles on a second table that they had pulled from the far end of the vaulted chamber. A large jar stood heavy with quicksilver, and small ingots of tin, copper and lead were stacked on the table-top. He had a thick volume of loose parchment folios held between two hinged boards that served as book covers and constantly referred to this as he primed his equipment with a variety of powders and liquids taken from a wooden box. The lid of this was intricately carved with symbols similar to those embroidered on his blouse-like garment, and though he did not mutter endlessly like the Moor, his lips framed the recipes and formulae from his book as he went about preparing his materials.

By the end of the second day's labour in the crypt, Alexander had reached the farthest point in his work which he had attained while in Bristol. He now wanted to push forward from there, hopefully inspired by the parallel discoveries of Nizam. But his initial optimism was soon to be confounded.

The next morning, soon after dawn and a frugal meal in the hut above, he came down to his bench. Instructing Jan to heat up the furnace with the leather bellows, Alexander melted the contents of a small crucible half filled with good Devon tin, which had previously been alloyed with mercury. With much murmuring of esoteric spells, he added a variety of powders from small bags of soft doe-skin, then weighed out some copper and silver filings on a small brass balance. The little alchemist sprinkled these into the crucible and added carefully counted drops of various coloured fluids from small flasks. Then he placed the crucible back in the furnace and listened to the sizzling until it subsided. Turning a sand-glass over to time the reheating, he waited for the final part of his process to be completed.

By now, the three Turks had arrived, the two sinister assistants carefully ignoring him. Nizam, bleary eyed and dishevelled, seemed only partly aware of his surroundings and bumped into several stools and the corner of the table before reaching his own workplace. Alexander thought he might be drunk, until he recalled that those of the Mohammedan faith eschewed all alcohol.

Nizam dropped heavily on to a stool and sat staring at his array of apparatus as if he had never seen it before, making no attempt to get started, in spite of Raymond le Blois's repeated exhortations the previous day to get some results. Alexander sighed with annoyance and frustration, but his sand-glass then ran out, so with iron tongs he removed his crucible from the furnace and plunged it into a wooden bucket filled with cloudy water taken from a nearby stream. With a sizzling hiss and a cloud of steam, the small clay dish cooled sufficiently for him to hold. Placing it on the bench before him, he took a flat iron rod and scraped off the layer of blackish encrustation that covered the walnut-sized lump in the bottom. As he expected, this revealed a shiny metallic surface whose colour varied from silvery white to reddish gold, especially when he took a wet rag and some fine white powder and polished the exposed surface. A final dip in the bucket rinsed the cleaning material away and he held out the dish towards the drowsy Saracen sitting near by.

'Ten years it has taken me to get thus far!' he said, with pride. 'I am almost there, so perhaps together we can achieve the final triumph.'

Nizam appeared to make an effort to pull himself together, and with Abdul and Malik squatting behind him, as impassive as usual, he managed to focus his eyes and stare into the crucible.

'Electrum!' he muttered. He spoke only the one word and that with a hint of contempt.

Alexander kept his temper with an effort. 'Yes, electrum! And electrum is an alloy of gold and silver.'

The other man shook his head and clumsily fumbled under his voluminous robe. Bringing out the package he had shown the Scot previously, he unwrapped it and held the small nugget out in his palm. Pointing to it with his other forefinger, he spat out the word 'Gold!', then indicated Alexander's offering and repeated 'Electrum' in dismissive tones.

Bristling with indignation, the Scotsman threw his crucible down on to the bench. 'At least I made mine here and now – and I can do it again under your very nose!' he snapped angrily. 'So let me see you make another of those knobs of gold, then perhaps I will be better impressed!'

Nizam stared at him for a long moment, then his eyelids slowly came down. 'Tomorrow. Not today. Today I must rest.'

He rose from the stool, moved in front of the hearth and lay down, curled up like a dog. His two henchmen crept forward until one was at his head, the other at his feet. Within a minute, he appeared to be sound asleep.

That evening, more than a mile away in the little village of Bigbury, a dozen freemen and villeins congregated as usual in the alehouse. It was a mean place, just a wattle-and-daub cottage of one room, with a lean-to shed built on to the back as a sleeping place for the ale-wife and a separate hut behind, where she brewed her indifferent ale. Only the ragged thorn bush, whose stem was jammed under the eaves of the thatch over the front door, indicated that it was a tavern.

Apart from the church, it was the sole focus of social life in Bigbury, and after dark, the men who had a spare halfpenny to pay their weekly toll for ale came to sit or stand about the fire-pit. Here they could gossip away an hour or two before going home to their straw palliasse or heap of ferns, to sleep the sleep of exhaustion until the daily grind began again at dawn.

As in most villages in feudal England, where the inhabitants were rarely able to stray more than a few miles from home, very little happened to enliven their conversation. Most of the talk was about murrain in the sheep or the probable father of the latest babe of the miller's daughter.

Tonight, however, there was something new to gossip about, a topic that gave rise to some apprehension and furtive looks over shoulders. The atmosphere of superstitious unease was heightened by a thunderstorm, which had threatened all day and now crashed and rolled in the clouds that covered the moon. Occasional flashes of lightning could be seen through the ill-fitting door and the gaps in the ragged thatch overhead.

'I saw them as plain as that big wart on your nose!' declared the sexton, who looked after the tithe barn, as well as the church and its burial yard.

The man with the wart glowered at the unkind remark. 'You'll poison your spleen and your guts if you drink so much – especially this ox-piss!' He held up his misshapen clay pot, slopping the turbid brown fluid over the edge.

The ale-wife, a blowsy widow who had scraped a living selling poor ale ever since her husband was hanged for poaching a hind, threw the core of a withered apple at him, catching him on the side of the head. 'Mind your words, Alfred Smith! Or go find your ale elsewhere, not that there's any as good as mine hereabouts.'

'No, Madge, nor none worse!' retorted the smith amiably. 'But our brave sexton must have been full of someone's ale when he saw three ghosts!'

Another villager, a stocky youngster, a conductor who led one of the eight ox-plough teams, chipped in with a knowing nod of his head.

'There's strange goings-on in that part of the forest. I keep well clear of it myself. It's all down to that old ruin that's in there somewhere. I went in as a child and saw such weird sights as made me shun it ever since.' He said this in a sepulchral voice that was accompanied by a loud peal of thunder.

'Last night, you say this was?' demanded Madge of the sexton. 'You didn't have much to drink then, as you said you had the runs from some rotten pork your wife served you for dinner.'

'That I did. I thought my very bowels were on fire! That's why I was squatting on the edge of the wood on the way back home.'

'We don't want to hear about your guts, Sexton,'

grunted the ploughman. 'What about these spirits or whatever you saw?'

'I had my arse towards the track, so I was looking into the wood. I was there for God knows how long, as I was straining fit to burst. Then in the moonlight, I saw three figures gliding through the trees, dressed in long white robes. One behind the other, not a sound from any of them.'

Alfred the smith should have been christened Thomas, as he was always doubting. 'How could you see them in the dark of the forest?'

'Because the bloody moon was up, that's why!' snapped the sexton. 'It was clear last night, before this storm came. I was on the edge of the woods, so I had enough light to glimpse these ghouls that were haunting the trees.'

He held out his pot to the widow and she trudged to the back of the room to dip it in a cask of new ale and bring it back to him.

'Here you are, you old liar!'

'I tell you I saw them! Fair shook me up! I hoisted my breeches and ran home, careless of whether I soiled myself or not.'

'There's strange things in that bit of forest, right enough,' said a new voice, a thin old man who had been the thatcher until a fall from a roof had crippled one leg. 'I recall a time when I was a boy when that old castle in the middle was pulled down by old King Henry's men. They set fire to the donjon on top of that hillock and pulled down the palisade around the bailey.'

'What's strange about that?' demanded the smith.

'Soon after, there was talk of ungodly rites being performed at the old priory next to it. The parson then – that's long before the one we've got now – had to go in and throw holy water about and chant prayers to drive out the Devil.'

The sexton nodded his agreement. 'I heard that from

my father. And who among us here is willing to go deep into the forest alone or at night? No bugger will, that's for sure!'

'That's because of the bloody outlaws and thieving vagabonds that are camped out in there,' snapped the smith. 'Look at what's happened these past few weeks! Chickens and sheep stolen, even a goat from up towards St Anne's. I even heard that winter turnips and cabbage had been taken from a garden of one of the agisters who lives on the north edge of the forest.'

The old man nodded sagely. 'The charcoal burners that used to go in there for coppiced wood say they're now too scared of the ruffians that threaten them. I don't know what the world's coming to!'

'Why couldn't these ghosts of yours be three of these outlaws, bent on a night's poaching?' asked the smith of the beleaguered sexton.

'Did you ever see outlaws in long white robes, like shrouds?' he retorted.

'What did they have on their heads, then?' asked Madge.

The sexton scratched his head through his sparse ginger hair, as he tried to remember. 'Not hats, that's for sure. Just trailing things, hanging down their backs. Never seen the like before – nor want to again!' Another peal of thunder and a brilliant flash gave emphasis to his words.

'Should we tell somebody about this?' asked the ploughman, with a concerned look on his round face. 'Maybe Roger Everard? 'Everard was the bailiff from Aveton Giffard, the larger village at the head of the Avon estuary, a few miles upstream from Bigbury.

The smith was contemptuous. 'Tell him what? That our drunken sexton, while having a shite in the forest, saw three ghosts dressed in white gowns! He'd have us up at the manor leet and get us fined for wasting his time.'

'Well, there's something odd going on in that forest,' mumbled the sexton obstinately. 'I know what I saw and it wasn't natural. We never used to have this trouble, things getting stolen and spectres wandering about the outskirts of our village. I reckon it's a sign!'

'Sign of what, you silly old fool?' sneered the smith. 'The end of the world?'

'Don't mock, Alfred!' snapped the ale-wife, who was also a pillar of the Church, as the priest was one of her best customers at the back door.

'The Apocalypse is not far off, according to what the parson said last Sunday.'

As if supporting her words, a shattering clap of thunder exploded overhead, with a simultaneous sheet of lightning that even in the gloomy taproom momentarily turned them all as white as the sexton's ghosts. Seconds later, torrential rain hammered down, bouncing under the ill-fitting door and spraying through the tattered thatch above. Thoughts of spectres in the forest were temporarily forgotten in their concern over getting to their homes along the waterlogged tracks in the cloudburst that would soak their thin garments – but when they all lay on their damp pallets later that night, images of unquiet spirits and terrifying ghouls in the nearby forest marched through their simple minds before sleep overtook them.

'But you can't stay here, John, it's not seemly!'

Nesta's eyes were round with concern, as she sat up straight on the wide mattress. Suddenly aware of her nakedness, she clutched the rumpled sheepskin coverlet to her rounded bosoms, heedless of the fact that her equally rounded bottom was exposed lower down the bed.

John de Wolfe, lying on one elbow alongside her, glowered defiantly at his mistress.

'Why not? I've stayed here many a night before. Almost all last week, in fact.'

'That's different, John!' she exclaimed with a certain

lack of logic. 'You weren't staying permanently then. What will people think?'

'The same as they think now, that you are my mistress. What's new in that?'

The Welsh woman floundered for an answer. 'It just doesn't seem right,' she said weakly. 'You're a knight and a law officer and I'm just a tavern keeper.'

'As we both were yesterday – and last week and last year, dear woman! Everyone from Dorchester to Plymouth knows that we are lovers.'

She flopped down on to the feather mattress and buried her face against his shoulder.

'Have you really left her, John?' she said in muffled tones.

The coroner slipped an arm around her shoulders and stared at the inside of the roof, where twisted hazel withies across the rafters supported the new thatch outside.

'Yes, *cariad*, I've left her,' he said in the language they always used together. 'Matilda said she wished not to set eyes on me again and I replied in kind. This is but the inevitable outcome of what's been building up for months, if not years.'

'But you've both said such things – and far worse – many times before. It always blows over, John.'

'So you don't want me either, Nesta!' He made it a statement, not a question. In answer, she nipped the skin of his chest with her teeth, then kissed it softly. 'Don't be silly, John. But this is really serious. How can you possibly live here, the King's Coroner?'

'It's an inn, isn't it?' he growled with mock ferocity. 'I'm entitled to a bed in a tavern, just as the King's Justices sleep in the New Inn when they come to Exeter for the court sessions. I'll even pay you my penny a night, if it makes you feel easier.'

This time she pinched his thigh with her fingernails. 'Everyone is entitled to sleep in an inn, but not in the landlady's own bed!'

'Right, then, I'll just pay for a bag of straw in the loft outside.'

She sighed and rolled over on to her back to join him in staring at the roof. 'Be serious, John, for pity's sake! What about your house and Mary and your old hound!'

'They will carry on just the same. Matilda is so fond of her stomach that Mary will be needed to keep it filled. And Brutus can sleep in her cook shed, just as he does now. I can call to see them every day.'

'How will I ever get any work done, with you under my feet?' she objected, though her objections were being weakened by his endless stock of excuses.

'I'll be at my duties every day and I promise to sit quietly in the taproom every evening. I'll be no trouble, I promise you, except when I get you in here at night!'

He made a grab for her and they rolled together on the soft goose-down bed. Later, as he slept and snored, Nesta lay awake to wonder how long this fancy of his would last.

The following day, John called at his house and found that, as he had expected, Matilda was still with her cousin in Fore Street. She often did this when they had had a bigger quarrel than usual, battening herself on her unfortunate relative for a few days until she pined for Mary's better cooking and the obsequious attentions of Lucille. He collected his few spare clothes from the chest in the solar and got the old man who chopped firewood and cleaned the privy to take them down to the Bush.

Mary took his news in much the same manner as Nesta.

'You can't leave home and live in an alehouse!' she snapped scornfully. 'You're the county coroner, they don't do things like that.'

John felt hounded, now with three women telling him how he should behave. This was supposed to be a male-dominated society, he thought. Norman knights and barons should have ladies who obeyed their every wish, on pain of chastisement. They were the sex that should be decorative and pliable, playthings of the solar, locked up in chastity belts when their lord went off to battle. Some chance! he thought ruefully. If Hilda took the same line, it would be four to one voting against his inclinations.

'I tell you, Mary, I'm leaving!' he shouted in exasperation. 'She's gone too far this time. We can't stand the sight of each other, so why prolong this charade of living together?'

'Because you are married, Sir Coroner,' said the maid calmly, using the faintly sarcastic title she reserved for when she was annoyed with him. 'You stood with her in that cathedral around the corner and the Church joined you with a bond that no one except God can put asunder. And he's not likely to come to your aid, I'll warrant!'

De Wolfe marched up and down outside her kitchen door in a ferment of passion. Brutus looked up at him warily, conscious that something unusual was going on.

'Why must I continue to live here in misery, Mary, when I can live happily just a few streets away in Idle Lane? Answer me that.'

'Because you are married and you have to put up with it,' repeated Mary, equably. 'It's the way life is, I'm afraid. You have many other blessings, sir. Money, position and power over the likes of me.'

He stopped pacing and glared at her. 'Well, it doesn't have to be like that, girl. I'm not bloody well staying here to be treated like a mangy dog by the de Revelle family. Don't worry, I'll see that this household carries on as before. You are safe in your hut here and I'll see you and Brutus most days.'

He turned to leave, but she laid a hand on his arm.

'Have you told the mistress what you intend?'

John looked at her blankly. 'She must surely have guessed that from the way we parted last night!'

Mary shook her head emphatically. 'You have to speak

to her face to face, if you really mean it. She deserves that, at least. Until you come to your senses when your temper cools, she will be expecting your step at the door every evening. You cannot just leave it like this.'

He stared at her for a long moment, then nodded abruptly. 'You are right, as always, good girl. Send word to me at the Bush when she returns from Fore Street and I will call on her.'

With that, he gave Brutus a farewell pat on the head and loped off towards the front door.

Commensurate with the severity of their falling-out, Matilda stayed much longer with her long-suffering cousin, and for the rest of that week John heard nothing to suggest that she had returned to Martin's Lane. Thankfully, the coroner's workload received a sudden boost after the previous slack period and he was too occupied each day to have much time to worry over his personal affairs. It also kept him out of the Bush until dusk, as even his somewhat insensitive nature was aware that it would not be wise to cling endlessly to his lover's skirts.

Monday was taken up by the county court, held in the bleak Shire Hall in the inner ward of Rougemont. He had cases to present to the sheriff, and Thomas was kept busy handing out his parchment rolls and whispering cues into his master's ear, as John's literary abilities had not yet extended beyond signing his name and recognising the date.

Tuesday and Thursday mornings saw more hangings, so again the coroner's team were busy at the gallows in Magdalen Street outside the city walls, recording the executions and the forfeited possessions of the miscreants. As with inquests, all this information had to be offered to the King's Justices when they eventually arrived to hold the Eyre.

Apart from these administrative tasks, there was the

coroner's usual workload of cases to be dealt with. Fatal accidents in the city and the surrounding countryside called him out a number of times. Children falling into mill-streams and drowning under mill-wheels or being crushed by runaway horses or over-laden carts were the staple diet of his inquests. A shop that caught fire in North Street was another case, though thankfully no one was killed. There was a rape in a village ten miles east, which turned out to be by the woman's brother-in-law – and a serious wounding occurred in a fight outside an ale-house in Chagford, one of the Stannary towns on the edge of Dartmoor. The last two cases involved some more travelling and John was thankful that Thomas was some-what faster on a horse now that he sat astride it..

The little clerk appeared to be rejuvenated after his visit to Winchester. All the months of depression and feel-ings of worthlessness had been banished by the brief ceremony in the cathedral. It was true that he still had no pastoral duties, but Thomas's main interests in the Church lay in the more academic and theological fields rather than labouring as a parish priest. The employment he had been given in the archives was an earthly form of paradise to him, as not only could he indulge himself in sorting through ecclesiastical records, but he could covertly read his way through the substantial library of books and manuscripts that lined the walls of the scripto-rium on the upper floor of the Chapter House. His daily Masses for his deceased patrons satisfied his liturgical needs and the weekly teaching sessions with the choristers allowed him to indulge his desire to impart his learning to others. All in all, life was now good for Thomas, but he never forgot his debt to the coroner, who had taken him in at the lowest ebb of his life and who had stood by him steadfastly during a number of crises, including an attempt at suicide.

The three men settled back into their routine and for a number of days John almost forgot his domestic troubles. He called at his house every evening to see Mary and to take Brutus for a walk. Each night that the cook-maid reported that there was no sign of Matilda, extended his contentment for another day. His hound was the only one who seemed to sense that all was not well, as he sometimes caught Brutus eyeing him reproachfully, as he cocked his leg against a grave mound in the Close or waited for his master to catch him up in Southgate Street. They no longer walked down to the Bush, as John would have had to bring the dog all the way back again each evening, so Brutus missed out on his tit-bits under the table in the taproom.

John restrained himself from going down to Dawlish again, though the temptation was always lurking at the back of his mind. Even when Hugh de Relaga urged him to visit their new partner, he made excuses and managed to delay the trip. The portreeve wanted him to let Hilda know the outcome of the shipwright's visit to the *Mary and Child Jesus*, as the man from Topsham had reported that the task would be easier and cheaper than expected.

'Together with the two ship-masters and a couple of crew, we can easily rig a jury mast,' he pronounced confidently. 'Pick a calm day and we can sail her round Bolt Head to Salcombe, before the winter gales set in. In that protected haven, the proper repairs can be carried out, ready for the spring sailing season.'

Hugh wanted John to reassure Hilda that all was going well, but John pointed out that she would have to come up to Exeter before long, to put her mark on the deed of partnership, which Robert Courteman, the only lawyer in Exeter, was drawing up in his office in Goldsmith Street.

De Wolfe did not want to risk making his love life any more precarious by stirring up the wrath of Nesta with any unnecessary dealings with the widow of Dawlish. One sword of Damocles hanging over his head in the shape of Matilda was more than sufficient.

Nothing further was heard that week from either

Shillingford or Ringmore, but the mystery was never far from the coroner's thoughts. Only one aspect of the killings was followed up – that of the two cross-bow bolts brought from Shillingford. John closely scrutinised the worn marks hammered into the leather flights of the short arrows, but could make nothing of them. Even Thomas, usually a fount of arcane knowledge, had to confess that they meant nothing to him, but suggested someone who might have a better knowledge of Levantine calligraphy. The jovial and portly chaplain of Rougemont, Brother Rufus, had come to the castle earlier that year from a similar post at Bristol, but previously had been with the King's forces in France, and before that, at the Crusade.

Thomas wondered whether Rufus, a literate man with a great breadth of learning derived from his insatiable curiousity, could throw any light on the markings. The coroner's trio took the quarrels down to the little garrison chapel of St Mary, but found no sign of the amiable priest.

'He'll be supping ale and swapping yarns in the hall, I'll wager,' grunted Gwyn, who tolerated this particular monk because of his down-to-earth manner and his fondness for drink and gossip. Sure enough, they found the Benedictine in the keep and showed him the bolts that had caused so much damage. Enthusiastically, Rufus peered closely at the inscriptions on the flights, his large red nose almost touching them.

'It's Arabic, no doubt of that. Very blurred, as the tool that stamped them must have been blunt – and there's been no gold leaf impressed into them, to make them more prominent.'

'So what does it say?' barked de Wolfe, impatiently.

Rufus fingered the leather, then broke off a splinter of wood from the edge of the rough table and used the tip to trace the shallow grooves.

'The same on both arrows. I'm no great scholar of

Moorish writing, but one set of signs is for Allah. And I think another is "just" or "justice".' He looked up at the coroner. 'Probably a quotation from the Al Qu'ran, meaning their god is just. That's about all I can get from it.'

De Wolfe nodded his thanks. 'But there's no doubt it's Arabic?'

The corpulent priest shook his head. 'No doubt about that – just the word "Allah" proves that. The Saracens are very proficient with these cross-bows, though they use the short hand-bow as well, especially on horseback.'

John smiled sardonically. 'I'm living proof of that!' he said, feeling the still-tender spot on his chest, a reminder of the prowess of Saladin's troops with the bow. This was another piece of evidence that strengthened his conviction that there was a Moorish connection with these crimes, but it got them no farther in finding the perpetrators.

On Saturday afternoon, de Wolfe sought out Henry de Furnellis in his chamber, as since the arrival of a friendly sheriff in place of the haughty and sardonic Richard de Revelle he had fallen into the habit of talking over each week's events with the older man.

'Has there been any reaction from the Justiciar or the Curia to Peter le Calve's murder?' he asked Henry. 'Surely the news must have reached London and Winchester by now?'

De Furnellis shrugged and set his pint pot of cider down on the table.

'Nothing yet, but I'm sure that Hubert Walter must know of it. I wonder if we should send him news of this Saracen involvement that you say is now all but definite?'

John nursed his own cider jar to his chest as he leaned over the small fire set against one wall. Kicking a log farther into the centre, he replied, 'It might be advisable, Henry. He was the one who sent us this idea about a Saracen connection, so maybe we should give him some confirmation from our end.'

'There's a messenger going up tomorrow. I'll get Elphin to write a note telling them of the attack on le Calve's son and the rest of the troubles.'

The sheriff, his drooping features looking more hound-like than ever, raised his eyes to the coroner. 'If this is all connected with Prince John, are we sure that my unlamented predecessor isn't mixed up in it? We all know that de Revelle has a strong inclination in that direction. God knows why the man hasn't been hanged for it twice over.'

De Wolfe gave another log a vicious kick that raised a shower of sparks.

'I don't trust him anywhere out of my sight, Henry,' he rasped. 'But I can't see any evidence of him being involved.'

'This Burgh Island where the ship was wrecked, isn't that within sight of Revelstoke?' persisted de Furnellis.

'Yes, in the distance, far across the bay. But there's no way in which Richard or his men could be connected with the slaying of the crew. The vessel would not have touched land since it left France.'

The sheriff looked unconvinced, but had to bend to the facts.

'Is there nothing you can do about all these deaths, John?'

The coroner noticed that Henry said 'you', not 'I' – or even 'we' – in spite of the fact that he had been appointed the custodian of the King's peace in the county of Devon. It was again patently obvious that the sheriff was content to let de Wolfe take the lead in any investigation – though to be fair, John knew that he would not then claim any glory for success or avoid any responsibility for failure.

'Where can I start, Sheriff?' he growled. 'I'm sure now that there must be at least a couple of hostile Turks lurking somewhere in the county. They probably came from France on poor old Thorgils' vessel, but God knows where they're hiding now.'

Henry, whose somewhat bucolic appearance concealed a shrewd mind, pulled at the jowls under his chin. 'But why are they in Devon, John? What good can a couple of damned Saracens be to John Lackland?' This was the sarcastic nickname that the ambitious prince used to carry before his indulgent brother Richard bestowed lands upon him, a gesture that John threw back in his face when he tried to usurp his throne.

De Wolfe had no answer to this. 'I'll ask them when I catch up with them, in the few seconds before I ram my sword through the bastards' hearts!' he grunted ominously. 'But first we've got to find the swine.'

'I'd gladly give you a posse of Ralph Morin's troops, if it would do any good,' replied Henry morosely. 'But until we get some clue as to where they might be, what's the use?'

John picked up his wolfskin cloak and slung it around his shoulders as he moved towards the door. 'My gut tells me they're somewhere down in the west of the county. But that's a hell of a large area, and unless some of the locals get wind of them, we've no chance of finding them.'

'Unless they make another attack and get careless,' suggested de Furnellis, unaware of his prophetic powers.

That same day, the former sheriff had a visitor at his manor of Revelstoke, to which Richard had just returned. He seemed to favour this manor now, much to Lady Eleanor's displeasure. The envoy from the French king, Raymond de Blois, came alone from Bigbury, covering the miles at a quick trot and occasional canter, so that he was at Noss Mayo well before noon. He made an impressive figure on the bay gelding that had been supplied by de Revelle. Tall and erect, he was an excellent horseman and in fact was a successful competitor in many of the tournaments held around Paris and farther afield. Much of his appreciable wealth came from his winnings on the tourney grounds, both in forfeited arms and horses and in ransom money for those he defeated with lance and sword.

When he cantered up to the gatehouse of Revelstoke, the porter peered through his peephole and saw a commanding figure waiting for admittance. Raymond wore a yellow surcoat over a chain-mail hauberk, all covered with a dark green riding cloak. Though his head was bare, a round iron helmet hung from his saddle, alongside a wicked-looking ball-mace. A large sword was slung from his baldric, as, travelling alone, he took no chances on the lonely lanes of this remote part of England. Like his mount, these arms had been supplied at Bigbury by Prince John through de Revelle, as Raymond had been unable to bring much with him on the hazardous journey by ship and curragh. He carried no emblazoned shield, nor did his surcoat display any heraldic device. He was an enemy agent loose in the country, and though no one was likely to challenge him outside the towns, de Blois prudently avoided advertising his origins.

The porter knew him from several previous visits and hurried to swing open the gate, yelling for an ostler to come and take the horse. Minutes later, Raymond was ushered into de Revelle's chamber off the hall and made welcome with wine and the promise of food as soon as it could be brought from the kitchens. Richard hurried in, resplendent in a blue linen tunic almost to his ankles, loosely covered with a green silk surcoat trimmed with squirrel fur.

'I returned here only last night, de Blois,' he said. 'My wife has decided to stay at my manor near Tiverton – she says she finds the winds from the sea too chill here, now that winter is threatening to descend upon us.'

The French knight had arranged this visit when he was last at Revelstoke with Alexander of Leith, and had been hoping now to report that the alchemists had made good progress. Instead, he had to deliver his misgivings about the whole enterprise.

'These Moors are uncontrollable, I fear,' he said, warming his chilled body with mulled wine. 'Our little Scotchman does his best, but he can get no sense out of this Nizam creature. Last night, Alexander came to me complaining that he fears that the man has no real expertise in his craft. He is also beginning to suspect that the nodule of gold that the Arab claims to have made has been planted there to sustain the deceit!'

The lord of Revelstoke looked aghast at his visitor.

'Surely that cannot be true? This Saracen was sent at the express wish of your king! He must have had credentials to prove his prowess?'

Raymond gave a Gallic shrug. 'I knew of the man in Paris. Philip Augustus brought him back when he returned from the Crusade more than two years ago. He claimed then to have discovered the Elixir of Life and was confident that he could soon convert this substance into its other form, with the ability to transmute base metals into gold.'

De Revelle began pacing up and down in front of his table.

'Yes, yes, I know all that! But the Prince in Gloucester is impatiently awaiting results. He sends a herald here every week or two, demanding news. Why is this God-blasted Nizam proving so difficult, eh?'

'He keeps vanishing for days on end, together with these mute ruffians he has as bodyguards,' explained Raymond wearily.

'What are they up to? They are supposed to lie low all the time, to avoid being seen. What can bloody foreigners like them want with skulking around the countryside?' He ignored the fact that de Blois himself was a foreigner to Devon.

'I wish to heaven I knew – but then again, perhaps I prefer not to know!' answered Raymond fervently. 'They are dangerous men. I fear no one in fair combat, I welcome any adversary before me with sword or lance. But these strange beings are so untrustworthy, I am reluctant to turn my back on them, in case they slide a knife between my ribs.'

Richard de Revelle stared anxiously at his guest. He respected him as a brave and honourable knight, even though he was spying for another king. For him to admit to fears about these men was serious indeed.

'What were they like when you brought them across the sea?' he asked.

'They were quiet enough until we came in sight of this coast. I brought them from Paris to the Vexin, which is in King Philip's hands now, then we slipped into Normandy dressed as black monks, for those white nightshirts and headgear they wear are hard to disguise.'

'Which port did you use, then?' asked Richard, curious to hear about the ways of espionage.

'We embarked at Harfleur, where I paid this ship-master well to drop us at Salcombe on his way home to some place near Exeter. He was a little suspicious of these hawk-faced "Benedictines", but I spun him a story about them being hermits from Sinai wishing to go on a pilgrimage to Glastonbury, via Buckfast Abbey.'

'But you never got to Salcombe?'

Raymond de Blois shook his head sadly. 'I intended that to be the plan, but after I explained to this Nizam that we would need to go back a few miles from Salcombe to Bigbury, they went into a huddle. As soon as the ship came close inshore in this big bay, they suddenly rose up and callously slew all the crew, apart from one lad who had time to leap overboard – though he must have perished.'

'What reason did they give?' asked Richard, uneasy that he had to deal with such dangerous people.

'Oh, Nizam said that the shipmen might give us away to the authorities and it would be better if they were silenced. They wiped their bloody daggers on the clothing of the poor sailors and then calmly put the small boat into the water and we paddled ashore.'

'Perhaps you were lucky not to have had your throat cut as well!'

Raymond shook his head emphatically. 'No, they needed me to survive. I knew the way to the hideout in the forest and without me they would have had no prospect of food or shelter.'

'And how are they to return when their task is completed – if it ever is, from what you have told me today,' persisted de Revelle.

The Frenchman shook his head slowly in bewilderment. 'I can't make them out, they seem so unconcerned. My plan was to make the journey in reverse, take them in their disguises to one of the ports and seek passage across the Channel, then work our way back to Paris. But they are quite incurious about this – at least Nizam is, for it is impossible to communicate with the other two, who are clearly nothing but ruffians recruited to protect the alchemist.'

He paused to drain the last of his wine cup. 'There is something odd about them. Often they seem drugged and sleepy, at other times they seem wildly excited. They chew some scented brown gum and spit filthy curds upon the ground. It seems to be some sort of opiate that affects their minds.'

At this point, two servants arrived with food for the traveller, and Richard joined de Blois in taking more wine while the knight tucked in to a roast fowl, grilled sea-fish, sliced mutton and boiled beans. Fresh bread, cheese and some fruit filled the envoy's stomach as they resumed their anxious discussion.

'So what's to be done about this?' demanded de Revelle. 'The Count of Mortain will doubtless be sending another of his messengers down here very soon, wanting to hear of progress.'

De Blois dipped his fingers into a bowl of water scented with rose petals and wiped them fastidiously on a napkin. He approved of the civilised style that de Revelle affected in his house, but his worried mind was occupied with their problem.

'I think that you should talk personally to these two alchemists, de Revelle. I can do nothing with them to bring them together and the Scotchman is becoming increasingly angry and frustrated. He is already talking of returning to Bristol.'

Richard paled slightly at the prospect of being closeted with an unbalanced trio of Turks who seemed all too ready to commit multiple murder.

'Is that really necessary?' he bleated. 'What can I say that you have not already demanded?'

'You will be a fresh voice with much authority. You are the direct agent of the Count in this enterprise and you can threaten them with dire consequences if they do not submit.'

Richard had his doubts about this, but his friendship with the Prince and the great prizes of power and advancement for him that were hinted at when John seized the throne were too important to jeopardise.

'Very well. If there is no improvement in the situation within the coming week, I will ride briefly to your hideout to talk to this Nizam. But make sure they behave themselves when I am there!'

CHAPTER TEN

In which the Widow Hilda makes a decision

Thorgils had built his house in a side lane off the main street, but the window of the upstairs solar faced back towards the sea, and the woman standing before the open shutter could see over the irrregular roof-line of the older buildings below. Though they blocked her view of the strand, she could see the sea in the distance, dotted to the hazy horizon with white caps from the stiff westerly breeze.

Beyond that horizon was the Continent, and Hilda stared as if she could see over the curve of the earth to the places where her husband had voyaged since he was twelve years old. He had brought wine from Bordeaux and taken Devon wool to Cologne, sailing to every port between them in the course of his long life. This fine house that was now hers had been built with the profits – and when she had opened his treasure chest and counted through the many leather bags it contained, she had been amazed at how much silver and even gold it contained. His three ships were now hers, and if John's and Hugh de Relaga's plan came to pass, she would want for nothing for the rest of her life – except, perhaps, for John himself.

Hilda turned from the window and closed the shutter, as the grey sky began to spit cold rain down on Dawlish. She sat on a padded chair near the small fire that burned in the hearth, the narrow cone of the modern chimney taking the smoke up through the tiled roof. Her embroidery stood neglected on its frame near by, as for the past few days she had felt too restless to bother with it. Elegant in her blue kirtle of fine wool, wide sleeved and girdled with low-slung gilded cords, she stared into the glowing embers and felt both sad and angry. She was sad over the loss of her husband, and also for the uncertainty of what life held for her – or what it might fail to hold. Her anger was for the way he had died.

Though she had never loved Thorgils in the way that she had loved John de Wolfe, she had felt considerable affection for him and respected him for his unfailing generosity and concern for her welfare. Though many years older, he had had a healthy passion, and she readily acknowledged that she had enjoyed their coupling in bed, though for the last year or two his advancing age had cooled his desire. She herself was very fond of lovemaking, and now she wondered whether she would ever feel those delicious moments of rapture again, with any man. Thorgils was gone, John was wrapped up in his marital problems and his infatuation with the ale-wife, so where did that leave her? At the moment, she could not even visualise going with another man, and though she knew without any conceit that she was still very attractive, her widow's wealth might prove to be a burden. Suitors would be easy to find, but would they want her for herself or for the contents of her treasure box?

These past few days, she had spent a lot time sitting alone and staring into the fire. Thorgils had been buried for several weeks and every few days she went to place flowers on the low mound of earth in the churchyard. She spoke to him under her breath as she bent over the grave, telling him that she wished she had been able to love him more, and pouring out her sorrow at his passing and her loneliness. Gradually, her self-pity was replaced by a slow but growing anger. He had been a good man and he had been stolen from her. As she had told John de Wolfe, she had long been resigned to the cruel sea taking him one day – but not the cowardly blade of some evil killer.

Hilda felt guilty as she stared into the reddened logs, guilty not because of her failure to truly love her husband, or even because she had occasionally been unfaithful to him with her childhood sweetheart.

She felt guilty that she could not avenge him, discover who killed him and for what reason. He deserved a better end than to be stabbed by some uncaring murderer, she thought bitterly. When would they be brought to justice, if ever? De Wolfe himself seemed powerless to discover the culprits – she would have heard by now if there had been any progress in his hunt for them.

Hilda was a determined, practical woman of peasant stock, daughter of a village bondsman. She was relatively young, both fit and strong – was there nothing she could do to avenge Thorgils? Getting up, she paced the chamber to recall what little she knew, as told by John. The key must surely lie down in the west, where her husband had met his death. She was under no illusions about the difficulties, not least the problem of a woman travelling about the countryside – but that might be the one advantage she had over the coroner and the sheriff and their heavy-handed investigations. Maybe a woman, especially a local Saxon, could better infiltrate the common folk of the villages and learn something useful.

At least she could try – and it would be something to fill an empty life. She avoided admitting even to herself that most of that emptiness was caused by the knowledge that John de Wolfe could never be hers.

The same Atlantic wind that whipped up white horses on the sea off Dawlish whistled even more menacingly over the bare island of St Michael de la Burgh. On the wind-ward side of the craggy isle, which was less than a quarter of a mile across, the waves lashed up in angry, snarling breakers, gouts of creamy spume flying upwards like feathers. The tide was ebbing, and already a line of sand was appearing between the island and the low headland that guarded the entrance to the River Avon.

In the anchorite's cell at the summit of the island, Joel peered out through the low doorway, a crude wooden frame closed by some rough planks of driftwood. It faced inland, away from the prevailing gales, and he could see the mouth of the river directly in front of him. A few days ago, in calmer weather, he had seen the rescued cog, the *Mary and Child Jesus*, sailing cautiously out to sea, with a half-size sail slung across a stumpy pole that did service as a temporary mast. Another smaller vessel, which had brought men and materials from Dartmouth, followed it like a sheepdog with a stray lamb, shepherding it down the coast and around Bolt Head to the safety of Salcombe.

It was late afternoon when the hermit crept out of his hut, his height making him almost bend double under the slab of slate that acted as a lintel. When he stood up, he could almost see over the roof, as the hovel was hunkered down so low in the rocky turf. Made of irregular stones set in a circle, it was topped with heavy flat slabs laid on stout branches dragged from the mainland. A turf roof could not survive the winds on that exposed crag as he had discovered the hard way, when he first came to the island more than twenty years earlier. When it rained, as it seemed to do for half the year, water poured in between the slabs and soaked everything in his hut – but as there was so little inside, this was no great problem. He had a pile of damp bracken to sleep upon, a crude fire-pit in the centre and a single milking stool on which to take his ease. A roughly carved crucifix jammed into one of the cracks between the stones completed the furnishings, apart from a handbell standing on the floor. A strict ascetic, Joel welcomed every personal discomfort, as for a score of years he had been trying to exculpate his previous sinful life by seeking hardship in whatever form he could devise. He drank nothing but rainwater and lived almost entirely on fish, feeling guilty when he occasionally ate a little bread given to him by one of the boatmen for whom he carried out simple tasks. Perched up on his rock jutting out into the bay, Joel could see when a shoal of herring or pilchard arrived from the activity of the gulls and the disturbance in the water. Then he would stand on his roof and clang his brass handbell to alert the fishermen. When they hurried to launch their flimsy curraghs, he would wag his arms about to direct them to the shoal, where they would scoop up the fish by the thousand.

This was almost his sole contact with the secular world, except for a monthly visit to the tiny church at Ringmore, where he would take the Sacrament and make confession to Walter, the parish priest. Joel never found this satisfactory, as Walter was dour and uninterested, always impatient to get away to his wineskin – but the hermit had little choice of confessor in this lonely district.

Now he stretched himself after being confined in the cramped hut and, from sheer habit, turned to scan the surface of the sea. It was too choppy to seek out any shoals and the fleeting rays of a low sun beaming through the gaps in the scudding clouds struck silvery patches across the angry swell. He turned back towards the mainland and picked his way like an old goat down the steep track he had worn over the years to reach the smooth sandbar which was now widening between the island and the low headland opposite. The winter was setting in rapidly, as a sudden swirl of snowflakes reminded him. Though he relished cold and discomfort, he knew that without a fire he would soon die of exposure on that bleak islet. That held no terrors for him, but he repudiated an early death, for it would cut short his self-inflicted misery, the atonement for his great sins of long ago, when he had killed and maimed – and, even worse, had revelled in the blood-lust of battle.

A fire required wood and he needed to replenish the

stock of fallen branches that he had stacked at the back of his cell, protected from the leaks by a torn fragment of old sail canvas. The nearest source of fuel was the woods around the corner of the headland, along the west bank of the river, where stunted trees and scraggy bushes had a little shelter from the prevailing gales.

He reached the sand and plodded across the isthmus, leaving a trail of bare footprints behind him. To his left the surf hissed as it surged forward, then retreated, while on the opposite lee side the water was much calmer. No one was about, the fisherfolk having gone back to their shacks at Challaborough and Bantham, after their day's work was done.

The anchorite reached the rocks on the mainland side and clambered up on to a path that ran around to the right, into the mouth of the Avon estuary. The start of the forest was half a mile farther, and he trudged along, turning over in his mind half-remembered stories from the Gospels and fragments of liturgy recalled from his youth. He had no Vulgate, so had to depend on his memory for all his religious experiences.

Murmuring to himself, he reached the first of the trees, just above the small inlet where the wrecked ship had been placed for safety. Hoping that the recent strong winds had brought down some more branches, he had started casting about for fallen wood when he saw an unusual sight for that normally deserted path. Three figures were advancing towards him, robed and hooded in black.

Though Benedictines were not uncommon anywhere in the countryside near one of their priories or abbeys, to see such a trio on the lower reaches of the Avon was rare indeed.

Joel dropped the few pieces of wood that he had gathered and waited for the monks to approach.

'God be with you, brothers,' he called when they were twenty paces away. They stopped and stared at him, only the dark shadow of their faces visible under their deep cowls. They said nothing.

'I am Joel, a solitary worshipper of Christ,' he said in his deep voice. 'I live a contemplative life on a small island near this place.'

This seemed to transform the leader of the three men, who stood a little ahead of the other two. He stepped forward another pace and threw back his hood to reveal a dark Moorish face, with a hooked nose and black moustache. With a sudden leap of intuition, the hermit knew why these men were here. A glad hymn of thanks coursed through his brain, as he realised that his long years of self-denial and suffering were over.

The coroner's period of uneasy peace ended in the middle of the second week after he had left home. Early in the evening of Wednesday, he called as usual at his house in Martin's Lane to gossip with Mary and take Brutus for a walk around the Close. The moment he entered the back yard, he sensed that things had changed. His cook-maid peered rather furtively from her kitchen shed and rolled her eyes upwards towards the solar high on the back of the house. As he followed her gaze, he saw that the door to Lucille's box-like room under the stairs was open and a moment later the weedy French girl appeared, clutching an armful of folded clothing. With hardly a glance at the pair in the yard, she clattered up the steep steps and vanished into the solar, the door closing behind her with a slam.

John stepped hurriedly into the kitchen, where Brutus was trying to look inconspicuous at the back.

'She's back, then?' he asked needlessly.

'This afternoon. It seems she's been in Tiverton with her brother, after leaving her cousin.' Mary sounded resigned, as, like her master, she had been enjoying peace and quiet for over a week.

'What sort of mood is she in?'

'Grim, from what little I've seen of her. She just asked me if you were at home, then vanished upstairs.'

'Did you tell her I was living at the Bush?'

Mary looked scandalised. 'Of course not! It's none of my business. But I doubt she is ignorant of the fact. There are plenty of wagging tongues both here and in Tiverton that would gladly relay such a tasty piece of scandal.'

De Wolfe slumped on to a stool, looking the picture of dejection.

'What do I do now, Mary?' he asked meekly.

The dark-haired woman laid a hand on his shoulder in an almost motherly fashion. 'You either come home and make the best of it – or you stay away and face whatever problems that brings.'

The coroner's dark face took on a stubborn look. 'I'm damn well not going to give in to her. Why should I spend my life in angry squabbling, when I can find peace and happiness half a mile away?'

The maid shrugged. 'You are the master of this house. Most Norman gentlemen would have their way, even if they had to knock their wives senseless twice a week – which many of them do, so I am told.' She said this with an undercurrent of spite, as she was from a Saxon mother, even if her father's identity was in doubt. Mary rarely missed a chance to make a caustic remark about the race that had conquered her people, even though it was five generations earlier.

'This past week was the quiet before the tempest,' he observed glumly. 'I knew it was too good to last. I suppose I'll have to face her sooner or later.'

Mary, as well as having political leanings, appeared to be a latent feminist. 'At least you should tell her that you have left her,' she complained. 'You just walked off the other day without a word.' She could have added that she thought this was a coward's way out, but even their former relationship was insufficient for her to push her luck with her employer that far. De Wolfe knew that Mary was right and his conscience pricked him on the issue. But before he could say anything in his defence, there was a familar bellow from outside.

'John! Are you there?'

Matilda was on the platform at the top of the solar stairway, gripping the rail and glaring down into the back yard. Realising that the sneaky Lucille must have told her mistress of his return, John reluctantly hauled himself to his feet.

'Wish me luck – or possibly farewell!' he muttered to Mary, as he left the cook shed and plodded heavy footed towards the solar. Lucille hurried down and, like a frightened rabbit, disappeared into her hutch under the stairs. As he slowly climbed up, his wife went back into the room and, when he entered, she was standing at the foot of their bed, fists planted on her wide hips.

'You've not been at home while I've been away,' she snarled. 'Where were you?'

Though he knew that she was perfectly well aware that he had been staying in the Bush, she wanted him to admit it to her face. As so often happened, his anxiety rapidly turned to anger when she confronted him.

'You know damn well that I've left you, wife!' he snapped. 'I told you so clearly enough when we parted.'

This was not exactly the truth, but he was working himself up to a rage so that niceties of speech counted for little.

'You've been with that Welsh whore – or was it that yellow-haired strumpet down at the seashore?' she snarled, her square face flushed with righteous indignation.

'What should it matter to you, Matilda? I no longer live with you, that's all you need to know.'

'The shame of it!' she screeched. 'A knight of the realm, the King's Coroner and a Crusader, living in sin with God knows how many women!'

Her exaggeration went unchallenged when he responded. 'Are you claiming that I am unique, woman?'

he snapped. 'I would find it difficult to name more than a handful of men who are faithful to their wives. Mostly those like me, who were pushed into loveless marriages by scheming parents!'

She opened her mouth to vilify him further, but he ploughed on.

'The sheriff, Henry de Furnellis, had a mistress that I know of, as did Ralph Morin, Guy Ferrars and half the cathedral canons!'

'I don't want to hear about your dissolute friends,' she raved. 'I have been humiliated by you before all the city. Even if you can shamelessly hold up your head, what about me? I have had to seek the shelter of my brother and his wife again this past week.'

'Ha! Your brother! There's a pillar of righteousness indeed! I rescued him from a brothel earlier this year and have more than once caught him with a whore in his bedroom!'

Suddenly, he felt tired and sick of this endless bickering. He pointed to his oaken chest which stood against the wall.

'I have taken my garments away. I will see to it that there will always be money in the purse that sits in that box. I will continue to pay Mary and your maid for their services and anything else you need will readily be forthcoming. Life will go on just the same for you, except that I shall not remain in your sight to offend you.'

He turned to the door. 'The Church bound us together in a way that cannot be broken asunder. But that does not mean that we have to endure each other's company, when you have made it clear over many years that all you feel for me is contempt.'

Such a long and eloquent speech was so out of character for her dour husband that Matilda was temporarily bereft of speech, but as he went out of the solar she found her tongue again.

'Yes, husband, contempt for the way you hounded my

brother and trapped him into disrepute! He has explained to me how you tricked and manoeuvred him over that treasure. I hate you for it! Do you hear, I hate your persecution of that good man!'

Knowing the truth about Richard de Revelle, this was too much for John, and he clattered down the stairs and hurried out into the street, determined to put as much distance between himself and his wife as possible.

Mary heard some of the heated exchange up above and saw the wrathful departure of her master. As she sat in her kitchen and fondled the soft ears of the old hound, she murmured, 'What's to become of us, Brutus?'

Alexander of Leith had more or less given up hope of gaining any knowledge or cooperation from the Mohammedan Nizam. The Moors were rarely to be seen in the old crypt and, when they were there, the Scot strongly suspected that the alleged alchemist was merely going through the motions of experimenting, to buy time for his other suspicious activities. Only once did he achieve any results, when he again produced a tiny globule of what appeared to be gold, embedded in a mass of dirty tin and silver. Alexander strongly suspected him of some sleight of hand in introducing the yellow metal into the crucible, and felt that the whole procedure was merely a sham to convince him that the Turk was a genuine alchemist. Raymond de Blois seemed more impressed and used the event to persuade Alexander to stay at Bigbury a little longer and not return to Bristol as he had threatened.

Now the Moors had vanished again for several days and the French knight was seething with impatience, as he wished them to be here for the visit of Richard de Revelle, for him to impress upon them the importance of achieving some results for the Count of Mortain.

With the others away, the little Scotsman repeated his own work, but once more failed to make the last vital transition from an alloy to gold. Disillusioned with the situation and the inferior facilities in the old priory compared with those he had at Bristol, Alexander turned to his other research, the preparation of the Elixir of Life. Claimed by other alchemists as a liquid version of the stone that would transmute other metals into gold, the magic fluid was supposed to cure every illness and prolong life almost indefinitely. In his view, this was a more worthwhile project than the Philosopher's Stone itself. If necessary, real gold could be dug from the earth, but a potion to prolong life and banish disease would be the greatest boon the world had ever seen.

In the quiet of the crypt, with no one else to distract him, he laboured to dissolve his almost-gold with strong spirits of salt, then neutralised it with soda. Two days of filtering and distillation produced a small quantity of murky liquid, similar to many he had manufactured before, though this time he used Dartmoor tin and Tavistock copper.

The problem was testing the elixir – if it prolonged life, how long would he have to wait to know that it was effective? He had tried previous batches on a few small animals, such as mice, rats and cats, but they either died straight away or after a few days – or there was no effect at all. Maybe, he thought, the latter group were signs of success, but none of them seemed to achieve longevity beyond what one normally expected for that type of beast. With a sigh, he filled a small phial with his latest creation and hid it away inside his shapeless tunic, hoping that some inspiration about a method of testing would occur to him.

The next morning, the Moors were back, as impassive as ever and equally uncommunicative. After the early morning meal in the hut at the old castle, Alexander expected them to be harried back to work in the crypt by an increasingly exasperated Raymond. Instead, they all saddled up and, dressed in their monkish robes, rode off again to some unknown destination. Nizam refused to answer Raymond's demand to know where they were going, just saying that they would be back before nightfall.

Later that day, sitting in the hut where they ate their meals, Alexander confided in Jan, a rather one-sided conversation, though the Fleming seemed attentive enough.

'We'll give them a few more days, Jan, then abandon this and set off home.' Tugging a bone from the rabbit stew that the serf Alfred had made, he brandished it at his servant to emphasise his determination. 'If this de Revelle fellow cannot instil some urgency into these damned Turks, the whole venture is a waste of my time,' he exclaimed. 'I'm not cowed by John Lackland, even if he is the King's brother. I'll tell him to his face that the French king is either mocking him or has been hoodwinked himself by these Arabic charlatans.'

The Fleming nodded and made some gargling noises in his mutilated throat which indicated agreement. He had been bored out of his mind by the enforced isolation, with only two Saxon simpletons for company. As for his Scottish master, he too was at the end of his tether, working with insufficient equipment in a dank subterranean chamber with a trio of uncaring Saracens for occasional company. In spite of his strange appearance and clothing, which in truth Alexander cultivated to enhance his reputation as an eccentric alchemist, he had a sharp and practical mind and felt that he would be far better employed back in Bristol.

And if he was honest, he was uneasy to the point of fear when alone with the three Mohammedans, as he sensed an evil aura about them all.

chapter eleven

In which the coroner rides yet again to Ringmore

The last of the evening light was fading from the western sky when the stout wooden doors at Exeter's five gates were pushed shut by the porters and the great bars dropped into their sockets behind them. The two city constables began their patrol of the streets to make their token inspection, ensuring that all fires were extinguished or damped down for the night. The fear of a conflagration in a town whose houses were still largely built of wood was real, and the curfew or '*couvre-feu*' was intended to protect the citizens as they slept. In fact, many fires were kept going overnight to save relighting them for the early morning cooking, but as long as no obvious flames or glow were visible, the constables turned a blind eye.

When they left their hut behind the Guildhall, the fatter of the pair, Theobald, turned up High Street to tramp the lanes in the eastern part of the city. His skinny Saxon colleague, Osric, made his leisurely way in the opposite direction down Fore Street, his dim horn lantern in one hand, his staff in the other.

He greeted a few people as he went, though most respectable folk were at home, either finishing their supper or already in bed, as the working day corresponded largely with dawn and dusk. From side lanes in Bretayne to his right and Smythen Street and Stepcote Hill to his left came the distant sounds of raucous singing and swearing from the more disreputable alehouses such

THE ELIXIR OF DEATH

as the Saracen, but tonight was no different from any other, and Osric stepped out unconcernedly past little St Olave's church towards the West Gate.

Halfway down the hill, he heard rapid footsteps coming towards him and from force of habit tightened his grip on his ash stave and held his lantern higher, though its pale light hardly reached his feet.

'Is that you, Osric?' came a breathless voice, wheezing as he hurried up the slope. The constable recognised Matthew, one of the night porters from the West Gate, which led out to the ford and rickety footbridge over the river to the main highroad beyond.

'Matthew? What are doing away from your warm fire?'

A portly man of middle age came into the circle of lantern light. He was dressed in a leather jerkin and incongruously wore a battered iron helmet as his badge of office.

'It's all right, Aelgard is on the gate. He sent me to fetch you. We need your advice.'

'Why? Have the French landed at Topsham to invade us?' Osric was only half joking, as in these uncertain times anything could happen.

'There's a man outside demanding to be let into the city, even though we shut the gates almost half an hour past.'

'Then tell him to go to hell – or come back in the morning.'

'He's very insistent. Come down and talk to him yourself. I don't want to get into trouble with the portreeves or the sheriff for either letting him in or keeping him out.'

Grumbling under his breath, the constable followed Matthew back to the lower town wall, which ran along the line of the river, with the boggy land of Exe Island in between. Aelgard, a younger man and a Saxon like himself, led him up the stone steps alongside one of the squat towers that flanked the gate. They reached the parapet fifteen feet above ground and peered over.

Though it was now virtually dark, a cloud moving off the horizon let through enough of the last streaks of grey light to make out a figure on a horse almost directly below them.

'It's after curfew, you can't come in now!' called Osric.

There was a whinny and a clatter of hoofs as the rider turned his horse to face the voice.

'I have to, it's urgent. I've ridden since early morning. This is the second horse I've worn out to try to get here in time.'

'Who are you and what do you want?' yelled the constable.

'William Vado, bailiff of Ringmore, here on the orders of the lord of Totnes, through his steward. I have to speak straightway to the coroner or the sheriff.'

Impressed by the credentials of the rider and the urgency of his tone, Osric weakened a little.

'What do you want with the crowner at this time of night?'

'To report a murder most foul – and one which Sir John will want to hear about from my own lips!'

The constable decided that this was a situation out of the ordinary and capitulated.

'Very well, we'll admit you and I'll take you to him myself. But no tricks, d'you hear – or you'll regret it!'

Though his ears failed to burn at his name being taken in vain, at that moment the coroner was only a few hundred yards away from the West Gate. He was sitting in his usual place in the taproom of the Bush, a quart pot before him and an arm around Nesta's waist. Across the room, Gwyn was drinking and playing dice with a few of his cronies.

De Wolfe's long dark face was more morose than usual as he described the return of Matilda that day. For the third time he recounted to his mistress every word that had passed between him and his wife, until it was glaringly obvious to Nesta that his conscience was troubling him even more than usual.

'Are you quite sure you shouldn't return to the poor woman?' she asked softly, her natural compassion for an unhappy soul vying with her desire to have John for herself.

'Never!' blustered de Wolfe, with a conviction that deep within himself felt rather hollow. 'I've made the break and I'm standing by it. She does nothing but upbraid and insult me whenever I try to placate her.' At least this part was true, and he used Matilda's abrasive rejection of his attempts at reconciliation to bolster his own confidence.

Nesta sighed and laid her red curls on his solid shoulder.

'What's to become of us, John? I love having you here and feeling the warmth of your body against me, especially at night,' she murmured in Welsh. 'But I feel every eye upon us and hear every mouth whispering when they see us together. I care little for my sake, but I fear for your reputation and your position.'

'To hell with them, *cariad*!' he growled. 'We have been together for almost two years now, so every soul in Exeter and half those in the county of Devon knows about us – not least my wife.'

'But living together, John! That's different somehow.'

'Why should it be?' he protested. 'What difference is there if we make love in the afternoon to making love at midnight?'

Nesta pulled away a little and shook her head at him. 'You are such a direct, practical man, John,' she said sadly. 'But a woman knows there is a difference. Being here all the time, forsaking your own home and hearth and turning your back on your wife, means a commitment far greater than a quick fumble when the chance presents.'

He looked down at her pretty face, a scowl trying to conceal his deep affection for her. 'Are you trying to talk

me into going home, wench?' he growled. 'Have you tired
of me so quickly?'

Little worms of doubt wriggled in both their minds, to
be stamped upon ruthlessly. For Nesta's part, though she
adored this big, gruff man, for several years past she had
become used to living independently. Now, though he was
hardly 'under her feet' all day, she felt obliged to sit with
him as much as possible in the evenings, keeping him
company when she should have been bustling about the
tavern, attending to her business.

John loved sitting with her, slipping his hand around
her to caress her and looking forward to climbing the
ladder to her little room every night. But he missed his
gossiping with Mary in the kitchen shed, fondling and
talking to his old dog Brutus – and even yearned for the
peaceful hours when he could doze in front of his hearth
with a pot of cider.

Just as their talk threatened to become too serious, the
awkward moment was broken by a sudden scuffle at the
back of the taproom, a squeal from one of the serving
maids and the crash of an ale jug as it fell upon a table.

'Bloody men!' snapped Nesta, jumping up to give a
carter who had drunk too much the length of her tongue
and scold him out of the back door until he had sobered
up. John had learned not to interfere unless things got
out of hand, as Nesta's powerful personality, often aided
by a few of her admiring patrons, was usually more than
equal to every occasion.

However, as she was haranguing the carter and pushing him towards the yard, another interruption came
through the front door. The lanky shape of Osric bobbed
his head under the lintel, closely followed by a shorter
figure swathed in a dusty riding cloak. The coroner
looked up in surprise.

'Bailiff! What the devil are you doing here?'

The two men dropped heavily on to the bench on the
other side of his table. William Vado looked exhausted,

and John shouted at old Edwin to bring some mulled ale to warm the bailiff. As the constable began to explain what had happened at the gate, Nesta hurried back, and as soon as she had gathered who the new arrival was, she sent a serving girl off to get some hot food for him. By now, Gwyn had been attracted by the arrival of the man from Ringmore and came over to stand listening at the table.

'. . . so I thought it best to open the gates for him, Crowner,' concluded Osric. 'He said he knew you and that he had come on the authority of the lord of Totnes.'

De Wolfe nodded impatiently, and as soon as Vado had gratefully taken a long pull at his warmed ale, he demanded to hear his news.

'Another killing, Sir John, a real nasty one!' he began. 'When you were in Ringmore last, you told us about the death of that manor-lord near Exeter here – the one who was beheaded.'

John stared at him incredulously. 'Was this a beheading too? Who was killed, for St Peter's sake?'

William Vado shook his head. 'Not beheaded, Crowner. But you said the lord was sort of crucified and this poor man was lashed to a branch by his wrists, then hung by his neck from a tree! It was Joel, the old hermit from Burgh Island.'

De Wolfe and Gwyn recalled the cadaverous recluse who had heard the dying sailor mention 'Saracens'.

'But he was a harmless old fellow, surely?' exclaimed John. 'Not worth robbing and surely no threat to anyone!'

'You say he was hanged from a tree?' boomed Gwyn.

The bailiff quaffed from his pot again before answering. 'Yes, but I doubt that killed him. He was covered in blood and had many knife wounds upon his body.'

More details came out bit by bit, as William related how, soon after dawn, one of the fisherfolk on his way to the beach smelt smoke. He soon found the hermit dangling from a tree, with a small fire still smouldering on the ground directly under the corpse, though there seemed little damage from the flames apart from some roasting of the feet.

'Bloody strange!' growled Gwyn. 'What's going on in our county these days?'

'At least Peter le Calve and his sons were Norman gentry,' muttered John. 'But this Joel was just some old anchorite, of little account except to God and himself.'

A steaming bowl of mutton stew arrived in front of the bailiff, but before he attacked it with his spoon, he looked up at the coroner.

'I wouldn't hasten to dismiss Joel as of no account, Sir John. No one knows much about him, except perhaps our parish priest, who took his confessions, but years ago there was a rumour that he came from a noble family before he renounced the world to live on that island.'

Between dipping a hunk of rough bread into his stew and chewing at it appreciatively, William Vado explained how the fisherman had hurried to Ringmore to report the murder. The bailiff had sent his reeve and some other men to safeguard the body, having learned from the previous episode that the coroner wanted everything left undisturbed. He had taken his horse and ridden hard to Totnes, where he had been given some food and a fresh gelding to get him to Exeter as soon as possible. Thanks to the dry roads, he had made the marathon journey of thirty miles in one day, just failing to reach the city before curfew.

When he had eaten, de Wolfe arranged with Nesta to give him a straw mattress and a blanket up in the loft and, tired to the point of collapse, William gratefully hauled himself up the ladder.

'Remember, we leave at dawn!' shouted John after him, and with fresh jars of ale and cider before them, he and Gwyn sat with Nesta to discuss this latest act in the drama of the mysterious deaths.

'This crucifixion thing,' began the Cornishman. 'Thomas must be right in thinking it must be an unChristian abomination. That must surely mean Saracens.'

'But why now and in a remote English county?' asked Nesta. 'There's no crusading going on that must be avenged.'

'It's quiet out in Palestine, I'll agree,' mused John. 'The King negotiated a long peace with Saladin through the Treaty of Jaffa, though skirmishing never stops out there.'

'And Saladin died more than two years ago,' added Gwyn. 'So I don't see why some Saracens should turn up here and randomly start killing us.'

John shook his head. 'I'll wager it's not random. There's some reason for it, though I'm damned if I can see what it might be.'

They talked on to little effect for some time. To be truthful, John and Nesta were secretly glad that their unhappy heart-searching about Matilda and their own emotional dilemma had been diverted by this news from the far west of Devon. Eventually, mindful of an early start and a long day on horseback ahead of them, the coroner and his officer finished their ale and Gwyn left for Rougemont, where he often found a place to sleep with his soldier friends. They had agreed to let Thomas carry on with his own business, as though his horsemanship had improved since he had given up the side-saddle, he was still an encumbrance when they needed to ride far and fast.

John took himself up to Nesta's small chamber in the loft, passing a snoring William Vado on the way. De Wolfe intended lying awake in anticipation of Nesta's warm body joining him after she had attended to various tasks in the cook shed and brew-house, but when she finally came to bed, he was peacefully asleep. With an affectionate smile, she crept in beside him and snuggled up close, uncaring for at least one night as to what the future might hold for them.

The coroner's return to the banks of the River Avon was not quite as swift as the bailiff's ride to Exeter. His destrier Odin was built for endurance rather than speed and this applied in lesser measure to Gwyn's big brown mare. They got further than Totnes on the first day and slept on the floor of an alehouse in a hamlet a few miles farther south. After another early start, by mid-morning they were at Aveton Giffard, at the head of the Avon estuary. William Vado took them on a track alongside the river which was only passable at low tide, bringing them out near where Thorgils' ship had been moored on their last visit.

'The corpse is just a bit farther on,' promised the bailiff, pointing to a swath of trees along the steep side of the western bank. A few minutes later, they saw a small group of men waiting for them, some recognisable as having been at the inquest in Ringmore. Sliding gratefully from their horses and rubbing their aching bottoms, John and his officer followed Vado into the wood, where gnarled and spindly trees, most covered with grey-green lichen and moss, gave the lonely place a mystical air.

They followed a faint track through the fallen leaves, the river still visible down to their left, until they reached an area where the trees were more widely spaced. Here they came upon a grotesque and pathetic sight which was even more weird than their imaginations had led them to expect.

Hanging by the neck from a branch of an old oak was a thin, naked body. There was a slight breeze and the corpse turned eerily from side to side as if scanning the scenery with open, sightless eyes. It was not very high above the ground, the feet hovering barely a yard over the remains of a small fire, where the unburnt ends of a ring of small logs projected from a heap of grey ash.

As with Peter le Calve, the arms were kept outstretched

by being lashed by the wrists to a length of dead branch passing behind the shoulders, though there were also lashings around each armpit to keep the branch in place. Again like the dead manor-lord, the chest was disfigured by stab wounds, though this time they were many more in number. There were also some on the belly, dribbles of dried blood streaking the skin below each stab.

For a moment, the new arrivals stared in silence at the horrific scene.

'At least he's not been disembowelled or castrated,' grunted Gwyn, as if this were something to the dead man's advantage.

'But he's just as bloody dead!' snarled de Wolfe. 'Poor old sod. Why do this to a harmless hermit?'

There was no answer to this, and they moved nearer for a closer look.

John noticed some scraps of part-burned cloth at the edge of the dead fire.

'That must be the remains of his clothing,' he grunted. 'Even in death they had to further humiliate the old man by stripping him naked!'

Gwyn was looking up rather than down, and nudged his master.

'No need to ponder if this is connected with Shillingford, Crowner! Look at those lashings and the cord around his neck.'

The coroner followed his officer's gaze and nodded. 'More red silk. And I'll wager two marks that those stab wounds are far wider than usual.'

De Wolfe felt nauseated by the evil nature of this killing. Though he had seen far worse mutilations in battle, this cold-blooded perversity both sickened and infuriated him.

'Cut the poor old devil down!' he snapped. 'He's suffered enough indignity.'

As Gwyn and Osbert the reeve supported the frail body, one of the younger men shinned up the tree and clambered out along the branch to cut through the thin but strong cord that was knotted over it.

'We left him there for you to see, Crowner,' said William Vado apologetically. 'There were those in the village who said it wasn't seemly to leave him hanging for two days, but in the circumstances I thought I'd best abide by your rules.'

'It's a dilemma, with Exeter so far away,' admitted John, with uncharacteristic sympathy. 'But you did right, Bailiff, we need all the information we can get to catch these bastards.'

'But where do we start?' growled Gwyn pessimistically.

'Have any strangers been seen around here?' demanded John of the bailiff.

Vado shook his head. 'This is a lonely spot, sir. Even the river fishermen rarely come up from the water's edge. Who's to see any strangers?'

They paused as Gwyn and the reeve went forward to gently take the victim's body as the lad finished cutting through the silken cord. The old hermit was laid on the ground away from the fire, and one of the men took off his ragged cape and laid it over the anchorite's body, a simple act of compassion that was not lost on the coroner.

'When was he last seen alive?' he asked.

'I saw him the day before he went missing,' volunteered one of the fishermen. 'About noon, it was. He was up on the top of his hut, looking out to sea. He does that for us, scanning the water for shoals.'

'Why should he be here?' boomed Gwyn. 'I was wondering whether he was brought here forcibly or whether he was ambushed.'

'Old Joel used to wander the woods looking for fallen branches for his fire,' said the reeve. 'I know this was one of the places he came for that.'

De Wolfe looked around as if for inspiration, but all he saw was the silent trees. If only they could speak, he thought whimsically.

'There are no horse tracks here. Whoever did this must have come on foot,' observed the bailiff.

'No mysterious hooded monks this time?' said John bitterly. This was a mystery with no clues, as far as he was concerned. They watched as the youth with the knife cut the cords holding Joel's arms to the crucifying branch and allowed the dead limbs to be pushed against his side.

'The death stiffness is passing off,' said Gwyn. 'That fits with him dying more than a couple of days ago.' He knelt down alongside the pathetic figure of the old man and gently pulled back the cape to look at Joel's face and trunk. The coroner came to bend over him, hands on knees.

'He didn't die of hanging, anyway,' commented John. 'His face isn't discoloured and there's no swelling around the cord on his neck.'

'Doesn't have to be like that, though I agree it usually is,' said Gwyn, unwilling to be overshadowed in his knowledge of violent death, even by his master.

De Wolfe pointed to some of the stab wounds, which, as he had prophesied, were seen on closer inspection to be very wide.

'The blood dribbling from some of them show he was lying down when they bled, not hanging from a tree.'

This time even Gwyn failed to argue, just nodded his head. He turned the body over and looked at several similar wounds on the back.

'Ten wounds all told, including those on his belly. Only one is needed to kill, so why inflict all these?'

'Does that mean the killers were in some sort of frenzy?' asked the bailiff .

John shrugged. 'Could be – though I've known of some cruel bastards stabbing a man many times just for the pleasure of it.'

Gwyn collected up the cut cords and stuffed them into the shapeless pouch on his belt. 'I'll keep these to add to the others. You never know, maybe we can match them with something if we catch these swine.'

There seemed nothing further to do in the wood, so John told Vado that they would take the body back to Ringmore.

'This is in your manor, I presume?' he asked, looking around.

The bailiff nodded. 'Only just. The boundary with Bigbury is over there.' He waved a hand vaguely. 'No use expecting them to do anything, anyway! They don't have a resident bailiff, he's in Aveton – and their reeve is a drunken idiot.'

They set off through the trees in the opposite direction to which they had come, moving down the side of the estuary towards the sea. The path was narrow and they had to thread their way through the trees, leading their horses by the reins. When they came out of the woods, it was about noon and the tide was in, so John's intention to go on to Burgh Island to look at Joel's hermitage was frustrated. They rounded the point and were able to mount their horses again for the mile or so to the village, leaving the others to tramp in their own time with the skinny body, which four men carried between them, a limb each.

In the old manor-house of Ringmore, William Vado soon organised food and drink and afterwards they sat around the fire-pit in rather muted mood, saddened by the apparently senseless murder of a penniless recluse.

'How long has this Joel been here?' asked Gwyn.

'Since I was a child, and that's more than twenty years ago,' answered William. 'I don't remember him coming.'

The reeve, Osbert de Newetone, was a decade older and recalled Joel's arrival.

'He just walked into the village one day. Autumn, it was, a real good harvest year. He wore a plain tunic and a pilgrim's hat, was bare-foot and carried a pilgrim's staff. He kept those clothes for years until they fell to pieces. Then someone in the village gave him the cast-offs he wore to this day.'

'And you know nothing of where he came from?' persisted the coroner.

The bailiff turned up his hands. 'He never said and it wasn't our place to ask. But he spoke well, and he could read words on parchment when someone needed to. I don't remember where this story came from about him being a former nobleman or knight, but I could quite believe it.'

'How did he come to settle on that island?' queried Gwyn, sucking ale from his moustache.

'When he arrived, he said he was a looking for a place of solitude to live out his life, praise God and atone for his sins,' said Osbert. 'The loneliest place we could think of was the island of St Michael de la Burgh. Our priest said there was no reason to object, so off he went and built that hut.'

Further questioning produced nothing useful, and when they had finished their ale and warmed up by the fire, John and Gwyn reluctantly shrugged on their riding capes and followed the local men outside, where the overcast sky was threatening snow or sleet, though at the moment it was dry, but with a biting east wind.

As they trudged up the road, John turned to the bailiff. 'I suppose your Father Walter will have housed the corpse in the barn again,' he said cynically.

To his mild surprise, Vado shook his head. 'When I told him what had happened, he said that as a solitary hermit and a man of God, he was entitled to be laid before the altar until we buried him.'

When they got to the tiny church, they found that this was indeed the case. The mortal remains of Joel, draped in a rather grubby linen sheet which was probably a spare altar-cloth, lay on a rough bier in the centre of the square room where God was worshipped in Ringmore.

'We'll have to carry him out for the inquest,' said John. 'It's not seemly to expose his wounded body to the jury in here.' It was too cold and windy to hold the formalities in the churchyard, so a couple of men carried the corpse-table by its handles over to the tithe barn.

Most of the men from the village, together with a few fisherfolk from the beach, formed an audience and a jury. John and Gwyn went through the usual routine, but when the coroner came to determine 'Presentment of Englishry', Father Walter interrupted him.

'I would speak to you alone for a moment, Crowner,' he demanded in a tone that anticipated no refusal. John walked over to the doorway, where the sour-faced priest had been watching the proceedings with apparent indifference.

'From what I saw at your last inquisition here, this "presentment" business seems aimed at distinguishing Saxons from those of mainly Norman blood?'

'It does indeed,' said de Wolfe. 'But in this case, his very name and the fact that he can read and write must indicate that he is unlikely to be a Saxon peasant.'

The florid-faced priest nodded, the bags under his slightly bloodshot eyes sagging like those of some old bloodhound. He looked around at his flock in the barn and nudged John farther towards the open air, to be out of their hearing. 'I can certainly confirm that,' he said in a low voice. 'Now that he is dead, I am not so concerned about keeping too strictly to the sanctity of the confessional. At least I can tell you his true name and something of his origins.'

The coroner waited expectantly. Any information would be welcome, rather than the void that seemed to surround these deaths.

'He would have been seventy years old at his death, calculating from what he told me some years ago. Joel's full name was Sir Joel de Valle Torta, from a noble family with estates in Normandy and Essex. He had been a Knight Templar many years earlier.'

De Wolfe uttered a low whistle of surprise. 'A Templar! Usually, once a Templar, always a Templar. How came he to be living in obscurity on a rock stuck in the sea?'

'I cannot reveal much of the detail, even after his death. But he said that his sins weighed so heavily upon him that he received a special dispensation to leave the Order to become an anchorite, cutting himself off from the world.'

'Then his sins must indeed have been unusually vile! Can you tell me what they might have been? It may have a bearing upon his murder.'

Father Walter pondered for a moment, as if communing with some higher authority – which he may well have been doing.

'It must suffice to say that it concerned his behaviour as a soldier. He came to confession regularly and it was always the same lament – his overwhelming guilt for his own actions in warfare. He was ever penitent and sought absolution.'

The coroner instinctively felt that this was important in understanding the man's death, so he pressed the parish priest harder.

'In which campaigns would he have served? There were bloody episodes in so many, from Ireland to Jerusalem.'

Then he had a sudden thought. 'But he has been here for over twenty years, so he could not have been with us in the last attempt in the Holy Land. Acre was the place where so many men have had cause for guilty consciences over the foul deeds that took place there.'

The heavily built vicar grunted. 'All I can tell you is that the cause of his anguish was indeed in Outremer – but long ago, for he was at the Second Crusade. That's all I know – at least, that's all I can tell you.'

The way his fleshy lips clamped shut indicated that no amount of persuasion would make him say more, but John was satisfied – though still mystified.

'The Second Crusade! The link that joins all these deaths!' he murmured.

As Father Walter swung away with an air of finality, John went back to complete the short inquest. Though it displayed the usual frustrating pattern of the previous enquiries into this series of killings, he left Ringmore with much to think about and to discuss with Thomas and Gwyn.

Two days later, the trio were breaking their fast in the cheerless room above the gatehouse in Exeter's castle. The cathedral bell was tolling for Prime, just before the eighth hour of the morning, and Gwyn was finishing a pork pasty, before tackling his bread and cheese.

Thomas had not long come from his early chantry Mass and was sitting at the table, preparing a palimpsest, a second-hand sheet of parchment. After scraping off the original writing, he was sanding and chalking it, ready to write a record of the Ringmore inquest, whenever the coroner was ready to dictate. But John was in a contemplative mood as he chewed on a strip of dried salt beef, which looked like leather. At least it gave him a thirst, which he quenched at intervals from a pint pot sitting in front of him.

'Thomas, you are a man of considerable intellect. Give us the benefit of that sharp mind of yours!'

The little clerk was unsure whether his master was being complimentary or sarcastic, but decided on the former. His peaky face creased into a smile of pride.

'On what, exactly, Crowner?' he asked, putting aside his parchment and rubbing his thin fingers together to rid them of the chalk dust.

'We have three dead men and one more injured, the only connection between them that I can see being the Second Crusade. Peter le Calve's father and this Templar, Joel, were actually there – and the steward of Shillingford and the injured son were part of the le Calve household. Is that just a coincidence, Thomas?'

The clerk pursed his lips in thought, but before he could reply, Gwyn interrupted.

'This damned Second Crusade – before my time. What was it all about?'

The teacher in Thomas leapt to the challenge. 'Giving such numbers to Crusades is unrealistic, really. God's war against the enemies of Christ goes on all the time – there's always fighting somewhere against the unbelievers. But yes, the ones where kings and princes get involved – or there's a major disaster – they tend to get numbered.'

'All I've ever heard is that this second one was a disaster, right enough,' grunted the Cornishman.

'Many of those who set off from the West never reached the Holy Land, as far as I remember,' said the coroner. 'Didn't they go off marauding on the way? And many more were wiped out on the journey?'

Thomas nodded energetically, his great store of knowledge bursting to be free. 'Many of the German army never even got out of Europe – they found wars to fight and cities to loot on the way.'

'What's this got to do with our killings here?' muttered Gwyn suspiciously.

'If this old Crusader, Joel, was so conscience-ridden that he sat on Burgh Island for twenty years, he must have been involved in something really bad,' observed John. 'What happened that could have been so awful? Something like Acre in the last Crusade?'

Thomas tapped his fingers excitedly on the trestle table. 'Damascus! I'll wager it was Damascus.'

The other two waited, impressed by their clerk's grasp of history, recently enlarged by his readings in the cathedral library.

'That's what caused the Crusade to collapse, the last straw in a catalogue of mistakes. Two kings answered the call to arms by Pope Eugenius and St Bernard of Clairvaux after the Mohammedans captured the city of Edessa. One was Louis of France and the other Conrad of Germany.'

'Didn't the English turn out for that one?' asked Gwyn.

'The country was too concerned with civil war then, between Stephen and Matilda. Quite a big English contingent set off from Dartmouth, but stopped for months in Portugal to kick out the Moors. That was about the only successful campaign in the whole Crusade.'

'So what's this about Damascus?' snapped de Wolfe.

'It was the final fiasco, both political and military. The two kings decided to besiege it, but their forces were so depleted and their tactics were so bad that they had to abandon the attempt after only three days. In their humiliating retreat, they inflicted terrible revenge and bloodshed on the surrounding inhabitants. I suspect that was the most likely source of the hermit's guilt.'

'This was all of forty-seven years ago,' objected Gwyn. 'None of us was even born then.'

'But Joel was! He would have been a lusty young fighter of twenty-three, if he was seventy when he died,' Thomas pointed out. 'And old Arnulf le Calve would have been about the same age.'

'As would Gervaise, Richard de Revelle's father!' added John.

The other two looked at him, puzzled looks on their faces.

'But his son's not been murdered, more's the pity,' rumbled Gwyn.

'No, but Peter le Calve's son was shot at – and no doubt the poor steward was mistaken for the other son,' retorted John.

There was a thoughtful silence as they pondered this until, as usual, the phlegmatic Gwyn acted as the brake on their enthusiasm.

'Hold on, wait a moment!' he grumbled. 'This is almost half a century ago, for God's sake! And we're halfway across the world from where it happened.'

He tore a piece of bread from the loaf on his lap and used his dagger to cut a wedge of hard yellow cheese to accompany it, still not convinced that all this speculation would help them discover who had killed Thorgils and the others. 'I still don't see what we can do about it! Who are the swine going to attack next?'

His officer's last question caused the coroner to feel a niggle of worry gnawing away at his mind. If this theory about vengeful Saracens was right, then they had dispatched a knight who had been in the Levant at the time of that ill-fated Crusade – and had killed the son of another, going on to wound a grandson and slaying his steward, probably by mistake. If this really was a blood feud involving the families of the perpetrators of some ancient evil, then what about the de Revelles? Old Gervaise had long been in his grave, safely beyond revenge – but if the pattern of murder was to be repeated, then was his family at risk? John cared little about Richard de Revelle, but in spite of everything he was certainly concerned about Matilda, the daughter of Gervaise.

Abruptly, he shook off the spiral of worry that had descended upon him. For God's sake, he thought, he was sitting in Exeter on a cold Monday morning, in a castle with four score men-at arms near by. His wife was either safely at home or among her friends in St Olave's church or the cathedral. This idea about secretive Saracen killers slinking about, intent on murder most foul, was surely a fantasy.

'You're probably right, Gwyn,' he conceded. 'We're letting our imaginations run away with us. But I'd still like to find the evil bastards who did this. I'm sure the answer lies out west, somewhere around Ringmore.'

chapter twelve

In which Hilda goes on a pilgrimage

The two ship-masters who had worked for Thorgils were now more devoted to Hilda of Holcombe than ever. When her husband had been alive, she had looked after their wives and families if things went wrong while they were at sea. Now that he was dead, Hilda had seen to it that the dependants of their comrades, the murdered sailors, remained housed and fed. The latest sign of her concern for them was the arrangement she was entering into with Sir John and the portreeve, which would ensure that they and their crews would remain employed in the only trade they knew. So when Hilda asked them to take her to Salcombe, they agreed without demur. After all, the ships were hers and they were her servants, but they did it willingly, rather than as a duty.

'We need to go there soon anyway,' said Roger Watts, the older captain. He was a short, rotund man with a weather-beaten face and bright red hair. 'Must keep an eye on those shipwrights who are repairing the *Mary*.'

He did not see it as his place to ask the mistress why she wanted to make even a short voyage so late in the season, but the other ship-master, Angerus de Wile, was not so reticent. A lanky man of about twenty-eight, with an under-shot lower jaw that gave him the appearance of a bull-baiting dog, he respectfully wondered why Hilda wished to brave the cold and the possibly bad weather.

'For several reasons, Angerus,' she replied, as she

poured them each a jug of cider in the kitchen room of her fine house. 'I have a need to see where my husband died on the ship he loved. Somehow it would help me to close off that part of my life. But I also wish to make some enquiries in the district, to know if anything has been heard of the villains who killed Thorgils.'

They knew better than to dissuade Hilda, as they knew from experience that her gentle manner hid an iron will. Once her mind was made up, nothing could divert her.

On a dawn high-tide two days later, the cog *St Radegund*, a slightly smaller version of the *Mary and Child Jesus,* sailed out of Dawlish creek and headed briskly south-west in a wintry east wind. Hilda had many times accompanied her husband on voyages to Brittany, Normandy and the Rhine, so was impervious to the pitching and rolling of the unladen vessel, but her maid, who was chaperoning her, soon wished she was dead. However, so favourable was the wind that her agony was short-lived, for they rounded Start Point by early afternoon and before dusk were safely at anchor in the calm waters of the Salcombe estuary.

Rowed ashore in the curragh, they were settled in one of the quayside inns by Roger Watts, who suppressed his concern at leaving his mistress without a male escort for some unknown purpose of her own.

'You will wait for me until I wish to return, Roger,' she ordered, giving him a purse of silver pennies to keep him and his crew fed for a few days. 'I may go on a short pilgrimage, so I cannot say exactly how long I will be away.'

With that he had to be content, and he went back to his vessel, where the crew slept in the hold, coming ashore to eat.

The following morning, Hilda was taken by Watts and Angerus to a boatyard in a small side creek just outside the town, where the *Mary* was beached, so that the shipwrights could check every plank. They were also restoring some caulking, lost during the buffeting she had received when driven ashore at Burgh Island. The new mast and main spar lay on the shore, ready for stepping when the hull was finished. Hilda clambered up a plank to her deck and tactfully the two ship-masters called the shipwright and his mates aside, so that she could be left in peace for a while. There was nothing to see on the small area of deck aft of the open hold. There were no bloodstains or scars on the timber from swinging swords, but the blonde Saxon woman stood silently for a few minutes, turning to slowly view each part of the little ship. She was remembering her voyages with Thorgils, and his amiable face came back to her clearly as she stared at the patch of planking where he would have stood to grip the big steering oar that rested in its bracket on the right side of the stern. She shed no tears, but her resolve to try to bring his killers to justice was hardened by the experience. After a time, she left the cog and had a few polite and intelligent words with the men who were making her seaworthy again, before asking Roger Watts to accompany her back to the inn. He left her there, still with misgivings about leaving such an attractive woman alone in a strange town, but resigned to falling in with her inflexible wishes.

Hilda then took her maid shopping in the bustling little town, which was becoming an important harbour and fishing centre. Wooden houses straggled along the steep banks of the branching estuary, but around the fine new church some stone buildings indicated the growing prosperity of Salcombe. Hilda's purchases were simple enough, and a short walk along the narrow winding lane that was the main street provided them all. At one stall she bought a long hooded cloak of brown wool with a cross sewn on one shoulder to indicate that she was a pilgrim. At a shop whose shutter hinged down to display its goods she haggled a little over a pair of strong walking shoes, and at another stall she bought a black felt coif, a close-fitting helmet that had laces which tied under the chin. On the way back to the tavern, they stopped by an old man who was crouching at the side of the street, amid a collection of walking sticks, shepherd's crooks, crutches and the like. From him she bought a thumb-stick, a holly pole with a small Y-shaped top, which would do service as a pilgrim's staff. Taking her purchases back to their tiny chamber, she changed into the sombre clothes she had bought and gave her bemused maid instructions for the next few days.

'I will be going away alone for a short time, on a pilgrimage. You are to stay here all the time, understand? Roger Watts will come every day to make sure that there are no problems. You can go as far as the church and you may look at the stalls and shops, but nothing more. I have left money with the tavern-wife so that you may eat and sleep until I come back.'

The maid, a meek and dutiful girl, adored her mistress, who had taken her in when her widowed father had drowned at sea. She too was worried that Hilda was going off unaccompanied, but like the ship-masters she knew better than to try to dissuade her.

The next stop for the determined widow was the church of the Holy Trinity, a fine new building dominating the surrounding houses. She stood inside the empty nave and prayed with bowed head and clasped hands for the soul of Thorgils and his crew – and for the help of the Almighty in giving her strength to seek out the identity of his murderers. When she had finished, she went in search of the parish priest, tracking him down in the sacristy that opened off the chancel. He was an amiable and sympathetic man, a Saxon like herself. Tailoring her story a little, she explained that her husband had died at sea off the coast in Bigbury Bay and she wanted to make a pilgrimage in memory of him as near to the spot as possible. She enquired whether there were any pilgrims going in that direction whom she might join for safety and company.

'Indeed there are, my daughter,' he said earnestly. 'We get many folk landing here by ship from farther east, in order to make their way across country to Tavistock Abbey or farther down into Cornwall. Groups of them leave almost daily.'

She also learnt that there was a small chapel and a holy well of some repute, only some seven miles along that route, which was certainly inland from Bigbury Bay, where her husband had been lost.

'There will be a group leaving here at noon, no doubt aiming to reach Aveton Giffard before nightfall. Travel with them and in the morning you will be at St Anne's Chapel, as virtually all pilgrims stop there to pray and take advantage of the holy well.'

And so it turned out, as she was welcomed by a dozen cheerful pilgrims who had come from Rye by sea, on their way home to the West Country after their pilgrimage to Canterbury. Hilda was surprised by their merry manners – they seemed more like a party coming from a feast than devout pilgrims – but she was grateful for their ready acceptance of her company and their hospitality. Five of them were women, mostly of mature years, and at least two of them were widows, obviously hoping that their pilgrimage might land them a husband. Indeed, she suspected that a number of the band assumed that she was on the same mission, but for the short time she would be with them, she was content to let them think what they wanted.

Glad of her new strong shoes, Hilda walked with them gamely as they covered the league between Salcombe and Aveton before dusk fell. The men in their broad-brimmed pilgrim's hats, the women in their warm cloaks and hoods or snug coifs like her own, they marched along robustly, all with staffs and sticks to aid them. Accompanied by one man who played his bagpipes and another with a flute, they sang a mixture of psalms, hymns and popular ballads, some of them rather roguish. Hilda's education was broadened, as her former image of pilgrims being dour and sanctimonious was shattered by these gregarious, cheerful people.

Aveton was a large village, belonging to the manor of the Giffards. All she learned that night was that the land had been taken from her own Saxon people by the Normans and given to Walter Giffard, the standard-bearer of William the Conqueror at the battle of Hastings. They stayed in a cheap alehouse that night, where a penny bought a plain but substantial meal and a bag stuffed with straw to sleep on. Next morning they set off after a bowl of oat gruel and a hunk of bread, marching the few miles to St Anne's Chapel, where they went through the routine of drinking the water from the holy well and kneeling in prayer in the tiny chapel at the cross-roads. It was little more than a wooden hut with a turf roof, but inside there was an air of sanctity that was almost palpable.

Here Hilda left her companions, not without some regrets on both sides. The pilgrim band were quite concerned at leaving this comely woman alone in the middle of what they considered a rural desert, but she assured them, with tongue in cheek, that she had relatives in a nearby village with whom she would stay.

As they plodded off into the distance, bagpipes wailing and singing their hymns, Hilda suddenly felt very much alone. She turned back into the little chapel and, after another prayer, sought out the elderly man who was its custodian, though he seemed not to be in holy orders, even of the lowest grade. Half blind and bow legged, the old man, whose name, she learned, was Ivo de Brun, was friendly enough, especially when Hilda pressed a whole penny into his arthritic fingers.

After some amiable platitudes, Hilda began asking him some questions.

'Apart from pilgrims passing through, do you get any strangers here?'

The old fellow's milky eyes fixed on her, to pick up the blurred outlines of her face.

'Lady, I think your presence here is not altogether as a pilgrim. You are the second person to ask that question,' he said with a knowing smile. 'The King's Coroner himself was here not long ago on the same mission.'

Although John had told her that he had been in Ringmore for the inquest on Thorgils, he had not specified all the other places where he had sought information, so she was surprised to hear that he had already ploughed this particular furrow.

'Would this also be connected with the deaths of those shipmen?' asked Ivo. 'That is the only matter which has disturbed the peace of this area for a long time.'

Hilda felt she should be frank with the custodian and told him that she was the widow of the ship-master who had been killed, come to visit the scene of his death.

'Then it is to Ringmore you should go, poor lady,' said the keeper of the chapel. 'They know most about the matter.'

'I will do that, good man. But what were you able to tell Sir John, the crowner, who is a good friend of mine?'

'Like you, he wanted to know if I had seen any strangers at around the time of the wrecking of your husband's vessel. All I could recall was that four cowled monks passed this way and strangely did not come into the chapel to offer a prayer, as is almost always their desire and indeed duty.'

Hilda's heart gave an extra thump. John de Wolfe had told her about such monks being seen at the time of Peter le Calve's horrid death, but had not mentioned any being seen down here.

'Where did they go? Do you recall?' she almost snapped.

'I told the coroner they marched straight off down the Bigbury lane there.' He waved a hand vaguely in the approximate direction. 'The gentleman and his officer went down that way to make enquiries, but I never heard any more of the matter until you came just now.'

Hilda felt a little deflated. The energetic John had already followed up every possible lead, so it seemed. She should have more sense than to think that a solitary woman like herself could achieve more than a highly experienced law officer like John de Wolfe. Still, she was here now, so she might as well make the most of the opportunity. But the day was wearing on and she felt that she must first go to Ringmore, which was her prime destination. Another penny made the custodian even more anxious to help, and he explained that the small village of Bigbury was about a mile along one of the arms of the crossroads, with Ringmore slightly farther down another.

With a final genuflexion, Hilda made the sign of the Cross towards the little altar and took her leave of the old fellow. With her thumb in the crook of her holly staff, she strode out towards Ringmore, apprehensive at being for the first time alone in a remote and deserted countryside, far from her familiar villages of Dawlish and Holcombe. However, after the first half-mile, in which she was neither robbed nor ravished by footpads or outlaws, her confidence returned, and she stepped out more confidently along the narrow track, rutted by cartwheels and fouled by ox-droppings, as were most of the country roads.

The lane began dropping, and she sensed the familiar smell and feel of the sea, though it was still more than a mile distant. Trees became lower and sparser, with gorse, broom and heather taking their place.

Then the track entered a shallow valley, where more trees were able to shelter from the gales, and soon some strip-fields heralded the edge of a village. She saw the tiny church at the top end of the hamlet and then the scattered dwellings, barn and manor-house that made up Ringmore.

A couple of bare-foot children appeared, guiltily clutching some scarred apples that they had obviously stolen from someone's trees, the last survivors of the autumn harvest. The sight of a strange woman in their village was enough to make them forget their crime for the moment and they stared open mouthed at this apparition from the outside world. Hilda asked them where she could find the bailiff, as William Vado was the only person that John had mentioned in Ringmore. Wordlessly, one pointed towards the stockade of the manor-house and she went towards it, soon meeting two men who came out of the gate, leading a pair of oxen. They stared at her curiously but said nothing, and she went inside the compound and peered in through the open main door. A couple of girls and an older woman were scattering new rushes on the floor, and stopped to stare open-mouthed at her as if she had just dropped down from the moon.

Within minutes, she had explained who she was to the woman, and as soon as the servant had assured herself that this was an earthbound woman and a Saxon as well, she was eager to help.

'I'll fetch the bailiff's wife directly,' she said in an accent so thick that even the village-born Hilda had difficulty in following it.

With much bustling and shouting, another woman appeared with a young baby swaddled across her chest in a shawl, two other young girls hanging on to her skirts. Once again, explanations were made and the bailiff's wife made Hilda welcome, taking her through to one of the rooms off the hall, where a couple more young women and an older grandmother were sewing and preparing food for the evening meal.

'My husband is out on his rounds,' explained Martha Vado. 'He has four vills to supervise for his lord's steward in Totnes, but he will be home well before the daylight ends.'

Hilda was pressed to take food and drink and afterwards offered to nurse the new baby, a job she remembered well from her days in Holcombe, where she

THE ELIXIR OF DEATH

had three younger brothers and a sister. With the other women clustered around, even though one was still plucking a pair of ducks, she explained all that she knew about the death of her husband and went on to tell them of the murder of the lord of Shillingford and the attack on his son and steward, which seemed to the coroner to be connected with the deaths of Thorgils and his crew.

The women were round eyed with wonder at these tales of mayhem from the world outside, which on top of the shipmen's killing and the murder of old Joel from Burgh Island gave them more to gossip about than for years past. Like the old man at St Anne's Chapel, they were concerned at an unaccompanied woman moving around the countryside, but Hilda impressed on them that she felt it her bounden duty to find out all she could about the death of her husband.

She said the same to William Vado and his reeve when they returned late in the afternoon. When he discovered that she was a friend and indeed now almost a business partner of Sir John de Wolfe and one of the Exeter portreeves, he became deferential and sympathetic.

'Tomorrow, we will take you to where the vessel was beached and also to where your unfortunate husband was found,' he promised. 'Also you may see the church where his body lay in dignified rest for a time. No doubt our Father Walter will speak to you to reassure you on that point.'

That night, Hilda was given one of the best mattresses, one stuffed with goose feathers rather than straw or ferns. She bedded down with the women and children in the side room, Martha and William Vado taking the other small chamber where the new baby slept in an old box alongside them.

The following morning she followed the itinerary that the bailiff had suggested, calling at the church for a prayer and a rather short, stiff interview with the parish priest, who seemed unimpressed by her pilgrimage to the

239

scenes of her husband's demise. Then William found her
a pony, which she sat on easily with just a sack for a saddle,
and they went down to the beach opposite Burgh Island
to view the resting place of the *Mary* and the place where
Thorgils and his men had been found. She looked up at
the now deserted cell on top of the island and was told
that Joel had been laid to rest in the churchyard at
Ringmore, where he had spent the last two decades of his
life.

'The parson revealed that he had been a Knight of the
Templars,' said William Vado. 'But no one seemed to
know anything of his family, and we thought he would
have preferred to be laid to rest among us.'

Hilda realised that she had learned nothing at all of
any use to her from these well-meaning people, mainly
because they had nothing to tell her. What now exercised
her mind was the shadowy image of three black-robed
monks, who seemed to have appeared too many times for
it to be coincidence. They had been seen on the track up
from the other beach near Ringmore, then at St Anne's
Chapel and once again far away near Shillingford. True,
it seemed at their first appearance that there were four,
rather than three, but she felt that these appearances
might have some significance.

Now this single-minded woman wanted to pursue their
last sighting in this area, which seemed to be down the
road from the chapel, according to the poor vision of the
old custodian. She needed to get away from Ringmore
now and with a twinge of conscience at her deception,
decided to fabricate a means of leaving her most recent
hosts.

'I am meeting another group of pilgrims at St Anne's
Chapel,' she lied. 'I met them in church at Salcombe
some days ago and they said they would be returning
from Tavistock to take ship at Salcombe again, passing the
chapel hopefully around noon.'

The Vado family insisted on filling her with food

before she left, and the bailiff sent his older sister and Osbert, his reeve, as chaperone and escort on the short journey up to the chapel. They wanted to stay with her to see her safely reunited with her mythical pilgrims, but she managed to dissuade them by saying that she would remain in the chapel in prayer for her husband and his men until the travellers arrived. Thankfully, the bandy old man did not blurt out his ignorance of any pilgrims due to arrive and, with expressions of genuine good feeling, the pair from Ringmore said farewell and left for home.

After they had vanished around a bend in the track, Ivo de Brun, the scarecrow that cared for the little chapel, gave Hilda a conspiratorial leer.

'I think, my lady, that you have other things in mind.'

She sighed and nodded. 'I have indeed! I have sworn not to rest until the murderers of my husband have been brought to justice. I need to follow every suggestion that might lead the law officers to them.'

'I told you that the crowner has already been here on that mission,' the old man pointed out. 'He went down to Bigbury, but I doubt he learned anything useful.'

'I know Sir John well,' she answered. 'He has told me of the monks you saw and he tried to discover more, but to no avail. Yet the itching of my thumbs tells me that some mystery attaches to those men.'

The custodian shrugged his pitifully thin shoulders.

'Go you then to Bigbury, lady. It is but a mile or so down the road, so I doubt any harm can befall you in that distance. Then return here and wait for more travellers who can see you safely back to Salcombe, for the roads are no place for a solitary woman, especially at this time of year. It threatens snow again today.'

The sky had a pink-tinged greyness that confirmed his forecast, but at least the cutting east wind had abated. Hilda pulled her pilgrim's cloak more firmly around her and thanked the old man before setting off down the other branch of the junction. She trudged along the narrow track, the ground firm where the mud had dried. On either side were scattered bushes and low trees almost devoid of leaves. There was no cultivated land here, and beyond the irregular tracts of heathland the edge of the forest stood in mottled shades of black and brown. There were no travellers on this path, and the only life she saw was a slinking red fox and a pair of circling buzzards. More used to the mild bustle of Dawlish, for a while she had the fancy that all humanity had perished and she was alone in a world deserted by all but the animals and birds.

It seemed a long mile, but eventually she came into the small hamlet, a dozen crofts and tofts around a church, a blacksmith's hut and a cottage with a drooping bush above the door, the universal sign of a tavern. Behind the village, a band of strip-fields ran up to the edge of the dark forest, which loomed oppressively into the distance, where it dipped down towards the valley of the Avon.

Though hammering came from the open front of the smithy, there was almost no one in sight, other than an old woman sitting on a tree stump outside her tumble-down cottage, spinning wool from a distaff under her arm on to a spindle hanging from one gnarled hand. She looked up curiously as Hilda approached, the sight of a solitary woman being unusual in these parts, even if she was wearing the garb of a pilgrim.

'Are you lost, good girl?' the crone asked, her bright eyes taking in every detail of the new arrival's appearance. 'There's nothing down this road other than the river and the sea.'

'I thought I could get back to Aveton, mother,' answered Hilda, putting on her strongest rural accent, honed in her own village of Holcombe.

'You can, if the tide is out,' replied the dame. 'Though you'll be hard pressed to walk there before nightfall.'

'Can I find some food and drink here, mother?' she replied. 'I have some pennies and that looks like an ale-house.'

'Madge will give you something there, no doubt. But a fair woman like you should not be walking the roads alone, especially these days.'

Something in the spinner's voice made Hilda take notice.

'What is happening these days to give you concern, mother?' she asked.

The old woman's brows came together and she looked somehow furtive.

'Strange things are going on in the forest hereabouts,' she muttered. 'Ghostly figures seen at night, food and livestock vanishing. Voices calling in the woods . . . I fear for our souls in this vill.'

Hilda felt a frisson of unease shiver up her spine. 'Have you seen three or four Benedictines come through here at any time lately?' she asked.

The aged woman shook her head. 'I hear that some king's officer came asking the same question not long ago. But we've seen no monks here, only ghostly shapes in white robes in the woods, according to our sexton.'

Hilda thanked the lady and moved on to the alehouse, where the buxom widow Madge told her much the same story after she had given her a plain but wholesome meal for a ha'penny.

'The village men are fond of their drink, but so they have been these many years,' she explained. 'Yet it's only in the last few weeks that they have been telling these tales about strange goings-on in the forest.'

Hilda had given a cautious version of her own story, of the widow seeking answers about her husband's murder. The ale-wife, a widow herself, had responded with sympathy, though she too was surprised and curious about an attractive woman wandering the byroads alone.

'What do you think is the explanation for these visions?' asked Hilda, as she sat at the only table and ate fat bacon, eggs and beans, with fresh bread washed down with cider.

Madge, her ample bottom overflowing a stool near by, lifted her hands in supplication.

'Who knows such things? Even allowing for the romancing of some of our menfolk with too much ale in them, something unusual is happening in the forest. Months ago, men sent by the manor-lord went into the woods on the other side from the village and stayed there a week or more. We heard distant hammering, but no one was allowed near – not that anyone wished to prowl, given the villains and outlaws that sometimes infest the forest.'

'Is there anything deep in the woods? Buildings or suchlike?' asked Hilda.

'Only ruins, those of an ancient castle and next to it what was once a priory in the old days. I've never seen them myself, I keep clear of such places, but my father spoke of these derelict remains. He used to go in there poaching, I must admit. Men are too afeared these days – one lad a month ago was beaten up and almost killed by some rough fellows in there.'

At that point, the landlady went off to pour a quart of ale for a ploughman, who seemed to have come in mainly to ogle this handsome woman who had descended upon their village. Left alone with her trencher of food, Hilda thought about what the two village women had told her about the surrounding forest and became convinced that something was going on in there that was connected with these crimes. Her feelings were mainly based on what John de Wolfe had told her about this whole area . . . the murder of the shipmen, the warnings from Winchester about a new Prince John rising, the possibility of Moorish involvement and, not least, the appearance in several sites of these hooded monks. To such an intelligent and determined woman as Hilda of Dawlish, this was a challenge that could not be ignored. If there was someone hidden away in those woods, then surely a circumspect reconnoitre might be well worth the effort?

'Can you give me a corner to sleep in tonight, goodwife?' she asked, when Madge had finished serving the nosy villein. 'I need to be at St Anne's Chapel tomorrow to meet my pilgrim friends and return to Salcombe,' she said, manipulating the truth again.

They agreed on a palliasse alongside Madge's own in the lean-to behind the inn, as well as another meal that evening. Then Hilda announced that she was going for a walk to familiarise herself with the village, while daylight lasted, it now being early afternoon. The ale-wife looked troubled at this and urged her not to stray too far.

'Certainly don't go into the forest,' she declared. 'And be sure to be back well before dark!'

Hilda demurely agreed, put on her cloak and, once out of sight of the tavern, made straight for the edge of the forest. The lonely atmosphere of deep woodland held no terrors for her, a country girl who had spent well over half her life around Holcombe. She found a deer path and, by a combination of natural instinct and observation of the motion of the drifting grey clouds above the trees, aimed her feet directly away from the village, towards where she gathered the old ruins lay.

After the better part of an hour, she began to wonder whether she was doing the most foolish thing in her whole life, blundering about an unknown forest on the strength of a couple of drunken yokels' fantasies about ghosts. She eventually stopped and began debating whether she should turn around and go back. Then she heard a horse neigh in the distance and wondered if she had come almost right through the trees and reached the other side of the forest. The next thing she noticed was through her nose, rather than her ears. A waft of wood-smoke reached her nostrils, and carefully she walked ahead again, tracking down the smell until she could see a thin line of grey smoke wavering in the wind. It seemed to be coming from the ground itself, and when she delicately trod towards it, saw that it was indeed rising from the centre of a larger thicket of brambles.

That was the last she saw for some time, as suddenly an oat-sack was thrown over her head from behind. Rough hands pinned her arms to her side, dragging her off her feet and carrying her bodily away, her cries of distress muffled by the smelly hessian of the dirty sack.

During the week that followed, life for John de Wolfe went on much the same as usual – at least, much the same as since he had moved out of Martin's Lane and taken up residence with his mistress Nesta. He was by turns happy and uneasy, then content and irritated. Life had changed radically, even though the people he was with were the same and the orbit of his life still revolved mostly within the same quarter of a mile.

He sat now at his table in the Bush, warmed by the same fire and drinking the same good ale brewed by the woman he loved, yet he could no longer slump by his own hearth, stroking the head of his old hound until it was time for a leisurely amble down to the Bush. He leaned now against the door-post of the inn's cook shed, watching Nesta and her girls preparing food for hungry customers, yet he could no longer perch on Mary's little stool in her kitchen, cadging hot pastries and gossiping about the day's events.

Passionate nights in Nesta's warm bed were a delight, and he certainly did not miss the barren mattress in Matilda's solar. But even up in the little room in the Bush's loft, he felt it was somehow unseemly for Gwyn or a castle man-at-arms to come tapping on Nesta's door when there was some midnight emergency, rather than being woken by Mary climbing the solar steps. In short, the familiar routines of the past couple of years had become so ingrained that this abrupt change to a different set of routines had unsettled him. He realised this well enough himself, but was powerless to shake off the mood of unease. John even daydreamed about giving up this split lifestyle and running off with Nesta to live in Wales or

Cornwall, making a fresh start. But the practicalities were insuperable. There was his obligation to the King to continue as coroner, as well as Nesta's attachment to her beloved Bush, which gave her both an intense interest in life as well as a fair living.

The cold light of every morning saw him back in his chamber in the castle gatehouse, and the familiar round of duties drove any decisions about the future direction of his life into the background once again. John called briefly at his house in Martin's Lane every day, choosing early afternoon when he knew Matilda would either be snoring in her bed during an afternoon siesta or on her knees in St Olave's church. He went there to check that Mary had sufficient money to meet domestic expenses and to replenish the cash in his chest in the solar for Matilda's benefit, even though she had an income of her own from her father, dispensed by Richard de Revelle. John's earnings came from his venture with Hugh de Relaga, which was increasing in value as the months went by, thanks to the boom in Exeter's economy.

On calling at the house almost a week after he had moved out, he learned from Mary that on this particular day he need not have timed his visit to avoid his wife, as she had had just departed again with her brother to his manor at Revelstoke, taking Lucille with her.

'She didn't say when she was expecting to come back,' added Mary, severely. 'So you just carry on back to your hideout until you come to your senses!'

Any other cook-maid would have received a whipping from their master for such forthright criticism, but given their past history, John knew that Mary was trying to be helpful – and deep down, he suspected that she was right.

Hilda was a very intelligent woman and she rapidly decided that her best chance of survival was to play the part of a simple peasant who would be no danger to anyone. It soon became clear that she had not been captured by common outlaws who were intent on robbery and rape. After she was thrust inside the coarse sack, a rope was tied over it around her waist, effectively pinning her arms. Then she was half dragged, half carried a short distance before being thrown to the ground, a heavy foot planted on her back preventing her from getting up.

Two gruff voices began debating her fate, using English with a coarse local accent. At that moment, she determined to speak only in that language and pretend to be ignorant of the French that someone else now began using, this time in far more refined tones.

The upshot of the discussion was that the two Saxons, Alfred and Ulf, had found a woman wandering within a few hundred paces of the camp and had brought her back with them. The two guards spoke abysmal French, but their master now replied in passable English.

'Take that damned sack off and let's have a look at her.'

The rope was loosened and the hessian bag hoisted over her head. Hilda found herself lying in long grass inside some kind of ruin, with remnants of old masonry and a few dilapidated shacks. A tall and rather handsome man was standing over her, as the two burly ruffians displayed her much as though they had brought in a deer from the hunt.

'Who are you, woman? And why were you spying on this place?' demanded Raymond de Blois in French.

She looked blankly up at him, pretending not to understand. The younger oaf repeated the question in English, ogling the blonde as he realised for the first time that she was attractive, even though she was almost old enough to be his mother.

Hilda rapidly improvised her story. Haltingly and fearfully, she claimed to be a pilgrim who had come to St Anne's well to pray and collect holy water to treat her mother's advancing blindness. She was staying in the village while she waited for her fellow pilgrims to return the

next day, but had got lost in the woods while out looking
for mushrooms. Ulf called her a silly cow for expecting to
find mushrooms this late in the year, but did not seem to
find this a significant flaw in her story. Raymond de Blois
studied her dishevelled appearance, and her plain rural
clothing and accepted that she was some pathetic Saxon,
of no danger to their mission.

'What shall we do with her, sir?' asked Ulf. 'Kill her,
perhaps? Alfred and me could have some fun with her
first. Pity to waste such a fair woman.'

The chivalrous knight was outraged at the suggestion
and ordered the two outlaws to lock her in one of the
small storerooms in the crypt.

'Put a mattress and a bucket in there, and find some
food and drink for her. If either of you so much as lays a
finger on her, you'll answer to me with your lives.' He slid
his sword halfway out of its scabbard and slammed it back
again, the hiss of metal on leather emphasising his determination to preserve the woman's life and honour.

Grumbling under their breath, they reluctantly led
Hilda away. Seeing no hope of escape at that moment,
she thought it best to stay passive and let herself be
pushed down the steps and through the gloomy undercroft, where the strange sight of three Saracens and
two other even odder fellows gave her plenty to think
about after she was locked into a small, almost dark
room. It was lit only by a narrow shaft in the side wall
which was almost totally obscured at its upper end by
profuse vegetation.

When her eyes became accustomed to the dimness,
she saw some crates and jars stacked in the chamber, the
rest being a floor of damp earth. After a straw-filled palliasse and a bucket were provided, Hilda sat on a crate
and considered her position. A brave woman, she
accepted that she might not survive this abduction, but
felt sure that this sinister camp in the forest was in some
way connected with her husband's death. She had not the

faintest idea what was going on in this place, but the presence of Moors and the general air of concealment and mystery told her that it must surely be connected with the scraps of information that John de Wolfe had told her about. There was no chance of getting out of this secure prison, as the light shaft was almost vertical and wide enough only for a dog. All she could hope to achieve was to learn more about this mysterious place and trust that she could somehow survive long enough to tell it to the law officers.

Hilda pulled a box across to the door and squatted on it, so that her ear was near the crack on the side where the rusty hinges were attached. Though the door was thick and strong, it was a poor fit in the frame, and not only could she hear through the gap, but one eye placed against it gave her a very narrow view down the long crypt. As figures passed to and from the hearth, they were fleetingly visible in the dim light from the fire and the rush-lights. Most of them were the white-robed Saracens she had glimpsed when she was dragged in, but now and then she saw a large man in a dark tunic and a smaller one wearing what appeared to be a thin jerkin over a skirted robe.

The snatches of speech were disjointed and hard to make out, as the crypt was long and the acoustics poor. The Turks were farther away, and she could distinguish almost nothing of what they said to each other, but she did a little better with the little man in the tunic. He was asking questions in French, with a strange accent that she could not identify. It seemed that the Turks also had a problem understanding him, as he spoke slowly, loudly and with pedantic correctness. Only one voice ever answered him, in slurred French, and she decided that the large fellow and the other two Turks spoke none of that language at all.

The gist of the questioning was at first about her and her presence there. When the small man demanded to know what was going on, the Arab informed him shortly and with apparent ill temper that this was some local woman who had been caught spying on them.

'She should be killed, for safety's sake!' he snarled, which sparked a gust of protest from the questioner. Hilda failed to hear much of the rest of the argument, as the men semed to have turned away from her. After this, all she heard were sporadic questions and even more grudging answers about some processes in which they were engaged.

In spite of her good intentions to eavesdrop indefinitely, within a couple of hours Hilda felt overcome by fatigue and worry and crept to the bag of straw, where she soon fell asleep.

De Wolfe had been living in the Bush for more than a week when one afternoon two worried men called at his chamber in Rougemont. They were Roger Watts and Angerus de Wile, the two ship-masters from Dawlish.

'We left it until now in the hope that Mistress Hilda would come back,' said Watts. 'But we waited at Salcombe until yesterday, then decided we had better catch a fine sou'wester and sail back home.'

John listened with mounting consternation as the two men related how their new employer had sailed with them to Salcombe, ostensibly to visit the *Mary and Child Jesus* and see the scene of her husband's death.

'But then she left her maid in the tavern and took off somewhere, dressed as a pilgrim,' declared Angerus. 'It took us a day to ask around and finally discover from the parish priest that she had left with a party for St Anne's Chapel.'

At this, de Wolfe guessed straight away that Hilda must have gone on to Ringmore to see where Thorgils had been washed ashore and laid in the church. Roger Watts soon confirmed this.

'We were worried out of our minds, Crowner,' he said

bleakly. 'We felt responsible for taking her there and letting her go off on this wild-goose chase all alone.'

'Not that we knew what she was going to do,' added de Wile, defensively.

They described how they had followed her route to the chapel and discovered that she had walked from there to Ringmore. They sought out the bailiff and were told that she had left there to return to Salcombe, allegedly with a pilgrim band, but the old custodian of the chapel had already told them that she had come back and gone down to Bigbury village.

'We hastened there and were told that she had arranged to stay the night with the ale-wife in a tavern,' said Watts dolefully. 'But she went out that afternoon and vanished. No one knew what had become of her, but she seemed to have this marked interest in the forest.'

The trail had petered out at that point, and though the two sailors had made half-hearted attempts to search along the edge of the nearby woods, they decided it best to hurry back to Exeter and report to de Wolfe, whose interest in Mistress Hilda was well known to everyone in Dawlish.

'Did you learn anything more from any of the people in that miserable village?' snarled John, now angry and worried at the news.

'Only that she questioned everyone she could about what might be in the forest there,' said Angerus. 'There were unlikely tales about ghosts and demons trotted out by the local folk, but they are a pretty backward and superstitious lot in Bigbury. We reckon there are outlaws and chicken thieves aplenty there, and the worry is that our lady might have been attacked by some of those bastards.'

This seemed all the two shipmen could tell John, but as they were leaving, Watts fumbled in the scrip on his belt and pulled out a crumpled scrap of parchment.

'When we were searching for Mistress Hilda just inside the forest boundary, I came upon this on the faint track that led deeper into the trees. I doubt it has any bearing on the matter, but I thought I had best bring it.'

He held out the parchment, which was stained with dried muddy water and had some shreds of grass stuck to the surface. John looked at it and saw some unintelligible writing, interspersed with strange symbols, which meant absolutely nothing to him. He thrust it at his clerk, who, like Gwyn, had been listening with avid concern to the ship-masters' tale.

'Does this mean anything to you, Thomas?'

The clerk smoothed out the small page of sheepskin on his table and picked off a few shreds of vegetation as he studied it.

'These are alchemical symbols,' he pronounced. 'I am no expert, but I recognise the signs for mercury, sulphur, lead, tin, copper and gold.'

'What about the other writing there?' demanded the coroner, now very worried about Hilda's disappearance. 'Even I can tell that it's not Latin.'

Thomas peered more closely at the soiled and smudged parchment.

'Some of it is Greek, but some is an oriental script that I have no knowledge of. It could be the language of Araby.'

'You are a great scholar. Can you make anything of the Greek?' demanded de Wolfe.

'I know only a few words of Homer and Aristotle,' said the little priest, defensively. 'I can make out "life" several times and "water" or "fluid" . . . and yes, there is "gold" again.'

Gwyn had a suggestion. 'Maybe the fat monk Rufus up at Rougemont could read it – he seems to be familiar with the Saracen world.'

Thomas bridled at this reflection on his linguistic abilities.

'I doubt he'll make much of these few words! It seems to me that the congruence of "mercury, lead, tin and gold" points to the main preoccupation of alchemists, the transmutation of base metals into gold.'

'What about the rest of it?' snapped de Wolfe.

'The words "life" and "fluid" may refer to the parallel search for the liquid form of the Philosopher's Stone – the Elixir of Life, which is supposed to confer health and everlasting life on those who partake of it.' Thomas crossed himself as he spoke. 'It is a form of blasphemy, seeking an alternative path to everlasting life other than through the love of God and the Holy Trinity.'

Gwyn was the usual dissenting party. 'Whatever it means, it doesn't help us find Hilda.'

John rasped his fingers over his stubble, a habit that seemed to stimulate his thoughts. 'I'm not so sure, Gwyn. Parchments like that don't land in lonely Devon forests unless someone is there to lose them. It tells us that someone is in that area who doesn't belong there. It smacks of Mohammedans with that Levantine script, adding to the suspicions we already have.'

'What about this alchemy gibberish?' grunted the Cornishman, still unconvinced.

'If someone can make gold from Devon tin, then Prince John can buy all the armour, pikes and horses he wants,' pointed out Thomas. 'This fits in twice over with what the Chief Justiciar said in his message.'

Even the coroner was scornful at this point. 'But that claim is nonsense, surely! Fools have been trying to make gold since Noah built his ark, but no one has ever succeeded.'

'There have been certain claims of success,' countered Thomas, cautiously. 'Though admittedly none has ever stood the test of time. But eventually, someone has to be first.'

'What about Mistress Hilda?' asked Angerus de Wile, who had stood with his friend in the doorway while the others debated the parchment. 'Shall we go back to Salcombe and start searching again?'

De Wolfe thought for a moment, then shook his head. 'I considered whether it would be quicker for you to take us by ship, but it's not practicable to carry our horses with us and we need them there. You go back to Dawlish and await events. I will seek out the sheriff at once and see what's best to be done.'

CHAPTER THIRTEEN

In which Richard de Revelle visits an alchemist

Matilda was tired of travelling, weary of being shaken about in an unsprung carriage that was little better than an ox-cart with a canopy, curtains and cushions. Admittedly, it was pulled by a pair of rounseys rather than an actual ox, but even that had its disadvantages, as the two horses went somewhat faster and so shook up the occupants even more on the rutted tracks of Devon.

Her sister-in-law, Lady Eleanor, sat alongside her, swaddled in an ermine-lined cloak, which did nothing to thaw the iciness of her tongue. They spoke rarely, and when they did it was with a cold formality that confirmed the antipathy that had existed between them for a decade and a half. Richard de Revelle's wife, the daughter of an Oxfordshire baron, considered that not only had she herself been married off beneath her station, but that her husband's sister had gone down yet another step in the social hierarchy by being wedded to John de Wolfe, the younger son of an insignificant knight from somewhere in the wilds of Devon.

Now they had to put up with each other in the close proximity of a lady's wagon, trundling between Exeter and Revelstoke, a journey of over two days halfway across a county, that, after Yorkshire, was the largest in England.

Richard had called at the house in Martin's Lane on his way to Revelstoke from his manor at Tiverton, to where he had again journeyed to fetch Eleanor. His aloof wife much preferred Tiverton, but he was insistent that he had urgent business down in the far west of the county and, with an ill grace, she was persuaded to accompany him. Her ill grace increased when she discovered that he had again invited his sister to stay with them at Revelstoke, but was slightly tempered by the news that this was because the scoundrel John had left her to live with a common ale-wife – and a foreign Welsh woman at that.

'You would be well to be competely rid of him,' said Eleanor, during one of their infrequent conversations. 'Can you not petition the Church for some sort of annulment?'

Matilda, who had no intention of either making it easy for John or losing a coroner-knight for a husband, had a ready excuse,

'He is too thick with the Archbishop of Canterbury. When he was a soldier, Hubert Walter was well acquainted with my knavish husband.'

'Then go straight to the Pope!' said her sister-in-law, airily. 'A man like that deserves excommunication, before hanging and drawing!'

Much as John de Wolfe was out of favour with her, Matilda resented Eleanor sneering at him. Insulting John was solely her privilege, and she relapsed into a stony silence that lasted for almost the rest of the journey. Eventually they reached Revelstoke, and Richard and his half-dozen men, who had been riding with the wagon, dismounted with groans of relief and came to assist the ladies from their conveyance.

'I hope by Christ and all his angels that they have a good fire going in our chambers,' were Eleanor's first words, as she stiffly descended the steps placed at the back of the cart. It was blowing fine snow again, and though this was unlikely to settle, the cutting wind and the grey skies of the waning afternoon made the manor-house a dismal sight. Amid the bustle of servants carrying their bags and bundles indoors and the chink of harness as the horses were taken away to the stables, the two women walked to the door of the hall. Here they were met by serving women with possets of warmed wine and honey, before they went wearily to their chambers – the large house had half a dozen rooms, apart from the main hall.

That evening, the three of them dined in one of these rooms, as, unless they were feasting or entertaining guests, Eleanor disliked eating in the hall with the commoners. For once, this was a sentiment with which her fellow arch-snob Matilda fully agreed, and they sat alone in the candlelight before a large log fire, working their way through fresh poached fish, roast pigeon, venison and a blancmange of chicken and rice boiled in almond milk, flavoured with cinnamon. Afterwards there was flummery of boiled oatmeal, strained with raisins and honey.

In spite of the good food and the excellent wine, which Richard imported through Plymouth from Anjou and Bordeaux, the trio was silent and morose. Eleanor had virtually exhausted her repetoire of condemnation of Matilda's husband during the long journey, and Richard seemed worried and preoccupied about something.

'I have to ride out again tomorrow morning,' he said eventually. 'But I will be back before nightfall.'

His wife scowled at him, just as Matilda did when her own husband announced another absence from home – which she always assumed was an excuse for drinking and wenching.

'We have only just arrived,' protested Eleanor. 'Why must you vanish again so soon?'

'I have urgent business to attend to, not far away. You ladies never seem to appreciate that a manor-lord has many duties and obligations. Revelstoke won't run itself, you know, and I can't depend on bailiffs and reeves for everything.'

'So you will be within the demesne, if we need you?'

Richard looked shifty at this. 'Not that close, my lady.

But I will be home for supper, I assure you,' he replied, evasively.

'Can we not ride with you, if it is but a short distance?' demanded Matilda. 'It would relieve the boredom of remaining within these walls.'

Eleanor scowled at her implication that their hospitality was tedious. Richard for once was on her side and soon squashed the suggestion.

'It is likely to be foul weather tomorrow, sister. This snow looks set for another few days and there is a keen east wind. You will be better off near a good fire. Next time, you may accompany me, if the weather improves.'

So the next morning the lord of Revelstoke set off with only two armed retainers. His steward and bailiff offered to accompany him as added protection, but he declined. The fewer who knew of his destination and the nature of his seditious business, the better he would be pleased. He even bribed the two escorts with a few pence and the threat of dire retribution if they gossiped about the expedition. They rode the ten miles towards Bigbury and, after they had passed St Anne's Chapel, de Revelle pulled them off the main track and on to a forest path, well before reaching the village. The half-blind custodian of the shrine had heard their hoofbeats and dimly saw three riders going by, but could not distinguish any details. He wondered again at the unusual activity that had disturbed his placid life these past few weeks, but decided it was none of his business, even when a couple of hours later he heard the same horses returning and vanishing westwards.

As soon as they had gone far enough along the forest track to lose sight of the Bigbury lane, Richard de Revelle ordered his bodyguard to dismount and stay there with their horses until he returned. He added a strict command for them not to wander off, but to rest there and enjoy the food and drink in their saddlebags. He wanted no witnesses to the activity at the old priory and castle, even two thick-headed peasants like these. He rode on down the narrow path, which he had travelled once before, when Prince John's men had come to renovate the crypt for the alchemists. Just before he reached the clearing, he almost fell from his saddle in surprise, as two men reared up from the bushes on either side of him, one with a longbow ready pulled, the arrow aimed at his heart. The other held a lance high up over his shoulder and seemed quite prepared to launch it at the interloper.

'Stop there, you!' yelled the one with the lance.

Richard now recognised the two Saxon ruffians who guarded the place. He identified himself in his usual arrogant fashion and demanded to be taken to Raymond de Blois. Still surly and suspicious, Alfred and Ulf let him pass, but followed closely, the bow and the lance still at the ready.

When he reached the derelict bailey of the old castle, Raymond de Blois came out of the kitchen hut and saluted him, sending the two guards away to continue their patrols of the area.

'I only wish the damned Moors were as obedient as those Saxons,' muttered the Frenchman. 'They come and go as they please, in spite of my orders that they keep out of sight as much as possible.'

'Where are they now?' asked de Revelle, noting that when they entered the hut for some food and wine, the place was empty.

'Down in the crypt – for once, they actually seem to be doing what they came for,' said de Blois grudgingly. 'I've had that weird Scotsman moaning at me ever since he came, saying that this Nizam has made no progress with his alchemy. In fact, Alexander suspects that he is a fraud.'

Richard drummed his fingers irritably on the rough table.

'The whole point of this dangerous enterprise is to produce gold for the Count of Mortain's future campaign to seize the crown!' he said. 'It seems obvious that my royal namesake is never going to return from his wars in France. The country is going to the dogs, being bled dry by that bastard Hubert Walter, just to fund the King's mania for warfare. England needs Prince John – and he'll be generous with his thanks to those who helped him.'

The French knight looked doubtful. 'Well, there seems little prospect of getting any gold nuggets out of these fellows here. I sense that Alexander is genuinely trying his best, but he expected that the Turks would be bringing new knowledge from the East to bolster his own efforts.'

Richard swallowed the rest of the inferior wine and stood up.

'You wanted me to speak to them to impress upon them the importance of this mission. What are they like, these Saracens?' De Revelle had never met any such people.

'Very strange indeed,' muttered Raymond. 'The two ruffians Nizam has with him neither understand nor speak a word of French or English, unless they are playing a very deep game. The alchemist himself speaks a little of both when he chooses, but I suspect he is far more literate than he admits. They are surly, secretive men, whom I wouldn't trust a hand's-breadth out of my sight.'

'What about the other two?'

'This Scottish dwarf is strange, but seems honest enough. He has a great dumb ox of a Fleming to look after him, lacking both a tongue and a brain.'

With these discouraging words, de Blois led his visitor across the overgrown compound to the hidden doorway to the crypt. At the bottom of the stairs, Raymond looked quickly to his left, towards the door to the storeroom at the far end of the long vaulted chamber. It was tightly closed and there was no sound from beyond. Richard de Revelle had no reason to notice his host's rapid scrutiny, as he was taking in the scene in the rest of the crypt. Many flickering wicks floated in their cups of oil on sconces around the walls, but nearer the hearth, whose fire itself contributed much of the illumination, a denser concentration of lamps and candles shed their light on the complex apparatus of alchemy.

Here three men stood with their backs to him, intent on the arcane equipment spread on two tables. One was a huge man dressed in black, with a face that came from someone's worst dreams. He was standing immobile, holding a flask under the long spout of a distillation flask, into which a short, fat fellow in a blouse and kilt was pouring a red liquid.

'That's Alexander of Leith and his servant,' said Raymond in a low voice, following the direction of Richard's gaze. 'And next to him is this Nizam fellow.'

At the second table, de Revelle saw a thickset man dressed in a belted white robe, a cloth wound turbanwise around his head. On the floor near his feet squatted a villainous-looking Arab with a hooked nose and nut-brown face. He was pumping away at a bellows connected to a small furnace that glowed at the edge of the hearth and on which was a pottery crucible. Beyond this Turk, another man of similar appearance was curled up on the floor like a dog, apparently sound asleep. In Richard's imagination, the dim flickering light and the glow from the fire and the furnace turned the scene into a ruddy representation of the lower circles of Hades.

'Alexander! Nizam! We have a visitor,' called de Blois. All the figures in this tableau from hell turned around at the sound of his voice, the one on the floor even waking and rising to his knees.

Uneasily, Richard de Revelle followed Raymond across the large chamber to meet them. The Fleming remained impassive, but his Scots master gave Richard an appraising stare, then raised a hand in salute.

'I am pleased to meet you again, sir. I understand that it is to you that we are indebted for our food and other necessities, for which I thank you.'

This civilised little speech help to restore de Revelle's confidence, but he was less sanguine about the attitude of the Saracens. When he turned from Alexander, he found that the three of them were now on their feet, staring at him, even the bellows-man having abandoned his task. All three gazed at him with their dark, piercing eyes, as if he were some exotic animal on show in a fairground booth.

As Raymond introduced him to the eastern alchemist, Richard stood unnerved by the intense scrutiny of the three Mohammedans.

'You are the son of Gervaise de Revelle?' were Nizam's first words.

Too bemused to wonder why the man had not asked whether he was Richard de Revelle, the manor-lord nodded. The three men now looked at each and Nizam said something in a strange tongue. The other two nodded and then all three turned back to give Richard their basilisk stare.

He cleared his throat nervously and launched into his speech about the urgency of completing their task as soon as possible. 'The Prince is relying upon you to assist him in a great endeavour,' he brayed. 'King Philip of France sent you here to work your expert miracles and produce gold for the purchase of weapons of war.'

Privately, Richard thought the likelihood of anyone making gold was remote, otherwise the country would have been awash with it centuries earlier. But his task was to facilitate whatever the Count of Mortain wanted – failure was none of his business, as long as his credit with Prince John was raised by his efforts to carry out his wishes. He was here today because Raymond de Blois wished him to exhort these people to greater efforts. Whether they were misguided fools striving for the moon or charlatans was no concern of his, as long as he did what was asked of him.

He harangued them for several minutes, and when he paused, Alexander of Leith was nodding his head in agreement. 'I am doing my very best, Sir Richard, you may be assured of that. I cannot say as much for these other men, though these past few days they seem to be striving more, though so far to little effect.'

Richard struggled to follow the strange accent from north of the border, but he was appeased by the small man's apparent earnest attitude.

The reaction of the Mussulmen was totally different, in that there was no reaction at all. They remained staring at him, until Nizam's guttural voice asked, 'You have sons and daughters?'

The complete irrelevance of this took de Revelle aback. 'No, I have not been so blessed. A wife and sister complete my family. Why do you ask?'

There was no reply, but the alchemist again turned and gabbled something to his men.

Richard launched once again into his prepared homily about the importance of their work and how at great expense they had been brought here and given every facility to succeed in their efforts at transmutation. Eventually, after much repetition, he stuttered to a halt, the faces of the Moors having remained totally impassive throughout his speeches.

'We'll do our best, sir, you can depend on it,' said the Scotsman, the earnest expression on his odd face a welcome contrast to the blankness of the others. 'Nizam claims to have made small quantities of the precious metal and has shown me little particles – but he seems to have lost the knack of doing it while I watch him.'

There was an underlying sarcasm in his voice, which produced no reaction from the Saracen.

Richard looked helplessly at Raymond de Blois. 'There seems little else that I can say or do,' he admitted. 'How long are we going to persist with this venture? It has been several weeks now, with no result.'

The French knight shrugged. 'I have no orders concerning that. We must see what the next messenger from

Gloucester has to say. It is up to Prince John how he proceeds.'

As Richard turned to leave, there was a sudden change of attitude from Nizam. His harsh voice cut across the crypt.

'You will come again in a few days. I promise you I will have gold then. Much gold. Enough for you to take, as well as plenty for your prince.'

De Revelle swung back to face the Turk. The mention of gold for himself had instantly concentrated his attention.

'You mean you are really near success? Are you sure?'

'I promise it. My experiments have been long and difficult, but maybe even tomorrow I will have gold. I will need more mercury, tin and copper later, to produce much gold.'

'I'll believe that when it happens,' muttered the Scotsman, loud enough for Richard to hear.

The lord of Revelstoke thought quickly, his mind suddenly stimulated by the thought of wealth. 'Today is Tuesday. Will you have completed your work in two days' time?'

'I will have finished by then. Come that day and see what has been achieved.'

Feeling relieved and excited, Richard left the chamber and climbed back up to the open air, Raymond close behind. Alexander pattered behind him, and when they reached the bailey above, the little Scot grasped the Frenchman's arm.

'This is foolishness! He has said nothing to me about suddenly attaining success! He has made no gold at all. How can he promise large amounts in two days' time?'

Again de Blois gave one of his Gallic shrugs. 'We must just wait and see, that's all we can do.'

'He seemed very sure of himself just then,' commented de Revelle, already counting piles of gold coins in his head, his former doubts about transmutation allayed by even the most tenuous prospect of becoming rich.

'It's out of character for the miserable fellow,' grumbled Alexander. 'He rarely says a civil word to me, just gabbles to those thugs in his heathen tongue.'

They waited until Alfred had brought Richard his horse, and as soon as he was mounted de Blois asked him whether he was really coming back in two days' time.

'For the sake of a ten-mile ride, I'll chance it,' he replied almost cheerfully. 'I think you'll agree that my visit today has moved us on a little, to say the least.'

As he rode off and vanished along the track between the trees, Alexander of Leith was in his most dour mood. 'I don't like it at all. I smell trouble with those Moors. That Nizam is lying through his teeth.'

He stared up at the tall knight. 'And what about the woman down there in that storeroom? What's to become of her? I'll not be party to any killing!'

The Frenchman shrugged again and walked away without replying. All of them were unaware that the subject of the Scotsman's concern had been pressed against the inside of her door all through Richard's visit. Her original intention had been to yell, kick and scream to draw the attention of this new and cultured voice, but as he passed across her narrow field of view, she recognised him as the former sheriff, whom she had seen on numerous occasions in Exeter, including times when she had accompanied her husband to guild feasts, fairs and local tournaments.

Knowing of John de Wolfe's endless antipathy to de Revelle and his tales of the man's faithlessness and treachery, she decided to keep very quiet and learn whatever she could about his presence there, as it was unlikely that any help would be forthcoming from him – indeed, if he discovered who she was, she would be in an even more dangerous situation.

CHAPTER FOURTEEN

In which Matilda goes to pray

On Wednesday, Richard de Revelle could not plead the
weather as an excuse to his sister. Though it was grey and
overcast, the wind had dropped and it was marginally
warmer. Reluctantly, he agreed to her demand to go
riding with him the next morning, and Matilda heard
with satisfaction the refusal of Lady Eleanor to accompany
them.

'Why, by Holy Mary's name, should I want to leave my
fireside and my tapestry to trudge through these miserable lanes for hours on end?' she said loftily. 'And might
I ask what you are going to do with your sister while you
attend to this mysterious business of yours?'

Richard's wife was well aware of his many dubious dealings, but though she chose to ignore their doubtful
legality as long as they increased their wealth, she could
not resist an occasional dig at his furtive behaviour.

To save him answering, Matilda rose to the bait.

'Richard tells me that there is an ancient chapel near
by, with a holy well claiming to offer healing powers. I
would like to stop there and pray for a time, while he is
conducting his affairs.'

She was careful not to enquire as to the nature of these
affairs, in case the answer was not to her liking. Eleanor's
supercilious sniff conveyed her opinion of Matilda's
devoutness, and there was a guarded truce between them
for the rest of the evening.

Soon after dawn the next morning, Matilda de Wolfe appeared in the bailey muffled in a heavy cloak of green serge, a wide hood pulled up over her wimple and cover-chief. She wore fur-lined gloves and boots of fine leather. Her maid Lucille, sniffing back a head-cold that seemed to afflict her most of the time, followed reluctantly in a markedly thinner cloak, a brown woollen scarf tied tightly around her head.

With the aid of one of the menservants, she helped her mistress on to her horse before clambering awkwardly on to the side-saddle of her own pony. Richard, elegant as ever in a long mantle of yellow linen lined with ermine, waited impatiently on his own white gelding for the two women to settle down, then gave the signal for the small party to move off. He rode with Matilda, with Lucille behind and the two armed servants bringing up the rear. Almost half the journey would be on his own lands and he had little fear of outlaws or footpads there. Beyond that, the land belonged to the Count of Mortain, though that was no assurance against trouble, which was why he had brought the two experienced men, armed with ball-maces and long-handled fighting axes. He himself carried a short riding sword and a mace hung from his saddle, though he fervently hoped that he would not be called upon to use either of them.

For such a thickset, inactive woman, Matilda was a sur-prisingly good horsewoman, a legacy of her youth, when she had been more addicted to exercise than eating and praying. She sat on her palfrey with a confident ease, unlike her maid, who clung to the pommel of her saddle as if it were the mast of a ship in a storm.

They set off along the lanes, passing through the empty fields, the strips now being ploughed ready for winter sowing or allowed to lay fallow, exposed to the frosts until spring. Soon heathland appeared, and beyond that the trees closed in, though this near the sea they were low and stunted, except where the track dipped into more sheltered valleys and where they passed other villages, such as Battisborough and Holbeton. Though there was no actual frost, the mud beneath their horses' hoofs had dried into a firm paste and the going was fairly easy. Crossing the River Erme upstream at a low-tide ford caused them no more than a few splashes on their legs, and once through Kingston they were nearly at St Anne's Chapel.

'I will leave you with your maid at the shrine,' said Richard firmly.

'You can come to no harm there in a House of God – though from its size, it's more like His privy!'

Matilda scowled at her brother for his frivolous sacrilege, but she had to admit that when the chapel came into sight, his remark was apt enough. The tiny building looked sad and neglected, but her devotion to anything that had been consecrated overcame her disappointment. Richard sent one of the guards inside and a moment later the bandy curator, Ivo de Brun, appeared, head outstretched like that of a goose as he peered at the blurred images of the visitors.

'I am leaving this good lady and her maid in your care for a few hours, fellow,' called out Richard imperiously. 'Lady Matilda wishes to see the sacred well and then meditate in your chapel for a while. There will be a couple of pennics for you at the end of it.'

Ivo kept his thoughts to himself as he leaned on his staff and watched while Lucille and a servant helped Matilda dismount. The two horses were tied to a fence rail outside the chapel, then the two women followed Ivo into the building as Richard and his men moved off towards Bigbury.

A few minutes later, he led them off the track and after another half-mile ordered them to wait. They were the same pair as before, and were quite content to squat near their horses and while away the time with the food and drink from their saddlebags, on the promise of a couple of silver pence when they returned to Revelstoke.

Richard trotted his gelding along the remainder of the track through the trees, savouring the thought of actually seeing some gold, as those foreign devils had promised. Though the whole object of the exercise was to provide funds for Prince John's forces, if gold was to be generated at will, then de Revelle was determined that part of the proceeds would drop into his own purse. He had no definite views on the veracity of alchemists' claims to be able to transmute baser metals into gold, but being a relatively well-read man, thanks to a good education at the cathedral school in Wells, he knew a little about the mystique of alchemy, with its emphasis on mercury, sulphur and antimony and the rumours of the famous 'Red Powder' that could work the miracle of transmutation.

Pondering this took him within sight of the ruins of the old castle and priory, and moments later he was tying up his horse outside one of the dilapidated huts used as a stable, as Raymond de Blois came out to greet him.

'Have they succeeded yet?' were Richard's first words. 'They promised to show me gold today. If not there'll be trouble.'

'There'll be trouble all right, for all of us,' grunted the French knight. 'Alexander has threatened to leave for Bristol tomorrow if there are no results – and he's going to tell the Count of Mortain that these men are frauds. That will do no good at all to relations between the Prince and my king – nor will it do much for my reputation in Paris!'

He led the way across to the concealed doorway in the wall of the derelict priory, behind which the trees formed a dense green barrier.

'There's another complication, too,' he continued morosely. 'We've got some damned woman held prisoner here. The two Saxon thugs we have as sentinels found her snooping around in the woods and dragged her back here. The Moors wanted to kill her, for they're a callous bunch, but I thought it best to hold her until we're ready to leave.'

Local drabs were of no interest to de Revelle, who had his mind firmly fixed on yellow metal. He stalked ahead of de Blois, down the narrow steps to the crypt below, and saw that both the Scotsman and the Turks were working assiduously at their benches. The red light from the fire and the furnace still made the scene look like one of the depictions of Hell that the more fiery priests were fond of declaiming from their chancel steps.

One of the Mohammedans was busy reviving the furnace with a large pair of bellows, the other was grinding something in a large pestle and mortar, while his master Nizam held a pottery crucible with a pair of metal tongs. On the other side of the fireplace, the weird-looking Scot was muttering to himself as he adjusted the long stem of an alembic that was dripping dark fluid into a glass vessel. His clumsy-looking Flemish assistant was holding a large book open, the pages facing Alexander, who glanced at it at intervals as he fiddled with his equipment.

De Revelle watched for a moment, Raymond at his elbow.

'At least they are all doing something!' said de Blois in a low voice.

At this, Nizam turned around and stared across the room. The man at the bellows stopped pumping and his fellow Turk ceased his grinding, both looking over their shoulders at the new arrivals.

'I hope you have something to show me, as you promised,' called Richard, with something approaching false heartiness. He moved across the floor of the arched undercroft towards the alchemists, and now Alexander of Leith and his man also turned to look at them.

'The wee fellow showed me another nodule of what seems to be gold this morning,' volunteered Alexander. 'Though I still can't fathom how he did it.'

Nizam's sallow face was without expression as he stared at the lord of Revelstoke. With the tongs he held out the crucible towards the former sheriff. 'In a very short while, you will learn something new, Richard Revelle,' he said, in an accent that was much clearer than Raymond was used to hearing.

'I am very glad to hear it,' replied Richard ponderously.

He turned back to the alchemists, concerned only with their news of success. 'What about you, Alexander of Leith? Have you made any progress?'

The diminutive man shook his strangely shaped head. 'I began to research transmutation much later than these Arabs claim to have done, for my main concern has been the Elixir of Life. Though the two are closely connected, I have a number of distillations to complete before I can say if success has been achieved.'

De Revelle was disconcerted to find the three Mohammedans staring at him with intense interest, as if he had just grown an extra pair of ears.

'Did you ride here alone?' demanded Nizam, abruptly. 'Did you bring escorts with you?'

Uneasily, Richard said that he had left them some way behind, along the track. 'There is no need for common men to be made aware of our business,' he added. 'The same goes even for my sister, who rode out with me. I left her at St Anne's Chapel.'

This apparently trivial intelligence appeared to greatly interest the Arabs, as Nizam rapidly spoke to Abdul Latif and Malik Shah. They stared at each other, then at the manor-lord, before breaking out into excited speech, incomprehensible to all the others.

'You have a sister, but no brothers?' demanded Nizam.

Frowning with annoyance at the man's impertinence, Richard nodded. 'My father was blessed with but one son,' he snapped.

This provoked another round of rapid-fire speech among the Saracens.

'What are you saying, man?' demanded Richard irritably. He turned to Raymond de Blois for enlightenment.

'Do you understand any of this heathen gibberish? Have they got gold to show me or not?'

Nizam, whose grasp of French was obviously far better than he had previously admitted, must have picked up the last words, for he beckoned to the two knights with a crooked finger as he placed the crucible on his bench and picked up the large stone pestle and mortar in which Abdul had been grinding something. The two Turkish acolytes crowded closer as their master offered the heavy bowl for Richard and Raymond to inspect.

'Here is your just reward, at last!' he said, triumphantly.

As the two men bent to look into the mortar for their gold nuggets, Nizam suddenly lifted the club-shaped granite pestle and struck de Blois a heavy blow on the forehead. The Frenchman fell as if pole-axed, as Richard de Revelle was seized by the two assistants, who had sidled alongside him and now grabbed his arms in an iron grasp. As he struggled and yelled, Nizam drew out a wide, curved dagger from under his flowing robes and held the edge to Richard's throat, drawing a thin line of blood.

'Keep still or you die now!' hissed the Turk, his face contorted in hate. The victim's yells of mixed rage and terror were silenced as Abdul slipped a noose of plaited red silk over his head and tightened it around his neck. Richard's cries were transformed into gurgles and gasps and his face became red, then blue. He began to sink towards the floor. With an expert twist, the two men threw him down alongside de Blois, tying his wrists together with another length of the red cord.

As if long-rehearsed, de Revelle, now only half conscious, was dragged roughly across the floor and, under the horrified gaze of Alexander and his Fleming, thrown through the other small door at the end of the crypt. After further shouted instructions in their language, Abdul came out with de Revelle's sword and dagger, which he threw contemptuously into a corner, then they lashed the wrists of the inert Raymond de Blois and dragged him off to keep Richard company. Slamming the storeroom door shut, Malik Shah tossed the Frenchman's weapons on top of Richard's and padded with Abdul back to Nizam, to await further orders.

Hilda was dirty, dishevelled and despondent after a number of days locked in her dismal chamber. Once a day, she had been brought some food and water, and twice Alfred had taken her wooden bucket away to empty it. She attempted to ask him questions and offered him money to help her escape, but he refused to speak to her, even in their common tongue. It was obvious that he was afraid, because when she increased the number of silver pennies she would give him, his eyes revealed temptation, but then with vigorous shaking of his oafish head he would back out and look over his shoulder to see whether any of the Turks were within sight. There was no chance of her overcoming him, as he was built like an ox – and in any case, there was his fellow Saxon, Ulf, the Frenchman and the three Arabs between her and any dash for freedom, as well as the other two peculiar people she had glimpsed on her way in, whose role in this set-up was beyond her understanding.

Hilda had long given up kicking and screaming, as not the slightest notice had been taken of her. She now sat either on her mattress or the crate, sunk in despair. Her hair was matted with dirt and straw from the floor; she had lost weight after the sparse diet of rough bread and a few lumps of tough, cold meat that was grudgingly provided. Her only company was a large rat who lived behind the boxes and a few mice who rustled through the straw that had escaped from the crates.

Listening at the crack in the door had also become pointless, as the Saracens were away most of the time and the small man with the strange accent talked only of his experiments. He never received a reply and Hilda began to be convinced that the other man must be unable to speak. All this changed with dramatic suddenness when Sir Richard de Revelle appeared for the second time.

As he entered the crypt, Hilda crawled listlessly to the spyhole, expecting to hear nothing more than fragments of conversation about whatever they were doing with all the apparatus near the hearth. But within minutes there was a commotion outside, cries and shouts and the sounds of a scuffle. All this was outside her slit-like field of view, but protestations from the small man were drowned out by cries of fearful outrage from the former sheriff, and soon the sounds of a body being dragged came nearer. She heard another door being opened, then violently banged shut. Muffled shouts of protest went on for some time, and Hilda gained the impression that de Revelle must have been thrown into a nearby chamber similar to hers.

The stone walls were so thick that no sounds came directly; only a faint murmur of noise percolated through the two stout doors. Much later, when she judged that no one was in the crypt outside, she tried calling out to attract the attention of whoever was in the other dungeon, but there was no response.

Dejected and now almost resigned to dying in this foul chamber, Hilda lay down on her thin pallet and tried to sleep.

Richard de Revelle tired himself out shouting and kicking against the inside of the door. His arms were firmly pinioned behind his back, but he was able to get to his feet to assault the thick planks, which he soon accepted to be a waste of time, as there was no reaction from outside. His throat ached from the effects of the ligature, and though the cut on his neck was very shallow, he could feel the sting and the stickiness of the drying blood against the collar of his tunic.

The ghostly green light that managed to percolate

down a narrow shaft was just enough for him to see that the small chamber was empty, apart from the form of Raymond de Blois lying in the centre of the mildewed floor. At first the Frenchman was breathing in short, noisy bursts, his lips puffing out at each exhalation, but after half an hour he became quieter, and de Revelle wondered whether he was dying. He had little sympathy to spare, as he was utterly fearful for his own life. Confused, frightened and furious by turns, he could make no sense of what had happened. Why had these strange foreigners turned against him? Could John de Wolfe be right in suggesting that this was some form of revenge for his father's actions in Outremer? He had supplied all that these men had asked for – food, horses, materials for their alchemy. They had been commissioned and presumably well rewarded by Prince John to come and perform their miracles with Devon tin, so why suddenly assault de Blois and himself? Richard, though a knight and a former sheriff, was no fighting man and often wished that he had been allowed to follow his inclinations as a youth, in becoming a lawyer or a court official. His father, however, an enthusiastic campaigner and Crusader, insisted on his only son following in his footsteps and a reluctant Richard was trained in all the martial arts, becoming a page, a squire and then a knight, and sent off to the Irish wars, where he was fortunate enough to avoid any serious fighting. He managed to ingratiate himself with several of old King Henry's ministers and eventually landed the post of sheriff, until his thrice-damned brother-in-law snapped at his heels until he was ousted.

His canny sense of politics had persuaded him that Richard the Lionheart was an eventual loser and so de Revelle had attached himself to the cause of Prince John – which had now led him into this unexpected and highly dangerous predicament.

Nervously biting his lip, he gave up shouting and hammering on the door and slumped to the floor, his back against the wall. Though it was cold, he was sweating with fear and trepidation. Spasms of shivering racked his body as he contemplated the end of his life at the hands of these Saracen maniacs. Would Eleanor mourn him? he wondered. He doubted that she would be crippled with grief, as their marriage had never been an affectionate one. In recent years, she had grown more and more impatient with him, content only when she was spending money on fine clothes and trinkets. He had more expectation of his sister Matilda grieving for him, even though her previous admiration had been tainted and diminished in recent months, thanks to the interference of her damned husband.

His self-pitying introspection was disturbed by a change in the noises coming from Raymond de Blois. His shallow breathing, almost as if he were asleep, became broken by grunts and then gargled sounds like attempted speech. From being as motionless as a tree trunk, he began to twitch. Again Richard almost indifferently wondered whether he was dying, but suddenly the Frenchman stirred and began moaning at the pain in his head, where dried blood had caked over a scalp wound in the centre of a patch of livid, bruised skin.

Soon, Raymond jerked himself up on to an elbow and began mumbling curses of which any quayside stevedore would have been proud. De Revelle decided that any live ally was worth cultivating and crawled to his side, to offer solicitous words.

'De Blois, are you recovered? What in Christ's name has happened to us?'

It took a few minutes for the other knight to gather his wits and push himself to a sitting position, still groaning at the pain in his head. He had no recollection of what had happened to him, and Richard explained that the three Arabs had suddenly turned on them and thrown them into this chamber.

Gradually Raymond's mind cleared, but the last thing he remembered was talking to the alchemists in the crypt outside. 'I thought this venture was doomed from the outset,' he muttered. 'I tried to dissuade the King's Chancellor from pursuing the idea, but he said that Philip had his mind set upon it.'

'What do these eastern devils want from us?' gabbled Richard desperately.

'Our lives, I suspect!' answered Raymond grimly. 'But there must be more to it than that. They have been up to no good ever since they arrived. Killing those poor bloody shipmen should have warned me from the start that they verged on madness.'

'What about this crazy Scotsman and his dumb servant? Are they in this too?'

De Blois gave his Gallic shrug. 'I don't know. This Alexander seemed suspicious of the Turks all along. It seems that he was right!'

'What are we going to do? They've taken our swords and daggers, even my small eating knife.'

With more groans, de Blois dragged himself on his hands and bottom across to the wall and leaned his back against the damp stones.

'In the time that I have been with these evil bastards, I have several times seen how oddly they behave,' he said thickly. 'Often they chew some foul paste and I have also seen them sprinkling a dark powder on to that mess of crushed wheat that they call food. Afterwards, they appear either drunk or glassy eyed and sleepy. Sometimes, it makes them chatter madly among themselves and they become agitated and start some outlandish dancing.'

Time went by, and all they could do was sit on the floor, shivering from the cold – and in de Revelle's case, from bouts of terror. They discussed the possibility of jumping whoever opened the door, in spite of their tied hands, but as the hours went by and no one appeared, even this desperate plan seemed redundant.

'Perhaps they've gone and left us here to starve?' suggested Richard, fearfully.

Again de Blois shrugged. 'What would be the point of that? They could leave at any time, without attacking us first. In fact, they have been absent many times, that was one of the problems. When they should have been working at their flasks and furnace, they vanished for days at a time, God knows where.'

Before long, it would become quite clear to them what had taken Nizam and his men away from Bigbury.

Following the incarceration of the two knights, Nizam al-Din led his pair of acolytes above ground, leaving a mystified and apprehensive Alexander down below with the stolid Fleming.

Striding to the kitchen hut, the leader marched in on the two Saxons, who were lounging on the floor, each with a hunk of bread and a piece of cheese in their hands.

'There has been trouble!' snapped Nizam. 'The lord with the pointed beard has attacked the Lord Blois. Both are locked next to that woman and now you will take orders from me!'

Even though his French was much better than theirs, it took several attempts and much waving of hands to get this through to Ulf and Alfred, but the display of a gold coin, a bezant from Constantinople, broke down all language barriers.

'Obey me and you will be given this,' he snapped. 'There are some of our enemies left on guard somewhere near. I want them found and then we will get rid of them, understand?'

The two Saxons nodded dumbly, their eyes still fascinated by the sight of the coin, the first gold they had ever seen, other than rings on the fingers of fat priests and noble lords. After more laborious explanation, they were sent off along the track and less than half an hour later returned to say with many gestures and a halting explanation that they had found two men-at-arms resting not far from where the forest track met the road to the village.

Nizam gave some rapid instructions to Abdul and Malik, who vanished into the sleeping shed and came out with a cross-bow. Beckoning to the Saxons to follow, they set off down the path. Nizam watched them go, then turned into the shed and began prostrating himself in an overdue prayer session, facing what he trusted was the general direction of Mecca. When he had finished, he went back to the entrance to the underground chamber and, with one hand on the hilt of the wicked dagger in his belt, went quietly down the stairs, where he saw that Alexander of Leith and his big, clumsy servant were standing near the hearth, looking extremely unhappy. The alchemist hurried across to him and demanded to know what was going on. Nizam regarded him calmly, holding up a hand to stem the flow of outraged recriminations.

'This is something that does not concern you,' he said harshly, in his thickly accented French. 'As a brother worker in the mysteries of our calling, I intend you no harm. What happens between myself and these other men is not your business.'

'Brother worker!' spluttered Alexander. 'You are no true alchemist, I should have known it all along! You are an impostor. God knows what you really are.'

The Mohammedan nodded gravely. 'Yes, my God does know who I am, but again that is none of your concern. You may leave here and do what you will in two days' time. I will not harm you, unless you dare to interefere in my mission.'

'Mission? What damned mission?'

'Again, that is not for you to know. You will stay here until I have completed my task. Tomorrow is my Sabbath, so I cannot act then until the fall of darkness. On Saturday, you may leave, as I will be gone.'

The little man glared at the Turk. 'And what if I decide to leave today?'

'My men and those two local peasants have orders to kill you if you try,' said Nizam in a flat, unemotional voice.

'What about those two men you have locked in there? One was injured, he may be dying. And what of the woman?'

'They must fend for themselves. The woman is of no account – she may leave when you go. The others will be dealt with when it pleases me.'

There was a sinister tone in the last few words which sent a shiver of dread up Alexander's spine, but the Saracen abruptly turned and strode away, leaving the Scot's clamour for answers unsatisfied.

As Nizam reached the bottom of the stairway, he pulled the heavy door behind him and the two men heard a bar being dropped into sockets on the other side. It was normally always left wide open and this final act of imprisonment impressed on them that their own lives dangled on the thin thread of Nizam's goodwill and perhaps sanity.

CHAPTER FIFTEEN

In which Crowner John goes to chapel

Once again, the long-suffering Thomas had to ride across half a county behind the coroner and his officer. He began to think that maybe his objections to Eustace de Relaga becoming an apprentice clerk to John de Wolfe may have been misplaced. At least the youth was a more enthusiastic horseman, better fitted to these long journeys than himself, even though he had now mastered sitting astride his horse instead of perching sideways.

They had left Exeter at dawn, the coroner forcing the pace in his anxiety to search for Hilda of Dawlish. They made an uncomfortable overnight stop in a mean ale-house near Luscombe, some distance beyond Totnes, where they slept rolled in their cloaks alongside the fire-pit in the only room. After another early start, they rode off into the cold, grey morning with its constant threat of snow, reaching Salcombe soon after noon.

John went straight to the inn where the ship-masters had said that Hilda had stayed, but learned nothing other than the fact that she had never returned there. The parish priest at Holy Trinity confirmed that she had joined a band of pilgrims going west, but had not been seen since then.

Before dusk, they arrived at Ringmore as weary as their horses, and once again a surprised bailiff resignedly provided food and shelter in the manor-house. He had had no further news since the two shipmen had visited him, there being no sign of the missing lady.

'I've been up to St Anne's Chapel several times,' said William Vado. 'But old Ivo de Brun has had no sight of her there – not that his sight is much use, poor fellow, but at least he would be able to tell if she had returned.'

'What about Bigbury village? Any news of her there?' demanded John.

The bailiff shook his head. 'I've not been that far, Crowner. My wife has been unwell with white-leg after the birth and I've not spent much time outside this bailey. Thankfully she's improving today, so if you want me to ride with you in the morning, I'll willingly come.'

Tired out, they sought their mattresses on the hall floor soon after a meal and a few jugs of ale and cider. In spite of his worries about his former lover – and Gwyn's gargantuan snores – de Wolfe was soon sound asleep. It seemed only a few minutes later that the cold light of dawn and the stirring of the manor servants jerked him awake.

'What's to be done today, Crowner?' asked the patient Gwyn, as they sat over bowls of pottage, which seemed to consist mainly of turnips and cabbage, with hunks of coarse rye bread to soak up the fluid.

'Follow the route she took again, I suppose,' grunted John. 'First check again at this damned chapel, then go down to this poxy village where she was last heard of.'

There was a pause as they scraped up the last of the soup with their wooden spoons, then Gwyn let out a breath of frustration that blew up the hairs on his straggling moustache.

'What in hell is going on with all this, Crowner?' he asked, dolefully.

De Wolfe shook his long head slowly from side to side.

'Gwyn, I wish to Christ I knew! So many deaths, bloody Moors, shipwreck, alchemists, crucifixions – and now a missing woman.'

Thomas de Peyne, sipping his ale as if it were hemlock, ventured into the conversation.

'Before we left Exeter, I took that piece of parchment up to Brother Rufus to see if he could make out any more words. He could not read the Turkish script, but confirmed what I said about the Greek and the symbols. It seemed to be some part of an alchemist's formula or notes, about some process to make the Elixir of Life.'

When they had eaten and had a final warm at the fire, they went out into the bailey, where William Vado had brought round their horses, ready fed, watered and saddled up. Together with the bailiff, they rode the short distance up to the crossroads. The tiny chapel looked forlorn in the morning mist, as a freezing fog was hovering over the countryside, with no sign of a sun to disperse it. Clouds of vapour hung menacingly over the clumps of trees, and even the birds seemed too depressed to twitter. The coroner reined in level with the small porch.

'We'd best ask that old fellow if he's seen anyone about here lately,' he rasped, his breath steaming in the cold air. 'Thomas, you are nearest to the ground on that overgrown goat you ride! See if he's in there.'

The clerk slid inexpertly from his saddle and trudged across to the door, which was partly open. Crossing himself as he approached this very modest House of God, he called out to the custodian, who lived in a lean-to shack attached to the side of the chapel. Getting no reply, he went inside, and the waiting coroner idly watched the doorway for the appearance of Ivo de Brun. Instead, he heard a piercing shriek which he thought belonged to a woman until he realised it had been made by Thomas de Peyne, who reappeared as if on a spring, his face as white as chalk.

'What the hell's the matter with you?' roared Gwyn, leaping off his mare and advancing on Thomas, ferocity masking his concern for the little clerk. John de Wolfe was but a yard behind him, and together they pushed past the priest and rushed into the small building.

'God's teeth, what's happened here?' shouted de Wolfe, as Gwyn and William Vado crowded alongside him. On the floor in the middle of the nave lay the crumpled body of the custodian. He was face down, but was easily recognisable by the bandiness of his bare legs, exposed below his worn cassock, which was rumpled up almost to his waist. The old man's arms were outstretched, as if in a final agonised supplication towards the little altar. He was ominously still, and even more ominous was the spreading patch of dark blood which had soaked into the earthen floor on either side of his body.

Gwyn knelt at his head and lifted it with a gentleness that was at odds with his burly, rough appearance. 'He's dead, poor old fellow. But look at his eyes!'

With Thomas hovering with an ashen face near the door, John and Vado moved around to crouch with the Cornishman and stare in horror at the face of the chapel's guardian. The nose and one cheek were flattened and pale from contact with the ground, the rest having the purple hue of death staining. But what was most shocking was his eyes – rather than showing the former milkiness of his cataracts, they revealed bloody pits where they had been gouged out, the remains hanging down his face.

'Did that kill him?' asked the bailiff in a voice hushed with dismay.

For answer, Gwyn heaved the body over on to its back, displaying a wide area of blood-soaked clothing covering the entire belly and chest. Pulling aside the brown woollen robe, the typical garb of clerks in the lower religious orders, he exposed the now familiar wide stab wounds, four in number, scattered over the heart and entrails.

'The same bastards again!' snarled the coroner, filled with anger at the ruthless killers who could do this to an almost blind and defenceless old man.

Thomas came a little nearer, one hand over his mouth

holding back his nausea, the other twitching repeated signs of the Cross at this further sacrilege of a holy place. Then something caught his eye which so surprised him that he forgot his sickness. He moved a few paces and bent to pick something from the floor.

'Crowner, look at this!' he said tremulously, holding out his hand to show what was coiled in his palm. Rather impatiently diverted from studying the wounds on the old man, de Wolfe glanced at it and his brows furrowed.

'A necklace? No, it's a string of paternoster beads. So what? This is a chapel – any pilgrim could have dropped them.'

Thomas shook his head, frightened but determined.

'Not any pilgrim, sir! These belong to your wife. I'd know them anywhere!'

'My wife's!' roared John de Wolfe. 'Let me see it!'

He rose from the side of the corpse and snatched the rosary from Thomas's hand.

'How do you know it belongs to her? How can it be, for according to Mary she's with her brother in Revelstoke!'

He looked at the long line of amber beads, threaded on to plaited horsehair.

'It is hers, sire!' repeated the clerk, in desperate agitation. 'I have seen her use it in the cathedral many times. She has five sets of ten beads, separated by knots. See!' He pointed to the sequence of amber globes. 'That is the new way of counting one's prayers, instead of a hundred and fifty single counts. Three are counted for each bead, in sets of ten.'

John, his face paler than usual, tried to talk his way out of believing Thomas.

'New it might be, but there must be many like it.'

'Not in such fine amber, master. And to put it beyond doubt, look at the end!'

He reached out and touched a small silver crucifix that dangled from the tail of the rosary. Next to it hung a small silver medallion, with a rather crude picture of a seated saint on one side, wearing a crown. On the reverse were some punched letters, which John could not read.

'That is St Olave, sir, the first Christian king of Norway. Your good wife diligently attends St Olave's church in Fore Street.'

Reluctantly convinced, de Wolfe stared about him wildly, his mood swinging between bewilderment and anger.

'So what the hell is it doing here, in a chapel with a murdered corpse? Who brought it here, for Christ's sake?'

Gwyn, who had listened silently until now, said quietly, 'Revelstoke is but a few miles west of here, Crowner. And your wife is mightily fond of making her devotions at any church or chapel that takes her fancy.'

De Wolfe calmed down with an effort, steeling himself to think rationally and act practically. Though he had more than once wished Matilda transported permanently to the other side of the world, he had never wanted her dead, which was now a possibility that he hardly dared voice. To his credit, the thought that it would make him free never entered his mind.

'But does the presence of her rosary have to mean that she was here herself? That amber is valuable – I recall now that she bought it herself many years ago, at quite a high price. Perhaps some cut-purse stole it from her at Revelstoke and then killed this old man for some reason.'

Gwyn rose and touched his master gently on the arm.

'Think how he has been killed, Crowner. With wounds like that, this can only be connected to those other deaths. This is no casual robbery.'

De Wolfe lowered his head and shook it like a bull being baited.

'So what do we do – where do we search?'

His two assistants had never heard him sound so hopeless and despondent. Then, almost as if in some divine answer to John's desperation, Thomas heard some faint sounds coming from the north wall of the chapel. Without saying anything to the other men, who were muttering agitatedly among themselves, he walked across to a small door that he presumed led to Ivo's living space. Putting his ear to it, he heard a soft keening wail and tentative tappings and scratchings.

'Crowner! Gwyn! There's someone in here!'

With huge strides, John hurled himself across the little nave, the bailiff and Gwyn close behind. He seized the rusted iron hoop that served as a handle and pulled and pushed without avail.

'Matilda! Matilda!' he roared. 'Is that you in there?'

The only reply was more pronounced sobbing and wailing from the other side of the door.

'Open the damned door, d'you hear?' he boomed, pounding on the rough panels with his fist.

Gwyn pushed him aside.

'Let me break it open, Crowner.' But as he backed off, preparing to charge the panels with his shoulder, there was a rattle of a bar being lifted and the door opened a few inches. A thin face peered fearfully out and John de Wolfe stared at it in deflated amazement.

'Lucille! What the bloody hell are you doing in there? Where's your mistress?'

Though Matilda was well used to being on the back of a horse, she was always sitting in the saddle, not draped across it like a sack of oats. She had to suffer the fearful ignominy of being laid face down with her belly on the leather, held on by a rope passing under the beast, lashed to her ankles and wrists. The weight of her own body made breathing difficult and by the time they had covered the mile and a half into the forest, she was gasping and purple in the face. Disoriented, terrifed and in fear of death, she used what little breath she had to whisper prayers, an endless series of paternosters and supplications to Mary, Mother of God.

The past half-hour had been the worst nightmare of her life, heightened by the fear that it might also be the last. Matilda had been on her knees in the little chapel of St Anne, praying peacefully. She had also asked the Almighty that the waters of the well, which she intended visiting would help cure the unsightly ailment of patches of silvery skin which had recently appeared on her elbows, knees and in the hair of her scalp. She was telling off the beads in her rosary as she whispered the endless round of prayers. The old man with the milky eyes hovered near the door to his pathetic dwelling, a hut built on to the chapel wall, far too small to swing a cat in it. Lucille crouched behind her mistress – bored, sniffing continually and pretending to pray, though Matilda knew that her devoutness was only superficial.

There was the sound of horses' hoofs approaching outside, and Ivo de Brun's head went up at the welcome prospect of pilgrims and more alms. But what his weakened eyes saw a moment later was an apparition out of hell itself, as three figures burst in waving long, curved daggers. Dressed in flowing robes with turbans coiled around their heads, they ran silently to the centre of the chapel and stood menacingly around the two women and the old man. Matilda and Lucille heard Ivo's cry before noticing the intruders, and turned to see the dark faces of the Turks glaring at them. With a terrified scream, Lucille shot away towards the north wall, while the heavier Matilda lumbered to her feet. Bemused by this unlikely intrusion, she glared belligerently at the hawk-faced Arabs.

She opened her mouth to protest and begin upbraiding these defilers of a holy place, but Nizam forestalled her.

'You are a de Revelle?' he snarled.

Matilda gaped at him, then became indignant. 'I am a de Wolfe, fellow! My husband is the King's Coroner and you will answer to him for this outrage!'

The oriental ignored her. 'You are sister to de Revelle?'

'I am indeed. My brother was the King's sheriff and again you will be held to account by him for your . . .'

She never finished the sentence, as with a jerk of his head to his two men, Nizam grabbed her arm and pulled her roughly towards the door. As Abdul and Malik closed in to seize her more securely, Matilda realised the seriousness of the situation and began to struggle and scream. While Lucille dived through the open door of the curator's hovel, slamming it behind her, Ivo himself stumbled forward with cries of protest and tried to launch himself at the marauders. Almost casually, Nizam struck him repeatedly in the chest and belly with his knife, and when the old man had fallen to the floor he knelt over him and with quick, practised movements mutilated his face. Having wiped the blade on Ivo's ragged tunic, the leader of the assassins followed his men out without a backward glance.

Now, half an hour later, Matilda was gasping for breath as she stared at the ground below the horse, seeing a narrow track covered with grass and weeds. She turned her head with an effort and saw that they were going along a path through dense trees, but a few moments later they came to a halt and the rope was untied from her ankles. She was pulled roughly off the saddle and fell in an ungainly heap on the ground, but was immediately dragged to her feet by one of the Turks tugging on the rope around her wrists. Stumbling and wailing, Matilda was pulled along by the man, the other two moving across to some derelict huts. As soon as she recovered her breath, she began screaming abuse, but all that happened was that her captor turned and smacked her hard across the face.

He said nothing, and even in her bewildered, terrified state, she sensed that he did not understand a word of what she was shouting. They reached a doorway in a ruined wall and she was pulled down some stairs, almost falling headlong as the villain tugged on the rope. In the dim light below, she hazily saw a couple more figures watching her, but within seconds she was hauled across to a door in the far wall. The Turk, who smelt strongly of sweat mixed with some aromatic scent, lifted the bar and thrust her inside, slamming it shut and dropping the wooden beam back into its sockets.

Sobbing with fear and shock, Matilda sank to the floor, her hands still tied with the rope that trailed beneath her as she lay on the dirty straw. Oddly, one of the thoughts that churned through her confused mind was that her new cloak would be soiled and hard to clean. Then a voice penetrated her consciousness and she felt soft hands trying to lift her shoulders.

'Lie here on this mattress, lady. Let me take these bonds from your wrists.'

As her eyes became accustomed to the dim greenish light, she was aware of a female figure bending over her. Gratefully, Matilda lifted her arms so that the woman could unpick the simple knots in the rope and then sank to her hands and knees as the woman guided her to a thin pallet in the centre of the room.

'Who are you? What are we doing here?' she croaked, as the face above her gradually took shape through the tears in her own eyes and the gloom of the chamber.

The woman with the bedraggled blonde hair did not reply at once. She had recognised the new arrival and was dumbfounded. An instant later, Matilda, even more incredulous, saw that the woman who was succouring her in her adversity was none other than Hilda of Dawlish, one of her husband's mistresses.

CHAPTER SIXTEEN

In which Crowner John meets a Fleming

It was many minutes before Lucille calmed down sufficiently to give any sort of coherent account of what had happened. Almost out of his mind with anxiety, the impatient coroner was inclined to slap the silly wench's face until she came to her senses, but it was Thomas who was best able to deal with her. He gave a meaningful glance and nod of his head at Gwyn, who took the hint and diverted John de Wolfe's attention, while Thomas led the maid aside and sat her on the old peoples' bench that ran along one wall of the chapel. Talking to her softly in her native French, for she came from the Vexin on the Seine, he soon reduced her hysterics to a steady snuffling sob, then began to extract the details of the recent tragic drama. As she haltingly mumbled and cried, Thomas beckoned to the others and they came nearer to listen.

'Poor Lucille here says that Mistress Matilda came here to pray and visit the holy well,' he explained. 'She rode out with her brother, who went off on some other business.'

'And what business would that be, out in this wilderness?' snapped de Wolfe.

Lucille looked up timorously at this stern, dark man. 'I know nothing of that, sir, but he told the mistress to wait a short while until he returned to collect us and take us back to Revelstoke.'

Gwyn looked at his master. 'So he must be somewhere fairly near, if they were waiting for him.'

'Then what happened, Lucille?' prompted Thomas gently. The skinny girl burst into tears once again and began shaking.

'Come on, girl, pull yourself together!' roared John de Wolfe. Though Thomas's softer approach seemed to have been successful, this outburst shocked the maid into lucidity.

'These three foreign devils burst in, sir! Terrible, they were! Huge men, dressed in long robes, cloths wound round their heads and waving great daggers.'

'What d'you mean, foreign?' snapped the coroner.

'Like Turks or Mussulmen. I saw some in a fair in Rouen once, jugglers and fire-eaters. Evil dark faces and hooked noses.'

'Then what? Tell us, quickly, for Christ's sake!'

'They seized Mistress Matilda – and I ran to bar myself in that room, otherwise they would have slain me as well. I saw them stab the old man, just as I was shutting the door.' She began shaking again and her eyes rolled wildly.

De Wolfe threw up his hands in desperation.

'What in hell is going on? These must be the same three Saracens. What do they want with my wife?'

Although none of them voiced the thought, it seemed unlikely that she was a target for ravishment, especially when Lucille, though skinny and unattractive, was a good twenty years younger.

'And where is Richard de Revelle, I wonder?' said Gwyn thoughtfully.

'I might have guessed that that bastard would be involved in anything underhand that was going on,' snarled de Wolfe.

'He would hardly want his own sister kidnapped,' Gwyn pointed out, reasonably.

John stalked to the open door, Gwyn and the bailiff behind him, leaving Thomas on the wall-seat with the snivelling maid.

'Where have they taken her, that's the thing?' he bawled, staring at the deserted road.

'And where's de Revelle?' repeated Gwyn. 'He can't have gone back to his manor without his sister!'

De Wolfe swung round to William Vado, who had been a silent and mystified observer of these strange events. 'Bailiff, you had better ride at once to Revelstoke, to make sure Sir Richard has not returned there. Then explain what has happened and get his steward to turn out with some armed men as fast as he can and come back here with them.'

'That will take a good few hours, sir. Where will you be when we return?'

'The answer to all this mystery has to be somewhere near here. Gwyn and I will ride to Bigbury to see if anything is known there, so look for us along these roads.'

As Vado hurried to his horse, John called after him. 'You'd best take that damned girl with you on the back of your horse. We can't leave her here alone with that eyeless corpse. I'll attend to him later.'

Now that he had at least instigated some action, however futile it might prove to be, de Wolfe felt better. But two of his womenfolk were missing – he hoped to God that at least Nesta was safe in Exeter.

Matilda de Wolfe was a very self-sufficient, almost hard-bitten woman, but the shock of her recent experiences had caused her to dissolve into racking sobs as she slumped on the mattress in the dim chamber. Though she was exceptionally devout and firmly believed that she would eventually be received into heaven, she had no desire to go there just yet. Hilda crouched alongside her, speaking softly as she supported her shoulders and stroked the wiry curls of her hair, for the older woman's cover-chief and wimple had been lost when she was thrown across the horse.

As she gradually calmed down, Hilda's story slowly percolated into Matilda's brain. How she had vowed to seek out details of her husband's murder, then had been captured when she was following up the villagers' tales of strange activities in the forest. Though Matilda had long been aware of her husband's romance and adultery with the Saxon, she now felt a grudging admiration for her determination to track down her husband's killer. She had immediately recognised the handsome blonde, as she had seen her in Exeter a number of times and, in common with most of the population there, knew that she had been de Wolfe's mistress since before she herself had ever met him. Matilda also knew, through the grapevine of intelligence provided by her snobbish friends at the cathedral and St Olave's, that for some time John had not been dallying with the woman from Dawlish, being too besotted with the Welsh cow from the Bush tavern.

Their common peril, together with Hilda's tender concern and sympathy, prevented Matilda from voicing the scathing antipathy that she would have offered in any other circumstances.

'But why are we here?' she sobbed. 'Who are these terrible men? What is this place? Why does my brother not rescue me?'

Uneasily, Hilda felt that she could no longer delay telling Matilda another uncomfortable truth.

'I am afraid your brother is indeed here! But he is also a prisoner. He lies in the next room, beyond this wall.'

She explained to a dumbfounded Matilda that she had witnessed the attack by the Arabs upon Richard de Revelle and the French knight. 'But I have no notion of what it all signifies,' she concluded.

Perversely, the news seemed to have the effect of lessening Matilda's distress and strengthening her resolve. She stopped weeping and sat up on the mattress, drying her eyes with her sleeve. 'You are a resourceful woman, or you would not have come seeking your husband's killers. Surely there is something we can do between us?'

Hilda sighed, for she had spent several days trying to devise some plan, without success. 'I have tried knocking on the wall and shouting, but I can get no reply from your brother or the other man. The stonework is too thick – I doubt they even know we are here.'

She explained about the two loutish Saxons who seemed to be servants or guards and the two strange men in the crypt, one who appeared to be dumb. 'I do not think they are as evil as the Mohammedans – I cannot fathom who they are or what has been going on in this place. All we can do is wait, hope and pray.'

After the sparse explanations had been given, the two women relapsed into silence. Tacitly, neither mentioned John de Wolfe, who, as far as they knew, was far away in Exeter going about his business, oblivious to the fact that they were imprisoned and probably at risk of their lives.

Outside the cell, the crypt was in silence and the feeble illumination was even poorer, as some of the rush-lamps had run out of oil and no one had replenished them. Alexander sat on a stool near the hearth, Jan squatting near by, the flames from the fire casting a ruddy glow on his bizarre features. All pretence at work had ceased. The furnace had gone out and the spouts of the distillation flasks no longer dripped into their beakers.

'They were bloody frauds, I suspected it all along!' muttered the Scotsman, for the twentieth time. 'They must have seeded those crucibles with blobs of gold, just as so many impostors have done in the past.'

Jan made some throaty noises which signified agreement. Alexander could recognise about a dozen different noises that the Fleming made, which gave him some degree of communication with his faithful servant.

'We are in big trouble, Jan, my lad,' he carried on, in his habitual monologue. 'I don't trust them when they say they will let us go on our way on Saturday.' He spoke in Gaelic, which Jan had picked up in his years with the alchemist. It was useful when they wanted to keep their conversation private. Jan made some signs and grimaces, using his fingers to denote running away.

'I doubt we'll get the chance, Jan. But you are the stronger and faster, so if you see any opportunity, take it and run. Find that village that we were told to make for – it can't be more than a mile or two away, through the forest.'

The Fleming nodded and Alexander fell silent, regretting again that he had ever agreed to take the generous payment to come here and try to augment Prince John's diminished treasury. The transmutation of base metals had never been his prime interest – the Elixir of Life was his goal, and he thought that he had now succeeded. He had a small phial safe in his pouch, but it was difficult to know whether the contents were potent as, by definition, producing immortality or even longevity was hard to demonstrate.

The thought of his little phial sparked a new idea in his fertile brain and getting up, he went to his work table and began tipping some powders and liquids from various stock bottles into a small mortar. Grinding them up, he decanted them into another empty vial. Carefully stoppering this, he placed it in an inside pocket of his loose-fitting blouse and went to sit down again to await events.

Some time later, there were heavy footsteps on the stairs and the door was unbarred to admit Alfred. The ungainly outlaw, who carried a long battleaxe, scowled at the two occupants and jerked his head towards the entrance.

'The Mohammedan says you had better have something to eat,' he growled ungraciously. Alexander shot a knowing look at Jan, who gave an almost imperceptible nod.

'What about the people in those chambers?' demanded Alexander, as he moved warily past the big oaf with the vicious-looking weapon. 'They need something, especially the poor women!'

The Saxon prodded the alchemist with the blunt head

of the axe. 'I don't know nothing about them, so get going and be thankful!' he snarled.

The Scot and his servant went out blinking into the daylight and crossed to the shack where they had their food, Alfred following them watchfully. Jan's eyes swivelled from side to side, but he decided that he had no chance of making a run into the trees with the guard so close behind.

In the hut, the three Turks were crouched in the centre, busy eating with their fingers from a common platter piled with a mush of boiled wheat and some unidentifiable vegetables. Ulf, the other local ruffian, motioned the pair to a low bench and dumped half a stale loaf and a wooden bowl of cold mutton stew between them. With some distaste, which was overcome by hunger, Alexander tore the bread in half and gave some to Jan, while he dipped his in the mess, in lieu of a spoon. The Fleming did the same, sucking at it with his toothless gums. When they had eaten, Ulf splashed some thin ale from a pitcher into a dirty pot and again slapped it down on the bench. The three Arabs continued to eat in silence and totally ignored the others, including the two Saxons lounging by the door.

Alexander took a deep draught from the pot, then offered it to his servant. As he did so, he caught a wink from his servant, who refused the ale, giving a series of loud belches. Then Jan groaned and bent forward, clutching his stomach and releasing several spectacular farts. This sudden activity caught the attention of Alfred, and even the Turks briefly raised their heads as the Fleming groaned again and made some retching sounds. He staggered to his feet and Ulf pushed himself from the door-post.

'What's the hell's the matter with you?' he demanded.

Jan groaned, gargled and rolled his eyes, then held his grotesque nose with one hand and pointed towards his backside with the other, before gesturing at the door and then fumbling with his belt buckle.

Ulf guffawed coarsely, also pinching his nostrils in a parody of the Fleming's discomfort.

'The food's not that bad, you dirty bastard!' he sneered. 'But don't go crapping in here, get outside.'

Jan stumbled outside, the alchemist watching him anxiously, as it was obvious to him what his man was intending. Ulf followed him out, holding a bare dagger by his side, watching as the Fleming seemed ready to drop his breeches. But then, with lightning speed for such a large man, Jan thrust the Saxon hard in the chest and sent him flying backwards, to stumble and fall on the ground. Ulf's yell of rage brought Alfred out with his axe, but by then Jan was hammering across the old castle yard towards the trees.

Inside the shack, the three Arabs shot to their feet in alarm and Malik dived for his cross-bow, which was leaning against the wall. They ran out of the hut, Malik cranking the lever to draw back the bow-string and fitting a bolt on to the platform. Screaming at the two hulking guards who were blocking his shot as they pursued the Fleming, he raised the bow and fired his bolt between them, careless whether he hit them or not.

Jan was just at the edge of the trees when the short arrow struck him in the shoulder, but he crashed on and vanished at full speed. The two Saxons lumbered after him, but a cry from Nizam pulled them up short.

'Leave him, I need you here! He is of no account and will wander the forest until he dies of his wound. Who cares about some dumb servant?'

Crestfallen, the two guards trudged back, and the Saracens returned to the hut, where, after some rapid discussion in their own language, they impassively resumed their interrupted meal. With a smirk of satisfaction, Alexander surreptitiously slid an empty vial back into the folds of his blouse.

With Thomas following somewhat apprehensively behind,

John de Wolfe and Gwyn rode down the track towards Bigbury, carefully scanning the land on either side for any signs of Richard de Revelle or the dastardly villains who had descended on St Anne's Chapel. It was now mid-afternoon and the sky still had its brooding grey appearance, though the threatened snow had held off.

'Not a damn thing to be seen, Crowner,' growled the Cornishman after they had covered almost a mile. 'Plenty of side tracks on to the heathland and into these bloody trees, but we can't explore them all.'

De Wolfe grunted his agreement. 'If it was wet, then we might see fresh hoof marks. But half-frozen ground like this is useless for such signs.'

He felt totally impotent and frustrated, knowing that Matilda and possibly Hilda might be in the clutches of these Turkish madmen, without any real notion of where they were.

Another mile brought them to Bigbury, the hamlet lurking at the edge of the forest that covered the plateau stretching from west of the chapel across to the banks of the Avon and up as far as Were Down, towards Aveton Giffard. As they rode down the track between the dozen tofts and cottages that made up the village, there was no sign of anything untoward. Across the road, an ox team was ploughing the hard soil to turn in the stubble of a meagre harvest, and at the side of the track a couple of men were repairing a dry-stone wall. De Wolfe reined in to ask them whether they had seen any strangers passing through that day, but received mystified shakes of the head.

'Few people come this way, sir,' said one, who recognised the coroner from his previous visit to Bigbury. 'The fisherfolk who go down to the river are all known to us. The only excitement we've had is that poor lady pilgrim who came and then disappeared a few days back.'

Thomas piped up for the first time since leaving Lucille. 'That means they must have gone either down to Ringmore or back towards Kingston.'

'Or vanished into the God-forsaken woods at any point,' muttered Gwyn, pulling ferociously at the ends of his bedraggled moustache. He was almost as worried about the situation as his master, even though he and Matilda could barely stand the sight of each other.

They rode on to the alehouse opposite the small church and confronted the clutch of people who came out to meet them, warned by the unfamiliar clatter of hoofs.

'Crowner, you're back again!' called Madge, the ale-wife. 'You'll be wanting food and drink?' she added hopefully.

There was nothing to be gained by refusing a short halt, as they had no definite plan of campaign. Inside the dim, smoky taproom, they drank ale and cider and chewed on some cold mutton chops, followed by bread and hard cheese. Urgently, John described the violent events at St Anne's Chapel that morning and explained that his own wife, sister to the lord of Revelstoke, had been abducted. Then he enquired about any strange events since the two ship-masters had come looking for Hilda.

Madge shook her head. 'Nothing at all, sir. Even our village scaremongers have seen no ghosts in the forest and we have neither seen nor heard anything strange in the woods.'

'Mind you, no one fancies entering there these days,' added the village smith, who sat watching them from a stool in the corner. 'Even the poachers have taken to going in the opposite direction, though the pickings are poorer there.'

'Where did the lady from Dawlish go, when she left here and never returned?' asked Thomas, sipping his cider cautiously.

The tavern-keeper held up her hands in bewilderment. 'I wish I knew, sir! I told her not to stray far, given the odd happenings here, but she was a wilful woman. She must have gone into the forest, for no one saw her on the roads.'

De Wolfe glared at Gwyn, as he slapped his empty pot down on the table.

'We'll just have to go in there ourselves and hope that we come across something. God knows when those men from Revelstoke will turn up, if they ever do. We need Ralph Morin and Gabriel and a posse of soldiers from Rougemont!'

'It would take at least three days to get them down here, if not four,' grunted Gwyn. 'It looks as if it's up to us, Crowner!'

The blacksmith, a large man in a leather apron scarred with burns from hot iron, stood up and offered himself. 'I'll go with you, sir. I know a few of the paths out there. A wife lost is a terrible thing. If the reeve was here, he'd come, but he's in Aveton today.'

Gratefully accepting his offer, John gave Madge a couple of pennies for the food and strode to the door. 'The sooner we get started, the better. It will be dark before long.'

Outside, one of the wall-repairers also volunteered his services and went off to get a hay-fork, a wicked-looking implement with two sharp prongs. The smith trusted to his hammer, a heavy-headed weapon with a long handle. John looked at these and then at his weedy little clerk, to whom non-violence was a way of life. 'Thomas, this may be a dangerous mission,' he said softly. 'You had better stay here and wait for the men from Revelstoke, if they ever come.'

The priest shook his head stubbornly. 'I will come with you, master. I owe my life to you and will willingly give my own in exchange. I may be useless at fighting, but maybe I can stand in the path of an arrow meant for you.'

John felt an unfamiliar lump come into his throat and he put an arm around Thomas's skinny shoulders and squeezed wordlessly.

'Let's go, then! Smith, where do we enter these damned woods?

Jan the Fleming was an unusually strong and powerful man, but the effort of fleeing from the old ruins eventually reduced him to a gasping wreck, and he was forced to stop and sink to the ground, past caring whether he was recaptured. However, all was quiet behind him and he crawled behind a moss-covered tree to allow the bellows of his lungs time to calm down. He had hardly noticed the impact of the cross-bow bolt in the tempestuous panic of flight, but now he became aware of a sticky flow down the inside of his tunic and a burning pain in his left shoulder. It was the dragging of the short arrow against his skin which caused the most discomfort and when his heart had stopped pounding and he could breathe without gasping, he felt with his other hand and discovered that the missile had lodged in the skin at the extreme top edge of his shoulder. An inch or two lower and he would have suffered a mortal injury, but as it was, only the loss of blood was a danger. The ever present risk of suppuration loomed, but for now all he could do was tear off a strip from the bottom of his tunic and wad it under his clothing against the wound, to help stanch the bleeding.

Jan again listened intently for any sounds of pursuit. All he could hear was a bird twittering and the soft sighing of the wind in the tops of the tall trees all around him. He had no chance of even guessing the direction in which he had been running. A trail of bent weeds and ferns told him how he had arrived at this spot, but that was of use only over a few yards. He might have been running in circles, and the danger was that he would go back towards the old castle and priory. Cautiously he got to his feet and started walking away from his former trail, looking back every few yards to try to ensure that he was at least going in a straight line.

He stopped every few minutes to listen for any Saxons

or Moors crashing through the woods after him. Thankfully there was continued silence for the next half-hour, then he heard something that made him freeze and crouch behind a fallen log that was slowly rotting under a tracery of thick ivy.

Ahead of him to his right, Jan heard a low voice calling out and an answering whistle from the left. He could not distinguish the words, but they were neither Arabic nor English. Then another voice came from farther to the left, more high pitched and certainly speaking Norman French. He shrank down even further to lie on the ground, ignoring the pounding throb in his shoulder in his fear of discovery.

A moment later, he was almost trodden on by a small priest, dressed in a black tunic with a short cloak around his shoulders. He sat up suddenly and the little man gave a shriek of terror at this ugly apparition that had bobbed up from under the ground.

'Thomas! Thomas, where are you?' came a deep bellow from near by. A moment later, a red-headed giant appeared, wielding a great sword. The sight of this apparition was almost enough to frighten the Fleming to death. With a roar, the new arrival dragged the priest out of harm's way and pointed the sword at Jan's throat.

'Who the bloody hell are you?' boomed the giant, as yet another figure appeared, this time a tall man dressed in black, also with a broadsword uplifted.

'He's no Turk, that's for sure,' snapped John, lowering his sword when he saw that the man was no threat. 'What an ugly bastard, though!'

The Fleming was used to such insults and was too glad to see someone other than his previous captors to take offence. He gargled his usual noises and pointed to his mouth.

'The poor fellow must be dumb,' said Thomas, always the most sympathetic to his fellow men. 'And he's wounded, too!'

The clerk dropped to his knees and gently lifted the end of the cross-bow bolt, which was hanging down behind Jan's shoulder, sticking out of the bloodstained fabric of his jerkin.

'He's been shot!' grunted Gwyn, now suddenly solicitous. He moved to bend over the man, but Jan held up a hand and, without help, climbed to his feet, grimacing now that the painkilling panic was wearing off.

'Hold on there, fellow,' said de Wolfe. 'We need to see how bad that wound is.'

They gently pulled down his jerkin and drew aside his tunic to expose the injury. 'Just caught under the skin, lucky chap,' announced Gwyn. 'This will hurt for a moment!'

With a quick snick with the point of his dagger, the coroner's officer cut through a small bridge of skin that was holding the head of the bolt and pulled it out. Even without a tongue, Jan gave a howl of agony, but the worst was over and Thomas slapped the bloody pad from the Fleming's tunic back over the wound to stem the fresh bleeding.

'Have we anything to hold this in place?' he demanded. Gwyn groped in the scrip on his belt and pulled out a length of red silk cord, which had been used to tie old Joel to the tree. As he gave it to Thomas to use to bind the pad around the shoulder and under the armpit, Jan became excited. Pointing to the cord, he motioned behind him, indicating distance, then pointed to the arrow that Gwyn was holding.

'The poor bugger is trying to tell us something! Thomas, you have the best brains here. Can you get some sense out of him?'

The clerk got the Fleming to sit on the tree trunk and perched alongside him.

'Can you understand what we say in French?' An eager nod led to the next question.

'You cannot speak?'

Jan pointed to his mouth and opened it to reveal the loss of his tongue. Then he performed a mime of running away and someone loosing a cross-bow at him.

'Ask him who did it,' snapped John impatiently, forgetting that Jan could understand him perfectly without Thomas's intervention. The man then went into a more complicated pantomime which left John and his officer bemused, but the sharp-witted clerk picked up the meaning.

'He's pointing to his head and winding it around, then at your sword and making a curving action. That could be a turban and a scimitar, eh?'

He looked at Jan, who nodded energetically, then did the turban mime again and held up three fingers.

'Three Saracens, is that it?' Again a nod, then he held up two more fingers, but shook his head while making the turban sign and pointed to them.

'Three Turks and two English?' The query was met by another wag of the head.

De Wolfe looked almost triumphant at this unexpected news. 'Where are these people? How far away?'

This was a tougher proposition for Jan's miming powers. He pointed vaguely behind him, then shrugged when he found he had no means of conveying time or distance. He saw a patch of bare earth near his feet, however, and with a stick, he used his good arm to scratch a crude sketch in the dirt, of a castle with a battlement on a mound. Then he mimed it falling down.

'Some old ruin, I would guess, Crowner,' ventured Thomas, and the Fleming nodded.

By now, the smith and the other villager with the pitchfork had closed in on them and were staring in wonder at the apparition sitting on the log.

'Where the hell did you find him, sir?' grunted the smith. 'His face is enough to curdle milk!'

'Never mind that, the poor man is hurt,' snapped de Wolfe. 'Get him back to the alehouse and ask Madge to dress his wound and give him some sustenance.'

As the second villager led the Fleming away, the coroner threw one last question after him.

'Wherever this place is, did you see any women there?'

Jan nodded and held up two fingers, then mimed the slamming of a door and the dropping of a bar. As a bonus, he also pantomimed by pointing at John and Gwyn, then at his bushy moustache to establish the sex, followed by the two fingers and the locking-up gestures.

'Two women and another two men, all imprisoned!' divined Thomas, unnecessarily.

'That's good enough for us!' shouted John. 'Come on, let's find this damned place. I don't know who that fellow was, but he was a godsend!'

The light was starting to fail in the women's prison chamber, as the short autumn day came to an end. The narrow shaft that was their only indication of the outside world was darkening, and Hilda roamed restlessly about, reluctant to sit while she could still see the dim shapes of the crates that littered the room. Matilda was slumped on the mattress, her head in her hands. She had been praying for several hours, but now seemed to have abandoned even that solace.

Hilda had already been through the contents of the boxes, looking for anything that might serve as a weapon. All she could find were bottles of strange-smelling powders, a crock of quicksilver and some scraps of metal, together with strange utensils that looked as if they belonged in an apothecary's shop. There were no knives or even heavy rods that could be used as bludgeons. In despair, she even tried to wield a glass vessel, a round flask with a long narrow spout, presumably used for distillation. It was far too light to be of any use as a club, especially as she then dropped it and it smashed on the floor. In the remaining light, however, she saw that one jagged fragment of the spout was at least as long as the span of her fingers and had a needle-sharp point at one end.

Tearing a strip of linen from the bottom of her kirtle, she wrapped this around the blunt end to form a crude hilt, so that she could grip it without cutting her fingers. Then she folded the whole thing in another piece of cloth and hid it in a pocket inside her cloak. Hilda was not sure what use this might be, beyond the half-formed thought that she might use it to kill herself and Matilda if they were threatened with rape or torture.

She went over to the older woman and put a comforting arm around her shoulders. 'Maybe they will let us go tomorrow,' she said, with a conviction that she did not feel in the slightest.

'I am well aware of who you are,' said Matilda suddenly, looking up at the blonde woman. 'But it doesn't seem to matter now. You have been kindness itself to me.'

Hilda was at a loss for words and merely squeezed Matilda's shoulder.

'I so wish my husband was here now,' murmured John's wife. 'With all his faults – and they are too many to speak of – he has a way of getting things done and never lets anything defeat him.'

She began sobbing quietly into her hands, but Hilda could think of nothing to comfort her. Suddenly, there was a clatter at the door, which had not been opened since Matilda had arrived the previous day. The bar was lifted from the outside and the door creaked open, yellow light from the crypt seeping in. The two Saxon outlaws were standing there, one with a heavy staff in his hands, the other with a bared dagger.

The younger one, Alfred, waved his knife at them. 'Come on, you two – out of there!' Again, Hilda tried her best, using her Saxon style of speech, to soften their hearts and persuade them to let them escape, but the two hulking peasants ignored her.

As they moved to the door, Ulf produced a length of thin rope and with a leer lashed it around their waists, so that they were joined together about four feet apart. He tugged on the long free end, pulling them like a carter with a pair of pack ponies.

'Move yourselves! We don't want you running off as well as that ugly Fleming bastard!'

As they stumbled fearfully towards the stairs, Hilda saw that the vaulted undercroft was empty – even the strange pair of men were absent. The fact that one of them seemed to have escaped, according to Ulf, raised a faint flicker of hope in Hilda's breast, but it soon faded. Outside, though it was getting dusk, the remaining light felt strange after the gloom of the chamber below. It was cold and both women shivered in spite of their mantles. Ulf tugged them across the weeds and nettles to the ruined bailey, and when they reached one of the huts he made them stand outside. The three Saracens appeared from within, and their leader stood in the doorway, rattling off a string of instructions to the other pair, their language mere gibberish in Hilda's ears. They loped off across the yard towards the crypt and vanished, leaving their chief to stare fixedly at Matilda. He ignored Hilda, but the older woman seemed to have a fascination for him.

'What do you want from us, man?' demanded Matilda, her voice quavering in spite of her best efforts to sound composed.

The black eyes of the Arab continued to bore into her.

'You will soon learn, woman. Now be silent!' he ordered, in heavily accented but easily understandable French.

'Where is my brother?' persisted Matilda, desperately frightened but stubbornly undeterred by this evil man. He ignored her, and she glared back at him, taking in his long white burnous with the dagger thrust through the belt and the green cloth wound around his head. The narrow black beard rimming his face helped to give him an even more evil, sinister appearance. He seemed to be swaying slightly, as if rhythmically dancing to some silent melody in his head.

Ulf, who still held the end of their rope, had taken up

a position at one end of the hut and Alfred went to the other. They appeared to be waiting for something to happen. A few moments later, the taller of the two Turks emerged from the doorway to the crypt, pulling on another rope of red plaited silk. This was looped around the neck of a haggard but handsome man in early middle age, who Matilda had never seen before, but who Hilda recognised as someone she had seen briefly when she had first been captured. As with their own bonds, the long cord travelled from this man to the neck of another, slighter figure – Matilda's own brother!

'Richard! What's happening, for God's sake? Who are these terrible men?' she screamed at him. She had at least been forewarned by Hilda that her brother was a captive, but Richard was astounded to see his sister there, roped to a woman he did not recognise.

'Matilda! How did you come to be here? For Christ's sake, you should still be in that chapel!'

Any explanations were brutally cut short, as Nizam stepped forward and punched Richard in the belly, then spat in his face for good measure. As the wrists of the captives were bound together behind their backs, there was no chance of retaliation. Gasping from the blow, de Revelle became even more short of breath, as Malik yanked on his end of the cord, tightening the noose around Richard's neck. He dragged the pair along until they were standing in line with the two women.

Raymond de Blois was not lacking in courage and yelled at the Saracen at the top of his voice.

'Nizam, why are you doing this? Have I not led you here and looked after you these past weeks? What do you want from us?'

The Arab walked across to him and stared coldly into his face.

'What do I want? I want your lives! Though you are not part of my personal jihad, did you not go to Palestine as part of your Christian armies?'

The Frenchman scowled at him. 'I was there for a year, yes! I was with King Philip at the siege of Acre. What of it?'

Nizam stepped back a few paces and then began marching up and down the line of prisoners, in a jerky, agitated manner. Alexander, peering cautiously from the doorway of the eating hut, again wondered whether he was under the influence of some sort of stimulant drug. Then the Turk abruptly stopped his perambulations and turned to face the prisoners, almost like some general addressing his troops.

'I have sworn a great oath and nothing will stop me from fulfilling that!' His French, though spoken with a guttural accent, seemed to be improving by the minute, though emotion shook him.

'Hear me, you uncaring spawn of looters and murderers! My father, as he lay dying from wounds made by your kind, begged me to avenge him, my family and all those who died by the hand of your ancestors.'

His voice rose in a ranting tirade, and he began swaying again.

'Damascus! Hundreds of your brigands, both lords and knights and common killers, descended on our city. I was but a child but the cries, the smoke, the blood, the despair – they will remain with me for ever!'

Raymond de Blois, though the cord was cutting into his neck, croaked out a disclaimer.

'The siege of Damascus! It failed miserably – and it was over forty years ago, we were not even born then. What has that to do with us?'

Nizam continued as if the words had never been uttered.

'The siege failed, but your rabble turned against the villages near by in their frustration and burned them to the ground. But not before looting, raping, mutilating, killing! My mother was ravished, then her throat was cut, three of my small brothers and two of my sisters were burned alive when our dwelling was fired. My father had

311

dragged me outside, bleeding from his belly and mouth, and I survived under his dying body.'

There was a silence, broken only by a low sobbing from Matilda, whether for the pathos of the Turk's story or her own mortal fear was not clear.

'We cannot be held responsible for these misdeeds of others!' shouted de Blois, but again Nizam ignored him. He seemed to be in a trance, his mind tracking back forty-seven years.

'Even as a boy, I swore to carry out my father's plea and seek vengeance, even if it took me the rest of my life. I have read that your own holy book says that the sins of the father may be visited unto the fourth generation. I cannot achieve that, so one or two generations must suffice!'

At last Richard de Revelle found his voice, even though the tight cord made his words even more hoarse than Raymond's.

'I have never set foot in Palestine! Why are you doing this to me?'

The Saracen seemed to notice him at last.

'De Revelle? Your father was a de Revelle, Gervaise de Revelle, who was at Damascus! Like this man le Calve, whose father was at Damascus! Like that Templar, Joel de Valle Torta, who was at Damascus!'

'How can you know this, after all this time?' croaked de Blois.

Nizam smiled, a twisted, sardonic smile.

'My father's dying demand to me, to avenge my family and my people, never left me. I have dedicated my life to it. It is my crusade, a far more worthy one than yours!'

He twitched his arms spasmodically and almost danced a couple of steps sideways, before continuing. 'When I was left an orphan in a burnt-out village, I wandered with a few other survivors until I was taken in by an imam of the Nizari sect of the Isma'ili. I grew up in their care and became a devoted servant of their master, Rashid el-din Sinan, in Syria. He learned of my unwavering desire for vengeance and fostered it. I became a fervent disciple of theirs and they put me to work, good practice for my vengeance. Many a Crusader has met his death at the end of my knife! Do you not recall Conrad de Montferrat, your so-called King of Jerusalem?'

'He was murdered in Tyre by two fanatics, dressed as Christian monks. Both of of them were killed,' countered de Blois.

'There were three, for I was waiting near by, in case the others failed. And in France this year, four more of your Frankish knights who were at Damascus – and two of their sons – died on our knives, like the rats they were!'

He gestured towards Abdul and Malik, but they stood impassively, unable to understand a word of what was going on.

'You cannot know that my father or le Calve or that Templar were involved in your tragedy in Damascus,' blustered Richard de Revelle, desperately.

'For years, our sect has sought information on who was present in that evil enterprise,' shouted Nizam. 'Gradually facts emerged, both in Palestine and in France. Those men were known to have been at the assault on Damascus and that is sufficient for us! They must die, and if death has already claimed them, then their sons and daughters must die, just as my father's sons and daughters died! After we have dealt with you, there are three more in your other counties who must be brought to account.'

Spittle appeared at the corners of his mouth and his eyes rolled wildly as a fanatical ecstasy possessed him.

'You can never return to your homeland – or even to France – without my help!' shouted Raymond. 'You are trapped here!'

The Arab gave an almost hysterical laugh. 'Escape! What care we about escape? We are dedicated to our task and will die joyfully at its end and pass into paradise! It is only because there were so many other rats to exterminate that we have not died with our victims, as is the usual way with our sect.'

His mood suddenly changed and he swung round to call out to his servants in his native tongue. Abdul dropped his end of the neck cord and vanished into the next hut, reappearing with a great armful of hay, which was stored there as fodder for the horses. He threw this into the dining shack, strewing it about as tinder. Then he came out again, holding a burning pitch brand which he had lit at the cooking fire. He held this high, the light of the yellow flame dancing over the desperate group, adding a macabre glow to the last remaining light of the dying day.

It was this light which finally guided de Wolfe to the old castle. After leaving the wounded Fleming to stumble with the villager back towards Bigbury, John, Gwyn and the smith, with Thomas trailing behind, tramped onward, trying to steer in the direction that Jan had indicated to the best of his ability. The light was fading fast, but there was enough to see the trail of crushed weeds and ferns, though where the trees were thicker there was more bare soil than undergrowth.

Every few minutes, John would raise a hand for them to stop and they would listen intently for any sound of voices, but all was silence, save for a few birds squabbling over a perch for the night.

After some twenty minutes, the coroner began to feel desperate. Both Matilda and Hilda were out there somewhere, but unless they could find this place that the dumb fellow had mimed, they might as well be back in Exeter.

'Shall we split up, Crowner?' suggested Gwyn in a low voice. 'Then we could cover a wider area than if we stick in a bunch like this.'

De Wolfe shook his head. 'If we get seperated this near to dusk, we'll never find each other again, without a lot of

shouting, which will give us away. Give it a few more minutes, walking straight ahead.'

The trail of bruised weeds had now petered out – or
was invisible in the failing light – but the movement of
clouds glimpsed dimly through the half-bare tree-tops
gave them some idea of direction. At least they could prevent themselves from walking in circles.

A few minutes later, John was beginning to reconsider
Gwyn's idea of splitting up when Thomas hissed a warning. His younger eyes had caught something away to the
right.

'I saw a flicker, Crowner! A yellow light, very faint.'

They all stopped to stare where his finger was pointing.
'There it is again!'

This time the others glimpsed a moving flare through
the trees.

'Must be a pitch brand,' growled Gwyn. 'Someone is
waving it around.'

With John in the lead, they carefully crept forward,
agonising when a foot snapped a dried twig. Two hundred paces brought them to the remains of a tumbled
stone wall, heavily overgrown with ivy and other weeds.
Now the flicker of the torch was easily visible, reflected
from trees on the other side of a large clearing. They
peered cautiously over the wall and in the last light of the
day, augmented by the dancing flame of the burning
pitch brand, a macabre scene met their eyes.

Before some half-ruined huts, a pair of large, scruffy
men stood, one with a staff, the other holding a mace.
Near them, a Saracen in a voluminous belted robe held a
flaming torch above his head, while another stood clutching a cross-bow, the string of which was cranked back
ready to fire. But the centrepiece was the line of captives,
two men lashed together by a rope joining their necks –
and two women, tied at the waist.

In front of them was a thickset Saracen, with a green
head cloth, holding high a wide, curved dagger, like a

priest using a cross to exorcise demons. His voice came clearly across the narrow castle yard.

'This was my father's knife! He gave it to me as he was dying and made me swear to avenge him and our family. It has never left me. I have slain a score of unbelievers with it, both for Sinan and myself!'

De Wolfe's brain had been paralysed for a few seconds by the shock of what he was witnessing, but now a deep rumble of pure anger rolled in his chest and he started to rise above the tattered wall, his hand already drawing his sword.

Gwyn urgently dragged him down, clutching the sleeve of his tunic.

'Not yet, Crowner! For Christ's sake, wait!' he hissed. 'They could knife your wife and Hilda before you could get halfway across the bailey. And that cross-bow could kill you, too.'

Even as he spoke, however, Gwyn was drawing his own sword.

'We must do something!' whispered John, desperately. 'Distract them somehow.'

'There are five of them to our three – and all we have are two swords and a blacksmith's hammer. That cross-bow is the problem.'

Frustrated beyond measure, they waited and watched the drama below. Nizam screamed some orders to his henchmen and the one with the cross-bow leaned into the hut and dragged out Alexander of Leith. He was pushed aside and the leader raised a finger, pointing at the alchemist.

'You I am sparing! Get yourself gone and thank your God, if you have one, that I am merciful to those who played no part in shameful events!'

The little Scotsman, whose appearance was another surprise to the watchers hidden behind the wall, sidled off and then ran on his short legs towards the track that led out of the bailey. He vanished from the view of the

Saracens, but from his vantage point the coroner could see that he had hidden in the undergrowth where he could observe what was going on near the huts.

'Who the hell is that?' muttered Gwyn into de Wolfe's ear.

'God knows! And who is that tall fellow roped to de Revelle?'

There was no time for an answer, as events began to move fast. Nizam rattled off more instructions to his men, who closed in on the captives. He gesticulated at the two Saxons, who were now looking more than a little anxious, but they started to pull the captives towards the door of the hut.

Richard de Revelle struggled to get nearer his sister, bellowing a mixture of prayers, obscenities and supplication, but a prod with the tip of Ulf's mace kept him moving. Then Hilda decided to come to a dead stop and refused to move, even though she was being hauled by the rope around her waist. Matilda cannoned into the back of her and then sank to her knees, sobbing on the ground.

'Who killed my husband?' called out the blonde woman, in a high, clear voice. 'Who slew the ship-master? I am entitled to know that, even at the last, before I die!'

This seemed to startle the captors into momentary silence, then Nizam laughed and translated her words for his two acolytes. Abdul, the one with the cross-bow, laughed in his turn. He stepped towards Hilda and indicated himself by tapping his own chest with his free hand, before bending forwards to spit in her face.

A second later he reeled back, as a long sliver of glass, exquisitely sharp at its point, was thrust deep into his chest. He screamed, raising the cross-bow to discharge it at the woman who had stabbed him, but then a great gout of blood shot from his mouth and he fell forward, the bolt fired harmlessly into the ground.

Pandemonium broke out, as Raymond de Blois roared

defiance and charged head down at Nizam, his hands still tied behind his back. It was a heroic but hopeless gesture, as his neck was still linked to de Revelle's. The rope brought him up short and the leader of the Arabs plunged his long dagger into his belly. As de Blois fell, dragging Richard to his knees, Nizam stabbed him repeatedly, then began kicking the twitching body as it lay on the ground.

He would have done better to look over his shoulder, as a warning cry from Malik and Ulf heralded the charge of two very large and very angry men brandishing long swords, followed by another swinging a huge hammer over his head.

Malik threw his pitch brand at Gwyn, who brushed it aside as if it were a fly and swung his heavy blade at the side of the Turk's neck, almost severing his head from his shoulders before the man could even attempt a thrust with his long curved knife. John had gone straight for Nizam, roaring with rage at this evil creature who had dared to abduct his wife, to say nothing of his former mistress.

The Saracen leader made no attempt to defend himself against this black shape that had appeared from nowhere, but in a desperate attempt to fulfill his father's oath, he launched himself at Richard de Revelle, who was still on the ground, crouching and still linked to the bloody corpse of Raymond de Blois. He put his dagger to Richard's throat, again drawing blood, as he screamed for his two Saxon mercenaries to come to his aid. But Ulf and Alfred were nowhere to be seen – they had melted away as soon as they saw how the battle was going and had vanished into the forest.

John raised his sword, ready to hack off Nizam's arms one by one, followed by his legs and head. But the Arab pressed his blade deeper into de Revelle's neck.

'Keep back or I will kill him!' he screamed, some vestige of hope suggesting that if he could stay alive long enough, he might get the sister as well. John stayed his sword-stroke in midair.

'Kill the bastard, for all I care!' he roared. 'I'm going to cut you into little pieces, whoever you are!'

'John, save him. Save my brother!' screamed Matilda, her tear-streaked face lifting from the crouch into which she had collapsed.

Indecision now clouded de Wolfe's mind as the red rage began to subside. Gwyn also moved cautiously towards Nizam, sword raised, but the Turk dug the point of his dagger into Richard's neck, making the victim utter a gurgling scream of terror. With a quick slash, Nizam cut through the cord around his neck, separating him from Raymond's corpse. Keeping the knife to his neck, he began to drag the manor-lord towards his sister.

'Stop him, Crowner!' yelled Gwyn. 'He wants her too!'

But the warning was unnecessary. Suddenly, Nizam's eyes rolled upwards in their sockets, exposing the whites, and he began twitching. He dropped the dagger and fell to the ground, black blood appearing at his lips. Then he had a full-blown convulsion and a great gout of dark fluid erupted from his mouth, before he finally became still.

There was a flurry from behind and the strange figure of the little man in the kilt and blouse rushed down from where he had been concealed.

'It worked, thank God! I was beginning to think I was losing my touch!'

CHAPTER SEVENTEEN

In which Crowner John returns home

Confusion reigned in the old castle bailey, as the survivors struggled to understand what was happening. John de Wolfe felt as if his head was bursting, as he tried to make sense of the chaotic situation, which was not helped by Matilda collapsing to the ground, alternately wailing and laughing, as she clutched his legs in an unprecedented paroxysm of gratitude.

Hilda also slid to the floor, still attached to John's wife by the cord, but she sat bowed over, staring blankly at the bloodstained shard of glass which she still clutched in her hand.

Richard de Revelle was bellowing for his wrists to be released and the blacksmith ran across to him to slash through the cords with his knife. Richard staggered across to John and grasped his arm like a drowning man clinging to a floating log.

'John, where in Christ's name did you spring from! You saved my life!' Though de Revelle was wild eyed and almost incoherent, the coroner noticed that he said 'my life', typically ignoring the salvation of his sister and the other woman.

'It seems to be becoming a habit, Richard!' he said cynically. 'Though I think this brave young woman deserves most praise.' He indicated Hilda, who was still slumped among the weeds.

Then he bent down and gently raised Matilda to her

feet, putting an arm around her shoulders, but forbearing to actually embrace her. Her almost hysterical keening subsided and she sniffed and rubbed her tear-stained face with her hand, making it even more grubby. Her cloak was soiled with dirt and bits of straw from her prison, making the contrast with her usual immaculate appearance all the more obvious. Gwyn, who sometimes showed more tact and sensitivity than his shambling appearance would suggest, took in the situation with John and his wife and went to Hilda, lifting her up and hugging her in his bear-like grasp, while he gently prised the glass dagger from her fingers.

'Well done, brave lass!' he murmured in her ear. 'Now Thorgils can rest in peace, wherever he is.'

Richard de Revelle belatedly acknowledged that others besides himself had survived and went to his sister, whereupon John readily relinquished her into his arms. Emotional women frightened de Wolfe beyond measure, but now he went to Hilda and rather self-consciously kissed her on the cheek. Rapidly becoming composed again, she put a hand to his cheek and said a simple 'Thank you, John!', but the look that blazed out of her blue eyes as she uttered the words was worth more than an hour's eulogy of gratitude.

At this point, the burly blacksmith appeared, grasping a squirming Alexander by the collar of his peculiar garment.

'I don't know who this strange fellow might be,' he announced. 'He's the only one left. Those two big bastards seem to have run off and the rest are all dead!'

Thomas de Peyne, a horrified observer who had kept well back from the recent mayhem, now came closer and pointed to the strange symbols embroidered on the Scotsman's tunic.

'You are an alchemist, I presume?'

'Ay, I am indeed! And sorry I am that I ever left my chamber in Bristol to come among these madmen!' He waved at the four corpses on the ground. 'Though that gentleman was civil enough, he just fell into bad company with those Moors!'

'How does that dumb giant with no tongue fit into all this?' demanded Gwyn. Alexander seized on the words with delight.

'You know of Jan the Fleming? Is he alive and well?' he shrilled.

'Certainly alive, and well enough for a man with a cross-bow bolt through his shoulder,' snapped John. 'He should survive, but who the hell was he? And who who are you, for St Peter's sake?'

'I am Alexander of Leith, a humble alchemist, searching for the Elixir of Life. That poor man Jan is my servant and assistant.'

Belatedly, the alchemist began to realise that his presence in this camp might take some explaining when law officers started to take an interest. This was rapidly reinforced when de Wolfe declared that he was the King's Coroner for the county and was determined to get to the bottom of whatever had been going on here.

Richard de Revelle also got the same message and his devious mind began to plan evasive action. As he held a linen kerchief to his throat to mop up the blood still oozing from the shallow cut, he glared at Alexander, then gave him a covert wink that was not lost on the Scotsman. Both of them had the same desire to draw as heavy a veil as possible over their activities. In this, they were greatly aided by the fact that all the Saracens were dead and Raymond de Blois was also beyond providing any explanations. If possible, it would be a considerable advantage if the coroner never learned that he was French, rather than Norman.

Richard looked down at the man's corpse, lying on its side in a pool of blood that had welled from the multiple wounds in his chest. Thomas was crouched alongside the body, making the sign of the Cross over it and murmuring suitable incantations in Latin. De Revelle, justifying his self-interest, thought it was just as well that he had been killed, as a spy found in England in the service of Philip of France could look forward only to the gallows.

Gwyn was still comforting Hilda, but he gestured to the brawny blacksmith to drag the four corpses into one of the huts. The man pulled the three Saracens unceremoniously by their heels into the kitchen hut, still strewn with the hay that was to have started the conflagration that would burn their captives alive. Their turbans had come off in the grass, revealing lank black hair coiled into plaits. When Thomas had finished shriving the Frenchman, the smith was more circumspect in handling his corpse, fetching a horse blanket from the stable. He wrapped it around de Blois to smother the blood, then lifted it into his arms and staggered back to the stable with it.

For the moment, de Wolfe's priority was the well-being of the two women, his wife and his former mistress. As the fire of conflict died down and his mind began to function more coolly, he wondered how to manage this matter of Matilda and Hilda. He was aware that his wife knew the identity of the blonde woman, and in view of her caustic sarcasm and constant hostility over the past few years, he thought it best to separate them as soon as possible. He laid a hand on his brother-in-law's shoulder.

'Richard, there is much to be explained about this sad affair, but I feel that your sister needs rest and the solace of your home and wife until she is recovered.'

He was not being deliberately sarcastic in his allusion to the Lady Eleanor, though he was well aware that the two wives did not enjoy very cordial relations. 'Your manor is not that far distant and I have already sent Matilda's maid Lucille back there. She also had a bad experience when those bastards dragged Matilda from the chapel, so the bailiff of Ringmore has taken her to Revelstoke, where she can care now for Matilda's needs.'

He wondered what had happened to the rescue party he had ordered William Vado to rouse from Revelstoke – there had been no sign of them, though admittedly events had moved very fast that afternoon.

Richard readily agreed, as he felt it would give him more time to think up some credible cover story. His self-confidence was returning quickly, and he solicitously led his sister across the bailey, to where several horses were tethered to a rail outside the third hut, used as a stable.

John was wondering what to do about Hilda, when his wife stopped dead and spoke rationally for the first time. All traces of her recent well-justified hysteria seemed to have vanished.

'Hilda must come to Revelstoke with us!' she announced firmly. 'She has been kind to me and I cannot leave her cast adrift here.'

John was astonished at this change of heart by Matilda, but he was wise enough to conceal it. One problem was that none of the horses had side-saddles, but Hilda, rapidly recovering from shock herself, solved the problem by tearing the skirt of her kirtle up the front as far as her knees and accepting Gwyn's help to mount one of the smaller rounseys. De Wolfe experienced further astonishment when Matilda, after one look at the woman from Dawlish, bent down and did the same to her own gown, which John felt was akin to sacrilege, given the way his wife usually worshipped her garments. Almost too hastily, Richard de Revelle helped her into the saddle of another palfrey and, climbing on to his own horse, on which he had arrived, hurried the two women off along the path back to the distant road.

'I shall follow you shortly!' de Wolfe called after him. 'I need to explore this den of murderers first.'

He turned first to Alexander, who stood uncertainly in the midst of all this activity. 'Now, sir, what's been going on here?'

'Nothing but my art and my science, Sir John!' replied

the Scot, evasively. 'I was employed by this knight who now lies dead, to come from Bristol with my assistant, to join with another alchemist in attempting to complete my life's work, the preparation of the Elixir of Life.'

'You expect me to believe that?' snapped John, sarcastically.

'It is the truth, Crowner! I was deceived, for this Turk was an impostor!'

'Who was this knight?' demanded de Wolfe.

'His name was Raymond de Blois. I know almost nothing about him, he was very secretive. He sought me out in Bristol and offered me a sum I could hardly refuse to meet with an alchemist from the Orient – one he alleged was renowned for his expertise, as are many Arabic philosophers. He claimed to have met him in Outremer, when he was there as a Crusader. This Nizam turned out to be a brazen sham, but it took me a week or two to discover that.'

'Why should this de Blois give you money for such an unlikely enterprise, eh?'

Alexander shrugged. 'Various claims have been made for the discovery of the elixir – I have come very near it myself. Any man who succeeds would rapidly become rich beyond any imagining!'

De Wolfe regarded the Scot with a stony stare, unconvinced by his tale.

'God's guts, man, do you expect me to believe that some unknown knight hires a Scottish alchemist to work with three bloody Arabs in England, to discover a potion to give everlasting life? And why in a secret hideout like this? Do you take me for a fool?'

The quick-witted Scot had a ready answer. 'There is a simple explanation, Crowner. As I have indicated, such an elixir would be worth a fortune, which is why Sir Raymond sought to acquire it. Rivals would kill for its secret – as they have done in the past – so absolute secrecy is essential to avoid the theft of the formula!'

He shook his bulbous head sadly. 'Unfortunately, these Mussulmen tricked de Blois into giving them a great deal of money, though they were charlatans!'

John glared suspiciously at the little man. 'Are you trying to tell me that he brings them across the Channel, lets them slaughter a whole ship's crew to preserve their secret, just to conduct some half-magical rituals?'

Alexander shrugged. 'I know nothing of how they came here, sir! I just jogged in on a horse with my manservant. They were already here long before I arrived.'

Still unconvinced, John ordered Alexander to show him the underground laboratory in the crypt of the old priory. When they reached the bottom of the steps, he was at least reassured that some of the Scotsman's blather was true. With Gwyn and Thomas at his side, he looked in mystification at the flasks, crucibles, alembics and furnaces that cluttered the benches around the hearth.

He turned to his clerk. 'You are the one with most learning, Thomas! What do you make of all this?

The small priest had been peering with interest at the assortment of apparatus, especially several large parchment folios. 'It is certainly the paraphernalia of alchemy, master! The subject is foreign to me, but those books are full of the symbolism and cabbalistic texts of that art.'

'Of course,' said Alexander, somewhat huffily. 'I am well known among the community of alchemists, especially in relation to the elixir – which is why this Sir Raymond sought me out in Bristol.'

De Wolfe looked into the two storerooms where the prisoners had been kept. 'So how did all this apparatus appear here?' he demanded. 'Don't try to tell me that these Saracens brought it by sea, for they had to row ashore in a little curragh after the swine had slain the ship's crew! And where did your food and their horses come from? Did they make them by magic in their crucibles?'

Alexander shrugged, still looking innocent. 'It was all here when I came, Crowner. I presumed that de Blois arranged it all secretly. It was none of my business, though if I had known how it was to turn out, I would never have left Bristol, not for all the gold in Christendom!'

This expression was an unfortunate slip of the tongue if Alexander wished to keep the coroner well away from the truth. John seized upon it immediately.

'Gold? Is that not also of prime interest to alchemists?' he snapped. 'My learned clerk here tells me that seeking this fabled elixir of yours is closely allied to the search for creating gold from base matter!'

The Scot looked sheepish, but again did his best to wriggle out of a difficult situation.

'Some say that, sir, but I do not believe it to be true,' he lied. He waved a hand around the gloomy crypt, where the rush-lights were beginning to gutter and fade away. 'Look around here. You'll not find any gold, unless those scheming Arabs had some of their own.'

De Wolfe ignored the invitation and prodded the alchemist towards the stairs, from where they emerged into the twilight of the fading day. The blacksmith had relit the fallen pitch brand and stuck it in the fork of a bush, so that there was some illumination of the area in front of the huts. As they left the priory ruins, John had more questions for the hapless alchemist.

'You come from Bristol? You are sure that it is not Gloucester?'

On moderately safe ground here, Alexander contrived to look surprised as he lied once again. 'Gloucester? I have never set foot in the place.'

'So you have never had any dealing with the Count of Mortain or any of his retainers?'

This was dangerous territory, and for once Alexander was glad that Jan the Fleming had no tongue, for otherwise he might already have told a different tale to this sharp, grim law officer. He shook his head vigorously.

'Prince John? I am but a lowly philosopher, sir. I do not mix with people in such exalted circles. I know my place.'

'In that case, how did you come to be here with Sir Richard de Revelle, a knight and former sheriff of this county?' demanded the coroner.

Thinking quickly, the little Scotsman came up with an answer, and only hoped that de Revelle would tell the same story. 'I do not know him in any real sense, Crowner!' he answered gravely. 'He seems to have been a friend of this poor man who lies dead, Raymond de Blois.'

He stopped and assumed an air of sudden inspiration. 'I suspect they were business partners in trying to obtain the priceless Elixir of Life. Maybe it was he who provided everything here. This was his second visit to see de Blois and to try to get those deceitful Turks to achieve some results.'

De Wolfe rasped a hand over his stubble. The story was becoming more plausible as the idea of Richard becoming involved in any dubious scheme that would make him even richer was not difficult to believe.

By now they had reached the kitchen shed, where the faithful blacksmith was standing guard, still grasping his great hammer. Gwyn stuck his head through the doorway and looked down at the three white-clad corpses.

'What are we going to do about these devils?' he growled.

The sight of the bodies reminded John of something that until now had been driven from his mind by the urgency and confusion of the past half-hour.

'This bastard you called Nizam, the leader of this gang,' he rasped. 'Why did he suddenly keel over like that? I was looking forward to spitting him on my sword!'

Gwyn decided not to remind him that Nizam had a knife at Richard's throat at that precise moment and Alexander, with a trace of pride, answered the coroner.

'That was my doing! Though it was a close thing, as I

had no means of telling when and how completely they would finish that mess they called food.'

John's black brows came together in puzzlement. 'What the hell are you talking about?'

'When they went chasing my man Jan, I took the opportunity to dose their food with a lethal concoction that I prepared for such an eventuality. It would have killed them all eventually, but Abdul and Malik came to a more violent end before it could work upon their systems!'

De Wolfe and Gwyn stared at the weird Scot with more respect.

'What was the stuff you gave them, eh?' demanded Gwyn.

Alexander grinned, his impish face creasing into a knowing smile.

'Among the many experiments I have made seeking the elixir, I had many failures. Some of them dropped rats and cats dead on the spot, others had a delayed action. One batch of the liquid I accidentally proved to be effective on a human, though he was a condemned prisoner,' he added nonchalantly. 'I made up a small vial of that one yesterday and kept it hidden in case I had use for it.'

Gwyn roared with laughter and slapped the alchemist on the back.

'Remind me never to eat or drink in your company, old man!' he boomed.

De Wolfe seemed less amused and returned to the problem in hand.

'The Christian knight deserves a proper burial, for he was a brave man, trying to attack those bastards with his hands tied behind his back.'

Thomas crossed himself piously as he agreed and made a suggestion.

'If he was a friend of Sir Richard, then perhaps he should attend to his last rites. He may know who his relatives are and could inform them of his death.'

De Wolfe nodded. 'I will tax him with it when later we go across to Revelstoke. But what about these infidels?'

'Are you going to hold an inquest?' asked Gwyn, his doubtful tone suggesting that it would be a waste of effort.

John considered the matter for a long moment. His dogged adherence to orders which had always made him such a staunch follower of King Richard, inclined him to stick to the rules and hold an inquiry on the spot into the four deaths. But common sense was telling him that these were all foreigners and non-Christians, who seemed totally outside the jurisdiction of the Crown. What was the point of sticking to the established routines of First Finder and Presentment of Englishry – and what possible jury could he empanel that would be of the slightest use? Come to think of it, the First Finder was John himself, as much as any of the others present.

The whole process seemed futile, and the ramifications regarding this little alchemist, his dumb servant – and even Richard, Matilda and Hilda – were likely to lead to complications that none of them would welcome. Hilda had stabbed a man to death, and though it seemed wholly justified in the heat of the moment, if the event was recorded on Thomas's rolls, the justices would have to haul her before the next session of the Eyre, with all the attendant publicity throughout the county. Furthermore, he had no desire to have his own wife embroiled in any legal proceedings and suffer the malicious gossip of her acquaintances in Exeter.

He made up his mind, not without some misgivings. 'To hell with it. There's nothing to be gained by probing this open sore!' he growled. 'I must tell the sheriff and Justiciar something, if only to explain the deaths at Shillingford and of the crew of Thorgils' vessel. But I will trim the truth to sensible proportions.'

'So what are we to do with these cadavers?' persisted Gwyn.

'Have you searched them? Maybe they carry

something that shows who they were and where they came from.'

The blacksmith, who had stood guard while the others were in the crypt, pointed to some objects on the ground near his feet.

'I went through their clothing, but apart from that gold chain and three wicked knives, there was nothing, apart from these little pouches.'

He bent and handed over some small envelopes of soft leather, inside which were lumps of a dark, brittle substance and some grimy powder.

Thomas sniffed warily at one. 'This is some kind of aromatic herb, no doubt an exotic drug,' he declared. They all had a sniff at it, but were none the wiser, although Gwyn said it reminded him of the souk in Jaffa.

'Let's show it to that fat priest in Rougemont,' he suggested. 'Brother Rufus seems to know a lot about the seedier side of life in the Holy Land!'

'But what are we to do with these corpses?' Thomas repeated Gwyn's question, anxious to get away from this dark and forbidding place.

De Wolfe put his head inside the doorway again and looked at the still figures and the pile of hay.

'The sods were going to burn my wife and my woman alive in here, God curse their evil souls!' he said harshly. 'Let them go the same way!' He strode to the stunted bush and pulled the guttering pitch brand free of its bare branches. With a contemptuous toss, he flung it through the door on to the pile of hay and shoved the rickety door shut. They waited until John was satisfied that the flames were taking hold, and as soon as smoke started to seep through the many gaps in the planking and the thatch, he picked up Nizam's golden chain and crescent moon and beckoned to the others to move away towards the stables and their horses.

Alexander stood uncertainly by his mare. 'This is my steed and the pony belongs to the dumb fellow,' he said tentatively. 'I am fond of the big fool. I would like to see that he gets to Totnes very soon, to have an apothecary tend his wound.'

De Wolfe, having already committed himself to bending the rules, waved a dismissive hand at the little Scotsman.

'You should find him at the alehouse in Bigbury. Now make yourself scarce and forget you ever had the greedy misfortune ever to set foot in Devon. Get yourself back to Bristol and keep out of everyone's sight, especially law officers!'

Gratefully, Alexander took the hint and began to thank the coroner profusely. John ignored him, as he gave his own thanks to the blacksmith for his steadfast help. The smith offered to show the alchemist the way back to the village and, throwing a leg over the pony, led him off at a trot along the pathway.

De Wolfe and his two companions turned back to watch the kitchen hut, which was now well ablaze. Thick grey smoke belched up from under the eaves into the evening sky and flames began issuing through the dilapidated thatch. There was a rank smell of burning vegetation, mixed with another odour – that of scorching flesh. Suddenly the roof fell in amid a great geyser of sparks that shot up into the air, and within moments the walls had caved in and the hut was converted into a blazing bonfire.

'That's the end of those swine,' said Gwyn with satisfaction. 'Though nothing can repay them for such vicious cruelty.'

Their own horses were still back in the village, so they took the spare ones left by the inhabitants of the camp to ride around to Bigbury. A moon had risen and, aided by the last streak of daylight in the western sky, they followed the path back to the road that joined St Anne's Chapel to the village. Just before the junction, they came across further evidence of the Turks' murderous activities. At the side of the path were two bodies, each with a cross-bow bolt in the back. They were lying face down alongside a dead campfire, and some pieces of bread near by suggested that they had been shot while eating their meal. Each wore a jerkin carrying the insignia of a blackbird on a green ground.

'That's de Revelle's device,' said Gwyn, turning the bodies over to look at their faces, as Thomas dropped alongside them to murmur his compassionate absolutions. His return to the priesthood was getting plenty of practice, if only in shriving the dead.

'He must have left them here on guard, by the looks of it,' agreed the coroner. 'Pretty poor guards they turned out to be – their idleness cost them their lives.'

Gwyn was not so harsh in his judgement. 'Not a lot you can do, taken unawares with a cross-bow fired from cover! Those bloody Saracens were highly skilled with their weapons in Palestine.'

There was nothing the trio could do about the bodies, so they remounted and rode on.

De Wolfe commented, 'De Revelle must have seen them, as he passed here when he left. It's up to him to collect them – he can do it when he sends a party to bring back this de Blois fellow.'

This reminded him that the posse he had sent the bailiff to fetch from Revelstoke had never shown up.

'Maybe de Revelle will encounter it on his way home and get them to return with him . . . and to hell with us, now that the fighting's over!' said Gwyn cynically.

They rode down to Bigbury to collect their own mounts, discovering at the alehouse that Alexander of Leith had already collected his injured servant. The strange pair had vanished down towards the river to take the tidal path up to Aveton, keen to put as much distance as possible between themselves and the law officers. The villagers were relieved to hear that their ghostly neighbours in the forest had been eliminated, and even more grateful when the coroner left them the horses from the camp as a gift.

'If they were provided at de Revelle's expense, he's lost them for good now!' said John spitefully. He touched Odin's flanks with his heels and they set off westwards. 'Let's catch up with the lying bastard. But I feel that once again he'll scrape out of this affair with his skin intact.'

'But at least he's had a bloody good fright, coming within an ace of being burnt alive!' declared Gwyn.

'And he came nearer having his throat cut than any man I've known!' added de Wolfe cheerfully.

Gwyn joined him in a belly laugh, and even Thomas managed a weak grin.

Five evenings later, a group of people were huddled around John's favourite table in the Bush Inn at Exeter. The remains of a lavish meal provided by Nesta lay in the centre, surrounded by pots of ale and cider and a cup of the best wine for Thomas. The taproom, lit by flickering rush-lights hung around the walls, was warmed by a large fire and the fug generated by a score of patrons. Outside it was frosty and Idle Lane wore a patchy white mantle. It had snowed that day, but the light fall had almost melted away.

'They'll be able to travel in this,' said Gwyn confidently. 'By tomorrow, Hilda will be safely back in Dawlish and your wife will be home to make your life a misery once again!'

John de Wolfe caught Nesta's eye and looked away uncomfortably. She smiled and put a reassuring hand on his thigh under the table. That day, a servant from Revelstoke, on his way to the other manor at Tiverton, had called at Martin's Lane and left a message with Mary that Matilda and Hilda were on their way home, attended by a strong escort.

As well as Thomas de Peyne and Gwyn, the garrison

chaplain, Brother Rufus, sat at the table. After several years as a military priest, the burly monk had no qualms about visiting alehouses and accepted with alacrity Gwyn's invitation to join them that evening. He was examining the substances in the small leather pouches that had been taken from the bodies of the slain Arabs. After sniffing at them and cautiously tasting a fingertip rubbed on the brown lumps and dipped in the dirty white powder, he delivered his verdict.

'The dark stuff is what they call hashish, made from a feathery kind of plant. I tried it once, though I admit a few cups of brandy-wine had more effect on me!' The jovial Benedictine gave a loud belly laugh and nudged the disapproving Thomas in the ribs.

'What about the powder?' asked John.

Rufus hunched his big shoulders. 'I don't know. It's not opium, as far as I can tell. But those fellows out there have all sorts of strange concoctions made from herbs and plants.'

'So why do they eat them?' demanded Gwyn. 'What's the effect?'

'It varies a lot – some just send the devils to sleep, to dream of Nirvana or wherever they fancy spending eternity. Other drugs are said to give them lurid dreams or else make them fighting mad. I'm not an expert, but I've seen some strange goings-on out in Palestine, as I expect Sir John and yourself have experienced.'

Thomas was proud of his own scholarship and unwilling to surrender all the explanations to the monk, especially after his recent hurried researches in the library over the Chapter House.

'This "hasish" gives rise to the *hashishin*, the common name for this murderous branch of the Nizari sect of the Shi'ites,' he said importantly. 'They have been slaying both their Sunni rivals and Christians – especially Crusaders – for years. They even had three attempts at Saladin himself!'

This was something de Wolfe knew about. 'Count Conrad de Montferrat, who was to be King of Jerusalem, was murdered by them when we were out there, Gwyn. Remember all that scandal?'

The Cornishman nodded. 'Two Saracens, dressed as Christian monks, stabbed him in the street. Didn't that bastard Philip of France try to put the blame on our King Richard, because he favoured someone else for the throne of Jerusalem?'

John nodded. 'He also claimed that the Lionheart had sent *hashishin* after him, even all the way to France. He had a permanent bodyguard to protect himself.'

'But there was a letter sent by the Old Man of the Mountains, the chief of these *hashishin*, exonerating King Richard,' declared the all-knowing Thomas.

'Yes, and it was declared a forgery by the French!' added Rufus, determined not to be outdone.

De Wolfe scraped at his stubble before he spoke. 'Hilda said that this mad leader, Nizam, claimed that he was also there at Conrad's murder, as a back-up in case they failed.'

Nesta shuddered, and not just at the mention of Hilda's name. 'These people sound completely crazy!' she said. 'Are they always under the infuence of this horrible stuff?' She pointed at the leather pouches on the table.

This time, Thomas got in before Rufus.

'I have read that members of this sect are persuaded into complete obedience to their master by being drugged, then taken to his hideout in the Syrian mountains, where they are given the best of food and the company of seductive women. Then they are sent out to kill certain targets, whereupon they are always slain themselves, but die gladly because they have been promised entry into a paradise where these promiscuous delights will last for eternity!'

'Sounds good to me!' jibed Gwyn, receiving an outraged punch on the arm from Nesta.

'But this terrible man and his accomplices surely had no such political ends when they came to England?' she asked, with wide-eyed concern.

'According to Richard de Revelle, who seems to have the best recollection of those awful hours at Bigbury, this Nizam was on a personal crusade of his own,' growled de Wolfe. 'Just before he was going to kill them all, he claimed that all his family had been butchered by Frankish and English knights during their retreat from the siege of Damascus, back in 'forty-eight.'

'That was a total disaster, like all of the Second Crusade,' cut in the monk quickly, with a sideways look at Thomas. 'I remember my father talking about it – his cousin was a bowman there. The whole enterprise was ill founded, a political and military triumph of ineptitude!'

'But why would this Turk come all the way to Devon on account of that?' persisted Nesta, whose curiosity was as insatiable as the monk's.

'According to Richard, he had sworn an oath to carry out his father's dying demand for revenge,' explained John. 'This Nizari sect spent years seeking the names of those who were at Damascus. Eventually this madman Nizam got himself to France, where it seems he murdered a whole series of either those who were at the siege or their descendants.' He stopped and took a long draught from his ale-pot. 'Then he managed to cross to England posing as an alchemist, using some far-fetched deceit about discovering the Elixir of Life.'

There was a pause while Thomas gave them a short lecture on alchemy and the Elixir of Life, which provoked Gwyn into a gaping yawn.

'Never mind all that!' cut in de Wolfe, irritably. 'I have the gravest doubts about such a tall story, but as they are all dead, there is little I can do about it.'

John had debated long and hard about whether to denounce his brother-in-law once again for involvement in some highly dubious scheme. He had taxed him about it in private when he had gone back to Revelstoke on the night of the drama at the old castle, but got nowhere with the crafty and evasive de Revelle. Richard freely admitted to being in partnership with Raymond de Blois in a venture to achieve the making of the Elixir of Life. On the defensive, conscious that his liberty or even life might depend upon convincing this incorruptible law officer, the former sheriff shed his usual contempt for John and was at his most persuasive.

De Wolfe had discussed the whole affair with Henry de Furnellis as soon as he returned to Exeter, giving him a somewhat selective account of what had happened near Bigbury. The sheriff, always willing to take the easier way out, agreed with him that they should give Hubert Walter, the Chief Justiciar, a suitably edited version of the truth.

John tried to keep Richard de Revelle out of the story as much as possible, as when he had gone to Revelstoke, Matilda had beseeched him to protect her brother from further trouble. She had done this several times before, and in view of the narrow escape from a terrible death that both she and her brother had experienced, he agreed to do what he could for Richard.

In any event, he had no proof that de Revelle had been involved with any new scheme of Prince John's. The Scottish alchemist's story of the mysterious Raymond de Blois joining with Richard to fund a search for the Elixir of Life was far fetched, but no more unbelievable than converting Devon tin into solid gold. The only gold that had been found was the ornament around Nizam's neck and John had quietly given this to Hilda, with instructions that it be sold to a goldsmith and the money shared between the families of the Dawlish shipmen who the owner had murdered.

'He said he met this de Blois fellow in London,' John now related to the group in the Bush. 'De Revelle was very vague as to what he knew about the man or even where he came from. But I can't prove otherwise.'

'So where did these alchemists come from?' asked Nesta, pouring more ale for the men.

'Richard said that de Blois knew of an Arab who he had met in Syria, famed for his expertise in alchemy. This man claimed to be within sight of suceeding with the elixir, but needed more facilities, so de Blois paid for him to come to Normandy and then fetched him across on poor Thorgils' ship.'

'Sounds a bloody thin story to me,' grunted Gwyn.

'So how did the lord of Revelstoke come into this?' asked Rufus.

'He says he funded the supply of food, horses and apparatus for this place in the forest near Bigbury. That was his part of the deal, in exchange for splitting the pro-ceeds of the elixir, when it was produced.'

'How did they get to be tucked away in this hideout?' asked the chaplain. 'Why all the secrecy?'

John shrugged. 'The explanation gets thinner and thinner! That land belongs to Henry de Vautortes, but he holds it as a sub-tenant from . . . guess who?'

Nesta looked at him blankly. 'Tell us, then,' she commanded.

'The Count of Mortain . . . Prince bloody John himself! But it's no crime to rent out a piece of useless land, so there's nothing I can do about it.'

Thomas, who had subsided after giving his sermon on alchemy, had another question. 'What about those two strange men, the Scotsman who poisoned the main vil-lain – and that grotesque foreigner with no tongue?'

De Wolfe ran his hands through his dense black hair, smoothing it down to the back of his neck. He was getting weary and also anxious about what he had to do very soon.

'According to my dear wife's lying brother, they were recruited to help this Arab alchemist in his final search for the elixir. He says Raymond de Blois found this Alexander in Bristol, where he had a reputation as a noted philosopher. I suspect that this is about the only part of the story that could be proved to be true.'

'So what are you going to tell the Justiciar?' asked Rufus.

'Nothing but the truth,' snapped de Wolfe. 'But perhaps forgetting a few details that will help no one.'

'And letting de Revelle off the hook is one of them,' grumbled Gwyn into his ale-pot.

'I'll tell Hubert Walter that the plot he was warned of no longer exists. Three dangerous Moorish assassins burnt themselves to death rather than be captured after failing in their mission – that's readily believable, from what we know of the members of this sect, who seem to relish dying!'

'What about the deaths of the old Templar, the shipmen and the two at Shillingford?' asked the chaplain. 'To say nothing of the blasphemous desecration in the cathedral?'

'I'll be able to resume all the inquests on those now,' answered John, with genuine satisfaction. 'The blame will quite rightly be attributed to these foreign assassins, who got into the country by stealth in order to carry out their murderous schemes against old Crusaders and their families. This is the absolute truth – all this nonsense about the Elixir of Life was a smokescreen and I see no need even to mention it!'

'So what about this Raymond de Blois?' asked Brother Rufus.

John shrugged. 'I don't know who he was or what he was doing here. I have my own suspicions, but they would only open a bag of worms that's best left undisturbed. He was a brave man, trying to save the others at the cost of his own life, so I will let him lie in peace.'

'Where is he lying, by the way?' asked Nesta.

'We buried him three days ago in that little church of St Peter the Poor Fisherman, at the foot of the cliffs in de Revelle's manor. Matilda and Hilda came with us and we saw him put in the earth in a most decorous manner, thanks to the priest that conducted the Mass in such a fine manner.'

Thomas blushed and hung his head in embarrassment at the unexpected compliment. The conversation went on for a time, until John had run out of explanations and the others had exhausted their theories about this strange business. One by one, they drifted away, Thomas to get ready for midnight Matins in the cathedral and Gwyn back to the castle for a game of dice in the guard-room. Rufus decided to join him, and at last John and Nesta were left alone at the table. He felt very uneasy and stared into his quart pot, turning it around restlessly in his fingers.

Nesta placed a hand over his. 'Come on, Sir Crowner,' she murmured, in the half-mocking, half-affectionate way she had when he was out of sorts. 'Up the ladder and rest your weary head. It's been a hard few days, especially for old fellows like you, well past their prime!'

He pinched her bottom in reprisal, but wasted no time in following her up to the loft, watched by the envious eyes of some of the patrons, who came to the Bush as much for the sight of the fair Nesta as for her excellent ale.

In the little chamber in the corner of the large space beneath the thatch, John slumped down on the large feather mattress laid on a raised plinth, just above the floor. He still regretted the loss of their French bed, consumed in the recent fire, and resolved to remind the new ship-masters in Dawlish that the new one he had ordered must be brought over from St-Malo as soon as sailing started again in the spring. The thought of Dawlish brought the beautiful Hilda into his mind and added to the turmoil there, as Nesta sank down beside him, her head on his shoulder.

Mentally gritting his teeth, he plunged straight into the problem. 'Nesta, my love, tomorrow Matilda will be back in Martin's Lane.'

He steeled himself to continue, willing himself to remember the words that he had been rehearsing since the messenger had brought the news of his wife's return. But the remarkable woman who was his mistress raised her head to kiss his cheek and laid her forefinger across his lips.

'Hush, *cariad*, there's no need to explain!' she whispered in Welsh. 'Of course you must return home. You can't leave the poor woman there after all she's been through.'

John looked at Nesta almost fearfully, his long-held suspicions that she must have the power of second sight confirmed.

'How did you know what I was going to say?'

She smiled sadly and patted his big, rough hands as they lay across his lap. 'I've known for a few weeks that you would not stay with me, John. You miss your freedom, your dog, your cook-maid, even fighting with your wife!'

John's long face flushed slightly. 'I would have stayed with you for ever, but for this happening. I cannot leave her now.'

Nesta nodded gently. 'I believe that you truly love me, John. If there were no Matilda and you could take your dog, your chattels and even your maid with you, we could go away and be happy somewhere else. But as long as you are married and are the King's Coroner, it cannot happen.'

'I'll not give you up, Nesta!' He sounded like a petulant youth, she thought affectionately.

'I know that, John, but home you must go! Let your wife get over this awful thing in her own time. To have been within minutes of being burned alive will have scarred her mind and will disturb her nights for months to come. I should know, for it almost happened to me not long past!'

He turned to her and seized her almost desperately, pulling her back on to the bed, kissing her passionately.

'You are *my* elixir of life, Nesta! Without you, it would have no meaning. My body may have to return home, but my soul will stay here!'

As they fumbled at each other's garments, she vowed that his body would also return to the Bush as often as possible!

It was late the next day before de Revelle's retainers appeared in Martin's Lane, ending the leg of the journey from Buckfast Abbey. As the sound of hoofs brought John to his street door, the sight of the blackbird devices on their jerkins gave him a momentary vision of the two guards on the track near Bigbury, with cross-bow bolts sticking from their backs. Then he was hurrying out to help a grim-faced Matilda from her palfrey, Mary following close behind to chaperone Lucille as one of the escorts hauled her from her pony. Leaving the two younger women to organise the bags and packages from the horses, John led his wife inside and took her into the gloomy hall, where a huge fire was blazing in the chimneyed hearth. Mary had placed food and wine ready on the table, and with uncharacteristic gallantry John led Matilda to her favourite cowled chair before the fire and helped her off with her heavy riding cloak.

'You must be chilled through after that long ride,' he said solicitously. 'I'll pour you a cup of wine and soon Mary will bring hot stew.'

He fussed over her for a few minutes as she silently warmed herself before the fire. Then he brought his own goblet to sit on the other monk's chair, wondering desperately how to find something to say that would not spark controversy. But as had Nesta the evening before, Matilda saved him the trouble.

'Are you living back here now?' she demanded, her gimlet eyes boring into his.

'I am indeed, wife! You need not fear any further assault now – those men are all dead.'

She turned to stare at the flames in the hearth.

'I am glad you are back, John,' she murmured tone-lessly. 'The house was not the same without you here to cause me trouble.'

ḣistorical postscript

The three assassins in this work of fiction are loosely based upon historical reality, which still has unfortunate relevance today. In the highly complex history of Islam, a major division occurred upon the death of the Prophet Muhammad in AD 632. The majority group, the Sunnis, declared that his successor was a caliph chosen by Muhammad's followers, but the remainder (the Shi'a or Shi'ites) claimed that shortly before his death he had appointed his nephew Ali, the husband of his daughter Fatima, as his spiritual and temporal heir. Later, other schisms about the succession occurred and the Shi'a split repeatedly, one sect being the Isma'ili, whose leader is still the present Aga Khan.

The Isma'ili had radical and esoteric views of their religion, and in the eleventh century the Nizari sub-sect under Hasan ibn Al Sabbah broke away, originally to kill leading Sunnis in Egypt, in order to restore the Fatimid Shi'a dynasty in Cairo. Hasan was viewed by the rest of Islam as a heretic, and around 1090 removed his sect to Alamut, a remote mountain stronghold in Persia, where he became known as 'The Old Man of the Mountains', though this is a mistranslation of Sheik al Jabal, meaning 'Chief of the Mountain'.

The Nizaris became known as the *hashishin*, because of the claim that they used hashish (cannabis) to excite themselves into a state of murderous ecstasy. The modern name 'assassin' is derived from this unlikely allegation. In fact cannabis does not have this effect, but they may well have used other psychedelic drugs.

Assassination became a potent political weapon, and for many years the *hashishin* imposed a reign of terror all over the Near East, where many leading Sunnis were knifed or poisoned by Nizari killers, who invariably died themselves during the attacks.

In the twelfth century, another Nizari, Rashid el-din Sinan, moved to a different mountain fastness in the Lebanon (then part of Syria) and became another 'Old Man of the Mountains'. From there he conducted a war of assassination against both Sunnis and the Christians of Outremer. A number of attempts were made on the life of Saladin (a Sunni Kurd), and he is said to have slept up a wooden tower for safety. They murdered numerous Crusaders and leading members of the Christian kingdoms, including, in 1152, Count Raymond II of Tripoli.

In 1192, two *hashishin* dressed as monks fatally knifed Count Conrad of Montferrat, the man who had been chosen as the next King of Jerusalem (an empty gesture, as the Holy City had already been taken by Saladin), in a street in Tyre. They were caught and killed, but before dying, one was alleged to have confessed that the assassination was ordered by King Richard the Lionheart, who preferred another candidate, Guy of Lusignan, to reign over Jerusalem.

The French king Philip, who had by now fallen out with Richard and had abandoned the Crusade and returned to France, took the opportunity to announce that he was also a target of the *hashishin*. He claimed that Richard had sent four of them to France to assassinate him, and henceforth he went about in armour and with a heavy bodyguard. However, King Leopold of Austria received a letter purportedly written by the Old Man of the Mountains, declaring that King Richard was not implicated, but this was declared a forgery by the Lionheart's enemies.

In 1194, Count Henry of Champagne visited Alamut and described how the assassins were trained – a story that was repeated by Marco Polo over a century later, though he visited the fortress several years after it was destroyed by the Mongols. These accounts told how young men were drugged with hashish and taken to a beautiful garden, with tinkling fountains, superb food and the seductive company of lovely maidens. They were later promised that if they carried out the murderous tasks set by the leader, they would inevitably be killed, but go straight to eternal life in a similar paradise. The Old Man was said to demonstrate their blind obedience 'by making a sign to these young men, who would instantly leap off a high cliff with a glad cry, to be dashed on the rocks far below'.

There is a huge literature on the Assassins, with some remarkable claims, such as that in 1175 the Nizaris offered to become Christian, so that they could ally with the Frankish forces against the Sunnis. It has also been claimed that there was some clandestine connection between the Assassins and the Knights Templar. Though Alamut was destroyed by the Mongols in the thirteenth century and the Nizaris dispersed, they survived in various forms and some still exist in India as the Khoja sect.

The Assassins have been the subject of many books, both fact and fiction, probably the most recent to feature them being Dan Brown's *Angels and Demons*.

For an excellent, detailed account of the Assassins by A. C. Campbell, see the following website: www.accampbell.uklinux.net/assassins